HE WHO IS A PROTECTOR

SADIK
BOOK 3

LOVE BELVIN

MKT Publishing, LLC

HE WHO IS A *Protector*

THE *Sadik* SERIES 3

ISBN: 978-1-950014-06-4 (Paperback)
ISBN: 978-1-950014-04-0 (eBook)

MKT Publishing, LLC
First print edition 2019 in U.S.A.

Cover design by **Visual Luxe**

I hate this part.
Dedicating a book to you doesn't seem natural.
I miss you more than I thought possible.
Your color so vivid, your brain so brilliant, and your light appealed so deeply
to my heart.

Shenedrea "Nena" Goshay-Colar

June 24th*, 1977 – May 20*[th]*, 2019*

∞|∞

"*Ashes to ashes. Dust to dust. Naked I came from my mother's womb, and naked I will depart. The Lord gave, and the Lord hath taken away*," the pastor quoted scripture over the descending casket. A small choir of seven softly sang a hymn about joining Christ in heaven.

This was it. It was the final destination. I thought seeing the casket in the church was the finale, psychologically. Just an hour ago, I believed the sniffles from the mourners in the pews and sorrowful words of eulogy were the dénouement of his life. I was wrong. Inside this cold ground was his official resting place—at least in the only form I'd known him.

The cold earth...

At the gravesite, standing amongst dozens of mourners, the wind blew aggressively, and the sun hadn't quite decided if it wanted to grace this day or to leave us in gloom. My thoughts were furthest from the pearly gates. A sharp memory rolled over in my mind. A wise man once told me if you were good in the illegal trade game, it wouldn't be the law that took you out. It'd be stress from the work, your heart, cancer, your hothead-ass lady, or a miscalculated loved one. Betrayal weighed on my heart, and vindication had purchased prime real estate in my mind. My family had taken a beating in the past two and a half weeks. Circumstances created by our decisions put us at risk of having this dynasty ravished.

Considering the occupant of that casket, I reflected on how fucked up the game was. Being in the illegal trade game like my father was a high-risk journey: thinking two steps ahead of law enforcement, working three times harder than your competitors, and operating twenty-*five* hours a day took a toll on the most solidly built men. It was never a burden I wanted to carry. I always knew whatever industry I went into, I'd grind harder than my peers. I knew it would take nothing less than that commitment to reach the Earl Ellis level of excellence. I'd been achieving it and still felt the loss from this death. Death to the game.

The small hand clasped in mine squeezed. I glanced down to my right. Bilan's brows above her dark sunglasses lifted, and she gestured ahead. The casket was six feet into the ground and on top were roses. I peered down to the long-stemmed one in my left hand, and that's when the realization was made. I tugged gently at her hand, and we smoothly gaited over to the unearthed hole to drop our flowers inside. I assisted her back to our respective places.

"How are you?" she whispered up to my ear.

With my eyes glued to the hole in the ground, I nodded my response. What more could I say? I was fucked up—for more reasons than one. I couldn't believe we were at a damn funeral. This shouldn't have been. It wasn't supposed to be. Of course, I couldn't articulate this to my fiancée in the moment. Instead, I tried focusing my attention on watching Monica and the girls go next with their flowers.

This period of time had been so fucked up for them. I struggled to remember I was still Monica's brother-in-law and Ivana, Iesha, and baby Irene's uncle over these two weeks. Bilan had been an invaluable help in covering my neglect. Monica looked thinner, almost lifeless as she struggled to keep up with two precocious school-aged girls, and a growing infant without their father. She was a fighter, but even these circumstances could rattle the best warrior.

Taaliba assisted my mother next. My queen, too, had been compromised by the latest set of unfortunate events. She appeared aged in just two and a half weeks. Like most of us in the family, her world had been delightfully enhanced by the addition of a new Ellis. We'd gained Bilan, finally, as well. Who knew so soon, we'd be wracked and disassembled by the ghost of death by natural causes and a suicide attempt before my son could make it to three months old?

My mother hadn't been herself. It was a good thing Taaliba flew in from Antigua when she did. Having her at the house with our mother gave me eyes on her, other than the staff's. Taaliba mentioned our mother had been prescribed a sleeping aid. A sleeping aid. Apparently, Taaliba's teas were no longer in supply or not as aggressive as my mother needed to rest.

Next to drop flowers onto the casket was Livia. Tiffany, along with Livia's mother, walked together to throw their flowers. It reminded me of how wide the web of my father's influence had stretched over the years. The few times my father's assistant, Palmer, had his young daughter on a visit, he'd bring her around my father's right-hand man's daughter, Tiffany, when they were my nieces' ages. I just didn't know they were still in touch.

"At this time, we're going to conclude the home-going service of our beloved," the eulogist announced. "On behalf of the family, thanks for coming out and celebrating the life of the dearly departed. There, in the church, the family has a repast prepared. Thank you." He nodded.

The crowd seemed to turn toward the church simultaneously at his last words. It was odd having a funeral and burial in the same location. You didn't see much of this in the metropolis. As we sauntered out of the graveyard, I held Bilan to me by the side of her waist. She wore heels out on the flaccid soil that would occasionally puncture the ground. As we meandered across the yard, her soft hand reached up for my chin, bringing my attention to her face.

"You sure you're okay? You held up well, but I don't want you suppressing," Bilan murmured as we trailed behind my mother and Taaliba.

I grabbed her soft hand and placed a kiss on her palm in a manner of responding. I didn't have many words to express today. However, I needed Bilan to believe I was fine. She should not suppose anything less than that. If I showed an ounce of weakness, it would have a domino effect on her as well as our family. I'd get through today and those after.

As we entered the church again, we were stopped by friends offering their condolences. Bilan and I stood behind my mother, just inside the door of the dining room, creating a line for greeting guests. I'd be a liar if I claimed to know ninety-eight percent of them. Quite honestly, it didn't matter. My mind was on the person whose casket was being covered in dirt as I forged my best smile while stringing together words of encouragement I didn't feel, and those of gratitude that were so distant to me.

Like she'd been at this for years as an Ellis herself, Bilan stood next to me, greeting attendees with warm efforts and sincere energy. She even completed many of my sentences when I stalled. Her small hand was at my back rubbing, comforting me while we were at work. I was trapped in a haze of remark-timing and recounting where I recognized faces from. It was so much easier with my father and brother. Everyone knew Earl Ellis, the infamous Double E Bags. And with Iban being the oldest and closest to my father's business, he knew far more associates than I did. I always stood third in line for events like this. I'd catch more conversations than the scary Iban Ellis, however, he'd give me a cheat sheet of names and connections by greeting them first.

Those were the times of yesterday. Today would be cemented in my life forever, and tomorrow, things will irrevocably change. Death may be a part of the game of life, but it was still a phenomenon most couldn't reconcile. I was one of them—when it came to someone so close. This shit hurt bad.

"I remember you," an elderly woman, no taller than four and a half feet with a gray and white Jheri curl claimed, peering at me over her glasses. Her eyes so aged, her pupils were bordered by gray spheres. Her voice carried over the line of people separating us. "You's the youngest boy." Her lips were tightly balled, tone accusatory. She moved toward me, cutting the line, but the people respectfully moved out of her way. Her one white gloved-hand pointed my way. "Earl was particular about you. I knew your daddy for *years*," she emphasized. "Met him over forty-five years ago, and I ain't never see him happy like he was when he brought you down here for Palmer's daddy's funeral. You was 'bout yay size." She removed the one glove and spaced her shaky, veiny hands out to the distance, representing the size of my son, Sadik.

My father brought me to a funeral in South Carolina when I was an infant?

"Where the oldest boy?" Her asking about Iban that way told me she didn't know about his accident. That, oddly, pleased me. She didn't wait for my answer before continuing. "I spoke a Word from the Lord to 'im whilst he held you in his arm. I told him the sun was on your head. The Lord poured a proportion of favor in ya momma's womb for you. You's a special one. Nothing like he ever made; nothing like he was ever gonna make again." Her eyes narrowed. "And you know what he said?"

When Bilan elbowed me, I blinked a few times, then shook my head.

The old woman's forehead lifted and a smile blossomed on her face, stained dentures in plain sight. "He said, 'I know.' Ha!" She slapped her hands together, laughing with her eyes as her short legs dipped. "Come on, y'all!" she commanded the crowd of people lined up to speak with my family. "Let the good people eat. We got food prepared for 'em at the tables. Let them eat, then y'all can give y'all condolences."

Almost in an instant, the line dispersed. My mother promenaded over to me, weariness painted all over her beautiful face. Taaliba, Monica, and the girls behind her, circling us, creating privacy as all eyes in the room were on us.

"Are you ready to call it quits, queen?" I asked her. "The limo's outside waiting."

Her arm snaked around my back as she moved in to hug me. "Just a few more minutes," she murmured. "I won't stay too long. Stacy's probably already started dinner back at the house."

"Okay. Just say the word and we can go," I informed.

She patted my back before ambling over to the tables a young man was directing them to.

I glanced down to Bilan, still at my side. Her eyes were pinned to my mother. She seemed concerned. I pulled Bilan into me by the side. "You want something to nibble on?"

Her eyes roved up to me, changing from concern to guilt. Bilan shook her head, grabbing my hand and leaning into me.

"I'm sorry for your loss, Deek," she whispered, squeezing my hand.

Deek...

Bilan only used that name under particular circumstances. This time, she was trying to finesse me.

I dropped my face to meet her forehead. "You're my gain—will always be my gain."

She rolled her eyes, fighting a grin. "Not like Sadik?"

"Sadik could never be his mother. He could never fulfill my needs like she does." Ever.

Speaking of our son lifted my spirit instantly. Now I missed him. The best thing was falling asleep with him on my chest for a nap and awakening to his little head lifted as he gazed at me. Within seconds, he'd smile, recognizing his old man. And when I'd ask him what he was smiling at, the rumbles from my chest would make him laugh. It was love expressed in a way I never knew possible.

I didn't see Tiffany approach, so I was surprised when Bilan squeezed my hand again. My eyes bounced around for a short while until landing on Tiffany's long blonde wig. It was parted in the center with the roots a yellowish shade. My eyes rolled down to her face.

"You mind if I talk to you alone?"

I gave her an empty expression. Would she pick this event of others to pull me from Bilan to speak privately?

"Please," she urged, then her eyes swept over to Bilan.

I followed her line of vision. Bilan's expression mirrored mine. Emptiness veneering disbelief.

Bilan pulled in a long, quiet breath. "I need to call and check on Sadik."

I watched her walk off, pulling her phone from her purse.

"Is it that fuckin' serious?"

I faced Tiffany. "What?"

"Her having to be all uptight. We just buried family!" Her arm swung behind her. "Why do I feel this divide now?"

"Are you implying Bilan is the cause of it?"

"Like shit, she is. Look at how she reacted to me just talking to you. We ain't kids; I get it. We fucked, but now you got a girl. I get it, but why the hell do I have to act like I don't know you?"

"Who asked you to do that?"

"That's basically what she wants!"

"Basically?" I challenged, calm demeanor opposite of hers.

"When I hit up Rory yesterday, asking where we was staying, she said the family was staying at your place in *Macen Beach*."

"Okay..."

"Okay? I ain't even know you had a place in South Carolina. So when I asked to be picked up from the airport and brought to the house, she gone say that ain't possible. She said the house belong to you and Bilan. What the fuck?"

"You think it's okay for you to stay at Bilan's house?" My voice was even.

Tiffany's jaw dropped, then her eyes. She balled her mouth. It took her a moment to rebound. "This is a family matter. We always come together: you know that. Everybody knows that! We can put our shit to the side and support each other. I heard Irene ain't doing well. It's fucked up that I can't be there with her."

I cocked my head to the side, lifting a brow. My father, yes, but

Tiffany didn't have the type of relationship with my mother to provide her comfort.

"Listen..." She took a deep breath, eyes rolling below. "Palmer was my family, too. He and my father was mad tight. I wanna be with my family this afternoon and tonight. Why am I being penalized because your girlfriend can't accept you had a past before meeting—when meeting—her?"

I changed stances, pulling my arms in front of my pelvis, clasping my left hand over my right wrist. "Let's get one fuckin' thing straight. You were before Bilan, not during. Don't you dare try to create that narrative. Secondly, you made clear who you are to her the minute you show up to my apartment requesting shit you left on my jet." Tiffany's neck snapped back as her mouth fell open again.

I nodded. "Yeah. Your lil' cute ass slip was hugely inconvenient for me. I almost had to share with her family business Earl wouldn't even want my mother knowing."

"And how was I supposed to know that?"

"By you simply keeping your fuckin' mouth shut and not taunting her."

"Taunting?" Her face balled. "Man, nobody was bothering that lil' girl!"

My eyes narrowed. "Little girl?" I stepped closer to her, hands still at my pelvic line. "What did you leave behind on the jet, Tiff?"

She blinked a few times. "I thought it was just my earrings, but I found them. Then I realized I left my slippers."

"You couldn't just buy a new pair of slippers?"

Her head reared. "They're *Ase Garb*!"

I began sauntering off. "I'll have Rory ship you a pair in every fuckin' color. See you back in Jersey, Tiff."

Palmer, my father's most trusted ally, was dead. A stroke. It took him out the day after Iban appeared in my son's nursery. It was too much. Two fallen soldiers; one guided him, and he protected and aided both. The law didn't catch up to Palmer. The stress of the game did.

The physical and harmonious rhythm of the powerful waves hypnotized me. It reminded me of the might of nature, versus the might of mortal stress. I imagined myself fighting against the fierce and angry waves, miles into the sea. *That* would be real danger. It would mean life—more like death. There would be no need to fight. Just concede to death. Whereas the drama I'd experienced in the past nine months since being kidnapped by Damien was optional stress, at least it was what I'd been telling myself. I'd survived it all. Even as the stressors kept rolling in, so had the blessings. I could choose to focus on the latter rather than the prior.

However, it would have to be a choice. Like today: I would have never thought Palmer's death would bring me back to my dream home that I now wrestled with for nostalgia. But I was here, with my two loves and their family: my family. I was worried about Sadik, the senior. He'd been under tremendous stress; more, I'd been learning, than ever as it related to his family. I'd never seen him so withdrawn and narrowly focused. This was weird because baby Sadik and I were saturated with his father's care, attention, and affection. He spent most of his time with us, though he continued working, sometimes during odd hours to make up for the time he put in transitioning our family from his penthouse after Iban's accident. He was present and in each moment with us, but...only to us and his work.

My phone buzzing on the armrest of the beach chair captured my attention.

Monica: *hey... please tell me you bought that YSL Rouge Pur!*

I glanced down to my bag I brought out here to the beach and dug through it until I found the lipstick.

Me: Got it.

After sending the text, I sat back in the chair, exhaling as I went back to the beautiful view. I could stay out here all day and lose time. That was proven when I heard Monica, just behind me, on approach.

"Girl, you been out here since you put the baby down!" she panted, having run the distance from the house.

I smiled while nodding then handed her the lipstick. "Sadik went for a run. I'll wait for him to come back, or for the baby to wake up first. Where are you going?"

Monica had changed into a cute velour sweatsuit, the pants cropped beneath her knees, showcasing her muscular calves.

"Into town. One of the security guys said there are a couple of restaurants there. I need to come up for air from the funeral." She waved back to the house. "Stacy, Taaliba, and Irene have the girls while I slip out for a couple of hours to call a few friends from school."

I observed her ample cleavage in the lowly zipped jacket. "Nice. You guys *FaceTiming*?"

"Yeah. Something different."

"Oh. Okay. Is this how you typically keep in touch?" I asked because Monica and I had several late-night girl chats since Earl and Iban had been down. It was clear to me she hadn't been in touch with many friends or family outside of the Ellis family, so it was strange to hear about this group of friends. "I mean... I hope I'm not prying."

"No! Not at all." She giggled. "I recently 'reached back' to them. They've been trying to keep in touch since just before Christmas. I guess I can now use them as a distraction from all of this. My heart is broken from the loss of Palmer."

That made my shoulders drop and eyes roll back out to sea. "Yeah," I breathed. "This is a tough one. But we'll get through it the way family's supposed to."

"I hope."

I supplied a smile of confidence. "We will. Are Stacy, Irene, and the crew done with dinner?"

Monica nodded. "Just had a small plate of her spring pork and noodles dish. *Mmmmmm!*" She hummed with closed eyes. "My favorite—at least one of them from her." I turned my nose up at that one. Monica laughed, turning for the house. "I'll see you later. Don't want to get the call while I'm in the car, on my way to the restaurant. This place is the bomb, girl. I don't know how y'all kept it a secret this long!"

As she jogged toward the house, Taaliba was dropping down the steps of the deck with a plate of food. I turned back for the glorious water, inhaling the salted air before downing the last of my wine.

"Mind if I join you?" she asked, plopping down into the seat next to me.

I grinned her way. Taaliba was a pleasure, no matter how much energy she required to interface with.

"I wouldn't have it any other way." I swept my feet across the sand.

"How do you sit out here so long with just a hoodie and coochie shorts on?" she asked. "It's not warm out."

I lifted my legs, realizing she was right. But I was fine. "I'm right at home out here. I love it."

"I suspect that's why you guys bought this place." She turned toward the water.

Sadik groaned in his crib, calling my attention to him.

"Is that my favorite nephy?" She picked up the monitor I brought out to keep an extra eye on my baby boy.

My heart smiled. Then I was reminded of how this all came about. I would have never imagined Sadik's family staying in our *Macen Beach* home. Sadik had Palmer's body sent back home after the autopsy had been completed. When Palmer's family, who resided in a small South Carolina town twenty-five miles west of *Macen Beach*, called about his funeral arrangements, Sadik only wanted to stay here. When he made that known to Irene and explained the home he'd purchased for us, she made clear she'd be staying here as well. That meant Taaliba, Monica, and the girls would stay here, too. *That* meant security needed accommodations.

I sighed deeply, eyes closing and mind absorbing the sound of the melodious ocean.

Taaliba pushed a carrot with some healthy-looking spread at the tip to my face.

I shook my head, declining. "All that good food in there—and back at the repast—and you're only eating cold veggies?"

"We must get picky eating from you." Taaliba snickered. "Nah. Mommy doesn't eat everyone's food, even if they're from the south. That's why she and Stacy planned on cooking this afternoon."

It was mostly Stacy. Irene hadn't been herself since Earl's heart attack.

"How is she?"

"Mommy?" I nodded. Taaliba's regard swung out to the water again. "Not herself at all, but I can understand why. Daddy's never been down like this. Iban's still recovering, and she had to leave them both to lay Palmer to rest properly. I can understand her being out of sorts. Those two are a team. Weird as fuck, but down for each other."

I nodded as the wind hugged my face. Palmer's sudden death completed the triad of misfortunes the Ellises had been hit with. Earl hadn't been excelling in healing as we all hoped for. The doctors weren't impressed with his progress either. Though they'd been assuring the family he'd still been in the normal range of recovery, it wasn't fast enough for such a vibrant leader as Earl was.

Iban, on the other hand...

My throat closed up at the thought of him. His suicide attempt was a thud, something I could only imagine the level of misery in that realization to him. The gunshot to his right frontal lobe toward the forehead lodged into the wall. It was horrific; the experience and the aftermath. The sight of his blood all over my baby's nursery would haunt me forever. But he'd survived. We'd been told his recovery, however, would be a longer road than his father's.

The bullet caused only minor damage because it passed through no vital brain tissue or vascular structures. Iban was lucky. Not only did he live, but he had a greater chance at recovery than my brother did because of where he shot himself in the head. Still, the doctors made no promises for full revival. It wasn't guaranteed he'd be one hundred percent at the other end of his healing process.

"They'll both pull through. I'm hopeful."

"I hope so, and soon. We're so vulnerable without them." Taaliba sighed as though in pain. "Palmer's gone, and Sadik does his own thing. Danny has promised his protection, but he's no Ellis. Only my family can truly protect me. I'm no fool. I know what my father's business is. I've been fully aware of what Iban helps him do to earn for this family like he has. In Earl Ellis' world, it's eat or get eaten. I don't want to be prey. I don't want my family to be prey."

I knew to consider my words before sharing them. Sadik made it very clear his mother didn't know all the details of his father's dark world. I had to assume that included Taaliba and Monica until Sadik told me it did not.

"Sadik would never allow any harm to come to you or this family." My eyes penetrated hers, chin dipped. "You know that."

With her regard sweeping away, Taaliba nodded, taking a deep breath. This was hard for her. It was a difficult time for all Ellises. As much as I hated the thought of Sadik participating in his father's dark world, I couldn't see him doing anything less than protecting his family and upholding the coveted Ellis name.

"Here comes bullet head now," Taaliba announced, gazing past me.

I turned to my left, and sure enough, Sadik was running down the beach, bare-chested with his t-shirt wrapped around his head. From a distance, the setting sun shined on his golden casing, his glossed skin reflected in the light. How he had the energy to go for a run after the workout we had this morning on the beach was beyond me. Not only did we do cardio, but Sadik had been increasing my self-defense instructions, too. I found my hungry eyes roving up from his striated legs to his cut chest. Instead of him heading our way, Sadik made a beeline for the house.

"I don't know what you find so appealing about all that?" Taaliba droned, snatching my attention away from her brother.

"Huhn? About all what?"

"That?"

"What did I do?" I was confused.

"You're damn near salivating, watching him do his *Baywatch* jog."

I rolled my eyes, finally understanding her point. "I've told you what I do with all of *it*."

"What?" Her neck snapped back as her face folded.

I motioned with my hand, by pumping my fist to my mouth.

"Ewwwwwww!" Taaliba's upper torso flew from her chair and her arms stretched wide with her plate in her hand. "Don't make me fucking puke."

A sharp croak upended my belly. "But *he* can make *me* gag!" I laughed from embarrassment to the point of tears. My vulgarity was funny, but my truth was severely serious. I loved the man and his cock—unapologetically.

"Sooooo gross, Bilan!" she pretended to cry out.

Or did she?

I really didn't care. The connection Sadik and I shared tran-scended etiquette. I conceded to my disease. I *was* sick. Sadik's love and ultra-alpha ways infected me for life.

"I'm sorry. I think my friends' crass personas have rubbed off on me after all these years." I feigned remorse.

"I think my big brother had something to do with that."

"He does." I nodded, unabashedly, wiping the tears of humor from my eyes. It felt good to laugh after all of the hell over the last few weeks.

"That'll never be me," Taaliba claimed.

"What?"

"Acquiescing to a control freak."

"And falling in love with him?" I amended.

"Yeah. All of that." She shook her head defiantly. "Never. No man or woman."

"Hence your asexual condition?" I rolled my eyes dramatically.

Her eyes ballooned. "You judging me?"

"Harshly," I returned quickly. She sucked in a breath. "How's Danny, Leeb?"

Her guilty eyes rolled away. "I guess he's...doing him."

"But not you yet?"

"It doesn't work that way."

"Who else are you seeing?"

"No one!" she groaned through gritted teeth petulantly.

"No one at all?"

"Well, Danny and I have been..." She shook her head. "He's been around since daddy's heart attack."

"That's nice. Supportive."

Taaliba shook her head. "It's too much."

"Why?"

"He's so controlling. I'm not built to be with men like my father and brothers. I need room to breathe...to make my own decisions."

"How do you not have that room when he's supporting you during a trying time?"

She pursed her lips, taking a deep breath with her eyes fixed to the ocean. "He wants to get married."

"Oh..."

That was alarming. Yes, I thought Taaliba was melodramatic when it came to simply entertaining people she shared a mutual attraction with, but I also knew she was in no way prepared for marriage.

"How does he propose that'll—"

"Girl!" she spoke excitedly over me. "And those shoes have only been out for a month, but I'm getting them. Let me show you!" She pretended to use her empty hand to go into her pocket.

It didn't take long for me to realize her jump in conversation. A standing body had flipped its leg behind me, over my chair. I glanced above my head before scooting up.

"Hey, you..." I greeted Sadik with my eyes on Taaliba.

A kiss at the back of my head was all the response I needed. Sadik handed me a fresh glass of wine. Quickly, I took a sip to distract myself from the awkwardness.

"I can't find them," Taaliba blackened her phone, stowing it back in her pocket. "I'll look later and send it to you." She beamed over to her big brother. "Hey, broski."

Maybe he acknowledged her nonverbally, maybe he didn't, but Sadik brought a forkful of food to my mouth. Without hesitation, I accepted it.

"Control." Taaliba shrugged with her shoulders and mouth, lifting her arms and dropping them.

I shook my head while chewing. "No way." I tried to quickly clear my mouth of the food. "Maybe a little, but it's actually balance at play here."

Taaliba rolled her eyes, blowing off my explanation. I enjoyed the food fed to me by her brother, not realizing how hungry I'd been. Sadik served himself, too. I leaned into his chest, loving the scent of his dried perspiration.

"Taaliba," he called to her.

"Hmmm?" She turned our way.

"My security has alerted me of your boy, Danny, announcing he's on his way to my turf."

Taaliba rolled her eyes again then let go of a hefty breath. "I swear I didn't know."

"Yeah. You let him know, I'll grant him courtesy this time, but if he tries it again, he'll be met by Rory," Sadik threatened.

"I didn't know he would come. I swear," she squealed regretfully.

Sadik didn't respond. He continued to feed me and himself until the plate was cleaned. I sipped the last of my wine, enjoying the patterns of the whitecaps. Then I felt his lips at the back of my head again.

"I'm going to shower and wake up Sadik. His little ass thinks he's going to be up all night again. I have a few calls to make. He can do it with me."

I nodded in agreement. Little Sadik talked well until two in the morning last night after sleeping most of the day away during our commute down here. Just when he'd began sleeping longer stretches at night.

"Okay," I murmured, lifting to give him room to stand. "I'll be in soon."

"Nah." He stood from behind me. "You stay out here and relax as long as you need. You want me to send out more wine?"

I shook my head. "Not right now."

Sadik nodded before taking off for the house. I felt Taaliba's eyes burning a hole in the side of my face and turned to her.

She rolled her eyes. "Controlling."

I snickered. "You think you have problems with a control freak? Try having your OB/GYN being the man who tests your lover and several of his lovers before you. If that ain't some mind-control, I don't know what is!"

∞2∞

"Hurry up, Bilan. Damn!" He laughs, running between trees. I struggle to keep up with him, my curiosity peppered with humor. "You're so slow."

"Jason," I shout, giggling. "Where are we going?"

My feet stomp over dried leaves and small tree branches. I'm sure to avoid the rocks I can see, afraid of the ones I can't. I have on no shoes, feeling light-hearted without a care in the world. Jason peers over his shoulder at me every once in a while, his amusement just as spiked as mine.

"Woman, hurry up!" he commands at high speed.

It's an overcast day, but the temperature is mild. My dress is sleeveless and flowing in the air against the fierce speed. I zip around trees and hurl over rocks the size of basketballs. We hit a valley in the soil, forcing me to adjust my speed to keep up. I nearly fall, but grace is ample and I'm able to resume my balance and pace.

"Jason!" I yell again.

We're now in an open field. The sun is setting to our right, which is weird. The sun hadn't been out a few strides ago.

"Come on, Bilan!" Jason yells. "You're so damn slow, you're going to miss it!"

My laughter begins again as I deepen my lunges, running faster. A quick glance to the corner of my right eye has my neck whip three times before my feet slow to a halt. The break is too fast and I tumble down to the ground, eyes squeezing to see what's far into the distance. But I see them. Irene...Iesha... Earl, Monica, Taaliba, baby Irene, Ivana, Iban, and—

"Jason!" I call to him.

Jason, though quite a distance away, glances back at me. The amusement in his face fades just slightly as he follows my line of vision. Then, as though he registers the family and why they're all on the ground with their bodies tightly coiled forming a protective circle, he maintains his stride.

He doesn't slow. Neither does he tell me to follow him. Jason continues to titter as he skips off.

"Jason!" I scream. "Help me! My baby is over there!"

He is. Sadik is in the inner circle wailing. I finally find my wits to go toward them. The ground is cold, the wind picking up, and my feet are being punctured by the rubble on the ground. But I ignore the pain and race to them. Though originally far, I reach them in no time.

"What's going on?" I cry, searching them for the cause of their huddle.

Each face is tear-stained, every eye in the same place and not on me. Sadik's cry pulls at something deep in my stomach, twisting torturously. He doesn't quiet down right away. As I rub his little back, I'm about to question the group again, but think to turn to see what's capturing their attention.

Instantly, I fall backward, too fast to break it with my arm. It's an animal...a wolf. Maybe a goat. It's huge, coat a dirty brown mixed with gray. Teeth exposed, thick saliva strands stretching from top to bottom. Heat expels as he roars threateningly. Sadik's cry shoots up an octave. I look around to Earl and Iban, but they're just as frightened as the children in the cluster.

Sadik. Where's Sadik?

My eyes comb the empty field. Why is he not here? The beast growls again, inching toward us. I'm perspiring all over, pulse beating a dangerous speed.

"No!" I pant, my palm stretched outward.

Irene and Monica's groans turn my stomach. With my eyes glued to the animal, I reach back and hand Sadik over to someone behind me. Anyone. Within seconds, the baby is being lifted from my arm.

I can now focus on the beast. The revelation of his kind finally bursts in my mind. A goral. I hadn't seen one since my middle school days. A goat of sorts. I can't negotiate with a damn goat. Slowly, I stand to my feet with one out-stretched palm. He lunges my way, forcing me to leap back. Strategically, I move away from the group. His fangs are exposed, growl shaking the ground beneath me as I amble backward away from my family.

Suddenly, it's cold, the air is thick and unkind. I can't focus on that. The goral's back is to the huddled group, its focus solely on me. It allows me to lead it away, the distance from my family's growing wide. My chest heaves, knees shake. But I make my decision. I break off on a sprint in the opposite direction of my family.

The goral's roar vibrates the ground beneath me. I could feel its gain on me. My death's imminent. I just hope the family took my baby and are seeking safety. Its paws pound the ground in a rhythm I'm focused too much on trying to flee. Then I no longer hear it. I hear a bestial whimper. Out of nowhere, a heavy fleshly weight falls on my head, knocking me to the ground. My entire frame recoils. I'm prepared to be mauled, or for the first puncture into my skin.

But...

Nothing.

The goral's whimpering over me. I feel a warm liquid running down my hips and legs. I struggle to get it off of me, feeling like I'm hyperventilating. Grunting, I push, twist my body. It wreaks and its bristle hairs on my skin are gross.

Then I feel its weight on me lessen. The minute I smell fresh air, I scramble from underneath. Before I can catch my breath, I see him.

Sadik.

Those kaleidoscopic-hued eyes are radiant with fury, lost in vengeance. He's holding a bow in one hand and using the other to push the goral from me. Two arrows are lodged into its body.

I'm out of breath, heart racing, eyes wild while swinging between my protector and the dying goral.

"Sadik..."

I turned over onto my side, eyes open wide to the dim room. The other side of the bed was empty. Harsh breaths dispelled through my nostrils.

What was that?

A nightmare about a goat. Out of all the things that could possibly freak me out; my brother's murder, my son possibly being killed or seriously injured by his uncle...another funeral in exactly six months. All these things could haunt me. However, it was a goral that got the job done.

I was now anxious. My mind slowing, but the adrenaline had already spiked my blood. I was fully awake. My eyes swung over to Sadik's crib, and I knew where I'd find his father. I knew Sadik would be in the same place he'd been falling asleep since Iban shot himself in our son's nursery. I shuffled off the bed and toed to the opposite side of the bedroom where Sadik lay sleeping in his crib as his father did the same beneath him, on the floor.

S.Q.E, the first lay on his side, facing the crib with just a pillow and comforter beneath him. With each step toward the father of my child, I could feel my sex liquefy and seep between my thighs. My pulse still raced, but my mind had settled on one thing, remnants of the nightmare in the distance. My breasts were heavy, nipples stung as I swung a leg on the other side of him and dropped to his hips. My mouth found his as I pushed him onto his back by the shoulder.

Sadik was momentarily discombobulated, but when my hand reached beneath the elastic of his boxers, finding his resting dick, he quickly awakened down there. He adjusted himself with ease, hands mechanically going to my hips. His squeeze on them was instinctive as he let me snake my tongue in his mouth. I managed his boxers down just enough for his cock to jut against my little pouch, spiking my temperature.

The sounds of the waves crashing at the shoreline helped keep the visions from my nightmare at bay. The breeze from the ceiling fan countered the boiling of my blood. I stroked him with my hands, kissing him while grinding my bare sex against his pelvis. Impatient, just when I felt he was hard enough I reared back to sit on him. The pulsing pressure fitting him in wasn't enough to deter me. I danced on him until I could fit half of him. Then I worked from there, pushing down and lifting until the glide was smooth.

My mouth found his again, his big hot hands guided my strokes. I saw the stars and moon when Sadik was inside me. I felt a brush of heaven when his breathing hiked, and his touch on me was filled with possession. It was what I'd grown to crave. What I could never do without again.

Effortlessly, Sadik lifted his torso; mine came up with his. Then he managed to his feet without breaking our carnal connection. My mouth busied on and in his as I felt us move. The tips of my hands pressing into his scalp, my back landed on the mattress as his torso lifted from me. Desperate for him, my arms reached high for his shoulders, hips bucked, desperate not to lose his fullness.

Sadik didn't break our nexus, but he did peer down on me with half passion, and half curiosity. I could read him so clearly.

Readily, I answered, "I will take a bullet for you." I panted. "I'll die for you and Sadik. I swear." I could feel my orchid opening for him even more. "I'm built for you—for him. I wouldn't think twice of dying, protecting—"

Sadik's mouth crushed mine, his tongue pushing through my lips with the same fervor he used to penetrate my world. I received him, pulling his hard body into me by his flexing wings. I loved him. With each beat of my heart, I did. Never did I feel so protected, so coveted as I did when held in this man's honeyed eyes.

His hardness rocked into me, the head of his dick beating into my core. It was a therapy like no other, a sensation I could never get enough of. My hips rocked against his thrusts. Our rhythm perfectly in tune, the cadence of our tongues synchronized. I was determined to match his pace, to meet his patience. The grimace on his lovely face told me, Sadik's focus was on the long haul. So desperate to be in harmony with him, I refused to succumb to the sparks lightning in my core. I wanted to prove my endurance...needed to go the distance with my lover, my protector.

My hand roved over his skinned head, his sculpted shoulders and back as we met mid-air with each passionate thrust. I bit his lip, pulling down the bottom one as I fought to hang on. The muscles in his face tightened, Sadik's pupils dilated before me. Then his eyes rolled back until they closed. Viscerally, my body knew it was time to release. And I did. I lifted my hips more to him and endured his deep plunges. Within seconds, I detonated. My flower opened to him.

"Shit..." he grunted, holding his last thrust.

I imagined he squirted into me in that moment. My hips bucked, breasts flopped, riding out my orgasm. My pussy rolled and rolled around him until the waves ceased. At some point, Sadik lifted me again. He crawled deeper into the mattress before lying me onto a pillow. I panted, zings shooting through my bare frame. My eyes went to the roof of the canopy, spotting the missing ropes.

I smiled. "When are you going to replace those?" Lazily, I pointed upward.

"Tomorrow," he grumbled, settling on his side.

I giggled, gloriously satiated and once again exhausted enough to return to sleep. "Tomorrow? We leave tomorrow."

It took a few seconds for him to return, "They leave tomorrow. We stay."

I lifted from my neck, turning toward him. "We...stay?"

Sadik yawned, seemingly tortured by drowsiness. "We won't be rushing back north."

A brief panic spiked my blood. "And Sadik?"

Again, it took a few seconds for a reply. "He'll be with his parents."

My heart relaxed, adrenaline dissipating from my blood. I lay back down on the pillow. Sadik I and Sadik II were all I needed for peace of mind these days. They gave me purpose and routine. As I turned to leave the bed, Sadik's semen beginning to leak.

"I'll call the office in the morning to let my team know I'll be remote."

And that was it.

No questions. No doubts. I didn't understand how Sadik wasn't ready to rush back to his ailing father and brother, but I trusted his judgment enough to not question him.

I made it to the landing of the staircase with Sadik cooing in my ear. I patted his little back, loving the sound of his shaky cords. After a late morning bath and warm bottle, I guess he was ready to socialize. I loved it. I loved him. He was so soft and smelled so good against my chest and shoulder as we traveled to the kitchen.

So many bodies of all sizes moving about on the main floor was striking. How we were able to fit the Ellis women in a three-bedroom cape cod, I still didn't understand. However, we did. Irene took the bedroom facing the front of the house and Monica and the girls took the adjoining second bedroom, connected to the master closet. Sadik had the house furnished with extra beds throughout the family and living rooms for Taaliba and Irene's staff. It was also a good time for him to tell me he purchased the house across the street when I was down last summer. It was for his security team to keep an eye on me. Well, now the house was occupied with his security and the Ellis women's.

"My sonshine!" Irene cried out at first sight of Sadik in my arms.

Sonshine was one of her nicknames for her only grandson. I smiled, seeing Stacy and another one of her staff members cleaning the kitchen and putting filled Tupperware into the fridge.

"You see your Nana?" I asked him, turning so he could see her over my shoulder.

When spinning, I caught his father, standing against the counter with a coffee mug in his hand. His face was tight and he was gloriously shirtless.

"Come to Nana, baby," Irene called out to the baby, stretching her arms and hands our way. "I need to get my share of kisses before I go. I don't know when I'll see you again." I handed him over to her. "It may be a week or more."

I scoffed. "It won't be that long. Just a few days, Nana."

Irene lifted the baby in the air as I floated across the room to his father. She made cooing sounds to match her grandson's before noting, "Or a week."

My face folded as I approached her son, big Sadik. "I doubt it'll be that long. I just hung up with Earl telling him a few days."

Sadik didn't respond, only taking a sip of his coffee.

Irene sang, "We'll see!" to the baby, though speaking to me.

"Queen, you're more than welcome to stay with us," Sadik offered.

"I have to get back to my husband, dear," she declined. "Two days away has been too much for me. Nurse Gladney told me Diane and Nena have been up there. Last night, they got so loud, the head nurse assigned to your father had to ask them to keep it down several times."

My face folded again. "What were they doing?"

Irene grunted she didn't know. "That lil' Nena is always loud. Young Diane is a mouthy one, too. They could've been arguing about the "usies" they took of him in bed. Which girl got to sit on which side of his bed, wanting their best angle captured."

I didn't know how to respond to that. Sadik didn't react, and I decided to follow his lead. No matter how well I'd been at acclimating to the Ellis family, those secondary affairs were hard realities to digest.

As I leaned against the countertop and Sadik, the alarm system chimed from the front door being opened. Seconds later, Taaliba sauntered in, appearing just as she did yesterday, but with a tight morning face. My eyes blossomed from shock when I recognized Danny on her heels. I felt Sadik tense against me.

"Hey, Ma," Taaliba greeted just before leaning down to kiss Irene. "Hey, pooh bear." She kissed baby Sadik's shoulder. "What time do we leave for the airport?"

Danny offered a neck bow to Irene. "Good morning, ma'am."

"Morning, honey," Irene returned, shock in her voice. It was clear she didn't know Danny had been in town since yesterday.

Taaliba gave her brother a once over. "You're not dressed yet, Hulk?"

Sadik continued to rubberneck Danny through slit eyes. The kitchen went silent, awaiting Sadik's answer.

"You come into my home and don't speak, Lopez?" he grated lowly across the room.

I could feel the vibration from his back. With a smirk, Danny began his way, extending his palm.

"I'm still adjusting to this, Ellis," Danny admitted. "I didn't expect to see you and so..." He cleared his throat. "Indisposed. Good morning. I would never disrespect you in your home."

Sadik's eyes roved down to Danny's extended palm, then rolled back up to his face. Sadik tossed his head back. "This is Bilan's home. You greet my woman first."

With a deepened smirk, Danny stepped past Sadik to offer me his palm. His humor was infectious, causing me to smile as I met his hand.

"Morning, Danny," I saluted.

"It's a pleasure to formally meet you, Bilan. Taaliba's had great things to say about you."

My smile widened with thoughts of pillow talks between him and my lover's sister.

"She's been generous to us both. She's spoken well of you, too."

I caught Taaliba rolling her eyes. She did the same with her shoulders, resembling a butch rather than a woman who'd been intimate recently with a man. "Again, Sadik, why aren't you dressed?"

"He's not flying back with us."

Taaliba's head bounced back, her eyes shot over to me. "What about you?"

I shook my head. "I'll be with the S.Q.E.s."

"*Shiiiiit*," Taaliba swore under her breath. "How are you guys getting back?"

"Sadik has his jet flying down," Irene answered.

Taaliba's eyes shot over to Danny. His brows hiked daringly.

Something was up.

Taaliba took a deep breath. "Mommy, ummmm..." She swiped the back of her tapered head. "I...uhhhhh. I'll be flying back up with Danny."

"The fuck?" Sadik growled.

Taaliba's palm flew into the air the same rate mine went to Sadik's bare back.

"Don't," Taaliba pleaded. "I'll be home by tomorrow. Mommy won't be alone."

"You damn right she won't be alone. Because you'll be with her no later than tonight."

"Sadik," Taaliba cried.

Sadik addressed Danny, voice controlled. "Tonight, Lopez. My family's going through a trying time. My mother needs her daughter. Whatever sniffing you want to do around her little ass can be done respectfully at *Elliswoods Palace*. Do I make myself clear?" His stormy eyes bounced between Taaliba and Danny.

"Sadik!" Taaliba tried again.

"No," Danny spoke firmly over her. "It's fine." He nodded. "He's right. Now is not the time to keep you from your family. We can head back this afternoon. You said it yourself, you're worried about your father. I can have you to the hospital this evening."

"But you're not even coming back?" Taaliba questioned Sadik's hypocrisy. "You just said you're staying behind."

"I have a fiancée and son to be concerned about," Sadik explained as Danny began tapping his phone, ambling out of the kitchen. "As you recall, my family's experienced trauma. We need alone time to regroup," he tried controlling his volume.

"Regroup?" Taaliba trilled. "You live together!"

"I'm trying to get married this year!" Sadik argued, voice on full blast. "Are you, sweetheart?"

I saw the moment she deflated. Taaliba's shoulders dropped in defeat and she marched out of the kitchen.

"I'll be fine, you know?" Irene informed Sadik as she played with the baby.

"She will, too. Right by your side." He took a sip of his coffee.

He worked out without me this morning. I could smell the dried perspiration on his skin. You would think a workout would mild his temper.

"Not necessary," I hummed so only he could hear me.

Sadik growled, blowing me off. Monica strolled into the kitchen with baby Irene on her hip and Iesha right behind her. The sight of both little girls swelled my heart. Iesha's attention was buried into her tablet.

"Morning, Uncle Deek," she greeted.

"Hey, baby," he mumbled in return.

I was grateful he didn't demand her to speak to me as well. I told Sadik we shouldn't make a big deal about Iesha's ongoing grudge against me in order not to fuel it. She was a kid and unless she got disrespectful, I could wait out her maturity. Seconds later, Ivana ambled in and greeted the room with a general good morning. Monica placed baby Irene in the high chair and went to the counter to prepare a bowl of pureed food. Iesha sat next to her grandmother and baby Sadik, remaining at task with her device. Ivana went straight to baby Sadik and pulled his little leg up for a kiss on his foot.

"Where's your iPad, Ivy?" Monica asked with her back to the table.

"I packed it," Ivy answered, giggling at baby Sadik as she played with his feet.

"Are you sure?" Monica asked. "We're leaving in less than an hour. What's left here stays."

"I'm sure, Mommy," Ivy continued with my son as their grandmother held him. "Uncle Deek, you wanna play chess on the way home?"

"I'm sorry, baby," Sadik issued regrettably. "We're staying behind today."

Iesha's eyes burst wide. "Oooh, Mommy, I wanna stay! Can we stay? I want to play on the beach some more."

"It's too cold out there for the water, honey," Monica answered, making her way back to the table with baby Irene's food. "Plus, you know daddy's still not feeling well. We need to stop by the hospital to see him this afternoon."

"Awwww!" she pouted, tears swelling her vocal chords. "Why do they get to stay down with Uncle Deek and not me?"

"Because it's *their* house," Irene hissed without skipping a beat.

"And if you want to be fresh this early in the morning about it, young lady, Nana will get those little legs."

Iesha began to cry. My initial reaction was to go to her, but I quickly reminded myself her mother and grandmother were better equipped to console and/or discipline her.

I murmured to Sadik, "I'm going out on the deck to call into work."

He nodded, raising the coffee mug to his mouth. "Camille should be back from the store any minute now. She can take Sadik while I shower."

Just as Iesha began to sob out loud, I slipped out of the sliding door.

"You believe this bitch saying she know who killed Haitian Ricky?" Tasche rasped into the phone.

My admiring eyes halted their gaze over the sparkling pool on the side of the house at that. For some strange reason, my belly fluttered and heart galloped.

Blinking, I hummed, "Really?"

"Yeah! This bitch been wildin', yo. I told you she been on one since his party."

"His party?" Tasche was right: she had mentioned Randi's peculiar behavior a time or two for months now, but not regularly.

"Yeah."

"What happened at his party?"

"You know Randi was tight about that nigga's wife coming to town. 'Member she left his crib and stayed with me? She basically stayed at my place since then."

"And now she thinks she knows who killed him..." I thought out loud.

"I told her ass a million people coulda murked that nigga—even the police. Haitian Ricky had mad enemies, yo."

From the corner of my eye, I saw a fleet of black SUVs pull up to the front of the house. I was on the deck when I called Tasche, and once we began talking, I found myself traveling to the side where the pool was. One of the men I recognized as Earl's security left the first truck and ambled to the front door, I guessed to announce their arrival.

"Did she say who, Tasche?" I asked into the phone, blindly watching.

"She said the streets but acted like it was personal." Tasche sighed. "I 'on't know, yo. I 'on't really be paying ol' girl no mind now. She just be...zoned the fuck out. I ain't gone front like I miss having that bitch around, 'cause these last four days by myself been fuckin' heaven, but I hope she okay."

"I wonder how long she'll be away. I tried texting her the day we flew out for the funeral, but she hasn't answered." As my regard remained on the SUVs that looked so out of place, a thought struck. "You think she's staying with her girl, Brenda? You have her num—"

My words were cut short when the door to one of the trucks opened and Tiffany climbed down in tall wedges, cropped cargo pants and a yellow cropped hoodie, exposing her midriff. Her hippy strut was purposeful, chin lifted into the air as she approached the front door.

"You there, yo?" Tasche asked.

I blinked several times. "Sorry. I was gonna ask if you have Brenda's number but just saw something that caught my attention. I'll call you back."

"A'ight. I'm 'bout to fall the fuck out anyway. Later."

"Bye." I pulled the phone from my ear with my eyes glued to Tiffany.

Slowly, I rounded the house on the grass, peering inside as Tiffany entered through the front door. I watched as she glanced all around when inside, taking in the place. For a while, no one noticed her, I imagined because everyone was busy gathering the last of their things to go.

I stepped onto the front porch, still undetected by Tiffany. Her head whipped left and right, seemingly with rapt curiosity.

"Aunt Tiff!" I backed up just before Iesha bounded the hallway until colliding with Tiffany's midsection. "You look so pretty!"

"Hey, baby!" Tiffany tittered with obvious delight. "Thank you! Where's everybody?"

"They coming. Mommy just packed the baby's bag."

"Oh. Okay."

"Hey, Tiffany," Taaliba called out, leaving the kitchen and headed for the stairs to the second floor. She was on a call.

"Hey, girl!" Tiffany's greeting was starkly upbeat. "I'm ready for this flight!"

Taaliba's attention of Tiffany didn't go past her two words to her. But as Taaliba ascended, her older brother descended. His face was blank, feline eyes impassive as he held our son to his shoulder.

Sadik stopped well before the landing, his head falling to the side, mutedly questioning her.

"I used the same transportation as the family, remember!" Tiffany explained with a smile in her voice.

"Iesha," Sadik called out. "Go help Mommy with baby NeNe."

Without a murmur of a question, Iesha skipped off into the living room.

Sadik dropped down a few more steps. "You had to ride to the house with transportation? Come inside with security to help with luggage?"

I felt the sting of his words in her hesitation. "Sadik," there was a croak in her delivery. "I had to use the bathroom."

I empathized with the abrasion against her soul from his scolding. Sadik was a lion protecting the peace of his home. Instinctively, I knew this.

Quickly, I stepped inside. "Right there to your left."

Tiffany turned to find me.

"Bilan," Sadik started.

I shook my head. "It's okay, Deek. She may really need to go," I tried to soothe the blow of clipping his leadership. "Besides, she's dripping syrup."

"What?" Tiffany demanded, alarmed.

"I said, once again you're somewhere I belong and you don't." I gazed directly into her perfectly lined eyes. "And once again, I'm granting you courtesy." I pointed and repeated. "Right there to your left."

Monica sauntered in with the baby on her hip and Iesha on her heels. Her expression was one of curiosity and discomfort from what she likely guessed right of what she walked in on.

"Hey, Tiff..." Monica stumbled on the emotion of her greeting.

Irene began down the stairs, appearing and sounding winded at the same time.

Tiffany supplied a quick and faint smile when responding, "Hi."

She took off right after for the bathroom.

I climbed a few steps to meet the Sadiks, asking for my baby with outstretched arms. His father handed him over without incident.

I murmured to him, "I may be warming to the Ellises, and my baby may be one, but I'll never concede to the Ellis way. Keep her away from my child, me, and your private parts."

I heard him suck in a breath as I turned to go back down the stairs.

I treaded out of the restroom to find big ass buggy eyes against the hallway wall. Understanding it could only mean news, I tossed my chin to her.

Rory waited until women leaving the restroom next to me passed by before sauntering my way. "I hit up Luis from the resort in Costa Rica."

"And?"

"He said they booked up, my nigga. The only way he could make something happen by tomorrow is if you wanna cop something."

I lowered my chin, brows hiked. "Buy property?" Rory nodded. "Luis must've lost his goddamn mind if he thinks I'm going to buy a villa just for him to accommodate me on short notice."

Rory shrugged. "Just act like you interested."

My face balled. "Fuck him."

"A'ight, then what? I can hit up Dawn in the Turks and Caicos." I shook my head at that possibility. Rory continued her push. "She still want you to come see some properties."

"Tiff was out there in the fall under the guise of testing out one of the properties for me. I'm not going to take advantage of Dawn like that."

"But Bilan ain't gone know Tiff was out there."

My head snapped back and a grin widened my lips. "There's no fuckin' way I'm taking Bilan to an island I had Tiff check out in a manner of sending her away for her birthday. Bilan would skewer my fuckin' balls! You're a woman; you should know better, Bean."

"Shit," she breathed, eyes rolling away. "I'm a different type of female, my G. Fuck that."

"Well, Bilan is, too. TCI is a no."

"Plus, you sent Tiff out there to keep her away from Bilan for Thanksgiving. B'll understand that shit."

I tossed my head left to right with closed eyes. "Hell fuckin' no."

I'd been in Bilan's good graces for a few months now, and the last thing I needed was to fuck it up, acting like a clueless ass clown. My fuck ups had been countless since making her mine; this would not be one of them.

"Then what?"

I took a deep breath, leaning against the wall in the long hallway. The restaurant was busier tonight than it was when Bilan and I visited here last summer. Even now in the spring, people visited *Macen Beach*. It made me think of "private and low key" accommodations even harder. Then it dawned on me.

"I forgot all about fuckin' *St. Justin*," I droned, hand going to my forehead.

It was where I wanted to take her after her brother passed away, but Bilan wanted to work.

Rory's head dropped at the revelation. "Shit! You right." She lifted her phone, her index finger going into the air letting me know I'd sparked a thought in her brain. Rory wasn't just a gun for me, she was a resource. I trusted her with my life, now I had to find a way to trust her with my fiancée's and son's.

Leaving her to do her work, I made my way back out to the

restaurant. From across the room, I saw Bilan had the phone to her ear while she rocked Sadik in his car seat. As I neared them, I could hear her conversation.

"I know," she breathed out. "Just like I understand you've been under a lot of pressure from what you've shared with me, understand he's been under four times as much—as far as what he's shared with me."

She nodded, rocking our son gently. His pacifier bouncing fast, eyelids melting while he succumbed to siesta. It was after nine o'clock, so I'd let his little ass live. Bilan was right: he'd been sleeping longer stretches at night. I just wanted to make sure we weren't hindering the process by expecting him to sleep all day.

"I know you love him, Leeb." Bilan's eyes met mine at that name. "I *know* you understand how he almost lost his son." A concoction of betrayal, pain, and anger lanced my chest at that reminder. "Losing your nephew *would have* been a huge loss for you, too." Bilan nodded, expressing her sympathy while listening, though my little sister couldn't see her.

"Being the only female and youngest sibling *has to* be hard on you at times. I can only imagine. Mmmmhmmmm..." She continued to listen as I rolled my eyes. I couldn't give a shit that Bilan caught me. Taaliba was being a brat, bringing her petty shit to my lady. "Girl, you know I know." She hummed, cutting her eyes away from me.

Know fucking what?

"Of course, I do!" Bilan emphasized. "I don't know much about Iban but being accosted by Sadik is like being run over by a bull-dozer. The man can be completely neanderthal!" She grabbed the phone from between her head and shoulder, placing her elbow on the table, never breaking her rhythm on Sadik's car seat. Her eyes narrowing devilishly, voice turned scandalous. "I ever tell you I think he got me pregnant on purpose?" she whispered conspiratorially.

My mouth fell and hand automatically went for her phone. Bilan moved faster, sitting back. Her eyes were pinned to mine. "Yup. The first time—" She shook her head, then quickly nodded. "I know it's gross, but if you want me to be graceful about your grievances regarding my lover, you have to reciprocate," she warned.

Lover.

So, I'm just your lover?

"Ewwwwww!" I could hear Taaliba cry into the phone. "Okay!"

It made me check my wrist for the time. Taaliba and my mother should have just left the hospital from visiting my father...or Iban. The thought was sobering.

"Girl, the first time we..." Bilan hesitated. "...did it, he made it clear: under no circumstance 'no condoms,' girl." Her defiant eyes still on me. "And his pull out game is garba—"

I reached across the table. "That's e-*fuckin*-nough!"

"Okay! Gotta go. Bye!" Bilan giggled.

"That was rather inappropriate, Bilan. She's my baby sister," I reminded her the moment I ended the call.

I was vexed, and for more than one reason, if I was honest.

"I know who she is, Sadik. I also know she's not a baby, and that she sees you as an energy versus a human being. You're not a tangible being to her, just a mighty force."

I sat back, fucking annoyed. "Taaliba's very much in tune with me." I'd known this about her. "That's not true."

She nodded, firm on her stance. "It's very true. She's in tune with your moods, probably to manage you. The same goes for your father and brother, *but* if I've learned anything in this Ellis family it's *you're* the upper crust, Sadik. You. She can't identify with you if she doesn't know who you are."

"As long as you and Sadik know who I am, I'm fine."

Bilan shook her head this time. "*That's* not true. Your father's down and so is Iban." She rolled her eyes. "Even if Iban wasn't... compromised, he wouldn't be the person they look to as Earl's proxy. You would."

"And what does that have to do with you telling her I got you pregnant on purpose?"

Her eyes fell away as she bit her bottom lip. "Because it's true." Her regard was on me again. "You wanted me pregnant," she whispered. "It's the Sadik Ellis way. I didn't know it then, but I strongly assumed it when I found the money at the house last summer."

But I didn't know she was pregnant, and that fact was still troubling. I'd miscalculated Bilan. That admission brought on another thought I'd been churning over in my mind.

"Why did you stay after finding that money?" It was a question floating in my head each night since I got the call she'd found it. "You could have run farther. Why stay?"

Bilan glanced over to Sadik, who was now sound asleep. Her rocking stopped as she thought about the question, it seemed.

She took a deep breath. "Because that's when I knew."

"Knew what?"

Her eyes rolled up to meet mine. "I knew you really loved me—and I don't mean that irrational claim of being in love with me you made the first night I stayed over at *Elliswoods Palace*. I mean the type of love that wanted me safe and protected. The type that includes provisions. The kind I haven't had since Asad and Idil." Her father and mother. "I subconsciously decided that day I'd stay and wait for you. I knew you'd come."

My head reared and eyes widened. I was confused. "But you gave me hell."

"Because I was scared out of my mind, Sadik." A crease appeared in her forehead.

"And now?"

She glanced over to my son. "Now, I have to embrace my reality." Bilan shrugged. "I'm a mommy to an Ellis. I can't think of a better point of inspiration to do so."

So badly, I wanted to ask if she was okay with that but hearing the wrong answer could send me over the edge. I decided against it.

Bilan perked up, opened an inspired smile. "You took mighty long in that bathroom! You had to unload?"

The air suspended as her lyrical chortle expelled. It was breathy and liberated, unlike I'd ever seen of her. My Nalib expressed humor at my expense and found it to be hilarious. My smile widened slowly, brows pinched.

I shook my head. "I don't shit in public, Nalib."

Her hands shot into the air as she cracked the hell up. "My bad. I forgot I was dealing with the super-human Sadik." She rolled her eyes dramatically. "Really?"

I nodded.

"Well, you're alone there. I wish I could align my mind and body as you seem to have the talent to."

I scratched the back of my head before leaning further into the table. "Are we really talking about shitting in public?"

Bilan tried laughing silently, covering her mouth. She didn't want to awaken Sadik. I saw tears form in her eyes. My Nalib found the topic particularly humorous. I shook my head, sitting back.

"I've been living with you for months. I know what your shit smells like. It's not a sexy topic."

Her eyes burst wide as she sucked in a breath. "And yours is, Mr. Feline-eyed, golden skin, ultra-alpha?"

A proper response tipped my lips but didn't reach my tongue. Instead, I found myself chuckling embarrassingly. "Why are we even talking about this?"

Bilan continued cracking the hell up. I allowed her, her time, enjoying her mirth.

"Why are you staring at me like that?" she asked breathily while wiping her eyes.

Because I've never seen this carefree side of you...

"I'm trying to remember how many times you've laughed at the apartment in the City."

Her silly smile dissipated into a sheepish grin. "I'm capable of laughing, Sadik." She rolled her eyes away bashfully.

"How can I witness it more often?" She shrugged. "Did you laugh a lot before me?"

Bilan's eyes rolled again, yet her grin remained as she peered over to our son. "Of course."

"Answer my question."

"What?"

"How can I see it more often?"

"I can't answer that, Sadik." She tried hiding behind clasped fists at her mouth. "It has to be organic."

"Does that mean you're not happy?"

Bilan shook her head. "I don't think so."

"Are you happy?"

She took a sip of her water. "All things considered, I'm in a good place."

"At the apartment in the City?" I repeated.

"I never thought I'd be living in one of your investment properties in Midtown Manhattan, especially the same place you took me after the Pixie concert last year." She nodded, processing that reality. We'd been there since Iban shot himself. There was no fucking way I'd have my family sleep there after that traumatic experience. "It's like more than less than half the space of your high-rise, but..." She took a cleansing breath. "I have all I need there. Sadik and Sadik."

I nodded, thrilled to hear that.

"How long will we be there?"

I tossed my head, in a shrug. "Depends on how long it takes us to decide where we'll build our family home."

Bilan nodded, eyes to the table. "I can look at the paperwork you gave me for my birthday tomorrow when we get back."

I shook my head, going for my wallet to finally pay the tab. "Tomorrow, we travel."

"Okay. So...yeah. When we get back to the apartment, I can look through them."

"Tomorrow we begin a getaway," I made clear.

Her eyes narrowed. "Where?"

"We'll see when we get there."

I didn't exactly have an answer for her. I just needed to get my family away from the metropolitan. To strengthen us.

"I'm not packed for a getaway, much less one without a named destination."

"Where we're going, you won't need many clothes, but I asked Kimmy to pack a few things for you and Sadik. They'll be flown down with the jet." I lay the cash on the table.

"Kimmy can't possibly know everything we'll need," she argued, but thankfully without anger.

"And whatever she doesn't, I'm sure we can pick up where we're headed."

Her eyes narrowed my way. "Is this what life will be like next to you?"

I pushed out my lips, eyes wandering as I considered that. A hum left my nostrils and my head bounced from side to side. "I suppose so." There was no need to lie.

Bilan blew out a deep breath, looking around her place setting and the bench she sat on. "I guess I'll get us packed then watch *Redeeming Souls'* archived service from earlier tonight on the back porch when I'm done."

She grabbed her purse and the baby bag before leaving the booth. I moved in after her and grabbed Sadik's car seat, careful not to rouse him. I followed Bilan to the door, noticing Rory and Johnson making their way out, too.

"Hey, Bilan!"

My head whipped forward, and I saw a brown-skinned woman intersect with Bilan. Her eyes were expectant as she smiled her way.

"Wandra," Bilan replied, somewhat surprised. "Brian."

The girl's eyes traveled back to me then down to Sadik's car seat. They landed back up to me, sweeping my frame from top to bottom, then sparkled once done.

Bilan caught on. "Hey, guys," she finally greeted them.

"Is this...?" the young woman inquired.

Bilan seemed stuck, unable to answer.

I extended my free hand to the young lady first. "Hi, Wandra and Brian. I'm Sadik, Bilan's fiancé." I lifted the car seat just slightly for reference. "And this is our son, Sadik the second."

The girl's eyes ballooned as they traveled down to Bilan's flat belly. "You...had a baby?"

Bilan sucked in a nervous breath, but her gushing smile was undeniable. "I did. He's ten weeks old."

"Holy shit!" She glanced my way again. "Bilan, you were..."

"Pregnant?" Bilan gave a firm nod. "Yup."

"Did Linda know?" the young lady asked, clearly blown away. "Jason didn't mention it."

"It wasn't Jason's announcement to share," I made clear.

The girl's head lashed toward me. The Brian kid's reaction was the same. I decided to make him the victim of my daring gape. His eyes fell away.

"It's late, Wandra, and we need to get the baby to bed," Bilan began the ending of this awkward exchange.

The girl, Wandra's, face fell as Bilan extended her arm protectively for Sadik and me to move in front of her.

"O...okay. I'll text you."

"Okay." I felt her soft hand at the waist of my shorts. "Goodnight, Brian," Bilan bade.

I could feel the girl, Wandra's, heated gaze on me, but didn't confirm it. Bilan's hand remained on my back as we gaited to the door.

Rory stood outside, waiting for us. I watched Bilan strut in five-inch heels and short denim shorts to the rental truck Johnson had pulled up that soon.

"That's them corny ass fucks she was chillin' with last summer?" Rory asked as I ogled my lady.

"Yup." Bilan hopped inside, allowing me to see the cheeks of her ass during her step up.

While that sight excited me, it annoyed me at the same damn time because others could see the same thing. Wisdom told me to keep it to myself because she'd assume I was referencing her weight gain from the baby. I would never utter a word about something as trivial as that. Bilan's slight gain gave her a mature look I enjoyed. Her legs were beautifully toned, making her ensemble consisting of a yellow and black, long-sleeved flannel shirt, jean shorts, and nude heels immensely appealing.

"We good?" Rory asked.

"Do me a favor." My eyes were still ahead on the truck. "Look into the pastor of *Redeeming Souls for Abundant Living in Christ*."

"That church shit B be watching?"

I guessed even Rory paid attention to the new target of Bilan's attention.

"Yeah. He's a client of *Ellis International*, but I need to know everything about him. Everything. Especially his marital status. Have Johnson look into his books...everything."

"You got it, sire."

I took off for the truck with Sadik in my hand and Rory on my heels.

Bilan

"*Markaad dhalatay oo aad u dhawaaqday...*" I sang to my sleeping baby as we strolled the beach.

Dhamaan jirkeyga ayaa iftiiminaya...

Dunida oo dhan," I breathed the last of the lyrics to the only Somali nursery rhyme I could remember.

Sadik was asleep against my chest. He'd given up on his pacifier almost at the start of our journey this evening. I held it on a finger as my hands were splayed on his back and tush. I sighed, peering out to the water. It was different than the body in *Macen Beach*. The water in *St. Justin* was clear and the sand was white and warm. At this hour of the day, the sun was forgiving. Still up, but dozing.

I glanced down at a bush of burnt orange hair. Irene told me his father's eye and hair color had changed several times before it settled, too. And just like his dad, Sadik was perfect. When I rose above the clouds of overwhelming responsibility, I still couldn't believe I was a mother. What was strange was, I couldn't vividly recall what life was like without him. He smelled adorable. His cry stirred my belly, and his smile swelled my heart.

Though he was fast asleep on my chest, this was a moment I'd carve in my heart forever. One day, he'd stay awake to observe the beauty of an oceanside view. Today, after staying awake the entire flight, my baby was exhausted. The first thing I did after being shown our villa was bring him out to the beach for a walk.

This was beautiful. I could never grow bored of watching the water while having my feet planted on sanded ground. In fact, I made a note to bring a book out once I put Sadik down for the night. Maybe a reread of *"The Alchemist."*

A moue formed on my lips as I gazed down to my orange-haired baby again. "But I want you out here with me," I groaned. "And your dad."

I was finally at that place in life where I didn't need much to relax and be content. I had my family. I had my Sadiks.

"Nalib!" I'd recognize that boom blindfolded and with an eardrum blown out. I turned to look behind me and found him and Camille ambling near me. "Time for Sadik's bath and dinner," he declared.

I began toward them.

"He's knocked out," Camille snickered. "He talked so much on the flight here. I told you he'd crash soon." She reached for him.

My initial reaction was one of hesitation. I wanted this moment with my baby. I'd just set my plans for the night. My son molded comfortably into my chest. He was the perfect size, not weighing my arms at all. This setting was my favorite; why would I not want to share it with him?

Nonetheless, I handed him over.

Camille smiled, receiving him. "I'll have him up, washed, fed, and back down within thirty minutes. I promise."

I forced a smile, missing him already.

"You know what to do if you need us," Sadik addressed our nanny.

"Of course." She gave a neck bow with a smile before backing away with my baby.

I watched her saunter off, regretting every moment of disconnect between S.Q.E., II and me.

"Do you not trust Camille?" Sadik's voice was thick, yet smooth as silk to my senses.

My eyes fell to the sanded floor. "I do."

"Because if you don't—"

"I do!" I needed to make sure he understood and so did I. "I just...I love that boy like nothing else, Sadik." I turned to him, my emotions in my throat.

"So do I, which is why I was okay with Camille being his nanny."

"It's just that he can't speak."

"He won't for some time."

"He's so precious."

"He'll forever be. He's our first and only."

I pulled in a deep breath and begged myself to get it together. Then I turned to him. "Was Rory able to get tampons?"

"Yes. They're in our suite."

"Are they the right brand?"

Sadik lowered his chin as though drawing patience. "*Kotex* is *Kotex*. And Kimmy sends her apologies for not packing them with your things."

My eyes fell to hide my unfounded irritation. "It wasn't her fault. She didn't know I'd be expecting my period this week, Sadik."

"Then your sudden mood change does have to do with being separated from Sadik," he theorized. "He's perfectly fine, honey. And we'll be here for a few days. There will be plenty of opportunities for us to spend time together as a family. You have my word." For seconds long, I searched his eyes for something unnamed. "But now, daddy needs his time with mommy. It happens, you know."

"You sound like a pro so soon."

Sadik formed a forlorn smile as he shook his head. "I'm just a man with an agenda, Nalib."

"What's that?"

He tossed his head to the side. "Come with me. I'll show you."

With less hesitance than with my child, I agreed.

"Easy," Sadik warned, assisting me into a rowboat.

It looked clean, possibly new from the inside. I felt guilty tracking sand from my feet into it.

"Have a seat," he ordered, waiting until I did.

My gaze went into the shallow water at the shore, observing the small sparkles inside, creating a majestic ambiance. Sadik sat down across from me and assumed the oars with a practiced pace and skill. He unclipped them from their fancy holdings and began to row. My eyes wandered all over, so amazed by the wonder of this island.

As we moved, I could see a lifeguard way out into the flat water. He sat high on a distant post. Other than that, there was no Ellis security; just me, Sadik, and our rowboat. The calm sky was dark out but for the stars and moon. The ambiance was stark from the pitch-black water with unusual scintillating turquoise lights.

"Oh, my god..." I breathed in amazement.

"What?"

"The water..." My eyes were transfixed on the sparkling water below. "It sparkles even more out here! It's like we're highlighting the water with our movement!" I'd never seen anything like it.

A guttural rumble pushed from his belly, echoing across the flat body of water.

"Of course, it does. It's the flagellates of the bay. The water's shallow and the mouth of the bay is small. The colored and minuscule organisms are trapped and protected here, making it very, very bright." My eyes danced around. "Each time we move, we create a disruption in the water and they glow. It's almost like how fireflies glow in the air."

Wow...

"This is gorgeous." I turned to him, eyes narrowing as I tried fighting my smile. "Are you going to save me if we tip over?"

"The water isn't deep." His eyes were lucent out here as he regarded the fluorescent water himself. "I'd say no more than five... six feet."

My gaze followed his before returning to his gorgeous face. The skin of his head glistened against the celestial illumination.

"If you're trying to impress me, it's unnecessary. You gave me my first child." A silly smile spread on my face.

"And I hope to give you more when you're ready." My belly

leaped. "But that's not the motive here. Here, I'm trying to make you fall in love with me."

I rolled my eyes, jitters now lancing my belly. "We're past that now, Sadik," I grumbled. "I've told you how I feel about you—more than once."

"You love me." He shrugged, eyes still out into the water as he rowed. "I want you in love with me. Helplessly." Then his feline eyes grazed me. "It's lonely out here."

"Me telling you I love you isn't good enough?"

"It isn't the same."

"How?" I argued.

"Of course, you love me." He scoffed. "Shit. I've given you a life of luxury and leisure. I've provided you a home and family...a child. Over the course of time, when receiving those things, why wouldn't you find a way to love and deeply care for me?"

"Okay. So, what more are you asking?"

"For your soul."

My heart dropped from my bottom, out of my body. My pulse raced and armpits misted. The muscles in my face held frozen. Sadik, noticing my reaction, stopped rowing.

"That request isn't unreasonable."

"Says who?" I breathed.

"The concept of having your soul in my possession isn't sacrilegious, Nalib. You own me: mind, body, and soul."

Anxiety spiked in my veins. "That's weighty," I croaked.

"That's what being in love entails. It's what I live every day."

"It's a lot."

He nodded, yet appeared unperturbed by my aghast state. "I told you outside of *Michelle's* when I finally decided against letting you go, I'm demanding, Bilan."

I nodded, mouth ajar. He did tell me that. But this wasn't *that*. Sadik was telling me I wasn't reciprocating his feelings for me, his love. That made me feel selfish and inadequate. The truth was I loved Sadik more than I believed was safe for me. Not only did I want the best for him, I also obsessed over his happiness. Was I not expressing these feelings?

"I was just cut from delivering my first baby, Sadik. A significant part of my being has changed. I'm still trying to find some of my mind after giving birth."

"And after watching my brother blow a bullet through his skull." His cautious regard was on me.

"Sadik—"

"Eventually, you'll have to deal with it, just like you'll have to sort out the loss of your parents, being kidnapped, seeing Damien die, and the kid in *Pulse* getting shot in front of you." He locked the oars into a holding apparatus as we sat in the middle of the bay. "You'll have to settle it all in your mind before I can expect you to accept me wholly. Until then..." Sadik stood, rocking the boat. He yanked his t-shirt over his head, dropping it into the boat. Next, he went for the waist of his shorts and pulled them down along with his boxers. "...we take a dive."

When he stood straight again, I was able to see his erection grow less than a couple of feet from my face. My mouth watered instantaneously. That quickly, at the sight of ripped and aroused Sadik, the previous topics of conversation were lost to me.

"I'll take care of that later," he answered an unspoken desire.

The swaying of the boat when he jumped naked into the water drove me into a mini panic.

Amazed, I watched the water around his descending body light turquoise. When Sadik surfaced, his smile was the first thing I saw.

Still in shock, face unmoving, a hum lit in my core, burgeoning to other areas of my body. His smile beamed against the neon water.

"You gonna have me out here alone, too?"

Slowly, my head shook. I bit my bottom lip and my eyes surveyed the area. This scene was reminiscent of our first night in Costa Rica, the first time I'd gone away and slept in a bed with a man.

"Unless someone's watching through binoculars, no one can see us. And if they're doing that, they'll have to answer to me, Bilan."

My eyes blossomed. "Don't say things like that."

"Why?"

"Because you're an Ellis. You actually have it in you to act on that threat."

Sadik laughed. "Then what do I have in me to get your ass in here?" His arm flailed in the water.

A rush of excitement coursed my veins and I took a deep breath. I stood and began to strip with a pounding chest. My shirt went first, and bra last. Sadik's expression of mirth disappeared from his golden face as I stood bared to him.

"Move," I commanded, nervous out my mind with my post-baby, surgery body, wanting to dive in and quickly cover myself.

"Hell no," he stated with a rumble in his cords.

"What?" I groused, my head extending past my shoulders in disbelief.

"Hell. No," he repeated. "Bilan, that's my body. It's been branded by me and my child. You think I'm going to spend a moment giving a fuck about a scar and pooch? That shit is mine; all of it."

"It's horrid."

"It tells the crazy muthafucka who tries after me that I demolished your ass, and his demise would follow soon after." His arms moved fluidly to keep him afloat. Another sign of his confidence. "You're mine, Bilan. I'm sorry to say. That scar is proof of it, baby girl."

"You don't mean that."

"You're marked. By me." His declaration was final. "Now get your ass in here."

I didn't wait any longer. I jumped in the water. My body submerged right away, and quickly, I felt his touch. Sadik grabbed me, pulling my body up and toward him before I hit the surface.

After the swishing sounds of emerging from the warm water, I heard him rumble, "You rocked that boat...'bout to hit your damn head."

My body brushed smoothly against his hard frame. I pushed my hair from my face, trying to catch my breath, but couldn't ignore the transmitter like zaps I now felt from this proximity, in these intimate conditions. I reached up and wrapped my arms around him. Unplanned, my legs enwound his hard body, too.

"*Shit*..." I heard him groan.

And I knew why. My hips bucked. The water was silky and at the perfect indulgent temperature to make me needy for him. Our lips found each other's and we did what we did best, giving into the mighty pull. When we withdrew, Sadik took me at the hand and we swam the bay together, reveling in the wonder of the bioluminescent water of *Saint. Justin*.

∞4∞

Her back arched deeper, the small of it dropping lower. She was tight. *Fuck...* She was tight, pussy throbbing around my dick. The view was delicious. The tiger stripes on her hips, dimples on her round ass cheeks, and the root of my cock at the rim of her pussy from behind. I could see her ass sphincter puckered, and a small patch of hair on the lips of her pussy open to me. A sheen of perspiration coated her back and neck.

"Don't cum," I grunted.

I reveled in the sight of her small waist above her wide mound. Her pregnancy weight had been melting off by the week, and I couldn't decide if I preferred it or not. I loved her body swollen and carrying my child, but a narrowed waist, wide ass Bilan drove me wild, too. Seeing her bent over the bed, arms stretched out, and fists clawing the sheet had me ready to explode. Her caramel skin glowed in the candlelit room. The breeze from the opened terrace door couldn't cool the heat from between her thighs.

My thrust into her was with strain. Her receiving it was the same. Bilan's ass cheeks squeezed, her hips vibrated as she tried to be obedient and not give in to the bliss awaiting her. I closed my eyes, squeezing them as I rocked into her again slowly, reveling the glide into her wetness. Her silkiness.

"Sadik!" she cried, her spine jerked, shoulders flexed.

"Wait, baby," I groaned, then slapped her ass.

"I can't!"

"You can," I assured her, not so confident myself.

We were both tired after the flight in and a swim in the bay. After a shower and me making her explode twice in my mouth, I suggested she finally go to bed. But my Nalib was greedy. She begged for my dick, and I figured she could delay her third orgasm.

And now...

Her breaths came out in long drags, body vibrating. I couldn't hold back any longer. My soft, intermittent thrusts grew to full plunges. I widened my thighs around her, going deeper inside.

"*Sa*—" she choked out, ass twitching in the air, pussy clutching me. "I can't—"

"Go!" I grunted, rocking into her.

Bilan's head dropped forward, shoulders flexed upward, and her ass moved into my thrusts, pounding me.

"I'm coming..." she droned deeply.

"Fuck..."

My head fell back as my balls heated and drew up. My explosion nearly knocked me over. I commanded my thighs to stand upright, squeezing as I plunged and plunged into her, splashing my gratitude of her all over her womb.

"I can't stop!" she whimpered, torso twittering violently.

I could feel the walls of her pussy convulsing, too. In that moment something broke, a barrier I was unaware of when it came to my woman. I was open to her, grinding into her too freely, too vulnerable. A lesser confident man would feel too stripped, too bare. But for one my age, I reveled in it.

When Bilan collapsed on the bed, taking me with her, her body still vibrated, partially laying beneath me. Her teeth shivered and brows remained pinched. I watched her through low lids as we faced each other. My heart continued to race, her entire frame still unsettled. I lay a hand on the small of her back to provide a point of connection.

"How can I ever come back from this?" When my eyes opened, I knew I'd fallen asleep. Bilan's freckles came into view first. Then her pooled eyes were clear. Her body still shivered slightly. "What comes after Sadik?"

Her tearing eyes were low; she was fatigued physically, yet overly-stimulated emotionally.

I didn't speak, didn't think it was appropriate to.

"You want my soul," she breathed, eyes struggling to stay open. "What if your absence from my life would destroy it?"

The muscles in my face tightened. "I'm not going to die, baby."

"You don't know." She tried shaking her head, her body yielding to another shiver. "I've lost the closest people to my heart. Losing the one who explored my heart and body—inside and out—isn't something I'd survive. Not even your son could replace my friend and lover."

I reached over and thumbed her tears away, then closed her lids with my fingers. "You won't ever have to live that nightmare."

I would continue to take care of myself, unlike Palmer. And I'd never belong to a high-risk lifestyle like my father.

Eventually, her breathing evened out and my eyes closed, too. It was short-lived from the knock at the door. My first thought was to ignore it. Whoever was there would get the hint and go away. It was after midnight. Then I remembered my number one man. I was a father now with endless hours of availability.

Letting go of a heavy breath, I slipped from Bilan, leaving her naked body sprawled out on the mattress. I grabbed a robe from the bathroom before heading for the door. On my way, the knocking sounded again. I opened it, expecting to see Camille. When I recognized Rory, I stepped outside, closing the door behind me.

"Just got a call from Dee over at Double E's warehouse," she whispered, wreaking of dro. "They think they being watched."

"By who?"

She shrugged. "He ain't sure. But they say the niggas sitting in the cars, tryna keep a distance is white."

"Who is they?"

She shrugged again. "Dee ain't say. He only said a couple of them niggas. They think it's them *FED*dy niggas."

"Why?"

Her head jerked back. "Why? My nigga, I just told you them muthafuckas all white."

I crossed my arms, widening my stance. "If you weren't so fucked up now, you'd realize Federal agents aren't all white. They're diverse and would be, especially for Double E Bags. They'd avoid discrimination lawsuits. And you know—*shit*, they should know—who the members are on the team assembled for my father's file."

Rory's face opened up in realization; her low eyes from being high were still big as hell. "Fuuuuuuuck!" she breathed. "You is so right, my G."

"Who's running shit over there anyway?"

Rory shrugged again. "Hell if I know. We just buried Palmer, and shit." Her voice turned regretful.

"Who's his second in command on the org chart?"

Her face balled again. "You know this ain't *Ellis International!*" she whispered hard. "They ain't corporate over there, my nigga."

I shook my head, brows going into the air. "They should still have someone named."

"I doubt it."

"Hit up Daz over there." He was a lieutenant in my father's organization. Over the past two years or so, Palmer had been spending copious amounts of time with him and one of my father's men who'd caught one in the Rizzo war. "Tell that nigga his crew is divided and isn't properly communicating. He needs to tighten up their org chart. Sounds like Popov staking out the place to test their strength now that their overseer is on his back."

"Shit, man!" she whispered again. "That's the first fuckin' step in attack." Rory nodded. I started back to the bedroom door. "Yo, sire," she called out to me on approach. I watched her sniffing me.

"The fuck is you smelling like, my G?"

I backed away. *Bilan.* "Mind ya fuckin' business."

When I closed the door, I heard her chortle down the stairs.

A draft hitting my chest had me turning over onto my belly. I lifted the blanket up to cover me. Then I reached for him.

Nothing.

I didn't smell him, didn't feel his heat. My eyes opened slowly to a blur. I rubbed the sleep debris from them, realizing how hard I'd slept. Sadik wasn't there. I lifted my head to glance around the suite, but didn't see any sign of him. Suddenly, I felt bereft. How could I not? Last night was...life-changing. Sadik had always been an incredible lover, however, I didn't have much to compare him to.

Last night, I came to the conclusion our sexual synergy was beyond his skill set. What Sadik and I shared was spiritually binding. I'd begun to feel at home with him in more than the physical realm. When I opened to him fully, the bliss was inescapable. I could no longer express jealous curiosity over what pleasure he provided women before me. There was no way he could have experienced this connection with another woman without giving her all he'd given me.

I ran my fingers through my hair, wishing to get over this fear of losing him. Normal women feared cheating or their significant others leaving, but they were not Ellis men. I feared Sadik's death and that of our child. I'd lost everyone I loved the most; I couldn't bear the lives of these two. The thought of it caused my belly to flutter.

My baby...

I leaped from the bed, holding my chest as I jogged to the bathroom. It only took a couple of minutes in the shower to wash off my lust session from last night, but washing my face and brushing my teeth took a little longer. By the time I was out of the bathroom and dressed in a fresh bikini, I was even more anxious to see my baby boy. I combed my hair back enough to toss on a beach hat, then grabbed sunscreen lotion and my phone from the dresser on my way out of the bedroom.

This place was larger than our villa in Costa Rica. There were three bedrooms here. Two were on the second floor and the third was just off the kitchen. That's where Rory, surprisingly, stayed. She'd made it clear in the past how she preferred her space away from her employer when traveling with him. But Sadik requested she stay with us this time. I had an idea it had to do with the baby.

The other bedroom on the second floor belonged to Camille and Sadik, II. I checked in there first and found the room empty. Only traces of my baby were there. I headed for the stairs next. The lower level was empty, too, but for a man in the kitchen cooking. His uniform revealed his identity and purpose for being here.

"Good morning, Mrs. Ellis," he attempted with a thick accent.

I managed a smile, not caring he addressed me by the wrong name. "Do you know where my family is?" My voice was too soft, too desperate.

He gave a neck bow, perceiving my unease, and pointed. "Out there, ma'am."

I could barely say thanks before barreling out the back door.

The beautiful tropical view was missed. The fountains, palm trees, sounds of the waterfall, and sparkling pool ahead was no more than props until my eyes were satisfied in their search. At first, all I saw of him was the designer scarf wrapped around his head and some of his golden muscular frame. He'd seen me, though. He shuffled around in his lounge seat.

"There she is," Sadik sang, standing with our cranky baby.

My baby made the stank face, snorting before the big cry. My feet led me to them before my brain could quite make the request.

"Yeah, yeah," Sadik croaked. "We know you're hungry." He handed him over to me. "It's perfect timing, actually. Your mom can feed you while I feed her."

My eyes shot from our son to Sadik's face. Unbothered, his friendly grin remained in place as I settled the baby on my chest.

"I didn't mean to sleep so hard and for so long," I tried to explain, very much embarrassed.

"Hey!" Sadik completely ignored me, addressing the baby. "You're gripping that thing like a pro. That's mine, partner," he warned, regarding my breast.

Sadik settled upon there, his face leaning into mine. His little lips in suckling position. I turned for the house. "I'll go get his bottle—"

The sight of Camille strolling out of the villa, shaking a bottle of milk broke my stride. She wore a solid black cover-up with flip flops. "Here you go," she sang. "Should I feed him or would you like to?"

"Please." I took the bottle. "Let me." As I turned for the chairs, Sadik wiggled in my arm sucking in air repeatedly, excited by the sight of his meal. "Mommy's so sorry for sleeping like that. I should have been up hours ago with you."

When I sat down and positioned the baby, Sadik chimed in, "But you were getting much-needed rest while daddy and Ms. Camille hung out with the young soldier." His tone was light and playful.

I tried for a smile, wanting to relax. Sadik was fine, and so was his father...bare-chested and tatted. He was so fine, I ripped my eyes away from him awkwardly. "What time is it?"

Sadik grabbed the baby's feet and wiggled them. "About eleven-thirty."

I winced, eyes closing. "I slept that late."

"Your body needed it. That's what this getaway is for. You need to be restored physically and emotionally."

I peered up to him. "Just me?"

"We do," he qualified. "All three of us." Before I could respond, he sighed. "Ah, here comes lunch—or brunch for you."

I glanced over my shoulder, where the chef was coming out

holding two trays of food in his hands. He headed straight toward us, and apparently, with a helper on his heels. He carried several tray tables in one arm and a platter dish in the other. They quickly set us up with food near our chairs. I watched as my baby gulped down his food while grabbing my nose and ears.

"What do you want to drink? A mimosa?" Sadik asked.

I couldn't think in the moment, needing to connect with my baby. "Sure."

He turned and mumbled to the chef. After they were done, Sadik took to the chair next to me. He yanked on my hat a bit.

"This is cute."

"My hair looks a mess. It was the only thing I could think of to not come down here looking crazy."

"You can't look crazy to us. You're our queen."

I snorted, observing the waterfall depositing into the aqua blue pool. "Irene's your queen."

He nodded. "Forever."

"I meant to call her this morning to check in. I haven't heard from her since they left *Macen Beach*."

"We called her this morning," Sadik murmured, his hand back on the baby. "She's consumed with my father's recovery."

"I bet."

"I offered her to come out to spend time with Sadik, but she said the doctors are considering releasing him soon. She doesn't want to miss that."

"I don't blame her. He's just my son's grandfather and I feel like I may miss something being out here. I'll call him today to check in."

Sadik didn't comment any further. Those gorgeous kaleidoscope-hued irises beamed when on our son, similar to the way they did when he desired me. I found myself awkwardly looking away again.

"I can't believe we have a baby," I muttered, so much running through my head at the moment.

When I saw Sadik's body, ripped in nothing but a scarf around his head and low resting swimming trunks, exposing his happy trail, it didn't seem real. My body had been shrinking, but it would never be the same; I'd had surgery. The first few weeks of postpartum, I felt violated. It took some time for me to recover emotionally from a last-minute emergency procedure.

"We do," Sadik made clear, his focus on the baby. "And it's my hope you'll let me have another chance at it." He stood. "What do we have for my Nalib to throw down on today?"

"Ha. Ha. Ha," I replied dryly.

Sadik turned back to me with a million-dollar smile. "The other night in *Macen Beach*. The night of the funeral, what woke you up in the middle of the night?"

I spent a moment recalling that. "Oh. A goat wolf."

He peered over his shoulder again. "A goat wolf?"

I nodded. "It's the only way I could describe it. It looked like a goat, but growled like a wolf."

"What about the wolf goat?" he jeered.

I took in a deep breath, recalling the details of the dream. "He had the family—your family—in a cluster in the middle of an open field."

"A cluster?"

"Yeah. They were in this like...circle...huddled in fear."

"Who?"

"All of the Ellises, including Sadik. But you weren't there."

He came back to the lounger next to me with a plate of fresh fruits and fajitas. "My father and Iban?"

I nodded again. "They were there. Irene, Monica, Taaliba, and all the kids. My baby was in the middle. I guess protectively, if you want to call it that. They weren't safe. All of them were fearful, waiting to be attacked by the goat wolf."

He pushed a forked piece of pineapple to my mouth, and I ate it. Then Sadik plucked a couple of pieces of fruit into his own mouth. I could see arteries in his temples raised as his eyes cast out into the blue sky. The baby's pulls began to slow, his little belly round and full, his hands still busy in their reach. When Sadik fed me more fruit, the baby attempted that, too, but was too slow. His father and I shared a chortle over it.

"A goat wolf," Sadik murmured, seemingly still processing it.

"Yeah." I swallowed. "It was weird. I was running in the woods until it opened to this field where I saw my—your—family."

I wouldn't share the part about Jason. Sadik wouldn't take to it.

His feline eyes hit me, likely in scolding of referring to his people as just his family. I still hadn't yet felt comfortable enveloping them. I'd gotten the impression it was what Tiffany did, and I was no Tiffany.

Sadik fed me more fruit just when the baby pushed the bottle from his mouth with his tongue. I pulled him over my shoulder to burp him. Sadik pulled out one of his phones and began tapping.

"Goat wolf hybrid," he muttered.

"Yeah. A goral."

Sadik's head shot up. "A goral?"

I nodded. "With a long tail." That memory was still fresh.

He returned to his phone, tapping away again.

"Good!" I encouraged little Sadik when he belched. He began to talk, tickling my heart. He eventually burped again. "Mommy's so happy your belly's full, S.Q.E.!" Sadik lowered his phone and went for the last piece of fruit on the plate. Then he lay the plate of fajitas on my lap and went to grab the baby.

"Eat," he commanded once my arms were free. "We're going to take my son out to the beach."

I took a bite of the fajita, then asked, "What did you find out about that ugly goral?"

Sadik's eyes were narrowed as he peered into the distance. "Long tail gorals can be found in Russia." His delivery was stiff.

"That's weird." I swallowed my food. "What would we be doing in Russia?"

He mumbled eerily, "Russians are in the States, too, my love."

His incessant babbling had me glancing up from my book to check in on him again. Sadik's eyes were fixed to the hanging fixtures over his beach playpen. He was engaged in heavy conversation with them.

I leaned over the pen. "Hey," I smiled. "I wish you'd talk to me like that." After processing my presence, his smile widened even more. "Hi, baby boy! Are you enjoying the beach? I told you, you would."

The weather was perfect to have him out here. I feared the temperature would be too hot, but his father assured he'd be fine underneath the tree, a shade, and another small covering his playpen built for the beach featured. Sadik had been a well-behaved baby out here. He'd even been awake the entire hour and a half or so we'd been at the water.

So lost in the joy of my baby, I didn't see Rory until she was upon us. She didn't speak either. Her short frame looked awkward in a tank with Bob Marley's face on the front and denim Bermuda shorts ducked beneath the umbrella. Her ears were plugged with buds and she held her phone in her hand. Her natural hair was braided back into a ponytail, making me wonder who did it. Per usual, Rory looked like a twelve-year-old boy.

"S.Q.E., II!" she chirped. "You out here chillin', lil' god? I can't wait to get you in that water...teach you how to dunk niggas in there." She gently yanked on his toe. Her smiled dwarfed into a grin. "I can't believe how big you gettin'. *And* ya ass still awake. That's what's up, king."

And *I* couldn't believe the love and adoration in her voice as she studied him from behind her sunglasses. She didn't address or acknowledge me as she adulated over my son.

"Rory," I called out to her, closing my book. She eased back from her knees to stand, returning to her guarded posture toward me. "you don't see me sitting right next to him? I don't see how not: I'm a whole fifteen pounds heavier than I was when you met and decided not to like me."

Rory rolled her head away, whispering a string of expletives.

"Why don't you like me? You've been spending more time with me than Sadik over the past eight months. His son has been here only two of them, and I still haven't had half the warmth he has from you. And not to mention, you've known Tiffany a lot longer, leaving me in between her and my son. I just don't know how to win you over."

"B," she groaned, hands going to her head. "why you always gotta fuck with me?"

Shocked by her disposition, I gasped, holding in a budding laugh. "Me? How?"

"You keep talking 'bout I 'on't like you—"

"You don't!" I finally released some of the humor.

Rory expressed no amusement at all. "But I fucks with you like every day."

"How?"

"When I'm driving ya mean ass all around!"

"Because you're paid to, Rory!"

Sadik began to cry.

Her arm tossed his way. "See, you fuckin' up lil' man's vibe, too."

I reached over and lifted Sadik from the playpen. "Don't worry, baby," I told him. "Mommy's used to this reception from her."

"Here the fuck you go!" she croaked, dropping onto the lounger next to me. "Why you always gotta fuck with me, B?"

"Because that's the only time I get 'color' from you." I rocked Sadik over my shoulder to calm him.

"What?" She shook her head like a male child. "I 'on't even know what the fuck that mean."

"It means you're mean to *me*, if anything."

For seconds long, Rory didn't respond. She gazed out to the water and I settled Sadik down. I grabbed a fresh diaper and wipes to change him. So used to having Rory around mutedly, I'd forgotten she was there momentarily.

That was until she murmured, "Don't be sayin' shit like that around them, B."

My eyes widened. "Who?"

"Them," she croaked. "The S.Q.E.s."

"So just live with the fact that you don't like me." I nodded, lips pouted. "Okay."

"Hell no! That ain't even true. That's why I'm saying don't say it."

"How isn't it true, Rory?"

"You know that shit ain't true, B. You and me both know if you thought I ain't fuck with you, my ass woulda been fired. That nigga don't play that shit." The grouse in her words concerned me.

"You think Sadik would fire you if we didn't get along?"

Rory chuckled, palms rubbing against her thighs. "I woulda been outta here before Lamont's ass got clipped. You 'on't see how open my G is?"

I nodded. "I think I have an idea, but that has nothing to do with you not liking me. Okay, I'm guessing you're dispelling my belief of you not liking me. Fine. But, Rory, I know nothing about you."

"Shit..." She scoffed and began counting off on her fingers. "You know the shit I like to eat, the brand of cigs I burn, where I live... where I work. All that shit, and you claiming you 'on't know me?"

"What's your real name?" I challenged.

Rory turned for the water again as I finished up on the baby's diaper change and went to lather him up again with sunscreen. "Rahdeah Smith," she muttered.

My eyes blossomed again. "Where does *Rory* come from?"

She shrugged, still facing away. "My uncle raised me. He said I looked like a fuckin' gnome."

I sputtered a laugh, glad she didn't catch it. "How did you meet Sadik?"

Another pause before she muttered, "Iban."

"Iban introduced you?" My body froze over the playpen when I reached in for his pacifier. Rory nodded. "How? When?"

"Back in the day. We was in a...probation program together. He saw me fight one night, then introduced me to his pops for work. S.Q.E. was there." Her forehead gestured to the water. "And when his pops passed on hiring me as a driver, S.Q.E. had other plans for me."

That was sobering. I knew Iban had a history in the penal system; he'd been convicted of murder. I could never forget the gory details in that search of him I did last summer in *Macen Beach*.

But Rory?

"What were you on probation for?"

"Shit." She spat into the sand and quickly swept sand over it with her foot.

"What type of *shi*—"

My words were lost at the rapid, shifting sight of watching him wade through the water for the shore. Water cascaded from his golden skin. His sculpted arms bunched into ropes as he wiped his face clear of it. His trunks were so low; they exposed his swollen abdominal oblique muscle. His sex appeal was a moving spirit, tickling my senses to awaken me for his coming presence.

"Look at ya ass," Rory snickered. "You be frontin' like that nigga ain't got yo head split the fuck open, too." My face folded. "Look at you! You rubbing ya lips!" She roared in laughter.

I couldn't help my eye roll. Before I could think of a snarky rebuttal, Sadik was upon us. He reached for a towel and rubbed it into his head. I watched with rapt interest as he dried himself off from his chest to his waist. Then I watched as his abdomen crunched when he bent over to clasp the baby's hand.

"Oh, you're just in time." I fixed a smile. "Rory was just about to tell me how you two met."

Sadik's mirthful expression dropped and he glanced over to Rory.

Rory quickly turned back for the water.

Sadik turned back to the baby and me. "Oh, yeah?" he asked before kissing the baby's feet. "Everything set up for this evening, Rory?"

Rory stood to her feet. "You know it." Then she took off, short legs, kicking up sand in her departure.

Interesting...

The baby started to fuss, snatching my attention.

"Oh, no!" I groaned. "What's the matter?"

When I holstered him in my arm to my chest, his father took him. "Sadik," his commanding alto lacked the silkiness I'd come to love. But it included a feature almost equally pleasing. "Hey," he called out to him again over the baby's cry as he tried catching his eyes. "Sadik!" My lover upped the authoritative bass found in a father's warning. "Where's his hat?" I searched through the bag and pulled out his little fisherman's hat.

Sadik placed it on his head. "Text Camille and tell her he's ready for a bottle and a nap."

"I can do that."

As he bounced the baby in his arm, Sadik shook his head. "I've got plans for you. Let her take care of him."

I sat back deflated. It wasn't that I didn't want alone time with him. I just hated parting from my baby. Torn, I watched the two Sadiks stroll down the beach. The senior eventually got the baby's attention and then for him to stop fussing. Hesitantly and with obedience, I texted our "nanny," Camille.

How am I going to adjust to this new life of mine?

∞5∞

"Alright." I slammed the shot glass down, then gestured with my head toward her plate. "Another bite."

Bilan giggled, trying to hide her mouth behind her fist. "No," she spoke around her food. "Now I feel bad."

I smiled. "Why?"

"Because that was your third shot!"

I shrugged with my eyebrows at the kitchen table in the villa. "I do what I gotta do."

She continued to laugh. "Just to get me to eat." Bilan shook her head, feigning rebuke.

"To encourage you to eat." I winked. "And let's not forget, you didn't work out with me this morning."

Her expression fell as she swallowed the rest of the food in her mouth. "And do more plank jacks on the sand? How could I sleep through those?" With hiked brows and her eyes rolling away, she grabbed her glass, taking a sip of water.

My smile widened, eyes narrowed. At first, I found her irresistible; now, I had to add hilarious to that growing list. "You're so silly." Bilan rolled her eyes, a smirk revealed in those high cheekbones. I glanced down to her plate at the leftover fajita from lunch she never finished. "Looks like..." I considered it. "Maybe two more bites left."

I poured two shot glasses and lined them up in front of me.

Bilan gasped. "Oh, my god. Sadik!" She reached across the table.

"What the hell are you doing?" I chuckled.

"I feel bad. I'll take these last two with you."

My forehead lifted in shock. "Really?"

"I can't have my baby's daddy out here in these *St. Justin* streets drunk off the tequila by himself."

That shit warmed my chest more than the previous shots had. I watched her toss back another glass. When she finally got it all down, Bilan took another bite of the fajita. My eyes were locked onto her mouth as she chewed. I was pleased. This was a fun attempt at getting her to eat.

"What are you thinking about?" I asked.

"If Sadik'll smell alcohol on me."

I shook my head. "It'll be out of your system by the time we get back from our excursion. He may be knocked out by then anyway."

"Where are we going?" she asked with a mouth full of food, going for the bottle of tequila.

"You'll find out when we get there."

She refilled the glasses. "Do I need to press out my hair?"

I shook my head. "Don't waste your time." Then I tossed my chin. "Looks like more than two to go. That last bite wasn't big enough."

Bilan's eyes rolled as her shoulders lifted in a giggle. "You did it again."

"What?"

She pointed to my mouth. "That thing you do with your lips when you want me."

"What's that?"

"Your tongue swipes the inside of your bottom lip. It's what you did the first time we met—I ran into you—at the diner."

"Did I?"

She nodded. There was a pregnant pause before she went for her shot glass. "Okay. I'm ready."

I followed her actions and downed the tequila. When it cleared her throat, Bilan took another bite of her fajita. Finally, there was just one more left.

As she chewed, she observed me. "I want to cook for you. Bake you something." Her tongue rolled over her front teeth, a move to clear her mouth.

"I would enjoy that."

"But..." She leaned into the table. "First, I want to ask you something."

My brows shot in the air again as I opened my palms over the table. "Ask away."

She took a drink of water, eyes never leaving me. She placed the glass down, eyes tightened. "How did you get into rope play."

Whoa...

Because it could have been worse, I rebounded quickly, sitting up in the chair. Bilan went to pour our final shot.

"An instructor."

"Instructor of..." she questioned.

"Well, let me clarify. I told you how, as kids, my mother exposed me to all sorts of shit. I did horseback riding, wrestling, baseball, karate, football, boxing, and boating."

"Boating?"

I nodded. "Eat the last of your food, baby."

Bilan's eyes landed below on the mostly empty plate. She started for the last piece of fajita then cut for the shot. She acknowledged me before lifting it in the air and tossing it back. I did the same.

"Now...boating?" she repeated. "That does require ropes."

"Yup. I didn't take a particular liking to it, but I finished the courses my mother enrolled me in one spring and summer. The crazy thing was, I was great at anchoring."

"Why that?"

I tossed my head in a shrug. "Likely because it was toward the end of each class, and I was ready to fuckin' go." I chuckled.

Bilan found that funny, too.

"Tying rope around the cleat, the dock lines, stern lines, spring lines, and tossing the anchor chain. I did all of that, and apparently well, making me comfortable with ropes: swinging...knots."

Her eyes narrowed as she appeared in deep thought. "I did peep how familiar you were when anchoring the boat after you went fishing for food in Antigua."

"Yeah. They let me do a little something, but I'm sure they went behind me to tighten up."

"Okay. Tying a boat at the dock doesn't turn you into a bondage king," she hinted to get on with the answer to her original question.

But I needed a moment to crack the fuck up. Maybe it was the alcohol in me, that in her, or just experiencing Bilan's sense of humor again, but I found her facial expression and words hilarious.

She smiled widely. "C'mon. I wanna know!"

"So, my...father got me a little job at a private pier, docking boats. It wasn't close to home, and I'm sure the amount I earned from the job was far less than the expense of my commute there. But my parents were impressed with my attempt at responsibility. I eventually quit, bored with it once the temperature dropped late that fall. In Irene Ellis' book, children must be engaged in extra-curricular activities—possibly more than one."

Bilan's eyes widened, seemingly wrapped up in this story.

"Ironically, my 'agreed upon' activity was aikido."

"What's aikido?" she asked.

"A form of martial arts. I'd done karate and collected a few belts. It didn't suit me, but when only having a few things to choose from, I selected that one. My instructor was a cool guy. He was a little younger than my parents, white, and weird. I hated aikido, but stayed the process as long as I could."

"What do you mean?"

"After five months, I told my mother I was done with it. I had to give a damn oral procès-verbal on why I wanted to quit. She eventually relented, but said I had to tell the instructor, Dan, myself." I swung my head left to right while gesturing with my eyes. "No fuckin' problem. The next day, I was driven to the school after class was due to end. I wanted to wait until I knew he was alone. I found him in the back. Through a cracked door, I saw him tying his assistant, Reba, to a chair. She was breathing hard, legs spread, shirt open, and tits exposed."

"How did you know he wasn't assaulting her?"

I shook my head. "She bit her bottom lip and her eyes rolled to the back of her head."

Bilan's mouth and eyes were wide as saucers. "So, you watched them?"

I nodded. "A little, until she saw me. It took her a while to alert him because she was ordered not to speak."

"By whom?"

"By him. It's one of many practices in BDSM."

She pulled in a breath. "Is that what we're—you into?"

I snorted, amused by her curiosity. "No, baby. We're not into BDSM. After that night, Dan and I communicated a bit after class—I stayed on a little while longer when I knew he'd teach me how to rope and tie a woman. It's what they in that community call bondage. Dan was into BDSM. My desires didn't take me that far."

"How old were you?"

"About fifteen/sixteen."

"Why wouldn't a fifteen/sixteen-year-old boy get freaked out over seeing a woman panting and squirming in ropes?"

"Because I'm nasty, Nalib." I found myself licking my lips, suddenly feeling self-conscious.

"Oh," she scoffed. "I know you are."

My head softly rolled left to right, infinitesimal movements. "You've only scratched the surface." I couldn't explain any further the depth of my sexual desires. However, she'd soon learn because I'd demonstrate each banked one on and with her. Almost as though she had a clue of my thoughts, Bilan's eyes fell to her lap. My phone vibrated a message from Rory. "C'mon, I want to show you something."

"Am I going to miss my baby?"

I stood from the table. "I promise to try and distract that longing."

The roads were bumpy the closer we approached our destination. I filled in the entire, close to thirty-minute ride typing drafts to return emails once I got back to the villa with Wi-Fi. While replying to one about my logistics team going to a convention, leaving for two days, I could see trees in the distance. It was clear I'd have to expense their attendance. However, it meant no coverage for the office. There was no way I could shut down operations for two days. So, I had to be diplomatic with my answer.

A few scenarios coursed my mind as we crossed into a forest. I placed my stogie in my mouth, taking a pull. I blew it out the open window. Feeling a draw from the left of me, I peered over to find Bilan's eyes low on my abdomen, wandering upward. Her lips parted with her curled fingers over them. When her roaming eyes made it to my face, Bilan's mouth snapped shut and her regard swung ahead.

I chuckled, dumping my ashes out the window. "You know there's nothing wrong with being madly attracted to me."

"Am not," she muttered, still looking away.

"You are, and it's perfectly fine. I'm going to be your husband." I put my phone away and shifted closer to her in the backseat. "If it helps, I'm wildly attracted to you, too," I whispered close to her face.

"Stop."

I snorted. "Stop what?"

"You're embarrassing me."

"I don't mean to. Here..." I scooted even closer. "Let me embarrass myself, too. I fantasize about the sight of your freckles, covered in my cum."

When Bilan sucked in a heap of air while turning my way, I covered her mouth in a kiss. The jeep jerked to a stop, rocking us.

She pulled away, wiping her lip. I chuckled again before scooting out, then handed Rory my cigar and phones before opening Bilan's door.

"We're here," I shared. She didn't answer, but her wary eyes bounced all around as she stood to her feet. I sidled behind her and whispered in her ear. "You're safe."

"I know," she countered, closing her eyes.

"Then why are you looking like a frightened puppy?"

"I'm not!"

Rory turned away from us, reacting to her hike in volume.

"What is that about?"

Bilan's eyes closed again. When she opened them, they rolled. "I don't like feeling you don't trust me."

"I don't trust you? You're my fiancée."

"Not like that." She turned to me. "Sadik, you don't trust that I trust you. You don't even believe I love you."

I scratched my brow. "Not this again—"

"Yes, this. It's frustrating. I've never felt so connected to someone—other than my parents—as I do you. I've never been so preoccupied with another human being until my baby was born. But I love you...dearly. I want to be with you. I know you'll be my..."

I stepped in front of her and ordered through gritted teeth, "Say it." Bilan's eyes remained on the ground. "Fuckin' say it, sweetheart."

"Don't call me that!" she blurted. "I told you not to ever refer to me as sweetheart as you do your former lovers. That's not who I am!"

"Then who the hell are you?"

Her index pushed toward the ground. "I am the mother of your child—"

"And?" I took a step closer, provoking her like the asshole I could be, feeling a loss of control. Bilan rolled her eyes again, scraping her teeth against her bottom lip. "And?" I yelped.

Her shoulders fell and eyes and chest, too, as she croaked, "You're my future husband—"

"And your goddamn protector for life!" I shouted even louder before walking off.

I hated fighting with him...now. It robbed us of peace and prohibited the bonding I so desperately wanted to do with him. But I hated the accusations, loathed the unsaid underscoring disappointment in me. It was beyond frustrating. *And...out of nowhere.* We were fine one minute, then the next, warring over unresolved issues of our relationship.

Now, hiking to what I was starting to recognize as a body of blue-green water, I followed behind his powerful, resolute steps to an unknown destination. As the sun beat relentlessly on us, I perspired between my thighs, under my arms, and beneath my breasts. Every few seconds, I glanced back to measure our distance. Rory, by the jeep, was appearing smaller and smaller.

Finally, Sadik stopped. I caught up to him and followed his gaze below. It was glorious. A hidden pellucid, turquoise cenote lay before us. The giant size hole in the ground was rocky, but such a revealing truth of nature.

Sadik reached for my hand. "C'mon."

Without hesitation, I followed him over to a rocky manmade staircase. There was no railing, so my steps were trepid as I held onto him with one hand, and the rocks behind me with the other.

"You wanna hop on my back?" he asked.

"No. I'm fine."

We were halfway there and descending at a good pace.

By the time we made it to the last few steps, Sadik removed his head wrap then tossed his chin to me. "You can take that off, if you want."

"We're getting in?"

"Yeah." Those kaleidoscopic-hued irises were shooting into me.

I glanced around. "Are there any lifeguards?"

Slowly, Sadik raised his hand into the air. When I rolled my eyes, trying not to laugh at myself, he swore, "I wouldn't take on a high-risk excursion, and would never encourage the mother of my child to either. The owner of the resort personally recommended this place as a hometown, little-known-of attraction. I had my men stake it out since we landed. Maybe a few people come and get spring water, but not many at all. You have to trust me."

That propelled an emotion. "I do!" I gritted then took my sun hat off and placed it near Sadik's scarf.

Next, I lifted my cover-up from my hips, pulling it over my head then tossing it, too. When my sandals topped the pile, I moved past Sadik and took the last few steps into cool water. It felt like silk against my overheating legs. Sounds of water dropping played the backdrop to my overwhelmed senses. I waded through, able to see clear to my feet, similar to in the ocean of *St. Justin*, only without the sand. The rocks inside weren't as prickle as those on the way down.

My eyes cut back to Sadik. He'd just immersed his entire frame in the water, going the opposite direction. Although I didn't want to, my better judgment told me to follow or stay close to him. As I did, I observed the stubble of hair growing on his head. It reminded me the busiest man I knew had been on a true vacation. Annoyed by my attention to him, I focused ahead of him. We were swimming to a...

Waterfall!

In fact, there were three. I didn't know how I missed them—*likely focused on my frustrating child's father*. However, they were there, falling fast and creating iridescent sheets. I swam over to the larger one, my mind freeing of all thoughts but this curiosity. The cool cascade pounded my head as I passed through. I held my breath until I made it to the other side.

It was a cave. Moving water sloshed over my shoulders until I stood to my feet, wiping my eyes clear. The acoustics were sharp on this side, and it was beautiful. The varying colors, the satiny, refreshing feel of the water, the mottled hues of the big cavernous rock—it, together, made me feel so small. It begged a spiritual awareness. Who envisioned this? Whose handiwork had this been? No way the Big Bang Theory could satisfy the majestic ambiance of this wonder.

It quickly reminded me of my lack of culture and the same of my travel. I'd never seen this type of nature. I'd seen the ocean more times in the past year than I had in all my life, thanks to an impatient ultra-alpha. I crossed my arms at my chest when a pang lanced my heart. I hated fighting. None of the beauty all around could distract me from that ineptness I felt at the core.

A man of Sadik's wealthy and influential stature wanted to marry me and I couldn't be a good enough fiancée to him. He'd given me my first child and I'd been unable to satisfy his need of security. How long could we go on like this?

A hard, golden arm snaked around my waist. Heat pressed against my back and my body tensed. His face moved to the side of mine, cool and wet, his audible breaths heavy.

My eyes closed shut. "I am in love with you." I couldn't feel my diaphragm with those words. "I love you so much, I'm afraid of losing you." Unexpected hot tears tracked down my face and my body trembled.

I felt when his arm fell away, but our bodies didn't disconnect. Then his hands were on me again, this time at the side of my face. Sadik was pushing a metal stem into my right ear. Earrings. I waited nearly breathlessly as he placed the first in and screwed the back on, and then the left ear.

"I'm impatient...jealous of your stubborn nature," he whispered. "I still need to know."

"Why?" I breathed, lungs vibrating.

"I can only think of it as one of my flaws. The woman I've lost my heart to should feed me her heart in return. I need your passion."

"You have all of me," I croaked, more hot tears staining my face. Waterproof makeup be damned. "You've multiplied inside of me. What more can I give you? Mere words?"

"Your everything."

"You *are* my everything. Can't you see?" My breathing turned heavy. "My heart is so settled right now, so at peace with all you've given me."

"Your tense body says something different."

I closed my eyes to a squeeze. "I know. I'm on edge with anxiety."

His lips brushed against my shoulder. "Relax, Nalib—"

"I can't!" My high volume made me cringe. "It's not that easy to control."

His fingertips danced onto my belly, causing me to bite my bottom lip. "You trust me?"

"Implicitly!" I was still defensive.

When I opened my eyes to try and control it, I saw Rory taking deep steps into water right at the steps on the other side of the waterfall. Then I felt Sadik's big hand on the back of my thigh. His fingers walked up and pulled my bikini bottom to the side. My knees buckled.

"Rory..." I whispered in a panic.

"She must've needed to cool off," he spoke to the side of my face, into my ear. "You know she keeps her distance."

His other hand was on my heavy breast, making feather-light strokes on the underside before rolling my nipple between his fingers.

My body quaked and head swung back, onto his shoulder. "Sadik..."

I struggled to keep my eyes open, feeling like I had to be our watchdog.

"Am I your lover?" The head of his cock was between my cheeks as he urged me to bend over with a gentle push. When I reached too far over my toes, he stopped me with a firm hold on my shoulder. After a few swipes between my lips below, he found my opening and pushed inside. "Fuck!" he grounded through heavy breaths.

Shamelessly, and without realizing it, I was unreasonably wet. After some time, he pulled me back to an upright position.

"Yes," I exhaled, finally answering him.

"And what else am I?" he panted, dick throbbing inside of me.

Bizarrely, I knew what he was asking.

After releasing a shaky, trembling breath, I answered, "My protector."

He thrust upward, breaching even more of my core. I yelped in response to the unexpected pinch of pain. Delicious pain. That internal massage was so familiar to the tissues he coursed, they responded, gelling. I was loose, too loose in my limbs. Even my sex was supple to him, little resistance at all.

Fighting to remain lucid, I forced my eyes open. Sadik thrusted into me, his hands covered each breast, kneading. I found myself unimaginably creaming for him even more. Each stroke inside me was followed by a rhythmic grunt from him. My lover, my protector was lost inside me. This made me fight to be more vigilant.

Through low lids, I was able to make out a moving dot, one growing larger. Closer.

I swallowed hard, feeling my body tense all over again. "Someone's coming," I panted. "A stranger."

"Rory won't let them near here," his words tumbled out under duress. "You gonna come, baby?" Those words were delivered helplessly, a little perverse.

My belly fluttered.

But I shook my head, needing to be honest. "No," I croaked.

I couldn't relax myself into it any more than I had—and I had a lot, involuntarily. Sadik had that magic over me.

"You sure?" I could hardly make out as his thrusts were coming faster as his body strained around mine.

I nodded, and before I was done, Sadik's legs were yo-yo'ing against me. His body suspended for seconds long before he jerked his hips forward again while releasing heavy mewls. The tips of his fingers dug deeply into the pouch of my belly. Feeling him explode like that, knowing he'd just shot himself into orbit relaxed me tremendously. I felt a dangerous concoction of excitement from nearly being caught, frustration from our earlier fight, and arousal. I also realized Sadik had never climaxed without giving me one first.

The moment he pulled out of me and shifted my bikini back in place, I leaped around to face him. My arms circled his golden frame and I nearly jumped him in the water. My lips flew to his mouth and my tongue soon followed. Sadik had to quickly adjust to my weight and oral action. I twirled my tongue all around his warm mouth tasting of cigar and tequila, spiking my yearning. I kissed him to express my need of him, my attraction to him, my frustration of him.

He held me with one arm crossing my lower back so his hand could palm my butt while the other clutched my shoulder. Sadik was raw, but for other reasons. After orgasms was when he was most pliable. He was most tender. He could never resist my affection, and that intensified my frustration. I kissed him hard and long until I could no longer feel the toes I put all of my weight on or my bruised lips.

Finally, I pulled back, lungs ready to explode and my belly filled with emotions. The moment I captured those feline irises, tears pooled my eyes. The muscles in Sadik's face lifted in concern.

I backed away, the side of my index finger going to my nose as my regard fell to the side. "I'm angry."

"Why?"

"Because I hate fighting with you!"

"We don't fight—"

"Don't talk!" I raised my finger in the air. "I need to explain this without your ultra-alpha." Sadik exhaled, eyes shifting toward the waterfall as he lifted the band of his trunks higher on his hips. "I hate this feeling of ineptness you cause when you want to tell me how to love you, or how to express my love for you. When you make claims of needing more, or for me to show it more frequently, it's a clear indicator that I'm not doing it right. And if by me giving you my all is not enough—" I whipped my head to the side, trying to control my emotions. After a few breaths, I continued, "Then it means I don't fit in and am not worthy enough of these."

I gripped what I knew were sizeable diamond studs he screwed into my earlobes. "It means I can be replaced by a Tiffany or... Ameerah. And it means Randi's been right all this time about me being over my head thinking I can maintain a man like you."

"Nalib," he sighed, stalking my way.

"No. I'm not an insecure woman," I needed him to know. "Jealous?" I flopped my head side to side. "I guess we've seen signs of it.

But not insecure. Becoming a mother has boosted my confidence tenfold. I am now a whole woman. I just can't have you unintentionally working against my efforts to plant my feet on planet Ellis."

"Baby..." he croaked, sifting through the water toward me. Sadik captured me in his arms, and I swear, there was no safer place on earth. He embraced me with a passion I'd only known from him. "You are planet Ellis for me. You give life to me and Sadik every day." The low hum in my ear set my core ablaze.

Snuggled in his neck, I twittered, "I don't think I need to be this close to you right now."

I felt his chest drop against mine. "Why?"

"Because I'm..." I hesitated. "You just..." I laughed. "I'm horny and still a little tipsy from those shots earlier."

Sadik backed up, expression deathly serious. "You want to head back to the villa?"

My eyes burst wide. "I'd love to see S.Q.E., II."

"No," that one syllable was firm. Sadik grabbed my hand. "His senior needs alone time with you more."

Sadik passed through the heavy and cool sheet of water, and I did right after him, feeling it beat on my skin. On the other side, he submerged, beginning a swim. I followed him with that, too. We swam the entire body of water, slowly, taking our time. When Sadik stopped to explore or observe, I did the same. More than anything, I observed him. I determined in my mind, I would do this intently to try and understand his needs of me and how to meet them.

Rory took pictures of us frolicking in the natural spring at her boss' request. She got into it and took more than I thought she'd ever have the patience for. But that was my fiancé's world. He got what he wanted on demand.

Including me.

Sadik

I opened the front door of the villa, allowing Bilan to step in first. After closing the door, I could hear the television in the main room going and movements in the kitchen. Bilan and I headed in there.

"Oh, you guys are back." Camille paid a glance over her shoulder. "I hope you had a good time this evening."

Bilan turned to me, cheeks likely heated as she grinned hard. "We did. Thanks for keeping Sadik. How was he?"

Camille gestured to a monitor on the counter. "He was a little fussy after dinner for some reason. But after a long burping session and a warm bath, he knocked right out."

"How long has he been asleep?" I asked.

"For close to thirty minutes now." She turned off the faucet. "I watched a little TV, and when I saw you guys were still out, I plated your dinner." She tossed her chin over to the oven. "I can warm it up for you."

"Actually," Bilan spoke up, eyes big and bright. I sensed she was apologetic for what was to come. "I'm going to shower, wash and blow dry my hair now. I think I'll have Sadik until the morning." She exposed her teeth, pushing back her lips in an exaggerated smile. "You can get some rest tonight."

I smiled. Bilan missed her baby, and I could think of far worse qualities in a mother.

"Okay," Camille smiled politely, likely sensing what I did. "Just let me know when you're ready for him. I'm going to wash a small load of his clothes tonight to prepare for tomorrow."

"Anything I can help with?" Bilan asked with heavy, red eyes. Her eyeliner smeared.

With a contained grin, Camille shook her head. "Not at all. Enjoy that shower. I have a great leave-in conditioner I brought with me if you need it."

"Kimmy packed one, but if it doesn't agree with me, I'll take you up on that offer." Bilan moved to the doorway of the kitchen.

"I'm gonna take a meeting with Rory," I announced to Bilan after following just behind her.

Her brows dropped. "Tonight?"

"I've been blowing her off since we've arrived. Lots of pertinent shit I've tasked her with I need to hear her update on. We'll probably stop by the bar." I brushed my thumb under her chin. "We'll be on the property. I won't be far at all."

Bilan snorted. "Okay." Then she reached up and kissed me sweetly. "In case we're knocked out when you get back."

I lowered my tone for only her to hear. "You need me to wake you?"

Her lips spread and eyes narrowed into smiling slits. "Tomorrow. Tonight's for little Sadik." She kissed me again and rubbed my abdomen affectionately.

"Should I heat up your food?" Camille asked when Bilan turned to take off again.

Bilan turned to face Camille first, then her eyes raked over to me. She ducked her chin. "Yes, please."

I smiled, head bounced back slightly. My girl was full of shit. She wasn't thinking past that little boy upstairs.

"Your ass better eat something, Nalib."

Then I was graced with another kiss. "I'll try."

"What about your dinner, Mr. Ellis?" Camille addressed me.

"I'll pick up something while I'm out."

When Bilan began to walk out again, I was sure to slap her ass. She jumped before giggling. I watched her take to the stairs then headed back out again.

Rory was waiting in the jeep. I stepped inside and closed the door behind me.

"He there," she informed.

Her big ass bug-eyes peering at me through the rearview mirror.

My attention went out the window to nothing in particular. I sat back in my seat, face hard, mood darkening as we pulled off.

∞6∞

"You ready?" Jamil's subterranean deep chords asked on my screen, though he was out of view. When I nodded, he rang the doorbell to the single-family home in Maplewood, NJ. After about a minute or two, the door opened. "Jason?"

After a moment of hesitation, I heard a feeble, "Ye-yeah."

Then there was a cacophony of sounds before the screen showed inside the home.

"What the hell?" Jason yelped.

"Goddamn," Jamil singsonged, clearly annoyed.

"What are you doing?" Jason shouted. "You can't—"

When I glanced up at Rory, she rolled her eyes as she twisted around, whispering into the mic on her headset. "Don't fuckin' be so brolic. You know he a bitch, my nigga!" she whispered harshly.

Amidst Jason's protests, Jamil shoved the phone to his face. "Somebody wanna word with you."

It took a few seconds for Jason to hold the device upright. But when he did, I smiled with my eyes, delighted to have his attention.

"You don't look as happy to see me as I am you," I began.

"I knew it had to be you, barging up in my parents' home. What the fuck, man?" he croaked.

"Your parents are on a quick road trip to Delaware. They're undisturbed at the moment. Nonetheless, now you know how it feels to have an unwanted person at your doorstep."

"What the hell are you talking about?" Jason was panting hard.

His pulse beating at the side of his neck could be seen.

Lovely...

I scoffed. "Oh, you know exactly what I'm talking about, Mr. Anderson."

"I don't know what you're talking about!" he cried like a bitch. "Please! Just don't kill me!"

Jason wasn't convincing. There were several levels of fear in a man when accosted. I could recognize when a man instinctively knew he was soon on his way to the afterlife. That's not what I was reading from Jason, which made him more of a concern. It didn't matter that I had no intention of harming him tonight. While he feared me to a degree, Jason thought he was smarter, as though he was in the lead on the chessboard.

I sat up in my chair and rested my elbows on the desk of a vacant office the resort manager offered for my last-minute request. "I have no desire to hurt you, young Jason, and I'd never send my men to do it for me." I shrugged with my mouth. "I learned you showed up to my home unexpectedly, and unfortunately my fiancée nor I was available to make your acquaintance." I opened my palms, observing Jason's eyes blossoming when the revelation hit. "I'm here now. What can we do for you?"

"I didn't come for you, Ellis. I came for Bilan, and you know it!"

Last night, Jason showed up to my high-rise, asking to be directed to Sadik Ellis' apartment to visit Bilan Asad-Yasin. When they determined he wasn't expected—as he wouldn't be since we'd moved out indefinitely, though I still owned the place—he was told she was unavailable and he could not go up. Desperate as the fuck he is, Jason left a note for her instead.

"Well, what I know is I'm her fiancé and the father of her child. Whatever business you have with her can be run by me."

The corny motherfucker gritted his teeth. "It cannot!"

"But it can. And to prove it, I'll read to you that bullshit ass letter you left her." I grabbed my other phone from next to me where a photo of the letter was stored.

Jason's eyes widened even more. "I didn't leave that for you to read! It ain't addressed to you!"

See...

There was more terror in that yelp than it was when he asked not to take his life. Jason was a fucking coward, the scum of the goddamn earth. He was the type to call the pigs on another Black man for building a fence in the yard that wasn't in compliance with the development's rules.

"See, this is what you don't understand, son. It was left at my high-rise for my fiancée. This makes it my business. Even the part here," I tapped and scrolled until I came upon the passage that struck me the most. "where you say you can protect her and her baby if she wanted to leave me."

"Don't read that!" he screamed.

"I don't care to read the other unrequited crushin' bullshit." I pushed my phone away. "I'm coming here to tell you explicitly to leave her the fuck alone. Stay the hell away."

"Let her tell me that!"

"She hasn't?" I asked.

"She hasn't said anything. She upped and left...stopped returning my phone calls, texts, and emails. How do I know she's safe? And the baby—"

"Don't fuckin' speak about my son." My delivery was as calm as I was capable under such circumstances.

"He's her son, too! I just want to be sure they're fine."

"If I texted, called, and email a woman to no avail, I'd get the hint of her not wanting to be bothered."

"What are you doing to her, Ellis?" His face enflamed, freckles darkened.

I sat back in my seat, tossing my head in a shrug. "All the shit you wanted, but couldn't get. Fuckin' her right, making her a mother, giving her the world, and making sure she's so happy and full of me, she doesn't have the time to take calls from boys like you."

"And you don't expect for me to just take your word, do you—"

"Don't ever try to reach out to her again," I spoke over him, yet keeping my voice calm. "From man to man. I'm asking you to never attempt to contact Bilan again."

"Or else what?" Jason's face tightened with indignation. "You going to send your father's assassins after me again?"

"My father has nothing of what you speak. Neither am I issuing any threats tonight. Please check in on your parents, though. Their trip has been delayed due to car issues."

"*Wha*—what?" he croaked just before the phone was snatched from him. "What did you just say, Ellis?" I could still hear him from a distance. "Ellis!"

Jamil's footsteps out the house could be heard, though the screen was dark. "Muthafucka pee'd his fuckin' pants," he muttered, annoyed.

The call with me was disconnected, and Rory continued talking with Jamil from her phone as he got in the car and pulled off.

Bilan

A deep breath expelled from my belly, awakening me somehow. I rolled from one side to the other, keeping my eyes closed. The riveting sounds of the ocean's waves breaking at the shoreline immediately brought Sadik to mind. The flutter in my belly brought Sadik to mind—the other Sadik.

My baby...

My eyes burst wide. Right away, my bladder cried. I shifted off the bed and took long lunges into the bathroom. The baby slept with us last night. As his father slept hard, I was up and down with Sadik, feeding and changing him, or simply adoring him as he slept in his bassinet. He was truly a beautiful baby, and I enjoyed taking care of him. Having a nanny had huge benefits, but there was nothing like meeting the needs of the creature you created.

I guessed being up and down during the night caught up to me at some point this morning, because I obviously slept so hard, I didn't hear either Sadik awake, or when they left. That concerned the over-achiever-mom in me. After washing my hands, I went to the deck and peered over the railing.

There they were, Sadik and Sadik, on the beach, relaxing under the overcast sky. Sadik cranked classical music from his device as they gazed toward the water. The sight eased something inside me. Peace. It's what I felt. It's why I decided to go back into the bath-room to shower and toss on a bikini for the day.

I did just that and headed downstairs to say good morning to the Ellis men properly and feed Sadik as his father fed me. We sat out there for hours, talking, listening to Sadik's instrumental tunes, and enjoying a break from the reticent sun. I couldn't think of time better spent.

I ambled out on the beach after putting Sadik down for a nap. He'd stayed awake all morning before finally crashing. Then I checked my emails and edited the last page of the final paper of the semester while indulging in a few tequila shots. Tomorrow, I'd go through the entire paper with a careful eye before sending it off, completing my first year of grad school.

Now, as I skipped down the warm sanded floor to the sexy orange man in the lounge chair my belly fluttered. I could see the billows of smoke over his head. Sadik was enjoying a cigar. My nipples tingled and feet moved even faster. When I reached him, I sat across his lap and grasped the stogie from between his fingers. In haste, I took a deep pull and nearly choked to death.

"The hell are you doing?" he cawed while stifling laughter.

I fought to breathe through constricted lungs, coughing until tears tracked down my face. When I was able to, I howled in laughter myself.

"How do you smoke these things?" I asked.

"For starters," he thumbed the tears from my cheeks. "by not inhaling. Cigars aren't cigarettes."

"Or weed," I managed while clearing my throat.

Then I tried again without inhaling. This time, I didn't choke, but my throat felt raw.

"What do you know about weed?" Sadik asked.

I giggled, readjusting myself so I could straddle him. "That it makes me paranoid and doesn't get me half as horny as your golden-skinned head does." I kissed him.

At first, it was a peck. Then his submission to the kiss made me want more. I kissed him again, this time pushing my tongue between his soft lips. They parted for me easily and the warmth of his palm on my hip aroused me even more. Our tongues slid over one another, lips brushed back and forth, and before I knew it, I was thrusting against his erection.

With closed eyes, he pulled away and rasped, "Your period come?"

I shook my head and leaned in again for more of his oral pleasure. My taut nipples pushed against his hard, inked chest. Sadik's grip on my hip pushed up to my cheek and his torso lifted to meet my face as though he was just as hungry for me.

He pulled back again, this time with opened, narrowed eyes and panting. "Unless you want to get fucked in front of our staff, you better stop."

Flustered myself, I climbed off of him with a puddle in my bikini bottoms and settled onto the lounge next to his. I planted myself practically beneath his hard frame, wanting to be as close as possible. This was frustrating. I didn't know how to reconcile my inherent attraction to him against the fighting we did, and the colored history we'd accumulated in no time. Being in a real, sexual relationship felt overwhelming.

Sadik pulled the lounger close to his with me on it. Then raptly, I watched him light his cigar. He pulled and blew a puff into the air, all the while his attention was back to the water.

Watching those simple things were captivating to me.

"How have you been enjoying your time in *St. Justin*, Nalib?"

I ripped my eyes from him. "Well, you allowing me to sleep late two days in a row, and not barking at me while working out..." I took a deep breath. "Sex with orgasms—and one I thought would kill me because it wouldn't stop..." My eyes flashed wide. "*Ooh!* And that romp yesterday behind the waterfall..." I nodded with a wide smile and narrowed eyes. "Just fine, I'd say. Mighty fine, Ellis."

Sadik laughed. "You're so damn silly."

I knew my smile was goofy and didn't care. I reclined more in my chair, my legs stretched out as I admired the roaring water. It was cooler outside today. The sun rested above the clouds. The breeze was relieving and humidity low.

"Yesterday, I thought you were going to miss the bullseye," I snickered.

"Pardon me." I heard the rumble in his chest and that tickled me.

"When you bent me over, I thought since you were being so covert, you were going to poke in error."

"Poke in error?" Sadik chuckled. "I'm too old to be missing the target."

I reached over and nuzzled into his neck, feeling prickles from the stubble on his cheek and chin. "I was hoping you would."

I felt his frame steel. After a beat, he asked, "Wished I'd what?"

I shrank, suddenly embarrassed. "You know."

"Do I?" His words reverberated in my chest, halfway splayed over his. "What? Fuck your ass?"

My butt cheeks squeezed and I nodded. Then my brazenness dwindled, I rolled back on to my lounge fully and scoffed, "You're probably too big for that anyway." My volume faltered as I turned away.

For the next minute or two, Sadik and I sat in silence. I regretted my liquid courage. It was a topic I should have held onto for a little while. It's what I got for reading so many romance novels with erotica. I rolled my eyes, careful of how heavy I breathed. I was shrinking by the second.

Stupid. Stupid. Stupid!

"I'll answer your every desire, Nalib," his smooth alto awakened me back to the conversation.

Those kaleidoscopic-hued marbles were on me, thick brows wild and narrowed. Sadik was as earnest as I'd ever seen him.

"You have," I muttered sheepishly.

He turned away, taking another puff from his cigar. My thoughts traveled. Being on vacation was new to me, too. The only concerns I had were finishing up the paper for school and deciding where we'd settle into as a family. The apartment in New York City, though contemporary and chic, was too small and not fitting for an active child. It wasn't even fitting for a larger-than-life persona like Sadik's. And there was that other issue of my period. It had been *long* overdue.

Then there was the Ellis family. Something felt off about them. Yes, the two eldest men of the family were down with ailments, but a shift had happened. The Ellis family's cohesiveness as a unit felt...weakened.

"Have you heard from your parents?"

Sadik nodded. "I speak to queen every day."

"How is she? I need to call your father today. Maybe *Facetime* him with Sadik at dinner."

"You won't be having dinner with Sadik tonight. You'll be with his father."

Ohh...

"Then I need to go to the store." I lay back on the lounger.

"For what?"

"A few things. No biggie. You think Rory can drive me?"

I felt his hand on mine, and I peered over to him. "We'll get you there."

That simple acquiesce gave me an emotional rush and I jumped him again. My mouth was on his, my arms and hands framing his head and shoulders. The pulse in my neck didn't concern me, neither did the clenching of my sex as I rolled over him. What did alarm me was my willingness to engage in public copulation with my fiancé.

"Marry me," Sadik asked between tongue laves in my mouth.

His heavy-lidded eyes held me captive. I wanted him so bad my body trembled as I rolled over his tight frame. His hand slipped beneath the band of my bikini bottom. The other stroked down my spine, causing me to shiver.

"*Yessss...*" I expressed with a sibilant at the end.

"Now?" He pulled my bottom lip in between his and roved his tongue over it.

I nodded, wanting him inside me immediately. Willing him to make it happen.

"Mr. Ellis, Ms. Bilan, your guests have arrived."

My head whipped toward the thick-accented voice and found three bellmen placing a wide coffee table and loungers next to us, and placing trays with drinks and food on it.

But the most surprising find was Julius and...

"Keisha?" I shrilled, halfway confident of getting her name right.

The Richards strolled hand in hand down the beach, smiling our way.

"Goddamn, Ellis!" Julius shouted. "And here I thought you were a dominant."

I clambered off of Sadik faster than I knew was possible, my mouth wide open and eyes not much different.

Keisha nudged her husband. Julius ignored the scolding and continued our way. They were intercepted by more staff members of the property, running in chairs and towels. I squatted on the opposite side of Sadik.

"I didn't fly your ass out to be a dick," Sadik grumbled as he stood then grabbed my hand and positioned me in front of him. "Come greet my lady properly before I fuck you up in front of Kee."

Without a moment of dither, Julius howled a laughter as his wife shook her head and rolled her eyes. Julius raised his arms as he trekked my way, his head tilted to the side.

"The grizzly's about to strike," he murmured before engulfing me into his arms. "It's lovely to see you again, Bilan," his tone completely humble.

I reciprocated his greeting, still shocked by his sudden presence. When we broke apart, I caught Sadik and Keisha receiving each other.

"Brother!" Julius proclaimed as he extended his arms toward Sadik in approach.

Sadik welcomed him with a dap. "You guys get settled in yet?"

"No," Julius answered. "Kee was beastin' to see the property before we unpacked. So we threw on our swim shit and came out here to check it out."

"There're drinks and appetizers here if you're hungry." Sadik then turned to me and murmured at a level meant just for me, "I think it's about time for us to nibble on something, too. We skipped lunch."

Still flustered, all I could do was giggle dryly as my eyes swept between the three of them.

"I hope you're okay with this," Keisha propose to me, obviously picking up on my state of surprise.

I didn't want to be rude. "Oh, my god! Yes! I'm totally fine. Just surprised—pleasantly surprised, though." I tried cleaning up as Sadik rubbed my lower back in comfort. "Really." I held my palm out pleadingly.

"Perfect!" Julius singsonged, using humor as he slapped his hands together and went to the table of food. "Drop your bags, boo," he told Keisha. "We're on a six-star vacation, courtesy of an Ellis. Eat and drink all you want!"

I laughed and Sadik rolled his eyes. He then turned to me, putting his back to his friends.

"Richards called saying he needed to talk, and in a circulatory manner mentioned being stressed with work and the election. I offered him a ride out. Luckily, they were able to get a couple of days off and it worked out with childcare. I wanted to surprise you." He observed me closely. "You sure you're okay with this?"

I nodded, maintaining my smile. "Yes. Just don't get the surprise part. You could have given me the heads up. It could've saved me from being caught molesting you."

He yanked me into his arms, our bodies slapping. "It's your job to molest me. Yours and only yours. Doesn't matter who's around."

He sealed that declaration with a kiss, and of course, I couldn't resist it.

"Nah," Julius chirped behind Sadik with a mouth full of food. "Fuck that!" He waved us over. "Now, I ain't gone stress you with the shit I need to say, but you ain't gone dry hump the woman in front of my lady. I need some bro time. Sit." He pointed to our loungers. "Eat. Everything's on my buddy. Exhaust his funds injudiciously."

Again, I spat out a laugh and Sadik rolled his eyes.

I began my way over. "How are the kids?"

"We're on the exclusive island of *St. Justin*," Julius groaned while chewing. "Those damn creatures don't exist for the next two days!"

Keisha laughed, nodding while holding a shot of tequila in the air. "You'll learn—especially if you have a second child."

I lay back on the lounger, facing the water. Sadik sat near my legs facing the table and the Richards, parting them so he could have more room on my chair.

"A toast to fortune materialized." Sadik raised his shot glass in the air. "Good friends and the woman I'd battle a thousand wars just to lay at her feet."

My chest dropped and eyes nearly popped out of my head when he kissed the unsanded top of my foot.

Sadik...

"Ah, shit!" Julius cried, waving off the sentiment. "She really got my nigga's head wide the fuck open," he shrilled.

Keisha and Julius took pictures and shot live videos on IG, showing the moon reflecting off the water, tiki torches lined festively, the small live band, white silk cloth with gold straps hanging from the canopy, and the beautifully laid table set for four. I glanced up from my phones occasionally as I typed up a proposal for my dispensary. Earlier, I received a draft of the new employee policy that needed approving. I was able to get this and more in while waiting on Bilan. I was happy the Richards had something to keep them busy. I couldn't blame them for savoring the ambiance. It was all a dope vibe.

"Yo, this how y'all been having dinner each night?" Julius returned to the table, taking a seat.

I snorted. "No. Just thought you and Kee would enjoy the ambiance."

"Shit, enjoy? You kidding me?" He rubbed his palms against his legs anxiously. "I 'on't know how I'm gonna top this when you ain't around."

I laughed. "Knock it the hell off."

"Oh, here she is!" Julius shouted over my head.

I turned as Bilan was toeing down the torched pathway to the canopy. She was stunning in a fitted tank dress, her skin bronzed with some shimmering coating, and her hair pushed back from her face. I stood to receive her as she drew closer.

"Hey," she murmured as her tempting scent drifted into my nose, shooting down to my groin. "Sorry I took so long."

"Is he okay?" Keisha asked, taking her seat next to Julius.

"Yeah," Bilan answered as I pulled out her chair. "He was unusually fussy tonight. I didn't want to leave him like that so after Camille bathed him, I gave him a bottle and rocked him asleep on the beach."

My eyes widened.

"Oh, wow," Julius remarked.

Bilan nodded. "He wouldn't stop fussing until we stepped outside. He burped a few times. Took over five minutes for him to fall out."

"Awwwww..." Keisha cried. "You remember those days, Jules?"

"Yup." He nodded dramatically. "It gets better. He was probably gassy then got worked up until he exhausted himself. He's fine."

It was good having tenured parents around at a time like this because I knew Bilan was uneasy about being away from Sadik. The last thing I needed was her to be in paradise feeling an ounce of stress. I was confident the baby was fine.

I rubbed her shoulder comfortingly leaning back in my seat. Bilan glanced back at me then leaned into my touch with a smile.

She whispered, "I'm trying."

I knew she was. My mother said it's difficult for new moms to separate from their babies. I guess I needed to be patient with her. It was hard to do when I had an agenda for her myself.

Julius snickered when I reached up to brush my lips against hers. I withdrew and glared at him for being an ass. Then I wiped her gloss from my mouth.

"Sadik, you know he's still adjusting to you having a woman," Keisha tried explaining his immaturity. "We may have seen him on dates or with someone he was seeing, Bilan, but we've never seen him in love. And believe it or not, Julius used to be unable to keep his skeleton hands off of me when we met." She nudged him as I cracked the hell up.

"The hell you laughing at, Ellis?"

"I remember those bony ass hands nibbling on the biscuits my mother's cook sent when my parents visited." I tried sharing while cracking the fuck up. "Your hungry, pole-looking ass would eat the whole damn basket."

"Stacy?" Bilan asked.

I nodded. "He used to come in from practices and inhale most of them shits before I could."

"Those shits were good as hell! I would've married Stacy just for that skill, bruh!" Keisha and I shook our heads as Bilan laughed. "I'm dead ass, yo!"

"Stacy wouldn't have given you those gorgeous babies Keisha did," Bilan teased.

"Shit," he droned. "Them biscuits would've been my babies."

"Are we ready to order?" The waiter arrived at the table.

We spent the next few minutes ordering our food. Throughout the appetizers and main course, Julius kept us entertained with his silly ass sense of humor. Bilan allowed me to feed her without much fuss, likely distracted by his banter. She seemed to have eased up considerably.

Dessert was served a few feet away on oversized beanie bags. They were large enough for Bilan to join me on mine as we sat at a bonfire, enjoying sweets and drinks. Julius and I indulged in cigars.

"These tarts are sooo good," Keisha moaned to the right of us.

I'd have to peer over Bilan to see her, so I didn't bother. As she and Julius mumbled about one thing or another, my eyes were out to the black water and attention was on several things at once. Rory mentioned men squatting around my father's warehouse. If it was Popov, how would that reconcile with his arrangement with the FEDs?

He could compromise his deal if engaged in a war…

Bilan's soft, warm lips brushing against mine snatched me out of my thoughts. I could see her eyes observing me while our noses touched. "I love the taste of a lit cigar on your lips."

"Lit?"

"It's muskier when it isn't. I love it so much, I always want to smoke."

"Why?"

"Because you do. And it's…" She swallowed, her lips centimeters from mine. "…sexy. You're sexy."

My face opened in a smile.

Bilan kissed me again. "It's not funny. It's only weeks away from one year since I lost my body to you, and I hate that I can't control my attraction to you."

"I hate that's all you can't control regarding me."

"You own my body; we saw that two nights ago," she whispered against my lips. "What else is there left?"

"I'll let you know when I get it." I pushed my tongue in her mouth.

Bracing herself, her palm rested on my abs where her nails dug into my exposed flesh. Bilan tasted sweet and in need. Our tongues rolled against each other. Her delicious breaths hitting my face as the violin cried out behind us. It was pure bliss.

"Hear ye, hear ye!" scratched the vibe like nails on a chalkboard.

Bilan's tongue ripped from my mouth. She whipped her head around, wiping her mouth. My eyes rolled up and forehead lifted in jest, though no one could see. There was no need to be offended by my friend being my friend. Keisha was right: Julius didn't know me as a man in a legitimate relationship. He never had to vie for my attention when I was with a female companion. No one held my attention as intensely.

"It's finally time for me to announce my reason for needing to meet with you...other than leeching off your wealth to woo my wife," Julius announced.

I sat up in my seat to give him my attention. Bilan adjusted her body so she was still affectionately attached to me. She pulled the cigar from between my fingers and drew from it with the confidence of a veteran. I was happy to see she didn't inhale this time, but peeped her attempt at appearing as a maven. I couldn't bear another man having the joy of her wanting to impress him to the degree of mimicking him. The thought made me murderous. It was why living in a world where the kid, Derrick, existed was intolerable. He stimulated her enough to open her legs and offer her pussy. My appetite to be her only was ravenous to the point of obliterating him.

"Okay, Ms. Bilan!" Keisha cheered her on.

I stifled my chuckle from my Nalib posturing because of me. On the low, I enjoyed it. I hoped Bilan's jealousy was a trace of her love for me that I craved.

"Well, I'm here to announce I've finally made my decision as to my chief of staff in the event I'm elected mayor in two weeks."

Ahhhh...

I sat back in my seat. This was the important news he called about a couple of nights ago. I knew something was weighing on my friend, but not exactly this.

I nodded for him to go on.

"And after countless conversations with you over the years about this occasion in my career, I'm clear on needing your counsel." He cracked a wise-ass smirk. "I need *you* as *my* consigliere." Jules wiggled his brows then busted out laughing when I hit him with the glacial stare. Then I waited for him to finish amusing himself. "All jokes aside; there's no other person equipped to guide me into this critical and life-changing role other than you. *But...*" I felt Bilan stiffen next to me. That conjunction may have concerned her, but not me. Like Julius said, we'd talked about this numerous times. "Due to your exhaustive schedule and various enterprises, I had to 'officially' choose a chief of staff on paper, and that will be Sofia Cruz." His eyes settled on me emphatically.

Keisha's regard swept between the two of us with caution.

Bilan took another pull of the cigar then grabbed her wine glass, likely oblivious as to the shift in energy. "What does that mean?" she addressed me as though they couldn't hear her.

"It means Sadik is way too busy with his own businesses to take on the official role," Keisha tried to explain while Jules gaped at me, communicating something other than what was being said. "He cannot oversee the staff, sign off on paperwork, handle the press, and all the other demanding roles of a chief of staff. Jules would need an in-office professional for the role. He'd be foolish to not have Sadik on his team with all his public policy knowledge, resources, and general vision for community building and...mobilization." She shrugged.

"It's not just that," Julius interjected with rare emotion.

I addressed Bilan. "Given the nature of my father's industry and my family's sordid reputation, it wouldn't be...appropriate for me to have such an essential role in his political career—"

"It doesn't matter in my book!" Julius screeched defensively.

This was a sore spot for him. His loyalty ran thick with me. He knew of my long ago, secret aspirations of public service. It was a significant point of our bonding at *Blakewood*.

"I believe that was a sagacious decision, Richards," I finally added, wanting to relieve him of the constant guilt. "You will do well in your fight to improve your hometown."

Julius stood, his expression solemn. "So, we're cool?"

I mirrored his action, after gesturing for Bilan to let me up. "Of course."

Our palms met in a firm shake.

"This means no decisions are made or actions committed without your approval," he qualified. "Sofia's contributions will weigh equally, and when there's conflict, I'll tip the scale. I've already explained the parameters to her and typed it up in my proposal. She's given me a definitive yes."

"That's wonderful, man." I saluted him. "I'm proud of you."

"My man!" He gave me another dap. "Now, let's hope my ass gets elected."

"For sure." I patted my chest while giving a neck bow. "It'll happen."

Keisha jumped from her seat, cheering while clapping her hands. "The deal is done and the band is headed our way! We have to celebrate!"

She grabbed Julius' hands and they began to dance. The band had drawn closer to us: a guitar, bongos, and maracas blended nicely for a rhythmic tune. Bilan appeared at my side, her eyes low and lips curved into a smile as she held the cigar.

"Congratulations, Mr. Ellis." My arms roped around her ass when her chest met mine. Bilan kissed me, using her right hand to cup the back of my head. "Now, I have to think of ways to reward you."

I chuckled at her brazenness, although it was attributed to the wine she had at dinner. Gazing into her eyes, I couldn't articulate how beautiful she was under the Caribbean moon. It was different from her usual splendor. Her high cheekbones were more pronounced; those freckles bronzer. The beach did her well.

"I can," I informed, pulling her closer into me.

"So can I."

"Let me hear your suggestion."

Huskily, she giggled. Fermented grape scent hitting my face as her palm slipped between us, groping my dick. "This..." Her hand moved to my arm behind her. Bilan directed it to the underside of her ass cheek and near the crease. "Here."

My eyes burst wide and mouth smacked closed while I tried controlling my shocked-humor.

She bit her lip, glancing away as she giggled. "Just kidding," she tried unconvincingly. I didn't contest her. When she got up the courage to find my eyes again, she asked, "What's your suggestion?"

"For you to exchange vows with me tonight."

Bilan's bright eyes dimmed and chiseled cheeks descended, all signs of coquetry and tipsiness gone.

∞7∞

His expression was gravely stoic, but for those intense eyes. Sadik was serious. Marriage. Tonight. Here?

My regard swept around, landing over my shoulder on the Richards, who clearly caught wind of the ultra-alpha's demanding request. Their expressions were similar to mine: shocked and uncomfortable. When I glanced back to Sadik, his chin dipped impatiently.

Why?

Why would he do this again? What was the big deal about waiting? It was a question I'd never ask because he'd return it with the usual or something to bring about those now, all too familiar thoughts of the lack of reciprocity between us. And it wasn't true. I now felt there was no way of convincing him of that.

Except to finally give him what he wants...

I pulled in a deep breath through my nose, nostrils widening and eyes piercing him.

I exhaled, conceding, "Let's do it."

Why not? There was nothing after Sadik. He was it for me. With his resources, determined attachment to me, and family's means to hunt me down if I tried taking his child from him, he was the end game. As hilly as this relationship had been, I wanted in his heart. I fantasized about being his forever. That reasoning made my submission simple.

"Tonight," he made clear.

I nodded. "Tonight."

"Now."

My heart stopped beating for about seven seconds. However, folding was not an option. I rebounded quickly.

Chin in the air. "Now."

"Oh, shit!" Julius mumbled. "How do we make this happen?"

Sadik's bulleting eyes finally left me and he motioned to one of the uniformed men standing just off our lounge area.

The man shuffled toward us and Sadik whispered something to him. I stood by, heart pounding in my chest.

"I'm so happy for you two!" Keisha was at my side. "You're doing it your way, and at your pace." Her shoulders lifted, matching her wide beam. "I'm so happy to be your witness!"

My brows shot into the air.

"I, Bilan Asad-Yasin..."

"Take you, Sadik Qadir Ellis, the first..."

"Take you, Sadik Qadir Ellis, the first," I repeated, trying to recall where I'd seen the elderly clergyman before.

"To be my husband."

I turned back to Sadik, who held my hands in his trembling ones. "To be my husband."

"To have and to hold," the officiant prompted.

"To have and to hold…"

"From this day forward."

I repeated. "From this day forward."

"For better, for worse…"

I bit my lip, nerved by Sadik's obvious unrest. He didn't move much, but the pressure of my hands inside of his was nearing unbearable. His were cold and wet from perspiration. "For better, for worse…"

The officiant continued. "For richer, for poorer…"

I turned to my baby sleeping in the arms of a tearful Camille as she watched. Sadik could have lost all his fortune and I'd still have mine in him and our baby boy.

With a little more confidence, I repeated, "For richer, for poorer…"

"In sickness and in health…"

And that's when I recognized him. He was the pastor of the church the Ellises attended.

My head whipped forward to Sadik. I wasn't sure if he knew what I'd just discovered. He likely didn't, considering his tense frame and pinched brows that hadn't adjusted since we began the "ceremony," as the officiant referred to it.

But I was determined to do this and had to move on. So, I vowed, "In sickness and in health…"

"To love and to cherish," the older gentleman fed me more vows.

"To love and to cherish…" That was easy to pledge.

"Till death us do part…"

I froze. Sucking in a heap of air that felt hot and dry, and still not enough. My hands went weak. *Oh, god…* Then my body began to heat.

"Baby, breathe…" Sadik was close…really close. Closer than he was just seconds ago. I couldn't see him because my eyes were closed. "In and out slowly. Deep." He coached. "Yes. That's it, Nalib. That's it." His voice was so soothing. It was more present than his touch. "Look at me, honey."

With great effort, my eyes fluttered open. Sadik was there. His palms holding my face, something I just realized as my senses returned.

Oh, my god...

"You okay, Bilan? You want to lay down?" I recognized as Keisha's voice.

"No, Kee," Sadik answered softly and soothingly. "She's perfectly fine, just like *we* will be." As my heaves transitioned into pants, I could feel my eyes widening. "And I'm perfectly fine, Nalib. I'm not going to die prematurely. I know it's a tall order, but it's not something I'll ever risk. I swear." He fought for calm.

I nodded, not necessarily believing he could keep himself from death, but appreciating he understood my fear.

After licking my lips, I tried again. "*Ti*—till death us do part..."

I heard a few sighs of relief. The officiant cleared his throat as he fingered through his small book to resume the respective page. He nodded as though he found the spot where he'd left off.

"According to God's holy law."

I pulled in a hefty breath and repeated, "According to God's holy law."

"In the presence of God and these witnesses, I make this vow."

I nodded. "In the presence of God and these witnesses, I make this vow."

"Amen," he cheered, signaling it was over. The officiant switched his attention to Sadik. "Brother Ellis, I believe you have your own vows to give tonight."

Sadik's eyes were low, not even regarding the older man. His hands on mine began tightening again. The lighting from the tiki torches allowed me to catch his eyes rolling beneath the lids.

"I've not been patient with you." There was a long pause before he continued.

"I've been forthcoming with some difficult details and less with others. But all the while I've been clear on how you're the woman for me. Beauty fades, and while that's what attracted me to you initially, there was so much more that fueled my curiosity with you. It was much more than your small waist and curvy hips and ass. More than your bright smile and those delicious freckles decorating your sculpted cheekbones. Even more than your innocence. It was your ability to commit."

My damn heart was about to pound out of my fucking chest, and I knew I was drenched with perspiration. Who knew revealing the most sacred thing could be so difficult?

Transparency is painful...

"You like to believe my family is a high pedigree, but you come from exceptional stock yourself. You know how to stay committed, enduring the worst circumstances life can throw your way. I've seen you journey through pain, self-doubt, danger, and betrayal—alone. I've watched you traverse the damnedest of events and remain the course. You didn't break, you didn't crumble. You didn't cry to the people around you. You walked with your shoulders high alone, until..." I stopped to think for a moment. "Well, I guess you still are. You're here with me in spite of the millions of reasons you could have turned me away.

"Why would I not want a woman like that at my side for the rest of my life? How could I let her pass by and not mother my children —not be my comfort each night and joy every morning I rise? Having you as just my child's mother wasn't enough. A woman like you should have rights to me in every sense; legally, exclusively, spiritually, and forever. You already own my heart, why not have me in matrimony?"

Jules patted me on the back the same moment I saw the first tear slipped from her eye, then the next. Bilan's hand pulled from my grasp. She reached up, and swiped something wet on mine. This felt maddeningly flustering.

She grabbed my hands again, cueing me to continue. "Bilan, I vow to love you with a fidelity you deserve, to take care of you with every resource I have, including my heart, and to honor your mind, body, and wishes. I promised to be your friend and keep your most guarded secrets. To be your lover and worship your body and mind. And to be your protector, keeping you from harm and the ugliness of life, even when it includes me."

There...

I'd said more than I should have publicly. This was a private moment. Only Bilan should see me so raw.

"Amen," Pastor Wright acknowledged with a smile. "Do you, Bilan, take this man to be your lawfully wedded husband?"

Bilan let out a shaky breath. "I do."

"Sadik, do you take this woman to be your lawfully wedded wife?"

Bilan giggled through her tears, I was sure anxious from my nervousness.

"With every fiber of my being."

"Then, by the powers vested in me, I pronounce you man and wife," Pastor Wright declared as Jules shouted. "You may kiss your bride."

There was a small round of applause as I released Bilan's soft hands. All I could do was stare at her. Unable to move, my body felt light as though I would float away. I continued to watch her cry while giggling. She'd done it. She cured my insecurity. Bilan was now my wife.

"Sadik," she called out while Julius beat on my back and shoulders, cheering.

Then she leaped over and wrapped her arms around me. Her lips pushed into mine, and my eyes closed in submission. Her kisses were gentle until she pushed her tongue between my lips. I opened, tasting her.

When she pulled back, her beam returned. "You meant all those beautiful things?"

"Every word." I managed to smile.

Painfully and embarrassingly so...

Bilan kissed me again, her eyes narrowing with wanton when she withdrew. "You got what you've been wanting. Now, give me what I've been wanting."

With the congratulatory shouts and whistles happening around us, it took a moment to catch her drift.

"I tried to wake him," Camille explained when she approached us with Sadik in her arms.

He was knocked out, oblivious to the ceremony that made his father a real man. I let Bilan down, knowing she'd go straight for him.

"Awwww! Baby Deek," Bilan cried heaving him into her arms. "You're tired, huhn?"

Pastor Wright approaching me drew my attention away.

He tapped his chest. "I have everything with me and will handle it all."

"I can expect the submission to be expedited."

"Yes. I'll have it to the clerk's office the moment it opens when I return."

I gave him a nod of confidence before he ambled off.

Jules approached next with his hand out, expression solemn. "I'm proud, man. So proud."

I returned his shake. "Thanks for this."

"I would've kicked your ass if I'd missed this," he threatened sans the humor. "I still can't believe you..." I waited. "You're really in love, Ellis."

Shit...

I shook my head. "It happens to the worst of us."

"But you, sir, are in a class by yourself. I'm honored."

My hand went to my overflowing heart. While I appreciated every heartfelt expression my man shared, I was still floating from the gift Bilan had just given me. I couldn't keep my gaze from wandering over to her and my son.

"So," Keisha sidling up to Julius and wrapping her arm around him caught my attention. "what are we doing to celebrate this union?"

"One of the busboys mentioned a club a few miles down. We can start the foreplay on the dance floor with a few drinks and dollar bills," Jules suggested. "I'll out-earn you there."

Keisha laughed, nudging him.

"I'm sure my wife would throw her money at you rather than me," I returned dryly. "but I'm going to start her foreplay in our villa."

"Awwwwww," Keisha gushed. "I don't blame you. That momma is hot with that post-partum body," she growled.

I chuckled before bidding them a good night. As the crowd dwindled, Bilan paid the Richards hugs before we walked to the villa with Sadik. My security, including Rory, and Camille strolled behind us.

I'd give Bilan her time with Sadik then she'd be mine for the rest of the night.

"Ooooow!" My face clenched and the trunk of my body trembled in the air. "You're too big, Sadik!"

I knew it! Knew this wasn't a good idea, especially when he'd never respond to my soft requests. My rectum was about to break, the sphincter stubbornly narrow.

"My head isn't even in, sweetheart," he grunted, body vibrated lowly behind me.

"Don't call me sweetheart!"

"Baby," he chastised, voice strained, cock throbbing against the rim of my anus. "You have to stay still or I'll hurt you."

You are *hurting me!* I wanted to scream but didn't want to fail this mission. It was what I'd been curious about, what I wanted to explore with only Sadik. He tried prepping me with three orgasms, sex in my favorite positions, slow, gentle kisses—even with my impatience at play. He was loving and strategic leading into this.

But I didn't know it hurts like shit!

"Nalib," his vocals were coarse. "Relax it or it'll lock up."

I felt an inch or so of him push inside, the pressure so extreme I thought I'd rip into two.

"*Sa*—deeeeeek," I panted. "I feel like I'm going to doo-doo on myself."

I was on the verge of tears. Defecate? On or around Sadik?

No way!

This was a terrible idea. I'd never forgive myself. And he'd never be attracted to me after that.

I could feel the low reverberation of his chuckle against me. "You're not. I promise." His hand pushed between my legs and he found my clit and rubbed. "Relax, Nalib."

He kissed my shoulder sweetly, a contrast to the ache of my poor tush.

My eyes rolled open. Immediately, I could feel my throat was incredibly dry. Daylight and roaring waters were my next senses. When I glanced toward the nightstand, I saw the time on the clock. It was almost eleven in the morning. I'd slept in.

Again...

I tried lifting to reach the phone and felt the ache in my butt. Suddenly, memories of Sadik climaxing inside of me while I tried to remain still came flooding through my mind. I'd done it. I saw anal sex through. Just as he assured me, it happened. I still wasn't sure he fit fully, but he answered my sexual curiosity with the deed. I also wasn't sure I'd try it again. Afterward, I ran to the bathroom and sat on the toilet, feeling something was going to seep out. All that did was his fluids. It was weird.

Out of nowhere, my belly fluttered at the memory, warming me. Now, I had to leave this gargantuan bed and get to my baby. Here was another day I hadn't exercised. My body felt tight and achy, likely symptoms of not working out. I lifted my head again to grab my phone and saw there was not only food on my nightstand, but a note.

Mrs. Ellis, thanks for last night. Everything about it blew my mind. Take your time coming down to the beach. Sadik is fine. But before you do you should probably address these. I guess it goes without saying you should refrain from alcohol until we know for sure.

Huhn? Address what?

I sat up to take a better look at the nightstand and saw four pregnancy tests. My eyes rolled hard at the realization. It was what I asked the concierge to look into yesterday when Rory took me to a convenience store a few miles from the resort, and they had no recognizable brands I could trust. He must've brought them by this morning while I was still sleeping.

I collapsed back onto the bed. Pregnant again? So quickly? That would be irresponsible of me, and unfair to Sadik. He wasn't close to a year old yet. How would I juggle two babies? I'd barely had a handle on one. Between the baby, school, and work there was no time. What would I have to sacrifice to include another child?

Feeling my bladder about to explode, I stood to my feet and grabbed all four tests. In the bathroom, I did the pee dance until I could open all the boxes and aluminum wrappings. I nearly pee'd on myself detaching the last tab. Though a messy catch, I was able to fill the glass found on the vanity then hold it until my bladder was empty.

I wiped and washed my hands. Earl popped into my mind and I decided to reach out to him this morning. That decision was why I moved on expeditiously to wash my face and brush my teeth. Next, I showered, tossed on a bikini then a robe. Finally, I dipped all four strips into the glass filled with my urine and lay them to the side while they processed. After washing my hands again, I went out into the bedroom for my phone and *FaceTime*'d Earl.

The phone pealed in my hands as I finished dapping gloss onto my dry lips. Within seconds, the call was connected and as I waited on the image to open, my breathing faltered and I grew emotional about who'd be at the other end. Earl didn't take his own calls. He had an assistant to do it when he was preoccupied like now, being in the hospital. But Palmer was no longer alive to do it. The thought saddened me.

The image emerged and after seconds of what looked to be the ceiling view, Irene's face came into view. She wore her hair back in a ponytail and only had on a little eyeliner and a blush lipstick. She didn't look well at all. Dark spots shaded the area beneath her eyes and her jaw appeared sunken in.

I panicked. "Is he okay?"

"Hey, Bilan," she tried for a smile. "I miss you guys."

Her response wasn't for my question.

I tried again. "Hi, Irene. Is everything okay?"

She blinked several times, expression starkly serious as she leaned into the phone. "Is everything alright out there?"

My eyes glanced around as I understood her counter. "Oh, yes! Just fine. We're all just fine." I didn't think it was a good time to catch her up on our getaway. "I'm just missing you guys, I guess. I haven't spoken to Earl in days."

"Oh," she chirped. "He's right here, just finished eating. Here."

She turned the phone around and traveled to his bed. I made out Earl's golden skin and salt and pepper hair right away.

"Hi, sweetheart," he greeted with a smile.

I couldn't help my own. "I didn't want you to forget what I looked like." He laughed. "I wanted to check in. How are you?"

He took a deep breath before answering, "Well, they say I can go home. We're just setting up the home care before I do. I need physical therapy and such. But I'm still here."

"Don't make it seem so morose." I scoffed. "We're happy you're coming home!"

"We?" His head reared back, brows hiked as he snorted. "Where's my legacy anyway?"

"Which one?"

"The one *you* made."

I stood from the bench and sauntered over to the balcony. It didn't take long to locate Sadik with the baby.

"Down there, enjoying the sun." I showed him.

Earl tittered a screech. "Don't look like neither one of them thinking about the old man."

I turned the phone back to me. "I meant to call when I had Sadik with me so you could see him live and in action. He's staying up longer and lifting up from his stomach more now. But now that you'll be discharged soon, he can see his PaPa face-to-face." I beamed.

"He better," Earl quipped. "I gave him those eyes that's gonna have the little girls sharing their animal crackers then their panties."

I snorted a laugh, covering my mouth. "Don't even! My baby's too small to go there!" My fake cry was horrible, but I meant each word.

"He's a Ellis. You better know it, young lady." He winked. "And thanks for those pictures of him on the beach. Made my heart pump stronger seeing him like that. He getting big, man."

Although I smiled, it occurred to me how Earl didn't look strong. He appeared compromised, something disconcerting considering his reputation. I couldn't believe I'd grown so attached to him in the past six months. He'd been a tower of strength, cheerleader, a provider...a father figure to me. I hated to admit it, but similar to Irene, he'd taken on a parental role since the announcement of my baby's arrival. It deeply troubled me seeing him outside of himself. Earl had a strong presence, full of vitality and authority. His alpha persona was similar to Sadik's, only more rigid and tenured. I'd seen how Earl handled his staff when spending time with him. It was with a heavier hand than I'd seen of Sadik.

However, he'd been sensitive and sweet to my child and me. Sadik was the apple of Earl's eye, similar to how his father was to him. That warmed me to him tremendously since the first time he waylaid me—I now knew in an earnest manner—outside of *Ellis Academy* headquarters.

"You got pictures of my grandbaby?" Irene shrilled in the background. "No one's sent me any!"

"That's because I gave him his best features, baby girl," he placated her in sound, but not in argument. "You only gave him that blond hair that's gonna turn gray eventually." Earl snickered in a flirtatious manner, if that made sense.

"And your eyes will turn gray eventually, too, with old age," Irene returned. "So what are you saying, Earl?"

Earl's response was a wink to me. His good-humored nature was welcomed but couldn't cover the undercurrent foreboding I felt was happening in the family. I'd been feeling it for days.

"So, when are they looking to discharge you?" I asked.

Earl looked over to where I assumed Irene sat. I could have been wrong: Earl kept a team around him.

After a beat, he answered, "Maybe tomorrow. They just waiting to hear back from the physical therapist about scheduling. The nurses on the compound is ready for me."

I nodded. "Okay. We'll be ready, too."

"When y'all coming back?"

I felt my face tighten. Sadik hadn't said. "I honestly don't know. Now, I'm feeling a bit embarrassed because I should. I have to get back to work!" My boss was Earl's wife. Not knowing when I'd return to work wasn't a good look. It didn't matter that Irene was practically retired and not involved in the day-to-day business of *Ellis Academy*. "Sadik hasn't mentioned when to you?"

"Honey," Earl exhaled hard and with conviction. "Sadik ain't been saying much to me lately. Unless he done said something to his mother..." His gaze went to the right of him, I assumed addressing Irene. I couldn't make out what she remarked or if she'd said anything at all. Earl's feline eyes returned. "I don't know. But tell him I said a call to check on his old man would be nice."

That was strange. Sadik mentioned speaking to his mother every day. Why not be as frequent with his father who had been ill, recovering from a heart attack?

Once again, something felt off about this family. Something unusual, even for them.

I heard voices—new voices. Earl's regard went above the camera frame as he listened. "Listen," he spoke eventually. "That's the nurse.

They wanna take me for another test. Give that Ellis baby a kiss from his PaPa. Tell him I'm getting better just for him."

"Okay. You can give it to him soon. We'll be right over, Earl."

"Okay, baby. Talk soon."

I nodded and he ended the call. My gaze went blindly into the distance as I placed the phone down. That was strange. It didn't feel good at all. I couldn't claim to know the Ellis family that well. I'd just met them a year ago. But this felt...off.

I leaned back in the armchair. Since I met Sadik, my life had been on fast forward. The gifts, travel, mind-blowing sex, meeting his volatile and dysfunctional family, getting pregnant, learning he's capable of murder, running from him, having his baby, and now being married to him.

Married...

I leaped into an upright position. I was now a married woman. How sporadic! The last thing on my mind when I woke up yesterday was that I'd be exchanging vows with Sadik in front of our son, his staff, and our witnesses.

"I'm so happy to be your witness!"

Keisha's enthusiastic words tumbled to the front of my mind. I considered that for a moment. Were the Richards my witnesses or Sadik's? I didn't know they'd be joining us in *St. Justin* until they showed abruptly. Sadik said he invited them out when Julius called, needing to vent about being stressed. But Julius mentioned last night his announcement was simply having a solid plan for his cabinet. He could have done that with a call, email, or text.

Then there was the officiant. I was absolutely positive of him being the Ellis' pastor. How was he here, in the Caribbean, on such short notice? Sadik's staff being present, including Camille with the baby?

I collapsed back in the chair. I'd been set up. My life was no longer my own. Sadik orchestrated everything, and so unnecessarily. I would have been his wife. And just like with being pregnant with S.Q.E., the second; he didn't have to declare no condoms with me to have him. I would have given him babies, too, just in my time. I've always wanted children. Just by the right man—

The pregnancy tests!

I sat back in the recliner with a glass of lemonade. The sun was bright and the breeze mild. We were so close to the shoreline; the sound of crashing waves was louder than the music Jules played on his portable Bluetooth speaker. He'd been rocking Young Lord since they joined Sadik and me out here a couple of hours ago.

Keisha played with Sadik on her lap while Jules was on his iPad. I took a break from the business of my devices to enjoy the view. Off to the left, I could see a vessel coming in, moving at a modest speed.

"That's us," Jules asked from the right of me.

I nodded. "They're early."

I hoped Bilan had awakened. We weren't due to set sail for another forty-five minutes, but she liked to wear makeup and jewelry sometimes on the beach and would need time for all of that. I thought to call Camille and ask her to give Bilan a heads up.

"Is that a yacht?" Keisha sounded surprised.

"Yup," her husband answered.

As I reached for my phone, she asked, "That's the one we're going out on?"

Jules replied, "You know who we're rolling with. Nothing but the best."

A warm hand pushed down my shoulder just as I lifted the phone from the table. Then her head was at mine and warm lips on my cheek. She smelled of vanilla and fresh fruit.

"You let me sleep in again," she murmured before clasping my earlobe between her teeth.

She lifted from me and ambled to the side of my chair where she sat with a plate of fruit and an omelet.

"Hey, Deeky," she called over to Sadik on Keisha's chest.

"Say morning to your momma," Keisha playfully told Sadik.

"You slept well, huhn?" Julius asked Bilan. "That dude forgot he left you tied to the bed?"

"Fuck you," I mumbled.

Bilan snickered. "When's the last time he's eaten?"

"Less than an hour ago." With his clenched fists wrapped around her index fingers, Keisha raised Sadik's little arms in the air.

"Did he nap at all?" Bilan asked me.

I nodded. "He dozed off for about thirty minutes before they came out."

"That omelet looks delicious," Keisha observed.

Julius glanced our way and pulled down his sunglasses to zoom in on her plate. "I think this is the first time I've seen you eat food not fed to you by that brooding nigga."

I took another look at her plate. It seemed she started eating before coming out here. My eyes climbed up to her face and immediately, Bilan's expression turned forlorn...expectant as her brows pinched. And that's when it hit me.

"Shit," I scoffed, unbelievably anxious. "You're pregnant, aren't you?"

Bilan nodded, body tense as she leaned into me. Her reach for me was needy. Bilan was emotional. It happened so fast. She was over me, wanting an embrace, and Jules was on his feet, removing her plate from her lap. I grabbed her into my arms, half stunned and half protective.

"What's wrong?" I whispered close to her ear.

Her body trembled. "I don't want to overwhelm us." Her delivery was muffled in my chest.

"You feel overwhelmed?"

Her head lifted, heavy eyes on me. "You're not disappointed?"

I snorted, appreciating her coyness as I raised her chin to meet her lips.

"Remember what you blurted to Taaliba about getting pregnant with Sadik?" I whispered. Her face folded. "I'm too old to be misaiming."

Bilan's jaw dropped.

∞Ɓ∞

"Seems like a lot of shit going on in your world right now, huhn?" Julius remarked while drying off.

I pulled the towel from my head and peered over to him. We were on the stern of the boat and had just come up from a deep dive. The water was exceptionally cold down there, so we didn't stay long. Now toweling off, the beaming sun was relieving.

"How do you mean?"

"You know..." He shrugged. "Just with your pops being down, you having Sadik, you getting married, and now the new baby on its way."

"It's life."

"A lot, though."

"Nothing I can't manage." I stood straight, facing him.

"But can Bilan?"

Shrugging with my lips, I asked, "Why wouldn't she be able to?"

He tossed the towel over his shoulder. "I'm not saying she isn't able to. I'm spot checking to be sure she understands the good, bad, and ugly of being Mrs. Ellis."

"I don't follow."

"You haven't mentioned Iban since you called to tell me he'd shot himself in your son's nursery." His forehead stretched. "In front of said son and his mother. The Sadik Ellis I know can't sleep with unaddressed infractions."

I smirked. "And what are you saying?"

"What I've been saying for years when I'm aware of the crazy shit happening in your other world; your Ellis world. And that is you have to find a way to process that shit before it turns you dark."

I closed my eyes, shaking my head. "Richards, you trying to stuff counseling down my damn throat again?"

"Look..." he argued with his hands in the air. "You're my number one guy. I give a fuck about your mental state. And while I know you have the mental capacity of the entire U.S. government, the reality is you're just one man. You now have everything a man could wish for: supportive family, wealth, several successful businesses, a wife, and now a family. All of that along with the bullshit of being Earl Ellis' son. That's a weight not many can carry. Shit, look at Iban. He's not even built for it!"

Placing my hands on my waist, really wanting to get back to Bilan, who was on the bow, I sighed deeply. "Thanks for your realness. I appreciate it, but Jules, I'm not the type of man to spill my fuckin' guts to anyone. No one can manage my shit better than me."

"That's what Tony Soprano thought at first, too."

I chuckled and started toward the staircase.

"Okay," He continued as he followed behind. "If you're not going to try to talk to someone about balancing your shit, then at least encourage Bilan to. Bruh, she had a panic attack last night, exchanging vows with you!"

I nodded. Bilan did have issues I wasn't quite sure how to term. I'd been looking into a skilled professional for her since she'd had Sadik. Now that she was pregnant again, I had to reconsider my stance. During the first pregnancy, I didn't want her seeing a shrink.

Now, I didn't think I could delay it for another nine or so months. I wouldn't share this with Jules out of respect of Bilan's privacy.

"All taken under advisement." I reached for his shoulder while extending my arm toward the stairs for him to go in front of me. "Now, let's grab a light snack before showing your city boy ass how to waterski."

Rolling his eyes, Jules led the way up the stairs. "Light-skinned, pretty ass-eyed muthafucka."

"I'm dreading leaving!" Keisha faux cried.

My face tightened as I sat reclined on the built-in padded lounger. "You just got here."

"I know. When Julius gave me the news about the opportunity to fly out to the Caribbean, he made clear it would only be for a night."

Utterly shocked, I parroted, "One night?" She smiled before lifting her wine glass to her mouth and nodding. "That's it?"

She swallowed, resting the base of her stemware on her thigh. "Yup. I was able to get a sitter and time off work at the last minute. That was a reach, girl!"

"Wow."

"We never get away unless Sadik is flying us out somewhere randomly." She paused briefly. "And not particularly with women. Sometimes, it's the only way he could spend time with Julius. And since we got married, Sadik would arrange for me and sometimes our kids. Other than that, Jules and I rarely get time away, especially since he'd been plotting on running for mayor of Paterson. For two years, our lives have been about this campaign year."

"I bet it'll be worth it. Sadik shared with me the latest numbers."

"It better be. Running for a political office is more enduring than waiting to have a baby. So much more money and worrying goes into the development and labor process. All of that and you don't know if you'll deliver."

My head bounced up and down as the motor of the yacht revved and we began to move. That meant the guys were done with their diving. I waited with bated breath for him. I saw Julius walk onto the bow first. My body opened as I sat up anticipating his bestie. Sadik's globular shoulders swung left to right as he appeared behind him. He swiped his nose as his eyes were set out on the water. I noticed the muscles in his face were rigid and I had a feeling it wasn't just the sun causing it. I smiled when those golden eyes finally meandered over to me.

I watched fixedly as Sadik sat on the sofa across from us behind a small table covered in vegetables, cheeses, crackers, and spreads. He began fixing himself a small plate. Unable to help myself, I stood from the lounger bed and wobbled over to him against the moving of the boat as we began to pick up speed.

"Bilan, your ass is nice!" Keisha exclaimed behind me. "And how did your waist go down so fast if you're not breastfeeding?"

If I wasn't so preoccupied with my...Sadik, I would have been self-conscious about standing without my cover-up.

"Sadik's boot camp class," I explained, partially joking. "You okay?" I whispered once seated next to him.

I slid as close as possible. Across from us, Julius laid out next to his wife.

Sadik kissed my forehead, I guessed answering that way. I watched him spread hummus and guacamole on vegetables and crackers. He ate quietly. I nudged him playfully, asking him to share. It was strange to see him eat without me. Sadik spread hummus on pita bread and pushed it toward my hand. That's when I knew something was off.

Good-hearted about his rejection, I smirked as I shook my head. Seconds later, he lifted the bread to my mouth and I took a big bite.

The moment it hit the roof of my mouth, my stomach growled. Food oddly tasted better from his hands.

"So how many kids do you guys want?" Keisha asked, leaning into Julius across from us.

My regard swung over to Sadik for his answer.

"Lots," he answered, spiritlessly. "As many as Bilan'll let me get in her."

If it wasn't for his words, I would be crushed by his mood. But I knew Sadik enough to know he wouldn't lie. He wanted a large family...with me.

"I'm thinking three...no more than four." I smiled his way. Sadik wouldn't grace me with his eyes. I squeezed his thigh, asking for more food. "I just thought I'd have a couple of years in between—at least a year." I giggled.

Jules chuckled and Keisha laughed, nodding in understanding, it seemed. Sadik didn't react.

"I still want one more," Julius confessed, regard raking over to his wife imploringly. "Just one more."

"How many years after you quit your political ambitions?" she challenged.

Julius shrugged. "We can do both." He pouted crossly.

I giggled at his reaction and Keisha rolled her eyes.

"Chile, these men only want to hump and spread their seeds. They don't see the other part of it, like your body recovering and resuming its original state that attracted them to you in the first place. And, by the way, in most cases, after having multiple children, the likelihood of your body returning to pre-partum state is damn near improbable."

I laughed again, gaze roving over to Sadik. He was now on his phone, attention lost to it. Sadik was drifting away. The question was, when did he start? We were fine when we left the villa, celebrating the incoming baby and kissing S.Q.E., the second goodbye. He seemed in good spirits when we motored over the water to a safe place for them to dive. And now... Sadik was off.

I reached to caress the skin of his head gently. "You okay?" I whispered.

Sadik's feline orbs swept slowly my way. He regarded me before kissing the tip of my nose. "Fine, baby."

Before I could probe, Julius asked, "How long before you guys move back into the high rise?" He scratched his brow. "Damn. That place is bigger than the apartment in the City, but not big enough for a growing family. Y'all need a damn edifice with your aspirations of having a school of babies."

After a few beats, Sadik muttered, "We'll be fine. Taking our time to figure out where to build. Bilan's still deciding between three properties, and my realtor just sent me a few."

Really?

"Nice. Where?" Julius probed, lightheartedly. "In Hunterdon County near the palace?" Sadik's face turned rigid as he gazed into his phone. Then he shook his head. "Central Jersey?"

Sadik finally placed his phone down and gazed into the open air as though contemplating. "I'm thinking upstate New York. There are a few impressive stretches of land out there to build on in Cove Neck and Sands Point." He sat back, shrugged with his mouth as he stroked the hair on his chin. "Shit. Or Connecticut. There're dope spots out there with the capacity to build big."

"*Daaaaaamn!*" Julius' head reared. "You must gone send the jet to pick me up. That drive could be a monster."

Unbothered, Sadik rubbed his eyes. He stretched back and yawned, "Life's evolving." He blinked several times, as though clearing his sight. "Time for some changes."

My face folded as I shook my head softly. "That's far."

"Far for who?" he countered.

"For you...for me. It's far away from your family."

"As it concerns my home, the only family I need to take into consideration is you and my children."

A chill ran through me at that declaration. Where did this energy come from? I could understand him still being upset about Iban's suicide attempt, but to the extent of drawing such a distance between us and the whole family? That didn't seem right.

"Mr. Ellis," the captain called out from the P.A. system. "We're about three minutes out from the destination. You can start gearing up."

Sadik raised his arm for the crew to see above us in the cockpit.

"Let's go, Richards. Let me show you how to trick on the water."

Laughing, Julius stood and kissed his wife. Sadik left with a trace of his fingertips down my arm. I shot to my feet to tell him to wait a minute. We needed to talk about this moving thing. He hadn't shared with me anything about expanding his search for properties to build on. The last we spoke, I was to decide between the three vacant properties he listed as a birthday gift. When did this change?

My anxious eyes burned into the back of his head, but my lips balled shut. I didn't want to be confrontational in front of his friends. We'd just found out about my pregnancy, something I still hadn't wrapped my brain around. I didn't want to sour the day with a fight that was more appropriate to have in private.

"Damn, so this where the tycoon spends his holiday, huhn?" Julius' regard swept the living room of the villa. It was plush in design. Rolling walls opening the rooms to aquatic nature. Even the floor-to-ceiling window in the master suite had a majestic view of the ocean. "Yo, you can see to the backyard. Your fuckin' backyard is the goddamn Caribbean Sea!" Sadik shook his head. Julius glanced down to Keisha, who leaned into him. "Our shit was dope as hell, but not this big, and with views like this! Do better, Ellis."

She laughed harder and I couldn't help but to do the same.

"Don't pay him any mind, Sadik." Keisha reached her arms out for a hug. "This was incredible. I feel like I've learned a whole new side of you after less than forty-eight hours out here." Her eyes closed as she squeezed Sadik at the waist. It was a sweet sight. "Thanks so much for having us."

"Anytime. Always good times," Sadik returned. "Thanks for chaperoning this nigga."

When they broke apart, Keisha graced me with a hug. "These are the rough days in relationships," she whispered. "Have patience even when he doesn't deserve it."

My eyes closed as we held on to each other. Her words were more than a heeding; it was a connection through wisdom.

"Thanks," I returned.

Julius approached Sadik. "So, we're good on the terms, bruh? You got my back?" He leaned into Sadik for a half hug.

"Always," Sadik assured. "Thanks for coming through."

"Easy." Julius pounded his chest with his fist as they withdrew. "I'll see you in two days?"

Sadik nodded. "No doubt."

Julius hugged me warmly before we walked them to the door. There was a car waiting to take them to the airport. We waved them off and Sadik closed the door behind them.

"What time does their flight leave?"

Sadik peered at his wrist for the time. "Captain Willie said about nine-forty."

My head jerked back and I blinked hard. "That's how they're traveling?" *Of course...* Sadik flew them out. "And what about the officiant from last night?" My tone turned derisive.

Sadik's bright eyes met mine and he nodded. "He's already at the airport. Rory left thirty minutes ago to drop him off."

"So, you're not going to deny it. Your family's priest."

"I think the more appropriate title in the Baptist facet is pastor." A sly grin crested his face.

"Whatever his title is, his presence was mighty convenient for a spur of the moment vow exchange—or ceremony, as he called it."

Sadik's bushy brows furrowed, his head tilted to the side. "Nalib, what the fuck is buggin' you? What am I missing here?"

"Missing?" I nodded with poked lips, trying it out for size.

"Yes."

"I think your question is exactly what these past few days out here have been about. Your friends magically appear only to officially offer you a non-official job. When my drunk ass talks about congratulating you sexually, you counter with a wedding on the beach where, magically, *your* friends are present, serving as witnesses, and your family's reverend is front and center to officiate it."

"So, I was a little strong-willed in getting you to marry me—"

"And then today," I spoke over him. "during one of your infamous mood swings, you tell your friends you're considering moving out of state?" My eyes widened in emphasis. Sadik's brows lifted with cavalier. "What a way to kick off a marriage!"

Sadik took a deep breath, appearing calm and too unmoved. That response amped my anger.

"Sweetheart, I don't know what's gotten you—"

"*Don't call me sweetheart!*" I yelled, body vibrating with anger.

His palms lifted into the air. "Bilan, I don't want to see you upset in your condition."

"Then be considerate, Sadik. Don't treat me like a second-class party in this union."

"How are you being treated any less than the woman I adore?"

"By manipulating me into marrying you! I would have done it!"

"When?"

"Soon!"

"How soon?"

My arms shot into the air. "Does it matter now? The opportunity is lost."

"It always matters."

"Then acknowledge your wrongdoing!"

"I'll never apologize for not leaving you on the table. I'm not a passive man, Bilan." His brows lifted with emphasis. "You know this."

"And I'm not a helpless woman, Sadik. It ever crossed your mind that I was perfectly content taking my time, figuring out my life as a new mom and acclimating to living with a man?"

"You never said."

"Because I was too busy acclimating!" I yelled.

"To what?"

"To *all* of you! To your wealth, your alpha, your...dark side, your tightly-knit family. It's been a lot, and I thought I was doing a good job."

His face tautened and voice cracked when he asserted, "Baby, you were. But you don't have to worry about my family. I've never imposed that on you. If I have, I was wrong. They are of no concern to you."

That hit me like a gut blow. Swaying, I backed away. "No concern?"

With a strong glare, he answered, "No."

"Sadik," I cried. "Your parents have been—"

"It's not my mother who I take issue with."

"Earl has been hugely supportive of me since learning of my pregnancy with Sadik."

"He arranged to have you killed."

And there was that. Sadik learned of that horrid detail the day Iban shot himself in the baby's nursery. I'd never told him I was shot at in my bedroom at my parents' last August. He didn't know Iban walked to the back of the house with the intention of killing me.

"But I wasn't!"

"Because Iban slipped, and Iban rarely slips." His hand went into the air as he approached me. "You could have been dead eight months ago. My son would have never been born!" he shouted violently.

I'd never seen his face color in this manner, or his throat lift and cords protrude. If I wasn't so angry, it could have frightened me.

"But I was not. He's here, Sadik," I tried to reason with him. "Your father is your father. He's not changed. Iban has issues of mental health. That isn't new either. What had changed was you. *You* fell for me. *You* took a risk with me they weren't willing to. It's called survival, Sadik. I could have run to the police. They didn't want to risk that!"

"Are you defending them?"

"No." My eyes closed and rolled behind the lids as I shook my head. "I'm yielding to their narrowed perspectives, something I do in this relationship every day to survive in it."

Sadik issued another penetrating gaze. The orange bush forming around his mouth was unruly and entirely impossible to battle.

"You think it's okay for me to accept my family plotted to kill my lady behind my back?"

I scoffed. "I think it's okay for you to forgive, considering the circumstances. We're alive. We're breathing." I raised my engagement ring to him to symbolize the new commitment to each other we'd just taken on last night. "In the end, you still got what you wanted."

"You make our wedding seem one-sided."

"You made it one-sided when you planned it without me!" His face opened wide with betrayal. I dropped my face into my palms. "You don't get it," I murmured.

"What you don't get is I'm not like you."

My head shot up. "What do you mean?"

"I mean, I don't allow my family to walk over me. I don't allow my brother to betray me so severely and turn the other cheek."

"It's not like Iban tried to kill you, Sadik."

"Hell, no. Not like Abshir did you when he set you up to die!"

Damien...

That jab winded me.

Tears blurred my vision and my lips trembled. "How could you pay for specialized care for him and have your mother arrange his burial if you had a problem with it?"

"I worked for the good of my best interest. I supported you."

"And that's a problem?" I needed to understand him.

"No, Bilan. It's not a problem. Not interfering in how you dealt with your brother after his betrayal was not wrong; no more than you not judging me for how I deal with mine. It's my family."

That stunned me, too.

"You made me feel your family was mine. Did you not? So, now the Ellises—even after our vow exchange last night—is just yours and Sadik's family, and not mine?"

Sadik's face balled viciously and he spat, "Of course, that's not what I'm saying! My mother, sister, sister-in-law, and nieces adore you."

"And Earl doesn't?" My question was sincere.

He took a deep breath, nostrils flaring. "Look..." Sadik shook his head then pinched the bridge of his nose. "I don't even know how we got here."

"Welcome to my world! Lucky for me, I do know how we arrived here. '*We're*' not going to make decisions regarding my life without me moving forward, Sadik. You tasked me with deciding on a home, I will do that. In New Jersey!" I stormed off.

"Bilan," he called after me to deaf ears.

The next morning, as the baby talked his head off to the small, hanging stuffed animals from his bouncer, I packed our clothes. Camille was doing a final load of laundry for S.Q.E., II. It amazed me the amount of clothes an infant went through in a day. As much as I wanted to feel in control of motherhood, Sadik was right to insist on a nanny. And now with two babies in my near future, I had to prepare to readjust again.

Sadik's hike in volume snapped me from my thoughts. I peered over my shoulder to find him smiling at the little stuffed elephant. His small arm flapped in the air as he tried reaching for it. My heart expanded.

"Hey, lil' boy," I called out to him. "You mind keeping it down and stop growing up so fast?"

Sadik's smile fell for seconds at the sound of my voice. Then he was distracted by the sight of the toys and his little face opened in wonder again. I turned my shaking head back to the task at hand. I'd just finished packing Sadik's clothes and needed to start my own next. The baby's would have to wait until his load was done by Camille.

We were due to return home this evening. Of course, this task of packing for three should have begun last night, but I was so angry with Sadik's bullheadedness, all I wanted to do was snuggle with my baby to sleep. I didn't even feel when he came to bed. I rolled over at some point in the night and he was there. Then I felt him get up and head to the shower this morning. He'd been a ghost since.

As I moved to the bathroom to start pulling together my makeup, a strong buzzing sound rang out. It grew louder by the second. Sadik's babbling stopped abruptly once it sprouted into a vibration in the air. I made my way to the opened floor-to-ceiling window leading to a lounge area and private pool. I arrived just in time to see aircrafts fly over the villa, south, toward a small uninhabited island that could be seen miles away.

There were three of them in formation. They circled in the air, diving then swerving. Two began emitting purple smoke. It took less than a minute to recognize the letters *M R*, and it appeared the one airliner was working on an *S*.

Airwriting...

The aircrafts were airwriting. It was clear to me when my first name started to appear. Minutes later, when they were all done, the sky read "***Mrs. Bilan Ellis***."

My mouth collapsed.

"What in the..." I mumbled, watching the planes fly away.

My attention returned to my name, spelled out in the air. When was this planned? How long will it stay? It was a sense of proprietorship, having my name over our villa. It felt like an imposition. It felt like—

Clicking sounds to my right grabbed my attention. Rory was off the living room patio, snapping pictures of the sky art. But before her, on the patio off the dining room was the man himself. In navy Bermuda shorts and a hunter green sleeveless knit sweater, Sadik could be an *Ase Garb* model. His shoulders were globular masses of muscle and his hands rested coolly in his pockets. I watched as his kaleidoscopic hued irises slowly descended from the sky to my frame.

My chest began to heave from unspoken words of gratitude and regret. But Sadik didn't wait until I was able to formulate them. He backed away before turning into the dining room, leaving my view.

"So the meeting with Miller next Wednesday?" I asked into the phone to my assistant, Tonya, while stepping onto the elevator. Rory was right behind me as I asked her, "You got that on your schedule?"

Rory was in the calendar app on her phone. She nodded. "At one-fifteen. Yup."

"We're on one accord with that, Tonya," I remarked as Rory pressed the button for the respective floor.

"Good. Another item: we're down a warehouse receiver," Tonya shared.

"How?"

"Why?" Rory asked, hearing from the speakerphone.

"Isaiah Green," Tonya explained. "He's been with us for five years. A few days ago, he was processing an incoming on the Kolwaski account. He said the contents of a couple of containers didn't feel like liquid. Said he couldn't allow something so blatant to pass on his watch. When he kept mouthing off, the foreman told him to pack it up. He fired him the next day."

My eyes met Rory's big ass ones.

Shit...

I didn't need this bullshit. While I knew Kolwaski would stuff his packages, I padded his account with the right warehouse people so we wouldn't feel it.

"I told Rashad to handle that account with gentle hands himself," I thought out loud.

"He's the one who appointed Green," Tonya offered.

"Then he fucked up." I gestured to Rory I had to handle Green.

I never had my professional world intersect with my dark inclinations, however, I knew this couldn't go by unchecked. That comment by Green was a red flag. The last thing I needed was the regulatory dogs sniffing around my warehouse. Never had I endeavored harming an employee, but this problem could spread like a wildfire. Who knew how many people Green shared this suspicion with.

Rory, understanding the risk, shook her head, motioning she'd take care of it.

"He clearly selected a hothead, and one untrustworthy." I pinched and rubbed the bridge of my nose, out to my eyes. "I'll talk to Rashad and the foreman tomorrow. Fit that into my morning, please."

"It'll be a tight squeeze, but you got it," Tonya answered.

It was close to seven at night, and after the longest day of work, I'd just arrived at the hospital to visit my father for the first time since returning from *St. Justin*. Although I'd been at *Ellis International* all day, I didn't have a chance to meet with my executive assistant about my schedule that had just gotten more demanding since I'd been away for over a week.

"Another issue I'm seeing," Tonya noted.

My empty gaze lifted to the floor number panel above. "Hit me."

"You asked, months ago, that your schedule begins later in the morning three days a week."

"Bilan's workouts," I thought out loud. "Yes."

"It's going to be impossible, especially over the next few weeks with the expansion transition. And especially with your commute from Midtown Manhattan, and your need to leave the office in time to get you home at a decent hour."

"Make the adjustments needed for me to get home by six," I replied. "I'll figure out something for Bilan." I could feel Rory's eyes on me but ignored them. Shit hadn't been right with the Ellises since she became one. It was a topic I didn't want to deal with now. "In fact, cancel that rooftop dinner for Friday."

"This Friday?" Tonya asked and Rory's eyes mirrored the same question.

"Yes."

The elevator chirped as it stopped.

"But we've signed with *DiFillippo's* for the food," Tonya warned. "It's non-refundable at this point."

I shrugged...at her comment and at Rory's annoying ass eye-regulating me. "Pay them."

There was an awkward span of silence as the doors opened. "Should I reschedule with them?"

"Yeah," Rory added. "I got that cello chick coming through."

Tossing my head with a shrug, I mumbled, "Do what you need to do to cancel. I don't have a tentative time or date in mind. Y'all can continue this scheduling conversation. Tonya, I have to go." I disconnected the call as I left the elevator.

After rounding the corner, I spotted my mother's assistant, Kema.

She waved me on as she took off. "She's this way."

As we neared the waiting room, I could see my mother's tight face etched with concern through the glass windows. Her eyes were narrowed, more hurt than angry. She ended a call as we entered the room and immediately passed the phone to Kema. Kema's response was a silent check-in of my mother's emotions.

When I didn't get the usual glow in her eyes the moment they met me, I knew there was a problem. My mother's demeanor had always lit up when I entered the room. This evening, it took her a few seconds to acknowledge me.

I headed straight her way with a three-word greeting.

"Who did it?"

∞9∞

With her fist to her mouth, her index finger over her top lip, my mother expelled a troubled breath, her brows pinched. She shook her head as she stared into the distance.

"Lia Rizzo and Iliza."

"What about them?" I demanded.

My queen shook her head resignedly again. "I've been asking for Iliza since Iban's accident and Lia's been giving me soft no's. Now that Sadik is back, I wanted to have pictures taken in the solarium with it being springtime. So, I reached out to Catena Rizzo, hoping she'd have a more mature take on the importance of Iliza spending time with both families. But..." She shook her head again, hesitating.

"But what?"

"I had Kema reach out to the Rizzo's to arrange a call for tonight."

"And?" I was past impatient.

"And Catena was there...with her son, Marco. He took the phone and said under no uncertain terms will Iliza be visiting our family until Iban is back and mentally evaluated."

My forehead stretched as my head reared softly. "Marco Rizzo said that? Directly to you?"

She nodded. "This is getting to be too much on me," she mumbled.

"What is?"

"Everything!" she trilled, sitting back in her seat. Those dark spots that developed beneath her eyes after my father's heart attack had not improved.

Her natural glow now an unseen before dim. I turned to motion privacy to Rory and Kema. They quickly abandoned the room.

I took a seat next to her. "What's everything, queen?"

I'd spoken to her nearly every day since the funeral and hadn't picked up on this anxious energy.

"Iban's still under. Every day I pray for his breakthrough. Your father's not one-hundred percent. They want to keep him an extra day because of complications with his lungs. Now that Palmer is gone, he's overwhelmed with work. And Earl doesn't need the stress, neither does Iban."

"And neither do you." I wanted to be clear. "Don't stress about Iban. He's dealing with more variables than you can control. He's receiving expert care with the best technology, and he has a wife to be his primary support as you are that for your husband. Don't try to take all of this on."

Her downcast expression deepened. Eventually, she patted my thigh and tried forging a smile. "Go see about your father. He's been missing you...needing you."

I nodded before standing to my feet. Leaving her like this wasn't ideal, but I understood the lioness wanted her space to pother.

When I entered the hospital room, Rodney and Travis, two long term associates of my father's both turned my way. They were on guard, which was good. One of the ideal features of this hospital was they catered to our unique needs, including having armed guards with my father, even in the surgery room. Security had to suit up and stand afar but was always present.

Both Rodney and Travis nodded their acknowledgments of me as I closed the door. My father peered up from his iPad then returned to it.

"Hey, baby. My son just walked in. I'll hit you later."

"Okay," a feminine voice acquiesced. "Don't forget. I'm bored."

His eyes were on me when he replied, "I got you."

Then he tapped the device and placed it on the side of the bed as he peered me directly in the eyes. They communicated displeasure. That aside, my father looked feeble. He was thinner, pale, and the opening of his gown exposed the wound of the incision down his chest covered in stubble. He was clearly shaven before being cut for surgery. Attached to his chest and arms were a gamut of patches and wires. I'd never seen Earl "Double E Bags" Ellis so vulnerable and compromised.

"Finally," was his one-word rebuke.

A silent scoff left my lungs. I approached his bed, my hands tucked into my pockets.

"It's been a demanding two days since returning from the Caribbean with my family."

"Too demanding to come see about your old man, I see."

I stood over him, the nail of my thumb scraping beneath my bottom lip. "Never, but as you know, I do have a family now."

"I see." He nodded. "But shit is thick on this side, my G. I didn't wanna bust up ya party with baby girl and my legacy, especially after the shit they seen—I swear to fuckin' god when Iban's back on his feet, I'mma put my foot up his ass for that shit he pulled. He fuckin' put us out there, bruh!" Abruptly, his head reclined as he sucked in needed air.

My father's eyes closed as he gave himself a minute to catch his lungs. "Shit's been wild since I been in here. And when Palmer took that *L*..." his voice faltered. "Let's just say I'm a lucky son of a bitch that I ain't have to put a bullet in none of my men for trying me yet. But you know they will soon. It's just a matter of time."

He took another moment to breathe. "The first shipment from

the Haitian boy's connect coming in soon. I can't fuck it up. Some shit go foul with that order, muthafuckas'll see it as a sign of weakness. I gotta get outta here. And now these fuckin' doctors scared to release me to the medical staff we hired for *Elliswoods Palace*! Top of the fuckin' line medical people, but they scared, and shit."

His gaze went out the window to the setting sun for a bit. "The kid, Daz, been steppin' up. He told me we gotta squatter outside the warehouse." His head rolled lethargically over his pillow. "I can't shoot right now. Can't risk hitting the wrong target. I doubt if the FEDs' goofy asses gone be outside the warehouse doing just shit." His eyes hit me. "Iban down. If he make it out this shit, he could be down for a while or forever. We don't know how he gonna come out on the other side. My men need to see Ellis leadership. A face and energy they recognize and know to be thorough."

I stood over him silently with my fist pressed into my hips, my suit jacket pushed back. Finally, my father recognized me. He unusually gave pause to my posture, something he hadn't done much of my entire life.

"What the hell is up with you? I see some shit." He regarded me with suspicion as I returned his gape. "Now that I think about it, you ain't been up here since that shit with Iban." His face folded slowly with suspicion.

My brows lifted. "Your point, sir?"

"My damn point?" His temper flared. "Sometimes, we need to prioritize things, son. I thought you knew."

I took a deep breath as I answered, "I actually do. I have a son to protect, and his mother."

"Shit. I expect you to. She's the mother of my goddamn legacy."

"A legacy that would not have survived much past conception if your son was a better fuckin' shooter."

His eyes bulged from his head in revelation. Seconds later, he ordered, "Everybody fuckin' out!" As they filed out of the room, Double E Bag's chest heaved and eyes were wild with irritation. "The fuck is you on? You bring this shit to my sickbed?" he hissed with strained chords.

My heart leaped from my chest when my determined mind

decided on the war. This war. The visit had turned into an out-of-body experience.

"You gave orders to kill the woman I told you I wanted to make my own." My mouth went dry with anxiousness. "You knew I had settled on her when you sicced your dog on her. Not only did you cross me, but you gave him a false sense of entitlement. You made Iban feel he could bully her, level her."

"I did no fuckin' such thing—"

"Iban told every goddamn thing! He came to my fuckin' home armed with intent of harming either her or my fuckin' son!" I shouted. With my hands remaining safely on my waist, I explained. "You fuckin' betrayed me!"

I saw the blood drain from my father's face as he processed those words. "The fuck is you talkin' about, youngin'? I ain't neva been with the shits when it came to you!"

"You put that fuckin' battery in his back to jeopardize the life of my son and lady, not once, but twice!" My body trembled, partly in fear for taking this tone with my commander and chief, and mostly from volcanic anger. "Are you going to lie to my face and say this isn't true, sir?"

"She was a threat to us. To our family, our brand! I couldn't risk that shit."

"But you could risk the long coming piece of happiness I told you I'd found." I scoffed again, moving closer to his bed. "You have a wife —and then some. Iban decided on his wife. But when Sadik finds his, he can't be trusted for you to want to keep her alive."

"I ain't know she was pregnant—"

"*IT DOESN'T FUCKIN' MATTER!*" My head felt near explosion.

The door pushed open, and immediately we yelled, "Get the fuck out," at the same time, same cadence, reminding me of how much of a carbon copy I was to the man I loathed in the moment.

Travis closed the door right away. My eyes shot into my father once again. This time, I was out of breath, but still fully loaded.

"All my life, in spite of our differences, I served you with honor, respect, and dutiful obligation—even at the risk of my independent businesses and my liberties as a free man. I've always served you against my better judgment, going against my own aspirations of wealth-building, and my strong inclinations of charting the path I'd dreamed of for myself. And after damn near forty years of honoring you...respecting you against the raging man within me... When I finally come to you, sharing my heart. Bilan..." Quickly, I caught my temper.

"I didn't know she was pregnant."

"Neither did I, but that isn't the point! Your actions were revealing. It told me you didn't respect me as a man. You viewed me as a tool to further your agenda, your business. I'm not much different in your eyes or world than Iban. You use me to further your ambition." My mouth tightened. "That shit is—"

"Bullshit!" he claimed.

"No! It's your truth. It's who you are. Nothing comes before your will and your way. We're all just pawns on the board. And all these years, I thought if no one understood my ambition, my need for dominance, it would be you. My fuckin' Nestor!"

His head dropped and rolled against his pillow again and my father groaned. "I don't even fuckin' know what that mean. All I do know is I love your lil' mama. Your child is my only reason to live nowadays. Ain't no fuckin' way I'll ever put them in danger. You know this, man!"

I felt my head shake, though I didn't recall telling it to. "You don't fuckin' get it."

"Get fuckin' what?" he demanded, panting.

"Get how you revealed yourself and your value of me the day you ordered Bilan's death."

"You know who I am, Sadik. You know my world. I gotta move... strategically. It's fucked up you don't get it. Real fucked up you think I did the shit thinking I was being underhanded. You know I 'on't apologize for the moves I make. It wasn't personal against baby girl."

My lips turned up in a shrug. "Just like it was nothing personal against you that I had the Ab kid resuscitated after Ib's weak ass gunplay, and worked on in this very hospital for over a month after your hit. How not only did my mother and I support Bilan here while he fought for his pathetic ass life, but my queen supported her in burying him underneath your manipulative ass nose. It's what I arranged. It's the type of compromise I provided for my wife."

As revelation illuminated his eyes, I moved toward the door.

"I love that fuckin' boy!" My father swore. "It ain't fair how I favor him!"

"Yeah." My smile was broken. "I once thought I had your favor. Turns out, I only had your most coveted interest in manipulation."

I strolled out of the room, not leaving him a moment of rebuttal. Once the door closed behind me, I heard a series of alerting beeps from his room.

"This shit good as hell!" Tasche declared while gobbling a mouth full of food. The waiter walked around the table collecting our discarded plates. "Yo, I gotta get this again."

As the waiter stood over her, I smiled. "She's not done yet."

"And what about you, ma'am?" he asked a spiritless Randi, whose head was ducked, attention to her phone.

Randi finally peered up, thick glued on eyelashes fanning her cheeks. "Oh..." Her eyes cut over to me.

I tried helping her out. "You want to pack that to go?"

Her regard bounced to her barely touched plate. "Ye-yeah..." She stammered. "I'll take it home."

"Okay. I'll get that packed up for you," he assured. "Can I bring out the dessert menu?"

"Ooh, yeah!" Tasche answered boisterously. "Let me see that joint."

I snickered as I nodded my head to the waiter.

When he took off, Randi spoke up. "Sorry about that. My appetite been fucked up."

My head bounced again. "I can only imagine. It's okay. We're just glad we caught up with you."

It had taken a full two days since returning from *St. Justin* to get in touch with Randi. She agreed to meet us here for dinner at *DiFillippo's* in Hackensack, near *Garden State Plaza Mall*. It had been the longest day for me. I visited three schools today for work and had missed my baby so bad, I asked Camille to meet me earlier and bring Sadik. I relieved her for the day and brought him to dinner tonight.

He was such a good baby, not fussing much at all. When I asked Rory to call for the reservation, I asked for a table off in the corner where we could have privacy and in case Sadik got a little noisy. Of course, I needed to flash the Ellis card for that request at a restaurant like this. I could have easily met Tasche and Randi at *Michelle's Diner*, but Rory recommended coming here as her boss wouldn't have been comfortable with the baby and me in Paterson. I thought it was ridiculous, but didn't fight. Sadik and I hadn't been right since that last night in *St. Justin*.

I reached down to my purse hanging on the back of the chair next to me. On the other side, Sadik talking to his hanging stuffed animals caught my attention again. He smiled, gums exposed.

"Damn, he so fuckin' cute, yo," Tasche gushed. "Let me hold him again. Auntie Tee want you to kick that game to me."

I placed the envelope I was reaching for on the table in front of me then leaned over to safely pull Sadik from his car seat without hitting his face on the handlebar. Tasche met me halfway, around Randi, to get him. As she began talking to him once seated in her chair, I handed Randi a thick envelope.

"This is for you," I started, but waited for her to pull her eyes from Sadik to hear me. She had been staring at him throughout the whole dinner, though she hadn't addressed him or asked to hold him. All she said in acknowledgment of him was she couldn't believe I had a baby. Randi's eyes reached the envelope in my hand. "I put together a few dollars for you. Some of it is here in cash. The other is a check so you're not walking around with all of it."

"What's this for?" she asked, opening the envelope.

"It's for you to get your own place. Like you said, Brenda's son is gonna be discharged next week. She's going to need his room back."

"How much is this?" She counted the cash, somewhat stunned, but more spirited than I'd seen her all night.

"Altogether, it's five thousand. There's a check in there for four. That's only one thousand in cash."

"Damn," Tasche breathed, holding Sadik on the table in front of her. "That's a down payment on some shit."

"Not exactly, but it could be for a one-bedroom...a studio apartment, or to rent a room. You said they're still holding your things at Ricky's apartment. You need to collect them before they're misplaced. This should help you get a place for you and your things and then look for work to maintain, then grow your personal space."

Randi didn't respond at first. She sat and counted the cash, though I had a strong suspicion she was processing my words.

"Ah-goo-goo," Sadik babbled to Tasche, demanding her attention as she held his neck securely.

He gazed at her intently, almost as though he awaited her response. It instantly swelled my heart.

"I know! He told me, too, man," Tasche played along. "And I told him next time he gotta beef with you, he gone have to see me."

"Goo-Guh!" he replied.

Tasche gasped, head falling to the side. "Word? Then we gone have to handle him, my G. Then this what we gone do—"

"You ain't have to do this." Randi's mumble broke my attention. She was still gawking at the money in her hand.

My forehead stretched, eyes narrowed. "I didn't think I had to. I'm doing it for someone I deeply love and care about." I reached for her arm. "I know it's not enough, but we have to start somewhere. You need your own space. And you must still be grieving. I understand all about those days where you just want to be left alone to sort it all out."

Randi didn't respond right away, neither did she give much eye contact as Tasche and the baby continued their conversation. But eventually, she did look my son's way in a manner of acknowledging him.

"How his daddy feel about you giving me his money?"

"That's not Sadik's money. It's mine. I may not have an Ellis' wealth, but I do have a paying job and a little cushion to fall back on. That's what I wanted to share with you."

Her attention went back to the baby, face expressionless. After a few seconds, she uttered, "I still can't believe you had a baby. Seem like just a few months ago, we was at your mother's spot waiting for her to finish cookin' that Somali shit we used to fuck up."

A wry smile spread on my face at the vivid memory. That was so many moons ago. My hooya had been gone for six years now. So much had happened since then. So many heartbreaks, so many twists and turns on my journey. Most days, I didn't recognize myself. Like today, I was having dinner at exclusive *DiFillippo's* with my friends so I could be a support to one. Oh, and I brought my baby along. I had a child. A child who owned my heart—along with his father.

"Yeah," I exhaled, brushing my hand down the back of my head as I rolled my eyes to prepare myself. "So, I have news to share with you guys, especially after the way you reacted to my changes last year."

"Bitch, you pregnant again," Tasche stated rather than asked.

Simultaneously, Randi blurted, "Y'all married?"

I took another deep breath, my chin lifting into the air, trying to cling to bravery. Exhaling while tossing my regard to the wall, I admitted, "Both."

"Both what?" Randi demanded.

"When you get pregnant again? I mean, daaamn!" Tasche cried.

This was as hard as I thought it would be. I wasn't used to explaining my decisions because none were ever so extreme.

"I'm not exactly sure when I got pregnant. My doctor's appointment is in a few days."

"How did you let him knock you up again?" Randi's tone was finally lively.

"That wasn't the intention." I shook my head. "It was partly my ignorance with my body. I didn't know how soon I should have started my period after a C-section, especially because I'm not breastfeeding. Then with all the craziness that happened, I really didn't get concerned until last week." I shrugged. "That's when I bought a few tests and found out."

"Crazy shit like Iban Ellis shootin' up your baby's room," Randi qualified.

The word had gotten out, and the last person I would be dishonest with about it was a friend of mine. So I didn't deny it.

"Yeah." I nodded with pouted lips, fortifying the next piece of information. "And before that with Sadik's father having a heart attack. That was a huge setback for the family." Licking my lips, I hesitated again. "I was there when it happened."

Tasche sucked in a breath and her eyes popped wide. "Say fuckin' word!" she graveled.

I nodded when I noticed Randi's expression of shock, even if not as much as Tasche's.

"Yeah." I swallowed, trying to decide what's necessary to share and what's not. The Ellises were a private family with a public reputation. I understood that and would protect them. "It was more terrifying than I imagined it would be for me. I felt that familiar pain of loss when I saw his body curl to it."

"Wow! You really in deep with them?" Randi inquired.

My eyes closed and I whispered, "I am. My son is one of them."

"They ain't like you, Bilan," Randi warned again. "Them mutha-fuckas kill people for fun." The blaze in her eyes had finally arrived after all this time sitting here. A flash of ire in them.

I leaned toward her, over the table. "I'd appreciate it if you didn't spit rhetoric like that in a public place when you're with me."

"It's true!" she screeched.

"Until you can prove it, please watch what you say in front of my son and me."

"C'mon, Randi," Tasche cried with Sadik cradled in her arm. "She just told you she married to the nigga with another baby on the way. Why you gotta bring that murky shit up?"

Sadik started sniffling, a sign of getting cranky. It was dinner time. I dug into his bag for his bib; his bottle had been warmed already.

"I'm just saying, I'm from the streets, Tasche," Randi explained. "Been born in them. You from Harlem, you know Harlem. Them Ellis niggas go deep in the streets. They bury bones underneath the fuckin' concrete!" she whispered hard as I extracted Sadik from Tasche's arms.

"Again, Randi, please keep that away from me and my son." I kept my voice low. "I know the Ellises aren't innocent, but they're a real family with real hearts and real issues. Don't dehumanize them. And at least when you're around me, don't discuss those things in public where others can hear."

The waiter was heading to our table with bagged food and the dessert menu.

"Take your time," he advised before walking away.

"How much I owe you for this?" Randi asked, digging through her purse.

"Nothing," I screeched, taken aback. "I invited you here. I'll take care of it."

"A'ight," she exhaled. "I gotta go. Thanks for everything. Sorry if you think I disrespected you." She stood, sounding very guarded.

After placing the bottle in Sadik's readied mouth, I watched her take off.

"Later, T," were Randi's last words.

Tasche shook her head, going for the dessert menu and sliding in Randi's chair, closer to me.

"Told you she was on one," Tasche murmured. I didn't respond right away, jostled by the energy that had just tornadoed at the table in that short time. Where had it come from? I knew Randi was off from the moment I met her outside of the restaurant, but I didn't have expectations of her being high energy, considering her loss of Ricky. "Let me tell you something, yo," Tasche whispered out of nowhere, eyes locked on me.

I swallowed. "What?"

"Watch out for her. I *never* liked the way she rolled witchu, but that bitch look scorned just now. And scorned bitches burn everybody around them. Don't be surprised if she flip on you. Sometimes, death bring the fuckin' demons outta people. The shit always been there, but been controlled until the lid come off. Ricky getting murked like that could be what blew the lid off that one. Be careful, B."

I nodded, chewing the inside of my cheek, gazing over Sadik, who was sucking hard and dozing off at the same time. Poor guy should be in the process of getting put down at this hour. I just couldn't resist having him with me now. I didn't want to wait until later tonight when he was fast asleep. He was my latest addiction—him and his father's sexual organ. That small fact annoyed me.

"I just don't get her. If I was a weaker person, I'd feel some kind of way about her disposition around me since Sadik. It's like she's angry with me for, at first, simply dating a guy. I thought we'd be beyond that by now."

She softly tugged on Sadik's clenched fist.

"I 'on't know why you let her fuck with ya head like that. Randi got some shit with her." Her eyes rolled to the menu book. "I know her kind, yo."

I peered down to Sadik to find him dozing off. He needed to finish the whole bottle so I wiggled it to rouse him. It worked, but I wasn't sure for how long. When he was tired, he was tired. So I rearranged him in my arm, disturbing his relaxed state more.

"Yo, I heard their crème brûlée be's the shit," Tasche rasped. "You ever tried it?"

I nodded. "It's the best." Considering the time needed to finish feeding and burping Sadik, we could definitely fit desert on the agenda. "Let's go for it."

"True dat." She closed the menu as the waiter returned. "Two crème brûlées, my man."

"Two?" he verified, eyes swinging between the two of us.

I nodded.

Tasche repeated, "Two." When he left the table, she turned toward me. "So, another damn baby, Bilan?" I nodded with a dry smile as I examined Sadik's half-mast eyes. "Another damn, blond hair, green...blue—" Her face folded as she gazed over Sadik. "Sometimes, I see hazel in there, too. But whatever color they is, another baby with them crazy features. You ready for that?"

I laughed at her description. Then I shook my head, humor escaping my face. "No," I answered honestly. "I wasn't ready for this one either, but it's been the single most creative thing I've done my whole life. Look at him. He's untainted...hope."

"Hope for what?"

I took a moment to consider that. "Hope for me to not feel like everyone I love dies or goes away." I shrugged, rearranging him again in my arm to keep him awake. "Hope that he'll contribute something good to this ugly world." Then I thought some more. "Hope he can change his family. Be the first agent of change for the Ellises," my voice but a whisper.

Tasche sat back in her seat. "I fucks with that." She nodded, picking up her phone.

We spent the next twenty-five minutes or so chatting about the new guy she'd been dating and eating delicious crème brûlée after I burped Sadik and let him rest into a peaceful sleep. Tasche kept me laughing to the point of needing to unbutton my pants at the table.

When we were done, I packed up Sadik's things as the check was being settled. She held Sadik's diaper bag as we trekked it to the front of the restaurant. I noticed the stumble in her stride when we reached the hostess' desk.

"Ezra?" she trilled, ghosted.

At that name, a distinct chill coursed up my spine, and not the type a bald-headed kaleidoscopic-hued, golden man caused. There was only one person with that name I'd come across in my life. But this couldn't be him. The tall, mahogany, bearded man with glasses perusing a menu glanced up at her. Slowly, recognition settled in his eyes as he removed the glasses with his marital banded left hand and slid them into the pocket of his blazer.

His smile was...accompanied by charm and warmth. "Tasche," he rasped deeper than her. "Good evening."

"Good evening? You mean night," she teased him, but with a softer hand than her usual. "Whatchu doing in Hackensack this late?"

He snorted, and—*holy something in heaven*—the man was gorgeous! Even with dark hair covering most of his head and face, his attractiveness was riveting.

No way...

"I had a late appointment and a certain friend of yours demanded eggplant parmigiana. In fact, she asserted if I did not arrive with this particular delicatessen in hand, I'd be addressed in the severest of manners."

Tasche snorted a hard laugh. "Lex ain't *that* tough, chief." Her one brow raised. "Is she, Ez?"

He sighed. "As a wife, I can assure without reservation, she unequivocally is."

Chuckling, Tasche scratched her brow. "I wouldn't know nothing 'bout that. As long as you ain't coming here for no cravings, I guess y'all good."

He chuckled lightheartedly as I stood dazed before him, clutching the handle to Sadik's car seat tightly to the point of red knuckles. I couldn't believe this was the preacher guy—the foreseer.

Or is he?

"No." He shook his head, boyish grin curling his lips. "Not that."

"Good." She gestured to Sadik's baby bag hanging from her shoulder. "Because seem like all my real ones having them left and right." There was a flicker in her eyes when they rolled up to me. "Oh, shit, E!" She turned fully to me. "This my girl, Bilan. She brought me out here with her baby boy for some grub tonight. We been tight since—" Her face folded. "Y'all met," she declared with conviction before turning to him. "'Memba last year...she came with me to one of your shows?"

The memory clearly lost upon him, his brows shot up in the air as he pivoted to acknowledge me. Oh, my god. It was him! The scowl forming in his eyes was definitely of the intimidating reverend I encountered last spring.

He extended his big hand. "You'll have to forgive me, Bilan. My memory doesn't often serve me well. It's a pleasure to see you again."

I placed Sadik's seat between my legs and reached for his palm. Something in me crushed with disappointment. He gave me a prophecy that shook up my world and those starkly engaged eyes were blank on me. Centimeters away from his hand, I panicked wondering if he'd spook me again.

I cleared my throat. "Hi," I breathed.

"You don't remember her, E?" Tasche asked with humor in her voice. She leaned into him and murmured. "You scared the hell outta my friend."

"Sorry to say I do not." He shook my hand then released it. "I am, however, saddened to have frightened you. The Word says in 1 Thessalonians, 'do not treat prophecies with contempt. Test everything. Hold on to the good.' So if there was any good in the message...any hope, let that be the focus, not the eccentric messenger." His laughter was colorful and rich.

Tactlessly, I couldn't join in on their amusement. I was pale with disbelief. He was here. The religious leader I stalked online, the one who inspired my spiritual revolution, and predicted with accuracy the rollercoaster of my life was before me. And he didn't remember me at all. I saw the apologetic emptiness in his eyes.

Tonight, he was...regular. My eyes danced around for an entourage, a handler. God knew Sadik had several of them. In fact, one was waiting on us just outside. Maybe his was, too.

"Told you, you hemmed her up when y'all met," Tasche tried to explain.

"Christ," he sighed, brushing his palm over his beard before his face collapsed forward. His head rolled up again. "Again, Bilan, I apologize for the awkward encounter." The depth of his apology was in the softness of his vocals.

And he'd remembered my name from the first time Tasche mentioned it in this conversation. That impressed me. Here I was, shattered from him not remembering me, but he'd been kind enough to memorize my name. I was being silly. He never asked me to troll him or subscribe to his church's *YouTube* channel or stream his services each week faithfully. I was victimizing the man through apparent guilt.

I breathed, "No! It's totally fine. I can only imagine how many people you encounter in your line of work. It's good to see you again," I admitted.

I wanted to ask about their new baby and how his wife had been adjusting to being a mother of three and married to a man with such a demanding lifestyle she didn't necessarily fit into, but that would have implied I knew Lex beyond that evening of our chance meeting. Tasche hadn't mentioned much to me, I was sure an oversight on her part. Over the past few months, our conversations were limited to Randi and the curveballs thrown in my life.

"Amen," he nodded, pleasant expression rebounding.

"Yo, she been wanting to pull up to ya church," Tasche chuckled nervously.

My heart stammered into my chest. I wasn't expecting that reveal; I'd still been stuck on seeing him live and in color.

He doesn't remember me…

Ezra's handsome face widened in a pleasant smile. "That sounds wonderful. We have *Family and Friends Day* coming soon. I'll be sure Alexis passes along the information. We would love to have you both. His eyes glided over to me.

I tried meeting him with a smile and was sure my nerves compromised it. As a last-minute save in his heavy presence, I opted for a nod.

Tasche twisted her face, an expression of doubt. "Yeah." She swiped the side of her nose. "I'll let you know."

Ezra gave her a knowing chuckle. His attention was snatched by a waitress appearing with a tablet in hand for ordering. After acknowledging her, he turned to us.

"Ladies, it was a pleasure running into you. Prayerfully, next time will be deliberate."

"A'ight, E," began Tasche's goodbye. "Kiss the babies for me and tell Lex-dawg I said waddup."

"Will do," he agreed before his regard reached me. "Hang on in there, Bilan." He turned to begin his order.

Suddenly jarred, I stood frozen, wondering if that was a "message" with special meaning.

"Yo, B," Tasche called out to me. When I found her, she was

standing closer to the revolving door of the entryway. "I think this ya peoples looking for y'all."

She was right. Rory was with Sadik tonight, leaving me with Johnson. He was kind enough to stay outside instead of hovering over us as Rory does.

Still dumbfounded about this encounter, I picked my baby's car seat up and began my way out of the restaurant.

We moved with cautious speed up the driveway. Rory ran inside the opened garage door first, gun drawn and ready. Jamil glided inside behind her, light on his feet. Retro 50 Cent played from a small sound system in the garage. Marco lay flat on a bench, lifting at least one hundred-fifty pounds of weight. I watched from beyond a bush right off the driveway when the guy spotting Marco Rizzo recognized Rory.

"Drop it on that nigga," Rory demanded.

The tall, shirtless white goofball looked scared, shocked, and confused at the same damn time. Jamil moved in closer with the fast cat, *Heckler & Koch G36*, because he liked to fucking show off. The guy's hands went into the air at the sight of that ogling him. That left Marco alone to lift, and he strained right away. The bar dropped to his throat and as he struggled to lift it, his feet thrashed into the air.

He grunted and wiggled until the bar graciously slid to his left and hit the cemented floor.

"Now back the fuck away, bitch," Rory grounded out, moving close to the spotter.

He backed away until his body hit the shelf on the back wall. Jamil's heat was trained on Marco, who, after a bit of an effort to stand while trying to catch his breath, eventually did.

"What the fuck!" he demanded, twisting as much as his body would allow, looking for his associate. Instead, he found a seething Rory. "Fuck!" Marco shouted, knowing what time it was.

"I wouldn't get too loud," I advised, striding inside, my *Glock* tapping my thigh casually. I smiled Marco's way. "We don't want to invite your family to this gathering. I made sure not to disturb them crashing this weak ass lift party. The fuck is a hundred-fifty pounds to a nigga weighing two hundred plus?"

Jamil scoffed, I assumed finding it funny himself.

"Look, Ellis!" Marco began, face beet red, perspiration dropping from his black hair strands. "I don't know what the fuck this is all about, but—" he lowered his voice. "my wife and kids ain't got shit to do with it. Right, brother?" He tried scoffing.

"That's where the shit gets tricky for me, Marco." I stood in front of him, hands crossed, the *Glock* 17 eye-length to his face. "I only have one brother, and I damn sure don't remember queen birthing you. Do you, Marco?"

"No, man!" he cried. "C'mon! What the fuck are you saying? I didn't mean it that way!"

"Then choose your words carefully." I tapped the tip of the gun on his head at each syllable. "In fact, that's my message to you tonight. It's why I'm taking away time from my damn family to be with a fuckin' Rizzo."

"What the hell are you talking about, man? This is my family's house—my wife and kids, Ellis!" he begged. "They don't deserve this shit, man. Not after how we lost my father! We're still handling that shit."

"Funny that you mention your family grieving and your father being down. My family's grieving, too, and we're compromised twice over. Our jefe is down, and so is our next in line. The last thing I would have expected from a, now, bastard like you was insensitivity. You should know how it feels to be compromised." I pushed the gun into his skull.

"What the fuck, man!" he grounded out through his teeth, breath choppy.

"You jumped the fuckin' board and spoke directly to the queen."

"Irene—"

Before he could finish her name, I smacked his fucking face with the gun in my hand. Blood splattered in a sheet against my clothing. "That's Mrs. or Queen Ellis to you, bitch." I groaned in his ear as he choked on his blood.

Once he gathered himself, Marco apologized, one palm in the air. "I'm sorry, Ellis! I'm sorry. I won't fuck that up again. Queen Ellis from now on!"

I shook my head. "That ain't what got you fucked up with me. The fact that you didn't acknowledge there're rules to this shit. I don't give a fuck what was established in *The Commission*, but in my universe, that you simply exist in, fucks like you don't have the right to speak directly to my mother on shit."

I stood straight while he held his gushing lip, panting out of control. Marco had no idea how inopportune his offense was. I'd been balancing a lot of shit and could use an outlet to offset the building rage since learning of my father and brother's betrayal. This shit was therapeutic for me.

"All I did was try to keep shit simple, man! Lia's been sick with worry since Iban tried that shit. I've got a mom, too, bro! This shit's been stressing her the hell out because it's stressing my little sister the hell out. My dad is gone. What did you expect me to do?"

"Mind your fuckin' business and let them sort that shit out. As sensitive as I am to my mother's feelings, I would have never thought to call Catena to get involved. I don't know how it's done in your community, but in my family, we protect our queen. She's fuckin' royalty to the family and the world at large."

"Shit!" he spat out. "And mine isn't! She's stressed as fuck, too. At least yours still has a breathing husband. Fuck that!" He stood to his feet, blood shooting down his chest. "My mother doesn't deserve the stress either. She's *our* fuckin' queen—"

I felt his teeth break from their respective holding spaces in his gums when I shoved the barrel of my Glock in his mouth. Marco's body dropped back on the bench, eyes looked to pop from his head.

At the same time, the tall cat with him leaped our way until Rory zapped him below with a silencer. He fell face forward trying to reach for his bleeding lower leg on the way down.

"Ah!" he screamed.

Jamil was down with the *G36* at the back of his head. "The first person coming through that door from the house is getting one straight in the head, no questions asked. If I were you, I'd shut the fuck up!" he growled.

My gun was still in Marco's mouth. I could see the ire in his eyes. However, it was over-powered by fear. Marco knew he was powerless, I'd weakened him in his own home. His grief surpassed my mother's earlier at the hospital. I could now sleep tonight. After a few strokes between his swelling lips, I pulled my *Glock* from his mouth then lifted it into the air, examining it.

"Shit, you've bloodied my tool, Rizzo." My gaze met his. Marco's mouth was trembling, hands shaking as he balanced himself on the bench, half his body in the air. "I should make you clean it, but I have to beat my old lady home."

"Nah. Fuck that," Jamil intervened. "Make his ass lick it clean."

My eyes lit with excitement. "How many licks would it take to make my *Glock* blow, Rizzo?"

Rory walked over snickering and handed me a ripped towel. I chuckled myself as I slowly backed out of the garage.

"Clean this shit up before your lady sees it," were my last words to him before we left for the waiting truck.

Kissing his warm cheek always brought pure joy. It was late. Late, and I'd had him out past his bedtime, but I didn't regret it. Seeing Sadik pass joy to Tasche at dinner made it worth it. I was blue all day at work, missing this little fellow. Now that we were...home, I could relax. My eyes swept over his new nursery. It was undoubtedly smaller than the one at the high-rise. Sadik was able to hire a designer who made this place a gorgeous, gray, white, and black nursery with a stripe and polka dot combo within two and a half days while we stayed at a hotel. It was without a doubt cute, but just as the entire apartment, too small and...not home.

Sighing, I turned for the monitor and grabbed it on the way out the door. After less than ten steps, I was at the end of the hall, walking alongside the small kitchen where Rory was crossing out, headed into the living room with a bowl of ice cream.

"You're going to be okay?" I asked her.

"Yeah, man!" she hissed, annoyed. "You act like I can't handle lil' man. You ain't going far."

Not wanting to get into it with her, I rolled my eyes and marched to the door, mumbling under my breath, "Fine. Let me go answer my summons."

"Mmmhmmm," I heard her hum behind my back.

Rory didn't want to push me tonight. I wasn't in the mood for her attitude. It was enough I had to deal with her boss. I closed and tested the lock on the door behind me. Then I gaited a few yards down the narrow hall, passing a small gate before heading to the metal door leading to the rooftop.

When the baby and I got in from Jersey an hour ago, Rory told me Sadik wanted me to see him outside. As tired as I was after getting S.Q.E., II down and showering myself, I decided on obedience. Things had been uncomfortable between Sadik and me since that last night in *St. Justin*. I had no idea why he needed to see me before coming to bed.

The moment I stepped outside, I saw him reclined in a chaise lounge chair. It was pitch black out, but the string lights hung around the perimeter illuminated the area. He wore a sweat suit, socks, and *Ase Garb* sliders. It was a casual look for him on a week-day. Perhaps it was telling of his mood. The sight of a tumbler with brown juice and a cigar resting in an ashtray revealed a relaxed state.

Maybe...

I took a seat on the chaise, next to his outstretched legs.

"Hey..."

He turned to me, feline eyes glistening against the glow. "Hey."

"What happened there?" I gestured with my head to his swollen fist wrapped in a soiled bandage.

Sadik glanced down at his hand with mild interest. He casually tossed the hand. "Busted it playing ball in hard bottom shoes at the office."

My brows lifted. "*Ellis International* has a basketball court?"

"Outside. On the concrete," were the words he used, likely lying. It was my gut intuition, but I wouldn't challenge him. Sadik was a layered man, capable of depravity deeper than my worst nightmares. The man I married had murdered and altered lives irreversibly. This may have been par for the course. "He's down?"

I nodded and pulled the monitor close to his face so he could see his son resting on his side, little fingers curled.

"How did he do at the restaurant?"

"Better than I thought. He carried on a full conversation with Tasche like they've been besties for years."

"My prince," he boasted while thumbing the screen affection-ately. "He understands the value in socializing already."

I couldn't help my goofy smile. "Tasche's understandably in love."

"How could she not be? What about your other friend?"

I took a deep breath, expression crestfallen. "Weird."

"Weird how? You give her the money?"

I called Sadik the day after we returned from vacation with the idea I'd come up with. Though I was still angry with him, I felt the need to bounce the idea of giving Randi so much money off of him. After a long pause of consideration, he suggested I go for it.

"Yeah," My eyes drew to the brick siding of the building. I didn't feel like rehashing it with him. Randi clearly didn't like Sadik, and I knew him well enough to know she was a peon in his massive universe. I also didn't want to tell him how I told my friends about our marriage and expectant child. That would mean me sharing their reactions. "I did. She was unusually quiet all dinner long. I guess I can understand...with her losing Ricky and all. She lost her home, too."

From my peripheral, I could see him nod with extended lips as he gazed into the NYC skyline. For a long while, no words were passed. There was a chill in the night air, causing me to tug on my thick housecoat. The city was polluted with heavy horns adding to the already teeming energy, even at this late hour. I hated living this deep into one of America's largest metropolises. It was never a desire of mine.

"Thanks for meeting at *DiFillippo's*."

"Huhn?" My head whipped to face him.

"Rory told me you were considering *Michelle's*. Thanks for changing your plans."

I lifted my brows in a shrug. It wasn't like I had much of a choice. Sadik and I had already been in a precarious place so soon into our marriage. His words in *St. Justin* wounded me. He'd scolded me for mourning my brother. Worst part of it all was I now agreed with him. I now questioned my judgment. That second-guessing didn't feel good at all.

"How was your day?" I hated the lack of bass and indifference in my voice.

This couldn't be how I behaved as a wife—as a woman. I couldn't allow Sadik to bulldoze my individuality.

He exhaled, bringing the tumbler to his full lips for a nip. "Long," he answered after swallowing. "Meetings back to back—on the way to the office, at the office, leaving the damn office," he mumbled. "I went to visit my father today."

A spark of hope flared in my chest. "How was that?"

He tossed his head in a shrug. "As to be expected. He's weak and tired, worried."

I swallowed hard, eyes falling away. "Did you tell him you're moving to New York?"

"No."

My regard shot over to him. Sadik was gazing the night air. "Why?"

"Because we're not moving to New York."

"We're not?"

Those multi-hued irises hit me, darkened with resentment. "No," the one-word emphatic. "My wife has made her desires clear. We're settling our family in New Jersey."

The unsaid emotion filled his eyes. They were so gripping it seared me, forcing me to look away. What was this thing with him? Never had I been so desired and admonished from the same source. Sadik's moods were always extreme and never misunderstood. He was angry with me. Good. I was frustrated with him.

Still...

I found myself leaning over his torso, hungry mouth taking me to his full lips where I brushed against him. My heart thundered in my chest when I caught his lazy regard roving from my lips and slowly up. His eyes closed in a rare sign of submission then his lips parted. The faint scent of brandy teased my senses. His breaths hitting my face intoxicated me, and I kissed him, pulling his bottom lip between my teeth. I slowly pushed my tongue in his warm mouth, and Sadik received me with a wide caress of his own. The woodsy tang of his cigar mixed with distilled grapes, apples, and berries of the *Mauve*, and the distinct taste of him brought me back to *St. Justin*.

When I could no longer breathe, I pulled back, wiping my mouth. "I miss you." Again, no bass in my delivery. My eyes slid over to find the tumbler frozen at his mouth, his regard examining me. Immediately, I questioned my decision to share that. "Well, some things about you."

A silent scoff escaped his chest. Monotonously, he demanded, "Show me."

She rolled and plopped over me, moving with inspiration. Her fingers clawed into my shoulders, pussy clenched my dick when she lifted, squeezing from her thighs. Her face was tight, eyes low, and tits flopping like a porn star's.

Bilan leaned over, tongue pushing from her mouth and swiped it over my lips. Her breaths were animalistic, her hips fast and fluid. She pulled me in as her thrusts propelled. Her grip on the back of my head enabled her to lift her bouncy tits in my face. I pulled one in my mouth, sucking her nipple as she jerked my cock, riding me hard trying to stifle her cries. Her second orgasm wasn't coming as expressive as the first. She didn't want to share it with me.

When it washed over her, she reclined, finding my eyes again. Her pussy slammed into me, the skin of her soft ass slapping against my thighs. It confirmed what I'd sensed. I'd been here a time or two. Bilan was fucking me. I'd seen this countless times in my life, just hadn't expected to see it from my...wife. From the woman I pledged my everything to.

I'd been fucked with desperation by women who were so close to their fate with me, they could taste it. Women who knew I no longer had use for them. Women who wanted to show me the best time they were capable of, determined to change their exit from my life. I had one who fucked with so much exertion she collapsed on top of me. One pulled a muscle, fucking so long while dehydrated from drinking to prepare to make her plea in this manner, *unbeknownst to me at the time*. All of this to communicate fears.

But this wasn't "them." This woman on top of me was my wife, the mother of my children, she even housed one in her now, though one couldn't tell by the way she lurched my dick with full gusto. My vision blurred, and her freckles danced on her high cheekbones. The sound of her wetness on my thighs, the feel of it dripping down my balls all hit me at the same goddamn time. My feet tingled first then my sac. I clenched the fat of her hips through the pain of busted knuckles, *thanks to Marco Rizzo*, holding on while she detonated the bomb in my fucking groin.

I sucked in air as I felt my cum jetting inside of her. For a long while, Bilan wouldn't slow. She held me to her chest, rocking over me deliciously. When she stopped, her lips were on me again, tongue demanding. Bilan didn't wait for me to catch on. She explored my mouth with hunger, hands all over my head, fucking owning me. The sound of our skin smacking together was replaced by our mouths. Bilan was "landing" me with this kiss as I throbbed inside of her.

She eventually released my mouth so she could breathe.

"You prove your point?" I asked, panting.

Her head rolled over to face me. "Huhn?"

"You weren't expecting that second orgasm."

Bilan's eyes fell as she lifted off of me, my receding dick slipping out of her. She left the bed and peeled on her robe before leaving out of the bedroom, closing the door. A few short minutes later, she returned with a washcloth for me to wipe myself clean of us. When I was done, I handed it back to her wordlessly and pulled the comforter over my naked body as she left the room again. I took a deep breath, resting against the headboard. So much was hanging between us. I hated the fragility so soon into our nuptials. I'd had enough on my mind with work.

The sounds of Sadik sniffling hard drew my attention to his monitor on the nightstand. He was stirring from his sleep. I expected to see him carried into our bedroom any second now. Instead, I saw Bilan in the camera leaning over his crib, placing his pacifier in his mouth and rubbing his back. When he fell back asleep, she left the room, returning to ours.

"Camille couldn't tend to him?" I yawned as she began pulling out clothes from the dresser drawers.

"She's not here."

"Where is she? Downstairs?"

When I moved my family into the apartment building, I had to move our staff, too. This was one of the larger units I did short-term corporate leases for. I did the same for a couple of apartments on the lower level. Two units so happened to be available when I needed them, however, both were just one-bedrooms. Rory took one and would occasionally share it with other security. Camille had the other and Kimmy, my housekeeper, kept personal items down there in the event she needed to stay overnight for convenience purposes.

Now that Bilan had returned to work, Camille was supposed to stay with Sadik most nights. It was too soon for Bilan to pull an all-nighter with him. She needed her rest for work.

"She's at *Elliswoods Palace*, studying with one of the girls for their exam," Bilan mumbled.

"She's not here with Sadik? What exam?"

She turned to me. "Camille and another one of your mother's staff are finishing up their master's program this summer."

"What master's program?"

She shrugged, ducking her head. "In nursing. You didn't know?"

"No. But her job is here with my son."

"The commute was a bit much on her from rural Jersey to the City. I told her to meet me at my office tomorrow to pick him up."

"And do another street pick up like you did today after work? Her job is here. She gets paid to be with him."

Bilan took a deep breath. "Look, boss." Her nostrils flared in anger, though I could see she was fatigued. "We're all trying to make this thing work."

"By her having you tired when you go to work tomorrow? What was the point of hiring her?"

"She has a life that was altered, too, with our move. If we were still at the high-rise, her commute from *Elliswoods Palace* that has a full, technological library would have been less taxing. Traveling over that bridge is no joke."

"Don't speak to me as if I don't have a fuckin' clue about the commute. I do it every damn day!"

"And so do I, as well as Kimmy. You ever think about her? She reports here every day!" She fucking shouted at me.

"She reports to work every fuckin' day. A job that also provides room and board for days when the commute is impossible."

"Does the word 'home' mean anything to you? Some people don't like contingencies, Sadik. They like routine, comfortability, their own space. The world doesn't revolve around you all the time! Did you know that?"

She's fucking screaming at me...

"You know how many people would kill for Kimmy's job...fuckin' Camille's?"

She stepped toward the bed. "Do you know how many people value normalcy and routine? You, Mr. Ellis, can't uproot the world at your convenience!"

"It's not just mine! I have a damn family to think about."

"And I don't?"

"What the hell do you mean by that?"

"That you're not the only person under stress here. I'm here! I have a duty to you, Sadik, and the staff, too."

"Okay?"

"Okay..." She folded her arms over her chest crossly. "By tomorrow noon, I'll have my selection of the property to you. What's next?"

I stood from the bed in search of my boxers. "Then we have to decide on a builder."

"And how does that happen?"

"I'm between two reputable ones. We have them tour the property and take a few days to come up with designs appealing to us. In the meantime, we close on said property. That can take a few weeks, I'm guessing."

"Okay. We select a builder and close on the property simultaneously. That'll take a few weeks. How long before the house gets built?"

After slipping on my boxers, I stood straight with my hands at my waist. "I don't know. It depends on the design and size. I can guarantee a year or more."

Her face tightened. "A year or more?"

When I nodded, Bilan's eyes bounced around the room, trying on the idea for size. "Here?"

"What's wrong with here, Nalib?" I was struggling to keep my cool.

Her lids closed for a few seconds and she took a fortifying breath. "This isn't home."

"I'm home, Bilan. Home for you and Sadik is wherever I am. My home is wherever you two are. Fuck addresses. We're all we need!"

She shook her head. "You need your nuclear family, too."

"Fuck them!"

"Why?"

"You know why!"

"Sadik needs them."

"Sadik has all he needs, and that's you and me."

Bilan dropped her head forward, pinching her nose. "We're doing this again."

"Doing what?"

"Fighting after making love."

I snorted, entertained by her categorical misinterpretation. "That wasn't lovemaking, honey. That was you fuckin' me, and very experientially, too!"

Her eyes ballooned. "Are you accusing me of manipulating you with sex again?"

"It damn sure feels like it."

She wasn't with me on this. She didn't trust my judgment to separate from my father. Bilan wasn't respecting my leadership, and that fucking insulted every ounce of manhood I'd cultivated over the years. How could I protect a family I couldn't lead?

"Sadik, thanks for the compliments on the sexual skills *you* taught me, by the way, but let's not forget I'm a novice at the act."

I shook my head, laying back on the pillows. "Hate to break it to you, but your pussy's a long way from Kansas, Dorothy."

I heard her squeak as I clicked off the light over the nightstand.

Bilan

It was close to six in the evening when Rory and I arrived at the hospital and I had to pee. Inconvenient pregnancy symptoms had returned. Almost as soon as we made it to Earl's floor, I escaped Rory for the restroom. Looking into the mirror as I washed my hands, I saw a woman I hardly recognized.

I was tired. God, I was completely exhausted and missing my baby as I dried my hands. Nonetheless, I couldn't cross over the bridge into the City until I'd seen Earl. I hadn't seen him since before leaving for Palmer's funeral, though I'd *FaceTime*'d him each day since returning from *St. Justin*.

The moment I stepped out of the restroom and into the quieted hallway, I was met by a man in scrubs. He wore a lanyard, displaying his hospital badge. His glasses were big, black plastic frames almost covering half of his clean-shaven face. He stood, holding onto a cart.

"You go see Mr. Ellis?" his accent so thick, I couldn't make out his nationality.

And he wreaked something awful of cigarette smoke. My pregnancy symptoms had indeed returned.

"Ye-yes."

"Can you take dinner?"

I gazed down the hall where his room was. "Ah... Sure, but you don't want to take it to him? He doesn't seem to have many guests."

He shook his head, thin lips balling. "No. They got too many guns. Scare me."

My eyes ballooned, recognizing that fear. I still hadn't gotten used to being escorted by armed security, and just as Sadik advised last spring, I'd have to get used to it. I was now married into the family. This was a life sentence as far as I could see.

"Okay." I pulled the cart topped with plates and bowls hidden in plastic salver covers, and a cup and mug upside down on the tray. "I'll have him call the nurses' station if he has any questions." I needed a distance from his scent. My stomach began turning over.

The man bobbed his head before taking off. In the opposite direction, I sauntered down the hall toward Earl's private room. The door was open and on the way, I caught a glimpse of him in a chair talking to Tiffany. I stumbled just a little, clutching the cart. One of Earl's security caught a glimpse of me, but I didn't approach the room. Instead, I took a seat in a chair outside.

"You ain't going in?" Rory asked, appearing again.

"He has a visitor." I wanted to roll my eyes.

"You ain't gone let his people know you here?"

"It's okay. I'll wait."

Before Rory could walk away, the same security I caught eyes with craned his torso out of the doorway.

"Ms. Bilan, Mr. Ellis'll see you now."

I hesitated before responding or moving. Then my eyes journeyed over to Rory, who'd just put her phone to her ear.

She balled her face. "The fuck? Go 'head."

This time, I did roll my eyes at her. If Rory knew who was in there, she'd understand my hesitation, but already she'd escaped into her real life, the one surrounding one Sadik Q. Ellis, the first. On a huff, I stood and gaited inside, wheeling the cart ahead of me. I was glad to have been dressed in heels, a pantsuit, and the *Chanel* lariat Sadik had bought me last year. I put it to non-sexual use every once in a while.

Tiffany stood across from Earl when I entered. I didn't spend much time observing her, but could see the powder blue blouse and white jeans she wore with cork platform heels.

Earl's feline irises lit the moment they settled on me. "And here she is."

His fragile arm lifted with a slight tremble. I parked the cart next to him. My chest opened as I accepted his invitation, moving toward him. I was completely shocked when Earl pulled me in for an embrace. He felt thinner in my arms. I could feel his heart beat against my palms splayed on his back while I hugged him. His kiss on my cheek was chaste, yet weird. It was intimate, something I'd never experienced from a man of his complex stature.

"I'm happy to see you, dear." The lines outside his eyes crinkled.

"I'm happier to finally see you again," I returned. My gaze found Tiffany. "I didn't realize you'd have company."

"Oh." His regard shifted to her. "Baby girl was just leaving."

Tiffany dithered for a moment before she smiled at the floor, possibly feeling like her ego had been clipped. "Yeah, Poppa Earl. Let me get outta here."

"You two can't say hello to each other?" Earl asked as he scoffed in laughter.

I pulled in a deep breath as I turned to her. "Tiffany…it's been a while."

That's all I had for her. I hated her. Really. It was mean, but I couldn't help it. She was Sadik's former lover who, like a bad scar, wouldn't go away.

"How's the baby?" She, too, circumvented inauthentic pleasantries.

"Fine. Just like his father." My smile found its way to Earl. "And we both know where they get it from." I squeezed Earl's shoulder.

"Shit!" Earl mumbled, dropping his head.

One of his security snickered in the corner of the room.

"Oh, I'm familiar with the beauty of the Ellis men," Tiffany reminded me while picking up her *Hermès* bag in a near chair.

"Not with my baby's," I warned, voice petite and eyes smiling.

"Goddamn," Earl grunted this time.

∞||∞

A snort sprang from his gut, barely pushing out of his nose. Earl curled over with a hand on his abdomen as he laughed silently and controlled.

"I 'on't know the last time I seen a catfight like that," he jeered. "Shit, I got three women to keep happy, and I can't remember the last damn time I had to witness that type of tongue whippin'. You a brutal one, huhn?"

"No." I let out a hefty breath, happy to be off my feet. "I'm just playing the hand dealt to me by your son."

"He's a good dealer, you know. I taught him."

My throbbing eyes opened. "And you know... That scares me nowadays."

"Why is that?"

I pulled in air, poking my lips. "Because I thought your ruling was solid. Thought your teaching and leadership was ironclad."

"It ain't?"

My eyes landed on him. The next words were hard to share. "He's not letting what you did to me last summer go."

"What?"

My eyes swept the room, and I whispered, "I believe you know." When Earl didn't respond right away, I qualified, "What you told Iban to do to me."

With a stoned expression, he sat back in his chair. "Yeah. He mentioned that shit yesterday when he pulled up." Earl batted off the idea with his hand.

My forehead wrinkled. "I don't think you should take that lightly." I trilled.

"And I ain't taking no fuckin' advice from a woman about my goddamn son, sweetheart!" he barked, taking my head off.

I literally flew back in my seat.

Oh, nooooo...

I could see his two security guards, left in the room, switch postures to be on guard seeing their boss had been ruffled. My heart raced and mouth dried instantaneously. The air staled to a familiar taste. I'd been here before; intimidated, frightened. Mentally, I shrugged it off.

"Excuse me?"

"You heard what I said! Sadik is my child," he spat. "I made him. What the hell I look like, taking advice from his lady. I'm the captain of this ship, sweetheart. I'm the head of this goddamn family!"

My mouth dropped. How quickly had his demeanor changed! Sadik really was his father's son. I was looking into the kaleidoscopic irises of my lover...my husband. The only difference from the Bilan of last year and the one now is I was no longer daunted by these unpredictable bursts of volatile emotions.

I leaned forward closer to him and grated, "First of all, never call me sweetheart again. It's a goddamn term of endearment you and your twin son use too loosely." My nostrils widened against his glare of fury. "Secondly, you may be the head, but I'm the neck that will turn his attention from your delusions of grandeur so fast you'll be needing that oxygen tank you were hooked up to for life!" I was out of breath with my finger pointing to his face, my eyes shooting into him like bullets.

For a while, Earl didn't move. And during the next seconds of eternity, I wondered if the Earl I'd gotten to know, the one who took his time defrosting my defenses, was an insignificant fraction of the real monster of a man the world knew. Here was his chance to confirm it. What he showed me right now would be who I'd believe he was moving forward.

"Out!" he barked, stabbing his index finger toward the door with the ruddiest face I'd ever seen of him.

All because of my big mouth...

Now, I was deathly frightened. Did I believe he would shoot me? No. Have them harm me? No. But I knew what the man was capable of doing to those he wanted to dispose of. The moment I told my legs to stand, his security began clearing the room in my peripheral. Almost instantaneously, the door was closed to just a violently frantic Earl and me.

What in the world was this? Then it dawned on me. *This* was Sadik. His temperament, his childish tantrums. I'd seen him speak to his staff insolently, dismissing them. And just like with Earl's son, I wouldn't be intimidated.

I watched Earl sit back in his seat, brushing the perspiration from his russet face. Those catlike eyes swept desolately to the window. His lips trembled as though he tried to speak, then shut. Seconds later, the same thing.

"Shit," he swore lowly. His gaze met me then rolled away. "This..."

I cleared my throat, fortifying myself. "It isn't easy for you to speak to me with respect when you're angry?"

He shook his head. "It ain't easy for me to say I'm sorry when I'm wrong."

"Not even to Irene?"

"Only to Irene."

I nodded, feeling my pulse slow. "I don't understand you people."

A guttural chuckle pushed from his nostrils. "Watch out now. You sounding like them white folk."

I rolled my eyes. "You know what I mean."

His laughter killed my anxiety. "I hope not that."

"Your family. You guys are African royalty one minute then the Black mafia the next. I was almost killed in my orientation into the family. Then I was seduced by your loyalty to each other. And now, I can't deny my heart breaking at the sight of a fissure in your bond."

Earl's face turned to stone as he peered out of the window. "Sadik," he uttered angrily.

"He's upset with you and Iban, and I don't know how to fix it."

"Then we in the same damn boat."

"Did you at least apologize—" My eyes closed when I realized the stupidity in that question. "Of course, not. You don't apologize."

Stoney. His face was hard as concrete, that's how resolved his stubbornness had been. More than that, Earl was struggling with something. It was clear these points of awkward silence were a sign of an internal battle.

"Have you and Sadik ever fought like this?" I chanced an ask.

"I been fightin' with my son since his dick outgrew his lil' ass hand, as the old fellas used to say. Sadik always been Sadik, and I've always been Double E Bags. He knew what he didn't wanna be since he was a boy, and that was me. He respected me 'cause I taught him to. Wouldn't have it no other way. But I got two boys and know there's different types of respect. Sadik respected me because he was taught to, not just by me, but by his mother. Iban respected me because he loved me...wanted to be me."

"There may be a difference, but the fact remains. Sadik has always made clear the honor it is being the son of Earl Ellis."

His head whipped to face me. "But what about the respect? What about obedience? Why the fuck he ain't here now when I need him more than ever?" he grated. "I'm weak, my second in command is down, and my right hand is six goddamn feet under. My whole damn life's work can crumble if I'm hit right." I could see an artery pulse in his temple, he was that lost in his emotions. His translucent eyes were opened to me again when he admitted, "I may not have the most noble way of getting that bread, but I take care of my family before anything else."

"I serve them with everything I ain't never have coming up. I even fought for Sadik's freedom, sacrificed my firstborn for that shit. I fight every day to make sure they ain't lost bastards in the streets, hustling to survive like I did. I told myself when I met my wife, my kids'll never be bastards like me. They had a whole mother, and I was gonna make sure they daddy leveled the fuck up, too. I made sure they was proud to wear that last name. Grinded all my life so they could walk with they shoulders high and straight. But not one day did I think they wouldn't respect me for the very thing that set them apart from everybody else."

The tip of his index finger pointed toward the ceiling. "My wife gave me three kids; two boys, and a girl. But she only gave me one child with a brain wired like mine, but more sophisticated. A man in my line of work gots to produce a heir. Gotta have somebody to leave these millions to." He leaned closer to me. "You know my child got the type of fuckin' brilliance that if he would've brought his talents to my empire instead of building his own, we would've been the first billionaires in the game underneath the government's nose?"

"But it's not who he is, Earl. He's his own man. He can be that and respect you, too."

"I get it. He ain't with this game: I accept that. But you know what fucks with me the most?" his words dripped slowly. I shook my head, though he couldn't see. "He can't respect me enough to accept me for who I am. He may be obedient once in a while, and even make me think he be falling for my manipulation, but behind each task he check off for me is a kind of judgment a son shouldn't have for his father."

With my eyes closed, fighting down my emotions, I shook my head. "That's not true, Earl. He has the deepest respect for—"

"Deep respect ain't saving *your* punk ass brother and keeping him alive in a private hospital I set up for emergencies and privacy for my family," he made clear. My heart dived into my belly. He was referring to Abshir. *He knows!* "Real respect ain't tryna move his family out of state, knowing damn well my wife and me forbid that shit."

"We're not moving—"

"And ain't shit deep about him getting married without my

knowledge." My eyes burst wide. Earl shook his head. "Yeah. I know y'all married on the beach in *St. Justin*."

"Wait..." This wasn't making sense. "He told you?"

"Yeah, but before he did, he made sure I found out, though. Our pastor been visiting me. He came by before y'all got back and told me. Sadik knew he would, which is probably why he flew Pastor Wright out there instead of using a local, who could've done the same damn thing."

I chewed on the inside of my lip, feeling outed. It's not that I wanted to keep it a secret, but I hated feeling exposed like this. Did he know I was pregnant again, too? I decided to let him tell that detail.

"It wasn't planned," I murmured, unable to look at him.

Earl scoffed. "Oh, it was by him. He's my fuckin' son, young lady. It ain't much on this earth we fix our minds on that we don't get. That boy felt fire in his belly when he came across you. 'Cause he ain't the type to cry a damn river about what he feels, I missed that shit and made the wrong call." That's when I did look his way again. "A goddamn call that could've..."

I gasped. "He's here. Sadik is here and healthy. Even after Iban's accident, my baby's alive and thriving. I'm so grateful for that, I can't focus on the what if's."

Or was I being naïve again and too forgiving?

Earl shook his head, fist going to his mouth. "I'm weak!" he grunted. "Fuckin' weak. I run the whole fuckin' state with a weak ass heart and troubled lungs. It's just a matter of fuckin' time before the vermin come and destroy everything I done worked hard for," he finished on a mere whisper.

My lungs seized. "What is it? What is it you're not telling me?" Considering his world, the possibilities were endless. My mind raced. "Is your family in danger?" I murmured with fear.

"One of Tiffany's clubs was shot up in fuckin' daylight this morning." I sucked in a heap of air. "That was just before some muthafucka snuck into my grandbabies' school and tried taking lil' Iesha when she walked to the bathroom by herself—"

I leaped up in my seat. "No!" I breathed.

He nodded. "Thank God the janitor so happened to turn the corner and saw a white muthafucka pulling her down the hallway."

"Who's doing this? Who wants to harm the family?" I began to panic. "What do they want?"

With his chin resting in his hand, Earl shook his head, golden eyes rolling away. Then he lifted, reaching for his tray of food. He plucked the tan cup that sat upside down. Beneath it was a folded piece of paper. Earl's eyes grazed me immediately in alarm. I could tell suspicion filled his mind. He lay the cup back on the tray and grabbed the paper. I watched him unravel it until it was fully opened.

Earl's eyes flashed wider than I'd ever seen them, and his mouth dropped.

"Yo! Travis...Rodney!" he shouted, allowing his wrist to go limp enough for me to see what was on the other side of the paper.

the untouchable can be touched. i could blow her head off

When the door burst open and his men charged in, Earl demanded, "Where did you get this shit?"

The stormy weather out was indicative of my mood tonight. I watched as Camille was escorted inside of *Elliswoods Palace* with Sadik's car seat in her hand. They had arrived seconds before me and were covered with umbrellas on their dash inside.

I opened my car door and jogged up the staircase, hurrying inside where it was dry. Immediately, I was greeted by the house staff and Rory. Several of them forming a perfect line in the grand foyer. My attention at this moment was singular. Camille removed her jacket then went to unwrap Sadik's car seat.

"Is he okay, Camille?" my voice boomed through the vestibule.

She turned to me, face initially tight from concentration, then smiled when recognizing me. "Oh, yes, Mr. Ellis. He's just fine. I'm going to take him to my room and feed him."

"Okay. As soon as I'm done, I'll call for him." I hoped the desperation in my voice went undetected.

Nothing would quiet my disposition more than holding my son securely against my chest. When we returned to the apartment tonight, he'd definitely be sleeping with his mother and me.

I turned to Elgin, head of security for *Elliswoods Palace*. "Good evening, sir," he greeted when finally prompted to speak. "All measures you requested have been set in place. I have about a half a dozen men en route and will assign them according to your wishes."

"And Brown?" I asked.

"I've contacted your security head and have begun coordinating routes for this week."

"Thanks, Elgin. You know to contact Rory and me directly should there be any problems."

He gave a neck bow before retreating.

Stacy was next. "Good evening, Deek. Your father's in his study. He arrived just over thirty minutes ago. The staff from the hospital is settling him and transitioning care. My nurses are up there being assigned roles as we speak."

"Thanks." I nodded, processing it all. "Nurse Gladney?"

"She has agreed to stay for a few days." Her fingers were laced at her pelvis as she spoke. "I just had her things sent for from her home."

"Anything she needs...or that of the staff. Whatever amenities we can offer. Are the rooms cleared for their stay?"

She nodded. "My girls are finishing up on it now." She checked her wrist for the time. "They have another thirty minutes to have the task completed. Dinner is underway as well. If you don't have anything more for me, I need to check in on them before the meeting."

"Thanks, Stacy. You may go." She took off with a few of her assistants behind her.

I turned to Rory next. She stepped closer. "They all in the dining room."

I nodded again. "I'm going to peek in on my father and I'll be right in there."

"Gotcha." She turned, hiking down the hall.

I motioned to Johnson my destination before taking off. We weaved the halls for the room on the lower level where we decided he'd be best suited for his medical needs. Yards away, I saw bodies swarming the hall. People in scrubs with clipboards and cell phones, using terms I wasn't familiar with.

"Mr. Ellis," Nurse Gladney called out to me as she headed my way.

"How is he?"

"He's fine. A little weak." Her expression was weary. "The doctor gave him something to induce rest before we left the hospital. Having him airlifted from there to here, and then transported in the rain could have been too much considering his agitated state. You can go in and see him if you want."

I shook my head. "As long as he's comfortable and safe."

"He is. The chief of staff has the hospital on lockdown. We still don't know how anyone got in there. They're reviewing surveillance video tonight."

"Yeah." I scratched my cheek. "I have my guy there now. He specializes in surveillance. In fact, it was he who built the system in the hospital years ago."

What I wouldn't share was it didn't matter who did it, just how. We knew the who right away.

Whose life is this?

That's all I could ask myself as I sat at the dining room table in *Elliswoods Palace* staring at the blackened face of my phone. My anxiety was through the roof, belly churning and groin stirring. Every muscle in my body felt tense from worry.

"Try this," Candy, one of Irene's kitchen staff murmured, placing a tray in front of me with a mug of steaming tea and accessories. "It's one of Taaliba's."

My eyes blinked, awakening me from my thoughts. For the first twenty-five minutes of sitting here, I waited for a text from Camille on her and the baby's arrival. That message had just come through and I didn't realize I was still holding the phone.

Placing the phone on the table, I murmured, "Thanks."

The table had been filling up. There were black and brown faces all around the room. Many I'd seen in passing when touring the property. Some I knew by name, most I did not. One older man took a seat wearing overalls and gardening gloves. A couple of men walked in with black captain style hats and matching livery. I recognized them as chauffeurs.

Across from me sat Monica, tapping away on her phone. Her expression so tight, creases would soon form. The more I observed her, I could see a slight grin behind the scowl. Clearly, she was engaged in a pleasant conversation. Everyone deserved a momentary break from the crisis surrounding the Ellis family at this point, I guessed.

Taaliba had been in and out of the dining room, the place we were ordered to plant ourselves and wait for Sadik to arrive. Apparently, there had been trouble with Danny. She'd been on the phone with his people, I knew. The details missed me, I'd been too preoccupied with settling what happened over the past few hours to listen in.

When Tiffany breezed into the room on her phone, my hackles raised. The only break I felt in anxiety was when she was in my presence. That's when heavy annoyance and anger dominated.

"No. Pack all my *Chanel* bags, *Hermes*, and diamonds...my pearls, too. Pack all that shit!" She listened in to the other party. "*Ase Garb?*

Fuck, yeah. All that high-end shit like my *Louis Vuitton* luggage and bags. I don't want nothing there." There was another pause from her listening as she sat at the far end of the table. "I 'on't know right now where I'mma take it. We waiting on Sadik now to tell the family what to do, but I can't stay there. Poppa Earl told me that earlier at the hospital. Just be ready. I'mma text you with the info. He'll probably say stay here."

Here?

That assumption upset me to the point my ears could pop at any moment. Then Rory gaited in, causing a blanket of silence to fall over the room. Following her was him. His medium build was yet powerful and commanding. He was in a full suit, navy blue with a crisp white dress shirt, burgundy tie, and cognac oxfords. He was all business with his stride, expressionless, and exuding authority. Those full lips were slightly perched, skinned head glistening, and green eyes spangled with agitation.

It was at that moment my anxiety eclipsed my anger, and the humming in my core had resumed.

When I entered my mother's dining room, my search of her began. She was seated toward the head of the table, slouched in her seat with a tray of tea in front of her. Her tapered cut looked fingered through at the top too many times, curls in disarray. All eyes were on me...except for Bilan's. Even still, I shouldered through, mentally preparing to address my family and its staff.

Rory pulled out the chair at the head of the table, and I took a seat. My eyes swept the room for the attendees.

Taaliba had just lowered into a chair with a swollen face and reddened, wet eyes when I asked, "Where's queen?"

Taaliba froze for a second, appearing discombobulated by the question. Her eyes squeezed. "She's on her way home."

"From where?"

"Tom took her away for his birthday."

Angered by the answer, I flexed my jaw. "Where?"

She shrugged. "Somewhere in Pennsylvania. But I spoke to her a little over an hour ago and told her you called the meeting. She said they were packing up to leave right away, but wouldn't be here in time."

Why in the hell was she out of town when her fucking husband was recovering from a damn heart attack? This didn't seem like my mother at all. She'd always been the gatherer, the most present.

"Tom insisted," Taaliba murmured, seemingly reading my mood.

I took a deep breath and began. "Ladies and gentlemen, if you're congregated in this room, I can speak with a loose sense of candidness. You all have an idea of the line of work my father's in, even if you don't know the specifics. I will not palliate the seriousness of the current calamity. It's my job to provide information on its status and present strategy which will change our modus operandi until the threat has been cleared. With that being said, as you all are aware, a series of events occurred today that my father believes to be an attack."

I ignored the hiked breaths and uncomfortable squirms in chairs.

"Can we ask what they were?" Joan, the head of housekeeping, had her hand raised toward the front of the room.

"Sure," I answered. "Late this morning, an intruder entered my nieces' school and attempted to abduct Iesha. Then a few hours later, this afternoon, Energy, one of Tiffany's clubs, was shot up. I've spoken to the lead detective and learned a few other stores near her suffered the same vandalism, but choose to not ignore the timing of it all. The last thing I can share is this evening..." My regard glided over to Bilan, whose eyes were straight ahead and not on me. "Bilan visited my father and was given a tray of food from an unsuspecting perpetrator. On the tray was a letter stating with specificity that my father's security had been breached by an enemy."

I gave pause for another moment of reaction from the room. "Upon discovery, my father was immediately packed up and transported to the compound by way of an aircraft. I'm sure you're all aware he has returned home. He's still under the watchful care of several physicians and specialty nurses, many of whom will be lodging here at Elliswoods Palace. You are to be at their complete disposal. Should any need arise, I expect you to go through the proper channels to have it met."

"How many people will be here with him?" Joan asked with the lifting of her hand again.

"Stacy will have an exact number for you soon." Stacy nodded at the table. "Also, please be advised, until further notice, Monica and the girls will be on the grounds. The same goes for Taaliba."

"Huhn?" Taaliba's face was etched in shock.

Expecting this from her, my head bobbed. "Elliswoods Palace was designed and built to be a secure compound in the event our family is in danger. This isn't news. Until I've had all incidents investigated and see no threat, the safest place for the family is here."

"And what about work?" Monica asked, uncharacteristically apprehensive. "I have inventory at the liquor stores. We have several being remodeled as we speak. It'll be an ongoing project until all eight are done. We have grand openings for two this summer. I can't quarterback all of that from Elliswoods."

"You're going to have to figure out who to delegate pertinent responsibilities to," I advised firmly. "This isn't the first shutdown of this nature."

"But I had Iban here to shoulder the responsibility with," she argued.

"And now you have a staff, all of whom should be competent enough to carry out your wishes with you being remote to their respective locales."

Taaliba's eyes closed as she shook her head. That highlighted her appearance all of a sudden. She'd been in distress of sorts.

"What's wrong, baby girl?"

Her head shook again, this time more rigorously as tears fell down her face. "La Cocina, one of Danny's father's restaurants, was burned beyond repair this morning. It was arson," she barely got the last words out.

"He's fine, though." Monica asked, grabbing her hand. "Right?"

Taaliba nodded, worried eyes stapled to my wife. "Yes, but only because he was delayed getting there for a standing meeting he usually has there three days a week with his staff."

Something passed between the two women. It was clear Taaliba was the cause of his delay.

Fucking disgusting...

"I'm sure Danny is handling it," I offered with wavering confidence.

"But you can't see why I can't revert to being a teenager and be confined to my wing in the palace like I'm fucking Rapunzel," she hissed.

I cracked a cheeky grin. "You don't have enough hair to be Rapunzel, baby girl."

"You can remind me of that while we're stuck here together—" Her eyes narrowed. "You're staying here, too, right?" Taaliba's eyes bounced between Bilan and me.

"No—"

"Yes!" Bilan answered emphatically.

My regard slammed into hers. Those high cheekbones were piercing, lips in a tight ball.

"We'll be with the family until the threat is over."

"We will not," I countered, then addressed the room. "My family is in the process of securing land and a property designer so we can settle permanently. We currently have our things between two residences as it is."

Bilan repeated, "We will be staying with the family."

She'd lost her fucking mind. "I'm sorry for the lack of comprehension on your part, but we will unequivocally not be staying here."

Bilan turned to me in her seat, her head falling to the side, puffy eyes squinting. "Am I to be an Ellis just on paper, or should I teach your parents' staff how to spell and pronounce Asad-Yasin?" She grated, "Either we stay here as a family or my child and I will get ghost so quick, no enemy of an Ellis—or ally—will find us."

My chest tightened and head spun. Never had I been spoken to like that at the head of a table. It wasn't a tone I was accustomed to in any facet of my life. She was fucking threatening me. I'd disassembled lives for less infractions.

"It's close to eleven at night," I reminded her. "We have nothing here. We can discuss this tomorrow."

"Kimmy's at the apartment," Bilan replied, gaze searing into me. "She can pack us a suitcase for pickup before she leaves. Sadik has more than enough to begin his stay tonight."

I understood right away what she was doing. Bilan was regurgitating the same logic I'd given her when trying to push her hand at my agenda for the impromptu St. Justin getaway.

"I think we should stick together, Deek." Taaliba's eyes were wider, expression now nervous. "She's right. It won't be forever. Just until you and Daddy can figure this out."

"No matter the length of time Earl needs," Bilan stated firmly, "we'll be here supporting him along the way." Then she righted herself in her seat and grabbed her teacup.

Before I uttered a word I'd possibly regret, I addressed Joan, Stacy, and Candy. "The rooms, food, and communication details for our guests will be ready shortly?"

"Yes," they spoke in unison.

"Fine." It was time to close this meeting. I felt like the fucking White House press secretary. "If anyone has questions, now is the time to ask. Otherwise, go through Rory."

Over the mumbles of the room, I heard a clear query. "So, what do you want me to do?" Tiffany asked. "Do I have my things brought here?"

"I don't see why that's necessary." Bilan's assertion was not a friendly one.

That comment jarred me momentarily speechless.

"Excuse me?" Tiffany asked her.

Bilan took a sip from her mug before speaking again. "We don't know that you're in danger for sure."

Tiff's face screwed with agitation. "How do you figure?"

"Earl said you told him the incident with your club happened this morning before Iesha's near-tragedy. Sadik is now saying it happened this afternoon, after the attempt at the girls' school. They've both said the stores aside your club were shot at, too. There's no reason to believe the threat involves you."

Someone in the room made a sound of scandal in reaction, inciting drama.

"I don't owe you shit in details," Tiffany began. "And I damn sure ain't asking you if I can stay at my godfather's place while I'm in danger just like the rest of our family."

"Danger, wanger. Wooh!" Bilan fanned her fingers in the air.

Several uncontrolled snickers sliced the thick air of the room.

The woman was in rare form. It was one thing to behave with jealousy, but to undermine me in the same setting wasn't Bilan's typical persona. That's when it dawned on me: her state of mind.

Tiffany's head whipped over to me. "So, you gone let her talk to me like this?"

"Bilan, sweethe—" I recognized the error in my words before her eyes cut over to me.

"Make the fuckin' call, Sadik!" Bilan demanded through clenched teeth, nose red and chest rising as she was prepared to burst into tears. "Now!"

I took a deep breath. "Tiffany, Rory will arrange a hotel suite for you until we have definitive answers." Ignoring her gasp, I addressed the room. "That concludes this meeting. I'll keep you all abreast as our status improves." I stood, dismissing the room.

Quickly, the room began to clear out. Only a few lingered. The table had emptied but for Bilan, who sat with her head bowed over the tea cup setting, face contorted, fists balled. Her shoulders heaved. A commotion near the door shifted my attention there. At least a half a dozen people had descended upon Rory, likely with questions and concerns they were afraid to ask during the meeting.

Taaliba ambled toward me, her hands expressive already. She, too, was visibly upset by the events of the day. I couldn't deal with her and my uncontrolled erection at the same damn time.

"Not right now, Leeb," I warned her while en route.

"Wait, Deek," she squealed, face still distorted. "Don't you think we need to go over—"

In my peripheral, Bilan rose from the table, hands still clenched tight. My fucking belly rolled in somersaults, dick fucking pulsing.

"RORY, CLEAR THE FUCKIN' ROOM NOW!" I shouted so loud, Taaliba stumbled backward and the room silenced.

Rory glanced back at me. My regard shifted to Bilan, who stood curled over the table, body trembling.

"A'ight!" Rory barked, forcefully nudging people back with urgency. She reversed in her journey, and grabbed Taaliba by the arm, pulling her toward the door. "Everybody, outside now! I can talk out there!"

They were just at the door when Bilan lifted her head exposing her glossed face and belted, "Sadik!"

The door closed as Bilan charged my way. I met her in the middle within three large strides. She leaped onto me, her soft, shaky hands pulled my face toward hers until our mouths collided. She shivered in my arms and against my chest. Her moves hysterical and urgent, and my body responded to it with strange familiarity. She clung to my torso as I marched her to the table, shoving chairs to the floor to make space. I lay her on her back and quickly, Bilan released me to undo her dress pants. She kicked off her heels and kicked her legs until she was freed of every piece of clothing, including her panties.

She lifted to yank my jacket off, and I knew if I didn't unbuckle my belt and free my dick myself, she'd possibly hurt it. We worked together until my cock sprung out. Her eyes seemed to dilate at the sight of me, rolling to the back of her head as she grabbed my cock, stroking. She brushed the head of my dick against her silken slit.

Fuck...

She was wet already. This was her alter-ego. The unpredictable, crazed woman who appeared when my Nalib wanted to escape her mind, perhaps. I didn't know for sure. All I knew was how to respond, and that I had better respond in the fashion she preferred if I wanted to keep her madness contained. This was my way of protecting my wife.

When she dipped my erection in her sweet pond, my shoulders shivered. With desperation, Bilan scooted up the table taking me deeper.

"Please, Sadik," she cried in a whisper.

She wanted me to fuck her. Pulling her closer to me, I did just that. I plunged into her with force. Sadly, I wanted to shock her, wake her from this frenzied state. How did I miss this? Why did I not see this coming? When Bilan felt threatened, she'd go into an aroused frenzy. Why did I have her sit through a meeting before addressing this? How could I be remiss on seeing about her first? How much of this episode had been my fault?

"Harder!" she demanded through clenched teeth.

Without a moment of faltering, I delivered, diving deeper, harder, pounding into her soaked pussy. I palmed her ass at the neck and fucked her hard, going balls deep. I fucked her for embarrassing me in front of my family and parents' staff. I fucked her for the threat she posed to me about leaving with my child without batting an eye. I pounded into her for forcing my goddamn hand publicly. I fucked her hard for the fear I felt of losing her for good.

When I saw her eyes roll to the back of her head again, her jaw collapsing, something in my mind broke, bringing me out of my own fury. That's when I felt her pussy contracting around me. Bilan was receiving her medicine. She was climaxing. Her hands clenched at my waist, the hem of my shirt balled in her fists as she lifted herself to me for a beating.

And I couldn't stop if I wanted to. My body took over, delivering the thrusts the way she needed. It didn't matter that my mind couldn't reconcile fucking my wife on my mother's dining room table. In the moment, it was Bilan's medical bed and she was demanding what she needed to pull her from this manic state.

I delivered thrust after thrust, losing myself in the task, ignoring drops of sweat from my head and face falling over her naked body and the table. Before I knew it, Bilan had rolled over into another orgasm, and then another not too long after the second. I didn't stop my drives until she let go of my shirt and the tension in her body abated.

When I slowed to a halt, my baby girl's body went listless beneath me. Her heavy eyes rolled to the side along with her head, her breathing still wild. I pulled out of her, ignoring my erection. My need was of her wellbeing. Bilan looked sedated and I would be okay with that if I was assured she was safe and satisfied.

Something in my chest ripped and I reached over her, brushing my lips against hers. I kissed her brows, cheek, and neck, grateful for her pulse. As my sweat coated her skin, she lay unmoving, eyes to the side of the room.

"Nalib—"

"I *lo*—ove," she hiccupped, a tear slipping from her eye. "you, Sadik," she murmured with little movement of her mouth.

With a pounding chest and vibrating frame from such hard drives, I wondered if she meant that or, if in the moment, what she wanted to convey was the need of protection from the woes of mine and my family's sordid lifestyle. She came so close to one of Popov's men when she accepted that tray of food. I would have been just as complicit as him had she been murdered. I didn't protect her, didn't prepare her for such invasions.

So, yes. I was angry at Bilan for reacting to my neglect, and I fucked her into oblivion for it.

My body, wrapped in his suit jacket, throbbed and pelvis ached deliciously as he led me out of the dining room. Sadik's strong arm enfolded me, tucking me at his side so close I could feel his heartbeat. I felt protected, even if temporarily. The tears had stopped, but my lungs continued to labor violently rigid and I sniffled successively and audibly under his arm. I felt empty, too, and completely drained. All I wanted was my baby and a bed.

The moment we crossed the threshold, I heard contentious mumbling. My heavy eyes lifted to Rory a couple of yards away, barricading the door from Monica and Taaliba. The sisters were angry with Rory. When Taaliba saw us sauntering out, she moved past Rory and charged our way. Monica was on her heels. I wasn't prepared to have my anxious state returned, couldn't endure another episode.

"Is everything okay?" Taaliba demanded under no guise of pleasantry.

Her eyes bulleted into her older brother.

"Yes," Sadik answered, irritated. "Of course, it is."

"Are you sure?" Taaliba asked me.

When her regard landed on me, I felt sympathy. Monica's mirrored hers, and then I knew.

"Bilan, are you okay," Monica blurted.

I felt Sadik's frame tense at the implication.

I hiccupped, unable to control my diaphragm. "*Ye*—yesss." My face felt stiff, swollen from anguish. "I'm *oh*—kay," I tried to assure them, tucking myself into Sadik's frame even farther.

"We heard you scream in there," Monica pushed.

"Yeah," Taaliba followed. "A lot. And you, too," she addressed her brother.

"And?" Sadik growled threateningly.

The last thing I needed was his temper to flare. The day had been too long.

"I'm just saying. It didn't sound good in there."

"Couples' fight, Taaliba." His rumble further rattled me. "Grow the fuck up."

I tightened my hold on his tapered waist, not wanting him to attack her.

"I am grown, big brother. And I've seen the thin line of violence occur between couples."

"No one knows that as well as I do," Monica tried chiming in with a calmer tone. "We're just worried. That didn't sound good in there, and we understand the stress today has put on the family. We just want to know you're good."

"You've got to be fuckin' kidding me." Sadik's full lips tightened, that cupid's bow more prominent than ever.

"That's what we thought when we heard Bilan scream like she was being attacked. And your toy Rottweiler wouldn't allow us to do our due diligence. We thought she was going to die for standing up to you or not fucking you, from the sounds of some of those screams!"

His brows narrowed. "Have you ever known me to lay a hand on a woman?" Sadik challenged.

"I've never known you to be a married man until tonight," his sister countered with lifted brows. "This day has been filled with discovery."

"And it's time for us to end it." He urged me to move with a soft push. "I need to put my wife to bed. As have you both, she's had a traumatic day."

We took off, leaving them standing there spooked.

"*Web*—we'll talk in the morning, ladies," I promised.

Sadik led us at a speed uninviting to further conversation.

Ameliorated...

Under the blanket of the late night, feeling the signs of life from the people I'm most responsible to, I felt a needed period of peace. The faint yet strong heartbeat I felt over my own as I lay in bed assuaged my rampant contemplations. As Sadik lay asleep on my bare chest, I could feel his soft breaths hit my skin. He'd been picking up weight, but not too much to soothe his old man with his full trust to sleep restfully on top of me. The cool night air flowing from the ajar door of the balcony was welcomed on this unusually warm May night.

What an eventful day. Popov had made his displeasure on being cut out as my father's arms distributor known today. I learned after speaking to my father's men earlier how Popov had been trying to contact my father and Palmer since my father's heart attack. However, with losing Palmer so soon after the general went down, the Ellis organization shut down in disarray. My father hadn't named a successor to Palmer until recently. Recently was too late.

Their world of illegal goods was small. Popov learned there was a new distributor in town when he reached out to Danny Lopez and was informed his services were no longer needed. It didn't take long to piece together he'd been replaced, and that made Popov a very salty Russian. My father was insistent on meeting with him, but I planned on arguing against it. He wasn't strong enough. Double E Bags never showed fear or weakness. Now wasn't the time to start. Iban's selfish actions at my high-rise put my father at greater risk.

I had my own shit to hold. Jefferson informed me two days ago, Jason reported to the *FBI* the visit I arranged to his home and his parents' car accident that night while on their way to Delaware. The *FBI* hadn't struck but were gathering up as much information as possible before deciding on charges, according to Jefferson. My lawyers assured me their pursuit was baseless, and I agreed. But I didn't trust being investigated.

Sadik's leg abruptly kicked out like an irritated horse, snapping me from my thoughts. He grunted as he stretched on his stomach then let out gas inside his little pamper. My chest vibrated with amusement as I counted down the seconds before I'd smell it. In the meantime, I stroked his little back, no longer than the width of my hand.

His mother stirred to my right. Her silky naked skin rolled over to me as she moaned softly in her sleep. Her hiked thigh brushed up my leg, her knee stopping near my groin. Her folded arm lay on my shoulder. She breathed a sigh of contentment against me. That soothed me, too. Bilan was safe. No matter how peril her day had been, she'd survived.

"You didn't cum," she mumbled.

My brows met. Maybe she was talking in her sleep.

"Sadik," she whispered.

"Yeah, baby?"

"You didn't cum."

"When?"

"In your mother's dining room."

"I didn't need to."

Her head lifted slightly and her eyes were upon me. "Why didn't you?"

My brow line narrowed even more. "Because it wasn't about me or my needs. It was for you, what you needed."

"I need you."

"You have me."

Laying down again, she snuggled beneath me. "You and this family are all I have."

"You have Sadik and me...and the baby you're carrying. We're all you need."

I felt her head shake against me. "You all are Ellises. The Ellises are a unit. I don't get to pick and choose." She yawned. "I want you all."

On a huff, I rearranged Sadik and my phone in my arm while gaiting out of Irene's office from a conference call with the administrative staff at *Ellis Academy*. We developed a tentative plan for my schedule for, at least, the upcoming week. My role required traveling to several schools a day to review mandated paperwork. Apparently, with the Ellis family on lockdown for the foreseeable future, I wouldn't be able to travel. According to Sadik, the more we were out assuming our regular activities, we were at risk of being attacked by Earl's unnamed nemesis. The risk doubled for the women in the family, as we were an easier target.

Sometime in the early morning, Irene contacted her executive assistant at *Ellis Academy* and requested the staff work with me to create an alternate method for my duties to the academy. The call took close to an hour to list all of the documentation I'd need for the schools to gather and send to me electronically for my review. We agreed to take it week by week until I was able to resume being out in the field.

Oddly, I felt unusually hungry. Or was it strange? This morning, when Sadik had awakened with the sun, I followed him into the shower. While our son slept soundless, I dropped to my knees and pulled him into my mouth. I stroked him with my lips, tongue, and hands until he exploded in my mouth. It was medicinal for me, considering my meltdown in his family's home last night. Having him exposed and needy for me may have been a showing of that sexual manipulation Sadik had accused me of in the past. I would take it just to be sure I could still affect him in a way that wasn't with disgust or embarrassment.

When he was done emptying into my mouth, I gave Sadik a minute to regain himself. Then I stood and fell into his arms, apologizing with invisible tears underneath the showerhead. He tried to assure me there was no need for the regrets, he would take care of me. But I still felt needy. The feeling of sickness had returned because here again, I saw violence in this family and yet had no desire to leave. I didn't want to leave *Elliswoods Palace*. It now felt like a tower of protection for my baby and me. We needed that protective covering from Sadik.

I still can't believe I'm married...

It took pilgrimage to make it to Irene's breakfast room. I could appreciate why she'd serve this particular meal in a room like this. The skylight ceiling illuminated the space better than any electrical lighting could, especially on a particularly sunny day like today. The room was sparsely empty this morning. Monica was alone at the oversized table, and behind her, a kitchen staff was at the buffet table replenishing a dish.

As we passed her for the buffet, I noticed Monica typing into her phone, completely engrossed. I took my time deciding on what to load my plate with. There was every American breakfast item I could think of before me. Another strange occurrence was how most of it appealed to me. I plucked a spoonful of scrambled eggs, home fries, and what was visibly labeled as turkey bacon. A stainless-steel chaffing bowl of Sadik's grits were nestled next to creamy oatmeal. Content with the little I selected, I carried the plate with one hand while Sadik quietly rested in my other arm. On the way to the table, I stopped for utensils.

"Hey, you," I finally greeted Monica.

She glanced up, expression quickly opening into a welcoming smile. "Hey! Oh, my god!" She acknowledged Sadik, dropping her fork into the plate to reach for him. "Bring that Ellis boy here!"

I handed him over, happy for the opportunity to eat quickly. As she spoke to the baby, I was able to scarf down some of my food.

"I'm so happy to see you," she finally broke from the baby talk Sadik seemed to have enjoyed. "I was so worried about you last night."

A nervous snort left my nostrils. I knew I had to answer for my actions sooner or later today. I wouldn't beat around the bush. "Thanks," I garbled, nodding my head as I chewed and cleared my mouth. "Yeah. Last night was crazy. There's no way I can dance around it. I don't want to talk about it exactly, either. I'll say this: I'm no stranger to violence, thanks to the Ellises. It sometimes pushes me over the edge."

Monica's eyes were wide, listening to me. "I was really surprised because Sadik is the only Ellis man to have an even temper when it comes to women."

"Trust me. Sadik is no saint. He's capable of harm, but nothing physical to me. Now, emotionally? I'm at his mercy. As far as violence to me, he's of no threat." I scooped more food onto my fork. "It's just... I'm still adjusting to all of this." My eyes gestured the room. "And I think he's adjusting to my adjustment, if you get what I mean."

The sight of Sadik's busted knuckles flashed before my eyes. My mind conjured several scenarios that could have caused that injury. I'd seen him vicious more than once. He and violence were bedfellows.

"And you guys are married!" Monica had a lot to unload.

I nodded again with a full mouth. "We've been married for five days and have been fighting just as long." My brows jumped. "There goes that adjustment thing." When I realized Monica was done with firing her questions, I asked, "So, how's Iesha?"

"For the most part, she's fine. But last night, she slept with her sister. She had a nightmare about what could have happened if the smelly white man had taken her." Monica's eyes rolled, clearly being distraught over the ordeal.

That mention of his scent filled my nostrils instantly in a wave before evaporating just as quickly. Suddenly, my appetite was effectively gone.

"If there's anything I can do, especially with the girls, please let me know. S.Q.E., the second and I will be here with you guys all week, or until this all blows over." My gaze dropped to him. My baby sucked his fat fist as though it was a well-seasoned chicken bone. He was my ray of sunshine. "I know vacations don't fix everything, but we just came back from paradise, and I swear I could go back to escape what's happened over the past twenty-four hours."

"Yeah," Monica sighed. "Tell me about it. I'd just gotten the girls to the point of not asking daily for their dad. It took a while to get them to understand he's in the hospital, and they're trying to get him well. And when he's better, it's going to take time for him to be a strong daddy again. What I haven't told them is he'll never be the daddy they knew."

"How *is* Iban doing?"

I wouldn't know because I was afraid to ask Sadik about his brother. And the conversation had gotten so ahead of Earl and me yesterday so quickly with his temper and lack of humility to do what's right and end this feud with his son, the opportunity had never come. I hadn't seen Irene in over a week outside of my *Face-Time* calls from *St. Justin*. She hadn't availed herself to me much lately, and I understood why. She'd had a lot on her hands with her family.

"There's finally been a change in his condition." Neither Monica's voice nor her body language gave a prelude of joy. "He woke up. The hospital called me an hour ago saying it happened just after four this morning. They want me to take my time coming to see him. They're cleaning him up, testing, and evaluating him to see what state he's in. The girls can't go. They don't want him overwhelmed with guests. Now I have to deal with that."

"Okay." My heart thundered. "He's awake. What happens next?"

"Rehab. I asked the same question. They said that's the best scenario."

It troubled me seeing her lack of excitement when delivering incredible views. I had mixed feelings for Iban. He'd threatened me several times and even put my baby at risk when acting out his disappointment with his family. But for his wife, this should have been the best news of the century.

Sadik began to fuss, so I took him from her and placed him over my shoulder to rub his back. Monica resumed eating quietly while my mind continued to turn over her situation.

"Monica, how are you doing with all of this?"

"Obviously I've seen better days, but since becoming the wife of Iban Ellis, I've learned to survive each time the ball drops. I've become quite a pro at it." She fed herself the last of her food, cleaning her plate. "Candy put her foot in this Quiche Lorraine," she moaned before leaving the table for the buffet table.

I didn't continue my questions because *where would you go from there?* My heart went out to Monica. Sadik calmed against my chest, so dissimilar to my mind in the moment. I began humming a song to him. I realized my eyes were studying the table when, in my peripheral, Monica's phone lit with a text. It lay right there, mere inches away from me. I didn't know I was reading the text that had come through until I was done.

the more i think abt it this is bullshit. if i can't C U like i want until UR fam figure shit out i at least need 1 more nite with you. please think about it.

My eyes blossomed wildly, then swiped to the opening of the room. I was jarred, my entire frame tensed with Sadik in my arms.

Oh, my god...

Monica had taken on a lover. I couldn't believe it because she'd always been the dutiful wife from what I knew of her. However, she'd also been the longsuffering wife. There was no way I could ask her about it.

Before I knew it, Monica had returned to the table. She sat down and forked into her egged pie. My rocking of Sadik picked up in pace again as I tried to appear unruffled. Thankfully, Taaliba sauntered into the breakfast room. She headed straight to the buffet table when I could feel Monica's head whip over to me after picking up her phone.

"Look, S.Q.E., two!" I cooed excitedly. "Your other auntie just walked in!"

Maybe my performance was believable because Monica shot to her feet and announced, "I have to take this in private."

She took off immediately, and I let go of a breath I had no idea I'd been holding.

Taaliba looked distraught as she approached the table. It reminded me of her demeanor last night. I couldn't fully appreciate it because I'd been upset and rising in a panic attack myself. I focused my energy on trying to hide it, suppressing the rise. Which could have been why I felt off today. Whatever it was that came over me when I got into those headspaces drained me, last night even more. From the moment I arrived at *Elliswoods Palace*, all I wanted was Sadik, but knew I couldn't have him until he was done with his family. Rory had given me the heads up well before Sadik arrived. I tried so hard to manage it, but barely. I was so wild and...angry!

I lashed out at Tiffany...

This morning, I had the capacity to ask. I waited until Taaliba brought her plate to the table, taking a seat across from Sadik and me. She wore no makeup, and her tapered cut bore no fancy curls, just slicked back. She offered a wry smile, though I saw the sparkle in her eyes when she looked at Sadik's pampered butt propped in the air.

"What's going on?" I asked, hating seeing her this way.

Her expression went hard, and she rolled her eyes. "I feel so helpless. I'm frustrated. Just sick of my family treating me like a little kid. Sadik's keeping me captive here on the compound when I'm a grown-ass woman! My obligation is to another family."

"What do you mean?"

"The Lopezes in that fire? It started in the kitchen. Bobbito, Danny's older cousin with autism, was the heart and soul of that restaurant. He was a cook and created many of the menu items. He was popular in the community, in general. He died trying to save the kitchen." Her eyes began to water. "People kept yelling for him to run for his life, like they were doing. But he was so determined to save the kitchen. They couldn't pull him back, he was a hefty guy. He ended up dying in there." She fell into a hard cry.

"I'm so sorry to hear this." I wanted to reach for her, but couldn't at our distance with Sadik. "I'm so sorry for Bobbito's family."

"That's the thing. It's not just his family missing him. It's everyone he's touched, like me. Over the years since I've been going over to the Lopez mansion, he's been very fond of me. If anyone knew of Danny and my relationship, it was Bobbito. He would sneak me these delicious dishes he'd make for me when I visited. Bobbito knew my favorite Dominican dishes. He would do it to make me happy."

"I'm sorry." It was all I could say. "Really, I am."

Taaliba shook her head. "He lived with Danny's father until he passed, and then Danny. Danny is so...incensed...so damn mad. And I'm not there. No one can reach him, calm him like I can, and I can't be there to do it. Once again, I'm the baby, bratty sister of the Ellises and I've been confined here. And I'm so fucking tired of it. I'm so ready to say fuck it all, and just leave."

I was speechless, afraid of saying something that would reveal my ineptness. "I can only imagine what it's like having to deal with them."

"I told you he wants to get married," she continued with her venting. "He swears I can bear the shoulders of a wife in his line of work. Little does he know, he's giving me more credit I don't deserve because I am not that woman. I'm still being treated as a baby. How can he view me as a wife or a wife in this business that I absolutely hate? I'm finally to a point where I'm thinking it's time for me to grow up. It's time for me to give it a try."

"Give what a try?"

Her chin dipped and she nodded nervously. "You know. Danny." There was a pause to give me the time to comprehend her meaning of marriage. "I don't know if we'll survive. Still not one hundred percent confident marriage is for me, but what I do know is Danny's my destiny. He's my soulmate, and I so badly—*finally*—want to be there for him. I don't think I can do it. Don't think I can deal." Her thick emotions had her whisper, "I hate this underworld. Since I've learned of it and understood it, I've abhorred it all. Here yet at twenty-seven years old, I'm still locked into this lifestyle I didn't choose. I absolutely hate it, detest it. I feel helpless, like there's nothing I can do."

"Have you spoken to your mom about it?"

Taaliba shook her head. "She's not the same. The shit with Iban and my dad has her so fucked up. Even now, when I want to go to my dad about it, I can't because Diane is always in his face, and he's on the phone, trying to talk to Nena."

My face folded. "Where's Nena?"

Taaliba's head whipped left in deep annoyance. "I don't know where the fuck Nena is and I don't care where Nena is, but apparently, my father does. And he acts as if he can't function if both his girlfriends aren't around him—*although* he lives with his wife. I am just fucking over all of them."

Sadik began to fuss against my chest. That seemed to have broken Taaliba's angry trance. Her face lifted in regret and she cried, "Baby, I'm so sorry!" Her eyes rolled shut. "Bilan, I'm so sorry. I have to go; I just can't deal." Taaliba stood from the table, food untouched.

As I rocked Sadik, I watched her leave, sulking as she sauntered out with heavy shoulders.

"Okay, baby," I murmured to Sadik. "Let's get you a bottle."

With Sadik to my chest, we traveled the marble halls of the palace, passing staff on the way. No matter how many times I'd visited, this place didn't feel residential unless I was in the bedroom assigned to Sadik. And even that was a suite, immense in size. I wouldn't complain, though. My focus had to be elsewhere. There were too many leaking faucets in this "home." Too many deteriorated pipes within the walls hidden by costly, plush Black art.

The Ellises were hanging on by a thin thread, so unlike the perception I had of them the first time Sadik brought me "home" and I experienced the biggest culture shock of my life. Yes, I was sick because instead of me leaving, my heart was set on healing. This family needed mending and soon. How could I bring another Ellis child into a family filled with chaos?

∞13∞

I drummed my fingers on the table as I waited, my chair facing the bathroom door. Not even the loud music pulsing the ceiling over us could distract me from this encounter. The muffled woman on the floor beneath Rory squirmed and moaned through her narrowed nostrils. Rory yanked her head back by her bleach blonde, silky locks of hair to shut her up.

When the door opened and a lone figure ambled out of the bathroom, I grinned in welcoming. His ocean blue eyes didn't land on me right away, they scanned around me first. He observed my men posted around the small room with guns drawn. I observed his tall frame, non-muscular build, sandy blond low haircut, and round face. His cheeks were blushed, nose its usual large bulbous size, and lips naturally thin as he considered his predicament. When his gaze finally landed on me, I smiled with joy.

"I've been waiting," I shared.

Popov stepped outside of the small bathroom in the basement of his strip club with his belt undone and found another one of his pastimes beneath Rory, seated on the floor. The other two were face down on the floor with Jamil's guns to their heads. They were also better behaved.

"You have lots of courage coming here," his deep thickly accented vocals mumbled as I summonsed him to the table with my fingers.

"This won't take long," I assured. "Have a seat."

Popov hesitated before obeying. He dropped into the chair across from me. "My men will be down momentarily." I nodded, not disagreeing with him. "They say you're the...suave one, not the crazy one." Popov's English was fair, having been in the U.S. for over twenty years, but his Russian intonation was still dominant.

One side of my face lifted. "I'm an 'Ellis' one." I sat up in the metal folding chair. "That's what you should never forget. Instead, you decided to play a petulant game, one my father taught us never to practice."

"And what is that?"

"To throw punches with closed eyes then run." It was clear Popov didn't understand. "You sent men to Earl Ellis' granddaughters' school, and one to the hospital where he healed with a note from you."

Popov scoffed, appearing relaxed for the first time. "Do not forget, burned down the fucking Lopez restaurant. It was very profitable, I heard." He shrugged, tossing his head, shoulders jumpy. "And the *negr* woman he's fucking? I have not touched her." He watched my expression darken. And with assumed victory on his breath, he leaned closer to me over the table. "Last week, when my men sent me footage of her sucking his brown *dik* outside, by his pool? I could have put a bullet in her head." Enjoying my deadpan expression, Popov turned the knife by bobbing his head over a closed fist, demonstrating.

I could choke Taaliba's little ass. Visions of slicing Danny's throat appealed to me to the point of increasing my heart rate.

"Wonderful segue," I complimented him. "That very admittance of stalking is what brings me here."

Popov straightened in his chair, appearing to be excited about what I had to say. "Please explain."

"You left a message for my father. You said—and I quote—'you're touchable.' Well, I was sent to model to you the Ellis way of telling a man heavily guarded that he's touchable. Earl didn't send an employee, he sent as close to his physical representation as he could get. He sent his own DNA." I dipped my chin, widening my eyes for emphasis. "He sent me. We don't punch with closed eyes, we show up to a fight like men. Since your route was childlike, Double E Bags is approaching you like a man. What message are you trying to convey?" I gestured, letting him know he could speak.

Popov placed his elbows on the table, attempting to get even closer to me. "Your father abandoned our agreement for services. He was a customer for many year. Loyal. The biggest seller in the state cut me off with no..." His tongue clicked the roof of his mouth as he searched for the appropriate word. "Note?" He decided on the wrong word, but I wouldn't correct him. "That is no good in my business."

"And what exactly is it you suppose he do?"

"Come back to buy my shit." Popov sat back in his chair and folded his arms. "This time, he pay twenty-five percent over market value."

I nodded with hiked lips, giving that thought a beat to drift into the air. "Okay. I'm glad you were able to communicate your thoughts like a man. I will share them with my father." I stood from the small table and pushed my chair in. "But you've got a bigger problem. Two actually."

Popov chuckled with arrogance. "What?"

He wouldn't look me in the eye. Another Earl Ellis rule.

"Earl Ellis doesn't entertain rats." I shrugged my shoulders with indifference, lips pouted. "He damn sure doesn't put paper in their pockets."

The nostrils on his wide nose broadened. I'd now had his attention. "What the fuck are you talking about?"

"We've long ago learned about your cooperation with the *FBI*.

My father has no ties to you because he's not in the same industry as you. I'm here simply to tell you he's no fuckin' punk and will not tolerate your harassment."

Popov's scowl was so hard, his lips stretched and the cords in his neck projected. "I'm not fucking rat!" he growled, pearly whites exposed, getting every bit of his Ivan Drago on.

At least, that was who Popov resembled to me over the years.

I swung my arms, another act of apathy. "I'm just expressing barbershop talk with you. It's what Black men do. I have no dog in the fight either way, and neither does my father."

He slammed his sizeable fists on the table in rage. "I'm not a fucking rat and I can prove it to you!"

"Again, it is of no concern to me. I've stated my purpose of being here." I needed that clear in the event the room was bugged which it likely was not. I wasn't expected here tonight.

"What's the other problem?" his thick tongue requested.

"That one's the biggest. The woman your fuckin' rigger targeted to deliver Double E Bags his dinner was my wife. You've put my wife in harm's way and insulted my only sister." I bounced on the balls of my feet, changing my stance. "You done fucked with the wrong Ellis, Popov. I'm sorry no one told you."

A feral shriek pealed from the noisy blonde. Rory yanked her head back with force.

"Easy, Ror," I mildly warned.

"Bitch tried to head butt me in my pussy!" Rory griped.

Jamil and Johnson snickered across the room.

I smiled. "She can feel your balls even if they aren't on you anatomically, is all." My eyes were on Popov.

His gaze rolled below. "I'll wait to hear on your father. My offer won't be so generous next time."

A struggle could be heard outside the door. A man shouted then quickly grunted. Next, a suppressed gun went off. I could discern all of this under the vibrations from the speakers above us in the club.

Popov chuckled. "I told you my men will be down soon."

The door opened and in fell a body. The man had fair skin with dark glossy hair. My regard rolled over to Popov and I watched recognition wash over him.

My smile returned. "It is my duty to deliver your message to Double E Bags. However, it is in your best interest to sleep with one eye open and make the most of your last days breathing."

There was a flash in Popov's blue eyes when he glanced up from his fallen soldier to me. It was good. Finally having his attention was good.

With the door still open by my guy guarding outside, I sauntered out, being sure to leave the private club patronized by mostly Russians and Ukrainians as discreetly as we'd arrived.

Johnson held the car door opened for me when I stepped outside. I glided into the cool air-conditioned space and loosened my tie. Seconds later, the front doors were closing after my security slipped inside. There was another issue concerning me. How could Popov be cooperating with law enforcement if he sent one of his men to kidnap my niece? That would never be a ploy of the federal government—the government in general.

A copy of the paperwork from the lead detective referred to the informant as USSR. That was an acronym for the Soviet Union. One of the republics it was composed of was Russia. The informant was a member of *The Commission*. The only party amongst them that could match the USSR nickname, something the agents used for anonymity of their source, was Popov. I allowed my mind to wrestle with that.

Thirty minutes into the commute, Rory sat beside me in the shadows of the dark coasting the highways. The lights from oncoming traffic on the opposite side cast moving illumination into the *Maybach* as Johnson relaxed to the lyrical expressions of Young Lord behind the wheel.

"What you thinking, S.Q.E.?" Rory asked as we wheeled into traffic.

I pulled in a hefty breath, brows lifting. "Soil my fuckin' hands."

I felt her big ass eyes on me but refused to acknowledge her. Rory knew the level of depravity I was willing to reach to extirpate the empire and livelihood of one Feodor Popov. It would take great implementation, however, combining the intelligence and tenure of my warfare team and the large number and strength of my father's, the Ellises could set the entire fucking Garden State ablaze.

"That nigga Popov ain't like weak ass Damien," Rory shared next to me. "He ain't low key like Rizzo, or sloppy like Lopez. That message you delivered was real clear...a fuckin' blatant threat." I nodded my acknowledgment of her heeding. "We ain't got shit on him. They army ain't deep like ours, but them muthafuckas sharp as fuck. They 'on't miss when they shoot, and trust me, them bullets gone fly soon."

"Say what the fuck you have to say," I demanded.

"I know we gets busy, but Popov is another level type of vicious. Them Russians'll turn you into the beast you swore you ain't never wanna be. Going to war with them's gonna put you in ya bag. It's gonna jeopardize the legit businesses—all of them shits."

I lay back on the headrest and emptied my lungs. My gaze was out of the window when I explained, "Rory, the man could've killed my wife. If he lives, I can't be her protector. I can't not eradicate him from the same planet my Nalib lives on. She needs peace of mind." There was a long period of quiet hovering over us before I informed. "No, I'm not the type of man to take on this war, but it's the one that chose me when that muthafucka came within an arm's distance of my wife, and I'll see it through."

I had to. Once again, being Earl Ellis' son had derailed my vision for my own life. For the first time, I feared for my son, my future children. What life was I birthing them into? Would they be free to choose a life of legal free will unlike me?

When the handle clicked on the door, I pushed up from the pillows against the headboard of the bed. Sadik quietly closed the door behind himself. He began into the room and those kaleidoscopic irises found me, causing my belly to flip over. His regard roved over me slowly from top to bottom. That's when I noticed the housecoat I was wearing—his—had slipped from my shoulder and opened at the thigh.

I tried hiding my pleased smirk when I used my finger to invite him over to me. With a casual pace, Sadik meandered over to me, stopping at the foot of the bed. I took to my knees and crawled over to him. His eyes traveled over to the baby asleep in his bassinet near the bed. When I reached Sadik, my lips brushed against his, catching the faint scent of brandy.

I reached for the hem of his black t-shirt, thinking it was unusual attire for him on a weekday. He helped me pull it up his torso and over his head. Then my hands reached the buckle of his belt. I kissed him again, loving his eyes closing submissively as I neared him. He didn't touch me as I released his belt and unbuttoned his jeans.

"How long's he been sleep?"

My eyes rolled over to the baby resting on his side. "About an hour. He tried waiting up for you. I told him Stacy would be sending your dinner up and I may eat with you."

Sadik's face cracked into a lazy grin. "And his sleepy head couldn't wait for his old man?"

I giggled. "Maybe he'll catch you when he wakes for a bottle in a few hours. Lay down. I need to inspect you."

He scoffed, but did as I asked. "Dinner's being delivered up here? I see you're enjoying the trimmings of *Elliswoods Palace*."

With a short giggle, I nodded.

When he was seated and scooted back as I instructed with a push, he asked, "Inspect? For what?"

"A few days ago, it was a busted hand. I didn't push for answers, but feel I should at least know your condition before I jump you like I did last night and this morning. I don't want to break you."

Sadik laughed as I removed his shoes and socks. He chuckled as I pulled at his boney toes to peep in between. Then I climbed his legs, enjoying the jollity on his face, thrilled I single-handedly put it there.

I removed the housecoat, revealing my matching black lace and satin bra and underwear set. His smile dissipated and eyes darkened to a molten miscellany of golds and browns. "You're not mad at me anymore?" he asked, gazing down my torso.

I didn't look pregnant, didn't regularly feel evidence of life in there either. But loose skin from S.Q.E., II hung over my pouch. Sadik didn't seem to mind or notice. He certainly still touched me with the same reverence he did the very first time.

"I'm frustrated about your views on your family, yes. But more than that, I want to be what you need as a wife and mother of your children."

My hands roamed all over his hard, golden case. I inspected the hairs and ink of his chest, each roll of his abs. When I made it to the orange trail beneath his navel, Sadik grabbed my hands with his busted one.

"Don't start what we can't finish," his warning was throaty.

It wasn't my plan to make love to him, I honestly only wanted to extend the olive branch. However, he was right. Me removing his pants could open a road I must travel.

"Okay," I gruffed, face folded animatedly. "Inspection passed, I guess."

Swiftly and smoothly, I was lifted and landed on my back. Startled, I was out of breath as I beamed up at him. Sadik's mouth was centimeters away from my own. The aroma of brandy could be tasted on my lips, he was so close. Those feline eyes examined my face with possession.

"You've discovered my weakness, Nalib?" He scowled.

I nodded, struggling to hide my mirth. "I have the power, Sadik." The confidence in those words gave me a new sense of strength.

Slowly, he nodded. Sadik grabbed my thigh, a piece closest to my sex with such authority. "That you do. Be careful how you execute it. I'm an Ellis; abuse of power won't be tolerated."

"Only if your authority acts in favor of my heart."

There was a moment that passed between our warring spirits. In his eyes, I saw a concoction of love, adoration, and mistrust. Sadik still doubted my feelings for him. Tonight, I wouldn't fight to defend myself: I'd have to allow my actions to.

"Have you heard the good news about Iban? He's awake." Sadik nodded again, still appearing entranced. "Did you visit him?" This time he shook his head then ducked to kiss my neck. My eyes fluttered and I clenched his arm, allowing the sensation of arousal to course through me. "Are you going to?" I whispered.

After a period of torture from his soft, full lips and viral scent around me, he murmured. "It's a consideration."

I swallowed, eyes blinking. "He needs you more now than ever."

"And I need you now more than ever," he shared between tongue strokes to my beating pulse.

He took my hand and guided me down his opened jeans to his growing erection. My legs widened involuntarily. His fingers crawled beneath the bed of my panties, strumming a purposeful cadence on my tight nub.

I've been wet all this time...

My head rested back and eyes closed. "Have you talked to your mother about this?" I asked, fighting the blanket of lust coming over me.

"Queen has had her hands full with other obvious matters concerning Iban and my father. Just like you have your hand full with...me," he croaked, and it was then I realized I'd been stroking his thickness.

I removed my hand then pushed him onto his back, straddling

him once again. "I don't want this feud continuing in my name," I made clear, almost touching his tempting lips.

A "V" formed in his forehead. "It's about betrayal, lack of boundaries, and decades of power tripping. If Iban had killed you and my son, it wouldn't have been because you were Abshir's sister. It would have been because of the power surge Earl enjoys when puppeteering his children's lives. It would have been because once again, I didn't do things his way and followed his path. In return, he sicced his dog on you. I still don't know what made Iban leave without killing you that night at your parents'. It's not what we do, not what we were taught. We shoot until our target is dead, or we are. We're still here because we're that good, Bilan. It's nothing short of a fuckin' miracle that you're on my lap now. That my child is just feet away from us."

My spine withered and I sighed. "But we are, Sadik."

"Months later, my brother, my so-called best friend, brought a gun into my home with the intent of murder."

"His own," I tried to remind him.

"I'm not convinced of his intent. That dog my father created didn't have enough of threatening my family, although his master did. I'm sorry I'm not a perfect man. Sorry you finally see how defective my family is. I've permitted your wishes to stay at *Elliswoods Palace* until this issue with my father's latest nemesis is settled, but don't push me beyond that, Nalib. Don't abuse the power."

"Sadik..."

He silenced me with the shaking of his golden head. "This conversation is closed. Tomorrow is a long day, from the meeting with the builders for our new property—"

I sucked in a breath. "New?" My eyes were large with surprise. "We got the property I chose?"

"I told you I'd search heaven and earth for the desires of your heart. We close on it next week. Tomorrow, two building companies will come to present their designs. You choose which one you like best. They're both aware of my desire to begin next week. *Elliswoods Palace* is my parents' home. We need to build our own for our family, create our own legacy."

I nodded in submission, eyes falling to his taut chest. "My O.B.

appointment is tomorrow afternoon. We find out more about the baby I'm carrying."

"Yup. Like how long he or she has been between us unknown," his delivery now gentle, tender. My eyes trailed down to his fingers caressing my belly, worshipfully. "I didn't plan this one either," he croaked. "but I'm so fuckin' happy you're pregnant again, Nalib. I want you to have all my babies."

I exhaled a trembling breath as my stomach flipped. "How many?"

Those inspired greens flicked up to me. "How many can you handle?"

"I don't consider myself a vain woman, but I don't want my body ravished by pregnancies." I stroked my sex over his hardness. "I'd rather be ravished by you."

His gorgeous orange hues raked from the point of where our bodies met to my face. "I'm going to fuck you now, Nalib," he announced, voice husky.

His hot hands gripped my hips on a slap, pulling me over his erection about to burst through his pants.

"What about your dinner?"

"They didn't tell you? After the second knock, the food is left at the door." He lifted to kiss me. "Now, turn over. Let me see that ass, Nalib."

My eyes blinked for clarity as my back was to the reception desk. I knew the nurses were ear hustling—more like ogling me; they always did when I came here.

"Pardon me?"

"Stop it!" my mother shouted into the phone, unusually angry and undoubtedly emotional. "I didn't ask for your help, Sadik. And you've made matters worse!"

"Because little Marco ran back to his mother about a busted lip?" I murmured.

"He didn't say a word! His wife did after she viewed the surveillance video of you and your men walking into his garage. His teeth are gone, Sadik!"

My eyes closed and I rubbed the corners at the bridge of my nose.

Shit...

What a rookie move that could have cost me. The last thing I considered when going to Marco Rizzo's home was surveillance.

"Why are you so upset, queen?"

"Because I just finished telling you how tired I am, Sadik! Exhausted!" Her screaming wouldn't cease. "I have a lot going on between your father and brother, I don't need any more dissension in my family than what we already have!"

"There won't be," I tried to assure her.

"There won't be?" A vile snicker pushed from her belly, it seemed. "It's too late for that, son. Catena Rizzo made it clear, Liza won't be visiting our family indefinitely." There was a pause as I switched the weight of my body from one hip to the other. "Did you hear me? I won't see her anymore. And what rights do I have if her father is incapacitated?"

I pinched the corners of my eyes again. "I'm sorry, queen."

"Yeah, Sadik, but do you understand sorry can't repair this mess? Every problem can't be resolved with violence or the assertion of yours, your father, or Iban's will. I thought if anyone understood this, it was you." That felt like a slap in the face. The last time I felt this level of rebuke from my mother was when she found me fucking one of her staff members in the pool house one spring break. She was evidentially hurt by it. This was no different. "I have to go."

Queen didn't give me a chance to acknowledge her request to end the call. The line went dead. I pulled in a long breath and turned toward Rory, handing her the phone.

"Think you need to get back in there, big bruh," she advised.

When I stepped back inside of the examination room, the first thing I noticed was Bilan's concerned gape on me as she lay on the table with her lower body naked but for the medical tissue sheet covering her. Her legs were spread wide, feet planted in the stirrups. Dr. Clifford didn't acknowledge my re-entry. He was too busy spitting medical jargon to his nurses.

"What's going on?"

Bilan pulled my hand to her chest. "You almost missed the heartbeat. We tried to wait. But something's wrong with the machine, and he's going to try again."

Dr. Clifford rolled back to the exam table with a squeeze bottle. "Okay," he chirped. "Let's try this again." He squirted gel on her belly, then rolled a handheld device over it.

Several galloping cadences could be heard. It was strange.

"Hmmmm..." Dr. Clifford hummed, listening in. "That's odd. It's doing it again." His hand roamed, trying to track a clear sound. After a while, he gave up. "Okay," he sighed. "Clearly something's malfunctioning with my equipment, but what we were able to catch was an undeniably clear heartbeat. It's strong and viable. Both my ultrasound machines are down, ironically. In a future prenatal visit, I'll take a look in there to see if big brother will be getting a brother or a sister." He smiled at Bilan.

My wife appeared uneasy. Her smile was devoid happiness, and that bothered me. Dr. Clifford not being his usual goofy self didn't help either.

"What's next?" I asked.

"Nothing. Just get plenty of rest and eat balanced meals," he warned. "Little time in between pregnancies can diminish the body's essential nutrients, putting mom at a higher risk for anemia and other complications. A year back, one client's uterine wall ruptured. Not taking care of yourself during this pregnancy because of how recent your last was can also put the baby at risk of low birth weight or premature birth. Not to mention, you're a whole year older than the last, and that small distance can make a world of a difference at your age. It's imperative that you take care of yourself."

"So, when do you think we conceived?" Bilan asked the million-dollar question.

"Based on the date you gave birth, your exams after, and the one I did today, you could very well have conceived seven weeks after birth," he explained.

Bilan's eyes flashed on me. "Seven weeks," she murmured, lost in calculations.

I'd already added the time up. It was when we left *Elliswoods Palace* to return to the high-rise. Bilan had been less patient than I was to resume sex, and I was grateful for it.

"After Easter." She bit her bottom lip when she'd finally come to her conclusion. Then she turned to Dr. Clifford. "That fast? I'd just been cleared of my six weeks."

He nodded, grinning bashfully. "It's all about timing, and with each woman, it's unique. For some, ovulation after giving birth happens before a period, making pregnancy possible for a woman before having the first postpartum period. And remember, you didn't breastfeed, which often prevents ovulation." He quipped, "You were out there with no defenses, young lady." He winked.

Bilan's gaze returned to me and she broke out in a fit of giggles. Had I been in a better mood, I would've explained to the doctor, it was me who needed defenses against her feminine wiles, and not the other way around.

Dr. Clifford stood and his face folded in concern as he glanced over to the machine his nurses were busy with trying to examine. "I'm sorry about my lack of technology today. I've never been so ill-equipped here. I assure you, we'll be prepared for your next visit."

Bilan nodded, unable to hide her happiness. She squeezed my hand. "We have to tell your family."

I didn't want that. At least not so soon. "And yours."

She rolled her eyes. "They care more about the news than the well-being of the baby and me. We need to tell yours. Tonight." When I didn't reply right away, Bilan pushed. "They can use the good news right about now. *Shoot!* We all can. I'm sure Earl will be thrilled." When the table inclined so she could sit up, I helped her upright. "Even if it's temporarily, let's use this to lighten the mood around the compound."

I considered it for a few seconds. The only person coming to mind was my mother. I'd like very much to lift her spirits. While I believed she was wrong with her position on the incident with Marco, I couldn't deny the sullen mood dive she'd done since my father's heart attack. Iban's accident increased the speed of it.

I mustered a smile to soothe an impatient Bilan. Then I kissed her gently on the forehead and murmured, "If that's what you want to do, we'll do it, Nalib."

"Yeah." Her smile broadened. "Let's do it, sire."

Rolling my eyes, I chuckled at the term she'd picked up from Rory.

As we trekked toward Earl's study, I grew nervous.

"We're so late. You think they're still gathered?"

Sadik's attention was to both his phones when he murmured with confidence. "Of course, they are, Nalib."

I didn't exactly believe him. On the way from the doctor, I sent a text to everyone in the family to tell them we wanted to meet this evening, where, and what time. That was before I suddenly wanted *B-Way Burger*, and once that desire was satisfied, Sadik needed to run to his office.

We were now entering Earl's study thirty-five minutes after I'd asked them to be here. Irene was present, rubbing down Earl's feet with oil as he sat in a wheelchair in house pants and a hospital gown.

Stacy was present in her uniform, sitting in a chair, tapping on her device. She looked adorable in her lime green framed reading glasses.

"Hey," I greeted the room nervously—more embarrassed—as Sadik waltz into the foyer of the study stiff and impatiently. I felt his mode switch instantaneously, even as he helped his mother from her squatting position to stand, and greeted her with a kiss. I hugged her as well as Earl. "I'm glad you all were able to wait. Sorry we're late." I sputtered a nervous giggle. "I guess I got so excited about the prospect of meeting you guys that I didn't consult with Sadik about his schedule this evening."

Sadik rounded me, placing his hands on my shoulders, applying light clenches for needed comfort.

"It's okay, baby," Irene offered, sadness etched in her flawless chocolate skin that couldn't be hidden by the smile she attempted.

The sight of her almost jarred me. Irene appeared aged and weighed down, so unlike the spirited, confident grace she exuded since knowing her. She was thinner, too. That change reminded me of Taaliba.

I glanced around. "Did we miss Taaliba?"

Just as I asked, Taaliba whirred inside the opening of the study.

"My bad!" she apologized, heading our way. "I had a call with a new art class I'm in. When I saw you guys were delayed, I finished it in mommy's office." She hugged and kissed me, then her brother. "Did I miss anything?" She grabbed a chair and plopped down.

"No!" I answered too eagerly as I pulled in a deep breath. My regard slid over to her brother, who was devilishly handsome even when brooding. "We just got here, and I guess shouldn't take up much more of your time than we have." I was struck with another realization. "Where's Monica?"

Stacy frowned in thought. "She was supposed to be here?"

I nodded. "She said she would try when I texted her."

"I served the girls a snack about an hour ago," Stacy added. "I haven't seen her since this morning, though."

"She's on the compound," Earl remarked. "So she can't be far."

My smile faded when the memory of the text on her phone from yesterday came to mind. "Oh, well. No need to be more dramatic than I've already been about this. I'll just have to share it with her and the girls later." I glanced over to Sadik for fortitude before announcing, "We're expecting...again!" I sang, swinging my arms out to expose a belly that had yet to arrive.

There was a delay before Irene cried, "Oh, my lord!" She cupped her mouth.

"Is that what this is about?" Taaliba demanded, shooting from her seat and reaching for me. She crushed me in her arms. "Girl, I thought it was more bad news!" I could feel her heart racing against my chest.

"I'm sorry," I tried explaining over her shoulder. "It's just that with baby Sadik, we waited months to tell you, and I didn't want that to happen again."

"Damn, big bro," Taaliba croaked teasingly and clearly shocked. "She just gave us a baby. You couldn't let her relax first?"

Embarrassed, I hid behind Sadik's shoulder.

"Shut up, Leeb," he growled, annoyed.

"Just saying." She rolled her eyes.

"When did this happen?" Irene's expectant gaze targeted her son, then rolled over to me.

I pivoted to his side again, feeling the need to explain. "According to the doctor, we conceived just after Easter."

"When you left the compound?" Stacy asked.

I nodded, unable to contain my joy. "Apparently, when we left, we procreated."

"Hmmmmm," Taaliba hummed suspiciously. "There's something about being out on your own that increases independence and growth." Her eyes rolled from her big brother to her father. "When's the baby due?"

"In January," I answered. "The sixteenth."

"That's pretty early," Stacy commented, still surprised.

"Yeah. With so much happening in the family, I forgot to get a script for birth control," I explained. "When we were away, the weight of forgetting got the best of me and I bought a test while we were in *St. Justin*."

Taaliba went over to congratulate her brother, making room for Stacy to hug me next. "I'm so happy for you and Deek, baby."

"Thanks, Stacy! I promise not to be any more of a headache than we are now."

"Oh, I enjoy it all." She pulled back. "I'll have to tell the cooks to keep more folic acid-rich foods available for you. I know you're not a big eater, but we'll do our best to make things more appealing to you for the sake of the baby." She rubbed my belly. "You're so tiny!"

"The doctor said not for long." I laughed.

"Well, hopefully we'll see to that!" She promised before going over to Sadik.

When my eyes traveled over to a quieted Earl, he motioned me his way with his fingers. I didn't hesitate obeying.

"You're making me happy," he whispered, green eyes gleaming.

"One baby at a time, huhn?" I teased.

Earl chuckled, possibly embarrassed, but not likely. "You're happy to expand my lineage. That's different from the cute little Halle Berry hair cut girl with freckles that was here last year. You're proud to be among us, and that makes me happy."

The smile on my face couldn't be broader than the one in my heart. "I'm trying," I shared, eyes glistening with tears I refused to drop.

When I stood from his chair, I noticed Irene breaking away from Sadik. She was wiping her eyes. "I thought y'all was gonna say you finally had a wedding date."

My regard went to Earl, who glanced away smoothly, swiping his nose. Stacy scratched the back of her head, announcing she had to get back to work.

"Uh," Taaliba stammered, eyes suspiciously wide. "I need to get out of here my damn self. I've got so much to do. I'm reorganizing my room."

Sadik's expression was as hard and steady as it was since he'd entered the room. That told me Irene didn't know Sadik and I had married. How could that be? Because of my episode the other night, many of the Ellis personnel knew. Irene had to be that disconnected as of late if she hadn't heard from *her* staff. What was more surprising is how neither Earl nor Sadik had told her. That left me feeling troubled.

Sadik laid a possessive hand on my shoulder. "Bilan and I have to go. We have to be in Paterson in a few hours."

"Yes," Irene chirped. "Today's election day. Julius has been on my mind all day. Please give him my best. I meant to send them something over, but..." She touched her fingertips to her forehead. "I guess the time got ahead of me. I'll have Kema do it tomorrow. Win or lose, I want to support him."

"We're hopeful for the win, queen." Sadik closed the visit. "You two enjoy the evening."

I waved my goodbye, eager to get to my baby. He'd sat through the meeting with the builders with us this morning, but at this hour the morning felt a day ago. I'd missed him.

As we headed to the door, Irene called out to me.

"Have you told your family, dear?"

My smile dried when I shook my head. "Not yet."

Irene's expression matched mine, revealing just how dim her spirit was. When usually she'd offer to contact them for me, she murmured, "Okay, honey."

My heart was heavy the whole way to the wing of our suite.

∞14∞

The place was so eruptive, I couldn't feel my phone vibrate in my hand. If it hadn't lit up, I'd have no idea I had two text alerts. The first was from Jamil.

E2: *Playdate confirmed for 2mor on the merry go round*

That was good news. It meant he'd recruited his final four men to train for the battle I planned on pursuing with Popov. My father had his means of pulling in men with failed interests in law enforcement to his team for assignments just like this. It was a practice I borrowed from him, but this time in greater number as typically, I had no need for large armies like he did. For Popov, we both needed it. He had more weapons, we had to invest our time and resources into training men for battle to conquer him.

The other text was from Rory saying Isaiah Green, the warehouse receiver from my 3PL, had been handled. That was even more good news, but what happened tonight reached my heart.

"And for the first time," the deejay shouted into the microphone. "Paterson's very own mayor, Julius Richards!"

Red, white, and blue confetti fell from the air, marking the moment as festive. The air cut with whistles, screams, and cries of joy. There were at least three hundred people in the ballroom of *Wilson's* banquet hall in South Paterson. I was insistent his victory party was at a Black-owned facility. The Wilson's had hosted many of my family's events over the years. They prided themselves on presenting an exquisite culinary experience, and an environment conducive to fine dining and escapism. I knew this from Mr. Wilson's constant claims of such.

When Julius stepped onto the stage with Keisha at his side, the pride on his face was downright giddy. We shouted him on, calling his name in the same cadence. Suddenly, Julius turned emotional. That made me laugh. Next to me, Bilan rubbed my thigh. We were seated on the second level of the room. Very few were up here, only my security, and occasionally staff from the venue to deliver food and such. I requested the space up here to be an eagle privately.

Keisha asked the place to quiet so her man could speak. The deejay lowered the music to give him room to prepare him. It took a minute, but Julius finally spoke.

"Just a kid from *Brooks-Sloate* Projects." The room exploded again. He waited before continuing. "Growing up in the eighties was terrifying for me. Drugs had come around and hit us bad. Maybe not as bad as *CCP* or *Alabama Projects*, but we were not left unscathed. My friends weren't as lucky. Some of them suffered at the hands of bad policing and slum lords. I can recall visiting my cousins and kicking crack vials around—remember they had vials before they had baggies?"

He was answered by a collective yes.

"Yup. Young kids on the block because no one shared the opportunities that were shared up the street in Wayne and North Haledon. I remember cops knocking me and my friends around for fun simply walking from downtown. Those same officers turning a blind eye to tricked out *Beamers* pulling into *CCP* by that side street off of West Broadway."

He nodded as everyone responded, affirming his point. "I didn't see a lot of the world coming up. I was raised by a two-shift-working single mother and retired grandmother living on a fixed income. The most travel we did was down to Jackson for *Great Adventure* in the fall when the price of admission dropped." He laughed.

"But they instilled in me hard work in school, of which I honored. I was rewarded with scholarships galore when I graduated high school. I began a new statistic in the city of Paterson. I took my academic talents to *Blakewood University*—" Julius was interrupted by the explosion in the room. *Blakewood*, a division one ivy league, was a big deal because it was the only HBCU of its kind. "Yeah!" He nodded, affirming their enthusiasm. "That's right. And in going away to school, the world opened up for me. I met people from all walks of life—on campus and off.

"I was exposed to so many cultures, experiences to counter my own. One energy I met, ironically, wasn't from afar. He was a Jersey-native himself. He came from greater means than I had but was a visionary, similar to me. He was the one to inspire me to dream big and to express them without apology. In spite of our polar lifestyles, he absorbed me into his world. He allowed me to travel with him, exposed me to creative minds—more dreamers. He taught me what my mother and grandmother couldn't. This peer of mine taught me dreams weren't limited to your pillow. Dreams were God's way of informing you of your purpose."

There was another round of applause. "And once God speaks, only fools don't answer the call. So, I shared with him my desire to make the world more welcoming and an open field ready for cropping. We'd stay up night after night cultivating realistic and attainable goals to get me there. We'd extrapolate honest, plausible, and hard-hitting policies. It's the *Blakewood* political science way, but with this friend, it was sport. It was my additional classroom." He cleared his throat. "It's a significant reason why we're here today. So salute to my dear friend and number two supporter, right behind my wife!"

Julius saluted me, timing it away from his words as to not draw much attention to the second tier. We were away from the balcony, making it difficult to see us unless you knew we were here. I returned his gesture. Then I felt a small hand on my thigh.

Bilan was on me, so close so fast. "He respects you," her voice was dreamy and filled with pleasant surprise.

I kissed her forehead. "The feeling's mutual." Then I turned my body to face hers. "But you know what's not mutual?"

"What?" She beamed just as she had been since leaving Dr. Clifford's office. "My love for you. I love you more than anything in this world." I lifted her soft hands to my mouth for a chaste kiss.

"Don't say that, Sadik," she purred.

"Why? I mean it." I reached over and kissed her nose. "No one makes me feel as complete and fulfilled as you do."

"Not even Sadik?"

I chuckled. "Would you stop with that?" I stood, holding her hands to mine as I did so. "Let's dance."

Julius was still on the stage performing his victory speech. But in my head was beautiful music to match a wonderful moment. I had my gorgeous wife in my arms, carrying our second child. And still, I couldn't believe I was a father in the first place. My dear friend had conquered his first political seat, winning by defeating five opponents in a landslide.

As we swayed to the rhythm playing in my mind, only with all the chaos alone, Bilan's head lifted.

"I just read on my phone they're still counting votes. The Spanish guy wants them all accounted for."

"Doesn't matter." I winked at her, enjoying her beauty. Her short, jet black hair carried a sheen at the top. The tapered back and sides were small waves, cut in a pattern. The diamond studs in her ears didn't compete with the compelling low cleavage in her gown. "He's up by five-thousand votes. It was a high turn out tonight, not many more residents can be counted to make a difference."

"I'm happy to be a part of this. Just a few days ago, I was drunk, horny, and married in front of him. Tonight, we're celebrating his mayoral win!"

Chuckling, I assured, "I'm sure I've experienced Richards in a wider range of moods and events."

"Why are we up here and not down there with them?"

I pulled her closer to me, curling over her frame. Having her this close relaxed me. Bilan was mine, every inch of her, making this celebration more enjoyable.

"I've told you. It's the price I have to pay for being Earl 'Double E Bags' Ellis' son. You don't always get to walk among noble men."

Her hands caressed my back. "What do you mean?"

"Because of my father's long-standing sordid reputation in the state, it wasn't possible for me to stand too close to Julius during his election."

"But you've been instrumental the whole time."

"My involvement has been behind doors. It was best that way." And suddenly, it felt good sharing this with someone without the pretense of emotional guards. "If people, particularly his opponents knew how involved I was, it would have narrowed his chances of celebrating a win tonight. How could he promise to rid the city of the drugs and mayhem my father is the cause of?"

"But that isn't your line of work, Sadik?"

"To many, it might as well be. People, particularly Black people, will always consume conspiracy before they'll give the benefit of the doubt. It's not different in business. I've been passed up on a number of opportunities...accounts the moment they learn the affiliation of my name."

Her arms squeezed around me, making my eyes close in content-ment. "But you're not Earl. I know you're not. And I've gotten to know him, too. He's planted himself in my heart, I can't lie. I adore your father, but you're your own man. And I love you for it. Sadik will love you for it, too. I'm sorry if others who don't know you believe what's so easy to."

"Yeah, especially those who it can hurt, like Jules."

She reared to meet my eyes. "What do you mean?"

"Not everyone is fooled. I've contributed modestly to his campaign and one report published it in the paper. That could have been the lethal blow to his career." But it wasn't. Under my legal name, I donated a meek three-thousand dollars. Through other means, like a few shell companies and distant associates, I contributed greatly and more than Jules knew. I preferred it that way. "Thankfully, the influencers around town shut it down because of the small dollar amount. But even now that he'll be in office, we have to continue to distance ourselves in public."

As the crowd cheered on the lower level, I pulled my wife even closer.

"But you know what, Mrs. Ellis?"

"What's that, Mr. Ellis?"

"This night would've been pretty lonely up here if I didn't have Sadik's mom to celebrate with me."

Bilan's face turned disconsolate. "I'll always be here." She swallowed a cry. "Always. It will be my honor." I stilled, eyes blinked. She smiled freely before nodding. "Earl isn't the only one worthy of the virtue. I'm privileged to be your partner, Sadik."

With so many emotions burgeoning in my chest, I couldn't speak. My only reaction was to gather her in my arms even tighter, allowing the warmth and gratitude I felt to hopefully permeate her. We danced and talked for the remainder of the party.

At some point, we returned to the table and I fed Bilan freshly baked churros dipped in milk chocolate and a strawberry syrup. Mr. Wilson delivered them up himself. The act was a difficult task because Bilan didn't want to disturb her lipstick, so her bites were exaggerated. Unwittingly, she moaned each time the dipped churro reached her tongue.

Her eyes were closed when she breathed, "These are so good."

I licked the stain of syrup and sugar from my fingers. "Nalib..."

"Hmmmm?"

"Your moaning's making my dick hard."

Her eyes flew open and dropped to my lap. For further inspection, she reached for me.

"Oh, my god, Sadik!" she whispered hard. "You're serious!"

I nodded, dabbing the corner of her mouth with a napkin. It was my intent to fuck up the lining of her lipstick later.

"Why wouldn't I be? I can't wait to have your mouth wrapped around me." Her face relaxed, shocked by my words. "Would you be okay with me coming down your throat in the limo?" I swiped beneath the seam of her bottom lip with my thumb.

Fuck...

I wanted her. The unadulterated feel of a man desiring his wife came full circle to me in that moment.

Bilan nodded, eyes bouncy, lips parted.

I reached over to whisper in her ear. "I want to fuck you now." With my eyes to the window behind her, I waited a beat before I asked, "Would you like that?"

I could feel her nod again, her face toward the floor, cheek against the whiskers of my beard.

My body froze at the touch of a small soft hand on my shoulder. My eyes trailed below to see both of Bilan's on my knees. My brain hiccupped at that juxtaposition.

Finally, I glanced up. "He stole the win with 9,891 ballots, and your arrogant ass couldn't come down and congratulate him properly in front of his constituents!" Sofia stood, swaying on one leg, an angry gleam in the one eye unexposed by her flip bangs.

I twisted to get a better view of her. "Excuse me."

"All night, I thought you weren't here—irresponsibly, but you never know with you—yet you've been up here cavorting with a belle rather than celebrating with your new boss like us commoners."

I took my time standing. From this vantage point, I saw Rory flexing in the background and Brittany trying to get through Johnson at the door. "First of all, we both know I have no boss, sweetheart. Secondly, you of all people know my position in this." When I noticed the glassiness in her eyes, it made sense. "And lastly—"

"Hey, Sofee." Rory took her gently at her arm. "Lemme rap to you right quick."

A soft body brushed against mine, rounding me. Bilan had her splayed hand out, offering it to Sofia.

"Belle, as in the mother of his children. It's my pleasure." Her delivery was with built-in confidence and smoothness.

Sofia looked confused as her gaze went from Bilan's face to her hand. Then she regarded me. "You don't have kids...with her!"

I took in a quick breath, hating the scene she was creating. Rory was back on her immediately.

"Come, mami," she urged. "We don't wanna make S.Q.E. mad." She tried reasoning with her.

"Why would she make your employer mad, Rory?" Bilan asked, smile planted on her face, nostrils flared.

"Maybe because he'd have to explain how I speak to him every damn week—sometimes several times a week—and had no fuckin' clue he was a father," Sofia shouted.

"It's time for you to go. Let her through," I called over to Johnson holding Brittany at the door. "She's drunk. Please get her out of here."

Julius and Keisha appeared at the door. Both wore expressions of concern at the melee now in action.

"Drunk?" Sofia spat. "No fucking way I'm drunk. I'm just asking how the hell can you be passing out seeds out of fucking wedlock—something you told me you were obstinately against to basic bitches."

"Basic bitches?" Bilan peered down at her engagement ring, the one I hadn't had a chance at accompanying with a band to settle our union.

"What's going on here?" Keisha demanded, jumping in front of Sofia.

"Oh, nothing!" Sofia stumbled. "Just asking the great Ellis here when did his rules change for engendering with random women, and supporting friends he's so-called backing!"

Julius positioned himself protectively in front of me. It was unnecessary, but I understood his position—we understood our relationship. Ironically, Sophia did, too. She was too drunk to reason against her alcohol-induced emotions.

"Sofia, please stop," Keisha begged. "You're embarrassing yourself in front of his pregnant wife."

Sofia's stumbling broke and her eyes widened. "Wife?" She stepped closer to me, her hair swinging into her face, heels clacking into the floor. "Your ass is married and you didn't have the fucking decency to tell me?"

My head reared. "I don't owe you the confidence of details from my personal life. What do you mean?"

Bilan propped herself in front of me. "That's what I want to know!"

I issued her a fixed glare of warning. She would not join Sofia in making a spectacle. Especially because Sofia's actions tonight had no bearing of the reality we lived in. I hadn't a fucking ounce of desire to lay a finger on Sofia. Even now with the way the silk of her wrap dress lay on her full breasts, narrowed waist, and round hips, I remembered why it all lost its appeal to me.

"You're fucking married with kids? Like how?" Sofia screamed. "You selfish, arrogant son of a bitch!" She snorted in mucus and cocked a spit aimed at me.

Before I could assess where it landed, Bilan leaped at her, grabbing her by the hair.

"Oh, shit!" Rory croaked. "B, easy!"

I grabbed Bilan, but not before she managed a fist full of Sofia's hair. As I pulled her back, she foolishly kicked Sofia in the stomach. My heart damn near jumped up my throat at the sight of that combo. If it were in reverse, I might have had to put a bullet in Sofia's head.

"Knock it the fuck offf!" I barked at Bilan.

"We need to get her out of here," Julius more or less shouted to Brittany.

Brittany leaped into action and with the help of Keisha, Sofia was being pulled toward the open doors.

"I can't fucking believe you!" she shouted, laughing. "I see what this is! You're no different from them. *Tu guapo manipulador!*" She spat into the air. "You remember who warmed your fucking pillows. Remember who was there when you thought you were going to prison after your brother!"

"Get off of me!" Bilan wiggled in my hold. She managed to turn in my arms, and I loosened. "Who do you think I am?"

Although I saw it coming, I was too weakened by her anger to protect myself. Bilan slapped the shit out of me.

"Yo, B, man!" Rory cried. "The fuck!"

"Fuck you, Rory!" Bilan swiveled and pointed in her face. "I dare you to call another woman my husband has fucked by a nickname when you're trying to comfort her as long as I breathe!"

When she took another daring step toward Rory, I understood what state of mind she was in. Angered, I reached to remove my tie.

"Fuck is you even talking about?" Rory tried understanding what I knew.

The way she addressed Sofia.

"I'm talking about *you* and you know what I mean! Don't ever fucking speak to me again!" She then turned to me. "And if you think I'm the Irene Ellis or even the Monica Ellis type, you've got another thing coming!" My dick swelled. "My name is Bilan Asad-Yasin, Ellis can be the concrete noun, but never the possessive. You speak to her every week and sleep with me each night?" she screamed.

"No, Bilan," Julius tried intervening. "It's not like that!"

With an aplomb demeanor, I approached Bilan, twisting her around and pulling her wrists together to link with my tie. My movements were lightning-speed swift, silencing her with confusion immediately. As I worked the strap over and between her wrists, I issued Bilan a gaze, communicating my lack of patience with her at this point. I was beyond my limit after being spit at and slapped in front of my staff and friends.

"What are you doing?" she finally shrilled.

I leaned into her, reaching her ear. "You say another fuckin' word, you'll be experiencing your first adult spanking. And trust me, it'll be public and painful before you feel a balm of pleasure. I dare you to fuckin' try me."

When I reared, resuming my natural height, I saw Bilan's jaw collapse.

"Your tie, please?" I motioned with my finger over to Julius.

His eyes brushed over Rory, astounded before he scoffed, "Excuse me?"

"Your tie. Please. Now!" I wasn't up to his ass trying me, too. With just seconds of hesitation, Julius began removing his tie. I glanced over to Rory. "Call the fuckin' limo around."

She turned, quickly pulling her phone from her suit jacket pocket.

Julius handed me the tie. "Dawg, you sure this the...move?" His eyes flickered over to my capricious wife.

"There would have been a better one if you would've made sure her drunk ass, like everyone else, didn't know I was here."

"Sadik," Bilan's cry was throaty when she realized she was about to be gagged.

Julius, perturbed by the sight, threw his shoulder into the air and turned away.

I whispered in Bilan's ear. "You used your hands to strike me and your mouth to spew filth. The next time you use your mouth to me it'll be to please me. Do you understand?"

"Sadi—"

"Do you fuckin' understand?" I shouted, causing her to jump.

Tears spilled from her eyes as she nodded. Her neck pulsed hard and chest heaved as I covered her mouth firmly with the tie, knotting it at the back. Then I removed my jacket, inspecting it for the saliva Sofia slung on it. Thankfully none landed on me, and I could use it to hide my erection.

I tossed my chin to Rory. "Get her shit."

With a firm yank of the end of the tie at her wrists, I urged Bilan to follow me, secretly praying she wouldn't test my endurance any further: I'd been unfairly patient tonight.

On the way out, Keisha appeared. With only the briefest glance at her, I picked up her shock of Bilan being bound at the hands, gagged, and pulled behind me. Julius whispered something to wisely mute her. There'd been too much fucking talking and not enough thinking already tonight.

The elevator arrived quickly, and my party boarded.

"I'll hit you tomorrow," I called out to Julius. "Congratulations." I bowed at the neck as the door closed.

We arrived on the lower level and moved quickly from the lobby to the limo waiting in front. The celebration had been over for at least thirty minutes so most had left, but some lingered. Bilan stumbled leaving the sidewalk for the street. It took a few seconds for me to catch on. She grunted, yanking back on the tie. When that didn't work, she struggled in her attempt at regaining her stride. Past infuriated, I lifted her into my arms. She squealed in surprise and I carried her the rest of the way. Rory held the door open while I helped Bilan inside.

Unbalanced without the proper usage of my hands, I traversed across the car. I could hear Sadik talking to the ungendered traitor.

"You see that?" Rory trill with concern.

"The flashing of a camera, yes," Sadik answered. "I heard the click, too."

I found my way to the bench, trying to settle myself against the hum of my body. It was happening again. I was living outside of my psyche. I was angry, scared, and dangerously aroused. He'd betrayed me. Sadik allowed that woman to disrespect him—*spit at him*—and she wasn't punished. Yes, logic prevailed and my better wits realized the nature of his relationship with his former lover was possibly exclusively professional at this point. But, momentarily, he'd lost his inviolability when he allowed her to attack him without consequence.

I heaved uncontrollably when he ducked to enter the limo. His scent led his presence and when his body passed through, my eyes closed as my senses were overwhelmed. A whirring sound had my head whipping behind me. The window to the front of the car was being rolled up. I turned to find Sadik pressing a button.

His disgusted glower on me bristled my skin. He sat motionless, legs spread apart, and one arm on the back of the bench. My head swirled with such unexpected need. I kept swallowing back thick saliva catching in my mouth held open by the tie.

I motioned for him to let me speak. Emitting a ferocious growl, Sadik reached over and unfastened the tie with two tugs.

Immediately, I began to roll my distasteful tongue around in my mouth.

"I thought you had something to say, Nalib," his vocals were coarse.

"I hate the scent of another man's cologne and body oil in my mouth," I managed around my stained tongue. "I was restrained. Publicly," I emphasized.

"I was assaulted by my wife...publicly. How the fuck did you want me to respond?"

"With compassion—the same grace you showed your lil' size two ex-pillow-sharer."

He snorted. "Compassion?" He nodded. "You define that as compassion. Okay." His head tilted. "I'll let you define how I respond to your disrespect tonight."

My body tremored. I was sick for sure. I still craved him, even in his bolshiness. I wanted Sadik.

"Please release my hands," my voice unrecognizably soft. "I want to touch you."

"No," he growled.

"Then punish me. Do something!" I screamed. "You know I'm sick for you! Don't shut me—"

Sadik was on me. Rough hands and abrasive touches as he yanked my dress to above my hips and my panties down to my thighs and ripped them off. The sting from the wrench pinched me in several places, increasing my feverish temperature to dangerous levels. His fingers ranged up my slit, then in my mouth, humiliating me with the reveal of my hyper-arousal. I was a puddle of gel without much work from his touch.

He scoffed, undoing the belt and button of his pants. My thighs spread wider for him at the sound of his zipper pushing down.

When I felt he took too long, I cried out, "Sadik!"

My groin shivered at the first thrust of his bulbous head inside of me. The flutter caused my head to hit the back of the bench. Sadik reared and plunged into me with unrepentant force.

"*Ohhhhhhh!*" I cried out, nearly orgasming so soon.

Sadik didn't stop. Almost as though he knew how on edge I was, he hammered into me with that scowl fixed into his face. The passing street lights illuminated his feline eyes, making him appear animalistic. I couldn't take the delicious massage and his scolding at the same time; I squeezed my eyes shut, feeling the limo rock according to his rhythm.

Life was moving too fast. I was married, pregnant again, and under guard twenty-four-seven. These events were directly related to a man whose lifestyle was extraordinary. He had wealth, popularity, and the wit to manage any adversary. Except a former Latina mistress. After coming down from the shock of learning he was in touch with her weekly, I understood the nature of their relationship. But seeing her so emotionally hysterical over the man who centered my universe angered me beyond logical thinking. Sadik was mine. He belonged to me.

Had he been hers in a similar fashion? Had he hammered into her with the same dominance and fervor he was performing on me now?

My frame tightened, pelvis lifted into the plundering. And I exploded, screaming his name in the same wild hysterics as his old flame. I felt needy, foolish, and over mental and emotional capacity as he thrust inside of me with determined force. He pelted until my cries slowed, then pulled out of me. I lay back awkwardly across the bench, breathing out of control with just one eye open. Sadik dropped his pants and boxers to his ankles. He sat back on the bench with his glare fixed on me.

Tremors still coursed my body like the aftershock from the orgasm. Now, staring at his raging erection beading with pre-cum at the head, that sense of satiation disappeared. I wiggled on my elbows to sit up and crudely dropped to the floor. On my knees, I shuffled to him greedily and pulled him into my mouth. I coated his lengthy, veiny muscle inch by inch, wetting him for my strokes. Then my drawn hands cupped him, fisting him while working him over with my mouth.

I knew what Sadik liked, he'd taught me. Sometimes, we'd go close to an hour with me between his legs perfecting his preferences while I was pregnant. I'd apply great patience, being eager to learn how to gratify him. I took pride in twirling my tongue, applying pressure in one thumb against the raphe line of the underside of his thick shaft. Sadik grunted over my head, thighs flexed around me.

That encouraged my fisting and twirling until I broke the cadence to take him deep into my mouth. I dipped over him, slowing when his swollen head reached my throat at the back of my tongue. Holding my breath, I pushed down, taking him farther, then pulled him out and did it again. Once Sadik caught on to my rhythm, he pulled down with me at the back of my head. Up and down I went with his urging from his hands. That was until he held me down longer than usual while he reached past my throat. I gagged several times, once to the point of tearing, but I was determined to endure the punishment.

I could feel his chastising pushes of my head onto him. It didn't matter to me. I was under the siege of guilt for my accusations. With a tear-stained face, I worked him over until his hands weakened, then dropped from my head. I readjusted myself on the floor and applied more fervor. Sadik was about to explode

"You think I've been disloyal to you?" he whimpered. My eyes shot up to him, but my dedication didn't slow. "To my *so*-son?"

My wide eyes were on him, but my brain hiccupped. I twirled, hollowed my cheeks and fisted. Moments later, Sadik's pelvis leaped then thrusted against my labor and I felt a warm creamy liquid at the back of my mouth and over my tongue. His head flew back and eyes closed as he released into me. My hands sped up and I swallowed when I could, rolling my tongue over him, jerking him as I observed him.

When Sadik scooted back in his seat just an inch, I knew he was done. I released him from my hands then popped him from my mouth as we gazed at one another. He too was out of breath. And like me, he was preoccupied with an unnamed emotion.

"You were mean," my voice coarse, entire face wet of tears and saliva.

"You did it again," his usual alto velvet was a throaty tenor.

"What?"

"You accused me of cheating on you, said you weren't my mother. You used my handicap against me."

It was the point he made to me in Antigua, on his father's private island the day Danny arrived. Sadik believed judging him according to his parents' mistakes was a form of discrimination. Maybe he was right. Or maybe he did have a handicap and was capable of the Ellis way of a lack of monogamy.

"It didn't feel like a handicap when she was just as emotional as I am now about my husband."

"And you damn sure didn't give me the benefit of the doubt. You jumped to the obvious conclusion. The easy one. You doubted me as a man."

A fresh hot tear raced down my face. A real one this time. I was struggling. I knew what my heart felt, but couldn't ignore my gut that was telling me there was something to what Sofia said.

"Why would you think you'd go to prison after Iban?"

It was rapid, but I caught it. There was a flip of fear in Sadik's kaleidoscopic pupils, but him being the wall of emotions he could be, his demeanor stonewalled. One side of his mouth lifted in a sinister leer, bearing strong resemblance to his older sibling. My frame tensed all over, mouth soured.

"Wrong fuckin' question."

"And what's the right one?"

"Why didn't I settle with her after those alleged pillow cries."

I swallowed, feeling another tear slip. "Why didn't you?" my murmur high pitched as we hit a bump in the road, causing me to leap on my knees.

"Because she wasn't you. She could never make me desire fidelity and wholeness in a woman the way you do. One day, you'll understand that and not give a fuck about extraneous matters that do not concern you."

His position was unwavering, leaving me gutted.

∞15∞

The moment Camille placed him in my hand, Sadik sniffled, unhappy about his sleep being disturbed. I was hit with guilt, but not enough. After the night I had, the comfort of my baby felt like the perfect remedy.

"Thanks," I whispered to Camille.

"No problem. Do you want me to feed him breakfast?"

I shook my head. "I'll take care of it."

"Okay. Text me when you need me, and I'll come get him."

"Alright," I agreed, leaving her room at *Elliswoods Palace*.

Having a nanny was still an adjustment. Camille was a huge help. She was always available and loving to our son. Her schedule was unbelievably flexible and practically catered to ours. Sadik was right in pushing for one. He was accurate about his need for my exclusive attention, similar to our son. There were times he wanted me in his arms all night without disturbances of having to get up with the baby.

Similar to tonight. We'd returned to the compound close to one-thirty in the morning. I was still an emotional wreck, crying in the shower. When I asked to have the baby sent up, Sadik said no, I needed the rest. I waited until he was lost in deep sleep before creeping out of our suite to get my baby. It was after three, and the need to have him near still lingered. Now, with him snuggled into my breasts, I felt a peace like none other. I'd deal with the consequence of disobeying his father later. For the next few hours, my baby would be with me.

Camille and other staff were in a parlor on the lower level, in a different wing from Sadik's suite. So, it took a great hike to get back. On the way down, I avoided the elevator and did so on the way back up, too. I could use the cardio from the stairs but decided to cut to the second level to break up the climb as I switched wings of the house.

The halls of *Elliswoods Palace* were their usual quiet and lit slightly dimmer for the hour. That's why I was surprised when I traveled down the one where Iban and his family's rooms were and saw a door open. Iesha's little legs moved swiftly, closing the door. My steps halted and I watched her trek down to the corner. Concern waved over me and my face folded. No one came out after her. Why was she even up at the odd hour? I took long lunges to follow her around the corner.

Iesha slipped into a room I wasn't familiar with. That wasn't unusual: I wasn't familiar with the estate yet. She didn't fully close the door, so I was able to peer through and saw her flick on a few lights and take a seat on the sofa, hugging her little legs to her chest. It was a lounge filled with beautiful paisley, yellow sofas with walnut finishing, high bright blue walls, and a plush area rug over dark wooden floors. I pushed through the door with my shoulder, not disturbing Sadik in my arms.

"Hey, you," I called out on my way to the sofa.

Iesha lifted her head, exposing her tight eyes. "Oh, hey..." She blinked. "...I don't even know what to call you, and I see Sadik's sleeping."

My gaze fell to my sleeping Black boy joy. "Yeah. He is." I couldn't help my smile.

"Your voice sounds different." She observed.

That fact frazzled me momentarily. I couldn't explain it was because I'd gotten into a fight with her uncle just hours ago. Moving to sit next to her on the plush sofa, I decided to redirect the conversation instead. "You can call me Bilan, Iesha. That'll never be wrong."

"But Mommy told me I can't. She said you're baby Deek's mommy, and he's my cousin. So, I have to call you..."

"Aunt Bilan isn't necessary if you don't feel it."

"You won't be mad?" I shook my head. "But Ivy calls you auntie."

"And I like that very much." I readjusted the baby so I could sit back comfortably like Iesha.

"But you won't be mad if I don't?"

I shook my head again. Iesha looked perplexed.

"You know what I want more than anything?"

"What?"

"To be cool with you again. I liked when we were friends." I twisted my lips, brows furrowing. "No. I actually loved when we were friends."

Iesha lifted a brow, distrusting. "You did?"

"Of course, I did. I told you, you were the first—besides your uncle—to welcome me into the family. You were so sweet and protective of me. I'm really sorry if by me having a baby you thought I betrayed you. I didn't mean to, Iesha."

Iesha's eyes dropped to Sadik's feet. She didn't have a response, and I didn't expect her to at her age. Iesha likely didn't recall why she'd stopped "liking" me.

"Did Uncle Deek and I move too fast?" I asked. "Did you need more time before I got as close to him as I did and have a baby?"

She nodded, although I didn't think she quite appreciated what she was admitting.

"Do you love your little cousin here?"

Her eyes roved up to Sadik, and Iesha nodded. "A lot. He's cute and sweet."

"He is, isn't he? Now, imagine not having him around. Doesn't he make the family happy, especially with all the craziness happening? We need little blessings like Sadik. You're a blessing to us, too, you know?"

"I know," she mumbled.

"You're such a blessing that everyone would worry if they woke up and saw you weren't in bed where you're supposed to be."

Her sleepy eyes met mine. "I can't sleep. Ivy keeps snoring and farting." She crossed her arms and pouted.

"Farting?" I giggled.

"Yeah. She let out a big one, and I had enough." Iesha let out a little scoff.

She was adorable in her little pink bonnet and long sleeve gown.

"You wouldn't have known she was snoring and farting if you were asleep yourself." I tilted my head. "Right?"

Iesha hung her head. "I'm scared."

"Of what?"

"Of that man coming to get me."

"He won't."

"He almost did."

"But he can't here."

Her face tightened. "How do you know?"

"Because your PaPa, dad, and uncle pay the best men around to protect you. That man may have gotten lucky and slipped into your school, but it won't happen again, and it definitely won't happen here. They'll make sure of it."

"But my daddy isn't here anymore."

"Do you think because he isn't here, bad things like that can happen?"

She nodded her head. "Daddies protect. My daddy's sick. He can't protect us. That's why that man tried to take me."

"Awwww, Iesha, come here." I waved her over to me. She didn't hesitate to scoot over. "Your dad wouldn't have been at your school even if he wasn't in the hospital. That foolish man would have tried anyway, and it wouldn't have worked because your parents and grand-parents put you in a safe school that would have protected you some way or another. Your dad did that. He made sure he and your mom thought ahead for accidents like this. And trust me, there's no hospital in the world that could keep your dad, PaPa, and uncle back if you were to disappear." I squeezed her to me.

"You think so?"

"I know so." I nodded, though she couldn't see me. "You know, before meeting your uncle, I used to live by myself. I was scared a lot."

She turned to face me. "Where was your dad?"

"My aabo—what we called our dad—died a few years ago. I was much older than you, but I think I felt what you're feeling now. There's nothing like a father's protection."

That wasn't my truth, though. I'd never felt as protected by my father as I had Sadik. I'd seen my father harassed and heckled several times; those experiences were where my fear likely cultivated. Sadik would never be tried the way my father had. I wouldn't tolerate it.

He did tonight...

"But you have what I didn't," I shared.

"What's that?"

"You have a PaPa and uncle that love you very much, and who will protect you against the world. When your uncle brought me to this place I felt like a princess in a castle. No dragon or army can overtake *Elliswoods Palace*. Your PaPa built it to be sure of that. We're here where no one can hurt or harm us. Look." I lifted Sadik's little leg and let it drop on my lap. "Even Sadik is so secure and feels so safe, he's sleeping like a log."

What started as a giggle ended in a yawn. "He's knocked out."

"He is. Those fears I used to have when I lived alone can't be brought here."

"Because of PaPa and Uncle Deek?"

I nodded. "Your Uncle would never let anyone harm me. Or his children, or his nieces who he adores."

"Why you say children? You mean baby Deek, right?"

The girl was sharp. My face opened in a reserved smile. "Uncle

Deek and I are having another baby." I hated the lack of confidence in my voice.

Iesha's eyes grew wide. "Another one?"

I nodded. "Another to love and lift the family," I reminded her.

"But could this one be a girl, 'cause Uncle Deek don't play with us like he used to?"

That broke my heart, and not because I thought she meant to slight me or my children. It was because she was feeling the effects of the rift between her father and uncle and didn't know it. Sadik hadn't spent time with the girls like he once had.

"We can only hope for what we want." I sat up. "C'mon. I hope your mom and sister aren't worried sick about you."

We stood and headed for the door. She held my hand all the way around the corner and down the marble hall to her room. When we stopped at her door, I knelt next to her, Sadik unbothered.

"I'm so glad I ran into you tonight," I spoke honestly. "I really missed having you as a friend."

"Can I tell you a secret?" I nodded. "It was hard not telling you how pretty you look at the table."

"Pretty?"

She nodded with a smile. "You're very pretty and nice. I didn't like when you stopped visiting that time." She was referring to my time in *Macen Beach*. "I'm happy you're back."

I had no more tears left from my bout earlier with her uncle, but my heart cried of joy. This felt like unsullied love.

"Thank you, Iesha," I croaked.

She opened the door and stepped inside the darkened room. "You should ask TiTi Stacy about that bug. She can help you with your throat with her teas."

My face opened in realization and I nodded. "Okay."

I stood to my feet as she closed the door. The goofy smile on my face was unfair, but it revealed my heart. I was grateful for that moment with Iesha. She may not have given me the prefix of *auntie*, but she sure felt like family to me.

"Let's go to bed, Black boy joy," I whispered to Sadik, who was still knocked out in my arm.

I lifted him to my shoulder and carried him that way. When I turned the corner for the east wing, a clear cut view of the south caught my eye. Monica was toeing up the stairs wearing a tight mini skirt and a low-cut tank exposing a generous portion of her cleavage while holding high heels in her hand. She was as quiet as a rose petal falling to the floor.

Adrenaline coursed my veins and my entire frame trembled as though in fear. But I wasn't. I felt utter astonishment from her boldness. Where was baby Irene? Why wasn't Monica here for Iesha's slip away?

Just when I allowed myself to feel hope for the healing of this family, I was doused with the reality of just, in fact, who they are. The mess they created.

Excessive vibrating of both phones awakened me. My eyes strained open to the dim room, the rising morning sun crept between the heavy curtains. I reached over to the nightstand to grab both. It was Rory, calling on each line.

"Yeah?" I answered, taking her call from one line.

"911 changing the morning itinerary," her commanding morning rasp made my face fold. "We need to move now. I'll meet you in the yard."

"Understood." After disconnecting the call, I checked for the time. It was just before six in the morning, and I was due to rise soon anyway. Waking early to a call of that nature was never ideal.

After returning the phones to the nightstand, I rubbed my eyes, trying to fully rouse. A heavy petite sigh had my attention going to the right of me. Sadik was on his side between two pillows. His mother was on the other side of the pillow farthest from me with her hand draped across his little torso. Bilan's lips were swollen and parted. Her freckles almost invisible on those molded cheekbones.

Sentiments from last night began to flood my brain. Sofia confronted me in a drunken rage, disgorging unbalanced facts. Worst of all, Bilan believed each one, including the possibility of me fucking around on her. Feeling remnants of anger, I turned away, rubbing my eyes. I'd told her not to bother Sadik. She needed the rest. We'd gotten in late last night. I guess a mother's love trumped father's orders.

One week...

We'd been married just over a week and fought nearly each day. This isn't what I wanted for her, for them. For us.

I leaned over and lifted my son from the bed. He stirred in my hands as I kissed his soft cheek, carrying him to his crib on the other side of the room. I placed him inside and watched him drift back off with pride. Sadik made me feel grand and accomplished. I had so much to look forward to in his development.

But first...

My gaze swept across the room to his mother still asleep. I traversed the room, arriving at her side of the bed. Laying asleep, Bilan appeared a different human being than she was when she flipped out. Last night wasn't her usual meltdown. It was her spazzing the fuck out. Jealousy was an unnecessary virtue with me as far as she was concerned.

I pulled down the comforter and reached for her leg, turning her onto her back. Slipping between her legs, I forgave her for the gown I had to roll up to get to her naked pussy. My treasure. The musky scent had my balls pulsing. I trailed my tongue between her thick labia. When I brushed over her clit, her pussy leaped into my face. I scooped her ass cheeks in my hands and lifted her closer to me. Bilan's puss first thing in the morning was better than any breakfast served on a plate. It was just as pretty as it was delicious.

Her thighs spread wider, hands found their way to my scalp in a deep grip. She rocked slowly into my face. Above the bed of her pubic hairs I found her gazing down on me with tight, lazy eyes and her bottom lip between her teeth. I stabbed my tongue into her wet cavity, causing a deep groan from her. She lifted the gown over her breasts, revealing beautiful mounds with pebbled apexes. Her eyes rolled back and back bowed over the bed.

When I started sucking on her swollen nub, her thrusts to my face increased. Her whimpers turned into full moans, the sound putting increasing pressure on my swelling cock against the mattress. Our cadence synced and that's when I knew she was ready to detonate.

I rose to my knees, releasing myself from my boxers.

"Sadik..." her cry was thick, guttural as I fisted myself.

I lay over her, swiping my sensitive head over her slit to wet myself. When I pushed into her, Bilan shivered similar to last night in the limo. This time, she had the benefit of her hands and her nails bit into my ass as I rocked into her wetness. She was warm, snug, and so inviting. Her muscles relaxed when I thrusted in and spasmed when I pulled out.

"New day, better us," I grunted, enjoying feeling the back of her walls.

One of her soft hands moved up to the back of my head while the other gripped my ass, inspiring my dives into her. Beneath me, she was soft, but not fragile; greedy, but collected. Slamming into her, I felt absolute and able to meet any need she may have.

"I want us to come...together today," I wheezed, my hands moved to cup her ass, mouth buried into her neck. The faster I rocked into her, the wetter she became. Her pussy clenched around me, propelling my explosion. "Come. Now, Nalib!"

I thrusted and thrusted and bit into her neck, then sucked it. Within seconds, Bilan shuddered beneath me, setting off my own flight into orbit. Her pussy quaked as she threw it on me over and over again. My mind whirred until all I felt was her. All that existed was Bilan and me. I could live here. Shit, I'd fight to live in an empty space with just me and my treasure: my wife.

"Took you long enough," Rory hissed as I gaited into the garage, pulling on my suit jacket.

"I had shit to address."

"Shit to address?" Rory asked as Johnson slipped behind the wheel of the *Maybach*.

"Yeah," I responded, straightening the collar of my jacket. "Pussy to eat to answer to the bullshit my wife witnessed last night."

"Oh, that?"

"Yeah." I scoffed as she held the door for me. "That. Now, what are you going to do to address it?"

Rory lifted her shoulders in a shrug. "I ain't do shit, and I got cussed the fuck out."

I shook my head. "You got cussed out because you handled Sofia with a fuckin' tucked tail."

"I was tryna be respectful!"

"It doesn't work that way with women in my world, particularly with my wife."

"Fuck you mean? You ain't never have a wife before—shit, a wifey either. How the fuck I'm 'posed to know how to handle shit?"

"Then imagine how the hell I feel every day. At least I use common sense and not make the old chick feel half as significant as the wife."

"The fuck I do?" she squealed.

"You called her 'mami' and 'Sofee' instead of addressing her by her full name, and you were pleading with her to leave. Even my *'fuck outta here'* game would've been better than that. But I couldn't use it because it would've looked very suspect to everyone around, especially to my wife."

There was no way I'd lose my cool over a woman other than Bilan. Doing that would make me appear emotionally attached, something I was not.

"So I was 'posed to manhandle shortie?"

"Eliminate the threat respectively. It's what you're paid to do, not fuckin' negotiate!"

"A'ight." She took a step back, cupping one hand over the other at her pelvis. "So what the fuck I'm 'posed to do now? I can't eat her pussy." Her big eyes widened, shoulders lifted, and head bobbled.

I chuckled at her being rattled. "You forget you're a woman, Bean? I'll let you figure that shit out." Rory rolled her eyes. I moved to get inside the car, then stopped with a thought. "I'm going to text you a link. Have it delivered to her this afternoon."

Her eyes ballooned. "Some shit from me to B?"

I snorted, "Hell no. *I'm* still trying to apologize. You ain't get started yet. This is my 'I'm sorry' gift." I laughed so hard, reaching for my stomach. "You're on your own with that one."

Her mouth tightened to keep the expletives to herself, but I knew they were seeping. "We got big fish today. Popov sent a special delivery to the warehouse." She tossed her head to gesture the house.

"My father's?"

She nodded. "I had Jamil lift it and take it to the hideout spot."

Finally, I ducked to get inside the running car.

"Fuck!" Johnson gawped, and Rory and Jamil leaned back from the large box.

We were at a commercial building I owned and used for privacy when my business buildings weren't appropriate. We'd just arrived to find Jamil here waiting with the white Styrofoam box taped shut. Johnson cut the tape and lifted the lid for an unexpected discovery.

"A head?" Jamil asked angrily. "A fuckin' human head?"

Then Johnson croaked, "His fuckin' eye missing!"

"This muthafucka crazy as shit." Rory laughed, clapping her hands. "S.Q.E., 'member we did some shit like this to them Bronx niggas?"

Ignoring that question, I asked, "And how do we know Popov sent this?"

Rory tossed her chin to Jamil, who grabbed a manila envelope and handed it to me. As I opened it, a phone rang. Rory walked to the corner, taking a call.

There were several documents inside the envelope, one the same of what I'd read from Jefferson's documented account. The others were complementary to it. They had a name specified as USSR "confidential informant" and the terms of his agreement. Farther into the details was *The Commission* with a list of its members' names. Paperwork from the *FED*s is limited information since their work is done surreptitiously and, nowadays, more electronically. However, it seemed Popov was able to get his hands on the official record detailing the relationship with this man and the *Federal Bureau of Investigations*. On one piece of paper was a number handwritten in large print.

"A'ight." Rory dropped the phone from her ear, turning to me. "That was J-Dot, saying he on his way in. Look like the nigga, Popov, sent another piece to *Ellis International.*"

Less than two minutes later, J-Dot pushed through the door, holding a smaller box. After the prompting of a nod from me, Johnson retrieved the box and cut the tape with a blade.

When he removed the lid, he nodded with puckered lips. "The muthafucka's thorough."

I shifted closer to the boxer and caught a purple tongue and bloodied eyeball laying on ice. Popov was making a statement. It wasn't him communicating with the *FBI*. It was *this* man.

I sat on the edge of the desk and took a deep breath. "Get him on the line." I handed Rory the paper with the number.

She dialed it and handed over a burner phone. In two rings, I was surprised to discover it was Popov who answered.

"So now we know, hmmm?" He breathed heavily, accent thick and voice taut.

"I don't know shit."

"Let me catch you up. I'm no rat. After your accusation, I needed to find out how true it was. So I did a sweep in my house. The face you're looking at is Afanasi. He was a driver for me. His time in America has been too long. He feared the fucking government here, so you have his head." He snickered. "What a joke, an embarrassment to Rossiya nation. He saw too much, so I cut out his eye. He spoke to the weak Yankee authorities, so you have his tongue. My gifts to Double E Bags. Now, our business can resume, hmmm?"

Unable to rip my eyes from the horror frozen on the head next to me, I allowed an abbreviated pause.

"No."

"No?"

"Your chauffeur boy here is a registered criminal informant with the FBI. You didn't just clean house, you gave that 'weak' agency an invitation to your front door. My father keeps a respectable distance from the authorities. But..." I turned to the blue head. "...your gift was generous. I would share how to profit off Afanasi's organs, but you Russians are far ahead in intelligence, right?"

"This isn't over, Ellis. You remind your father he's the largest disseminator in New Jersey. There's no way I can continue to lose that type of money. Who is his new supplier anyway?"

"Earl Ellis isn't in the business of sales or distribution of any illegal goods, Popov. This chat was cute, though."

I heard him snort on the line. Popov knew I was curving him as much as I understood his threat. This wasn't over. My father would have to answer to him. Popov had been losing millions without my father's business.

"*V kontse terpeniya smert' zhdet.* Do you know what I said?"

I scratched the back of my head. "I'm not fortunate enough to have learned your language."

"I said 'at the end of patience, death awaits.' When I'm done with Double E Bags, there will be nothing left for your son to gain. What's he? Almost three months now?"

A chill surged in my spine at the mention of my legacy.

With pouted lips, I nodded. "A wise man taught me to never overestimate your power based off of 'theater of the mind.' Do you know what that means?"

"Ehh," he hummed with condescension. "Enlighten me."

"Theater of the mind is what you imagine. Those thoughts that act out in your favor and entertain you. It's safer to stick with empiricism. The Ellis name has been tried and proven. I'm not the 'crazy nigga' you saw coming. I'm the persistent, calculating monster you'll meet at the end of your patience. When I'm called, it's personal and permanent." I motioned my men to wrap up the boxes. They'd be sent to an incinerator. "Wield your patience with wisdom."

I heard when Popov disconnected the call. When I pulled the burner back, it was black.

"What we 'posed to do with this?" Rory asked, holding her nose.

"Burn it." I stood from the desk. "I just bought us some time with him. How much, I don't know." I waggled the papers in the air. "These need to be confirmed today."

"You want me to hit Double E's peeps with a heads up?" Jamil asked.

"Nah." I scratched my chin. This was above my father. Popov had access to my wife and threatened my kid. "It's only going to get kicked back to me anyway."

"Facts." He nodded, pinching the hairs on his chin. "We got a dope ass round of soldiers for this war, boss."

"No fuckin' cap," Rory confirmed.

Music to my ears...

We may have just commenced the biggest war we'd ever undertaken.

"Take the money...
Take the fame.

Take this old body...

Change my name." I heard a chorus sang a short distance from the kitchen as I traveled the halls of *Elliswoods Palace.*

"And deep down inside, what you'll find...

Is a worshipper until the end of my time.

No, I'm nothing special...

Oh, Lord, I'm tired and through.

I'm decidedly your vessel!" I turned the corner to find the industrial-sized kitchen filled with working bodies, many of them engaged in belting harmonically.

A few shouted phrases of praise I'd heard at the Ellis' church when I visited. They seemed to be incited by one another.

"Hallelujah! Hallelujah!" one woman sang into the sink over and over again.

"Praise Him!" another declared.

One, with her back to me, waved a cloth in the air with sheer exuberance.

Someone shushed the group, two tapped others to get their attention.

"Ms. Bilan!" Candy approached me with a sheepish expression. "Sorry about that. We sing sometimes to help pass the time. Mrs. Ellis likes it and sometimes joins in."

Suddenly, I felt like an interloper. Everyone had faced away, carrying on with their duties.

"Please!" I laughed nervously. "Don't stop because of me. You guys sounded like the real recording—well, I know only Ragee sings that part. But your sound..." I was at a loss for words. Gospel music wasn't something I was too familiar with, but I knew all of Ragee's catalog. I'd followed him over to that genre when he'd include a 'psalm of worship' at the end of each album. He even had a full one I purchased, though I didn't listen to it as often as I did his others. "I can see why my mother-in—" I caught myself and covered my mouth with my fingers. "Mrs. Ellis enjoys it."

There was a light spirit in this kitchen filled with Black and brown faces.

"It's definitely a perk for working here," Candy replied with a warm smile. "Is there anything I can help you with?"

My eyes burst like a deer in headlights. I'd forgotten that quickly. Their music had me befuddled.

"I... *Uhhhh*..." I rolled my eyes, trying to get my thoughts together. "I'm done with work and the baby's napping. I'm bored out of my mind and thought to see if I could help with dinner. I thought it would be great to hang out with adults. I haven't been in a busy kitchen in forever. I can help with anything."

I was also hoping to catch Irene in here. She hadn't been around since we arrived days ago.

"Sure." Candy turned around, considering my offer. "You bake, right?" I guessed Irene shared that with her staff.

"Yeah."

"Mr. Ellis requested his favorite, which is sweet potato pie. His doctors okayed a small slice. The girl who does the best crust called out today. Think you can handle that?"

I sucked in a breath. "In a jiffy, yeah!"

When I moved to make my way to an empty sink to wash my hands, my name was announced from the other side of the kitchen.

"A package arrived for you. It's in the foyer," Stacy advised.

"Oh!" I chirped, finding that odd. "Candy, I'll be right back."

"Okay!" she called behind me.

My journey to the front end of the house was with impatience. I wanted to get back to the kitchen and get to work. I turned corners and passed rooms, feeling proud of myself for learning my way around a little more. It was typically quiet around unless the family was congregated in a room. So when I heard a deep voice speaking into a phone or such, I slowed my stride. It was near the opening of the formal family room, the same one I'd met the Ellis siblings and grandchildren in a year ago.

Who would be in there?

I stopped near the opening. "Your beard makes you look old." A woman on a device laughed.

"Old? How old are we talking?" I craned my neck just enough over the column to see Tom Banks with his back to me, engaged in a *FaceTime* conversation with a woman.

I couldn't make out much of her from my vantage point.

"Old like 40, old!" She fell into laughter again. "Your old lady is turning you into an old man."

Tom let out a breath. "Yeah. Okay! Ain't nothing old about me but my brain and experience between the damn sheets."

"Whatever!" she sang. "Are we doing the trip to Antigua, or what? You told us you had the hookup, plane and all. Or don't you have that clout over there in the Ellis castle?" She goaded him.

"Shit, I don't lie about a damn thing. I'm working on it. I don't think the island'll be in use for a while. So much shit's been going on around—"

"Speaking of," she cut him off. "How are you all relaxed, posted up in the royal melanin's tower so comfortably like this?"

"C'mon, Britt. Too many hours in that library's got your little indexed brain malfunctioning. Will Sofia be coming?"

My eyes ballooned.

Sofia, Sofia? Sadik's Sofia?

"I don't think she can be around anything belonging to an Ellis after last night's fight," the woman snickered.

That was Brittany, Brittany. Sofia's friend, Brittany.

Tom countered, "When she sees the inside of the *Bombardier Global 7500*, she'll be cured of all things Ellis instantly. You a member of the mile-high club?" He laughed. "That shit's different on a *Bombardier 7500*! You have to try it."

"With who?"

He cackled. "I mean... I do have experience."

I whipped my body away, unable to listen any further. How could he disrespect Sadik's mother that way?

And be so damn corny about it!

I was disgusted as I reversed and took another route to the foyer. A longer route. Much of my anger was because I had to bottle all of the "Sodom and Gomorrah" experience I'd incurred in *Elliswoods Palace*. I had no one to bounce them off of. I couldn't share with my friends, feeling a loyalty to this family who couldn't be faithful to each other, and during a trying time.

I fumed on my hike across the mansion, ignoring the two staff members I passed. When the foyer opened, there was a beautiful floral bouquet on the table next to the usual fresh one on display. A ginormous balloon floated over the flowers. It read in big print "I'M SORRY," and in between those two words were a smaller, different font that read "not" and "broke the condom." So on first glance, you think it said I'm sorry when in totality, it read "I'M not SORRY I broke the condom."

My hand flew to my mouth as it dawned on me, Sadik and I never used a condom.

"Cute..." I giggled to myself.

Next to the vase was a medium-sized, black *Chanel* shopping bag. Inside was a box wrapped in a white ribbon. I released the tie and removed the fabric, then the lid. Next, I unfolded the flaps to the velvet cloth, which revealed a long, layered necklace adorned with pearls and metal. My nipples tingled at the sight of its tiers. It brought images of erotica to mind. Sadik enjoyed me in *Chanel* necklaces and nothing else.

Tears upended from my belly and my hand shot to my mouth again. How could a gesture so thoughtful sadden me? It was because I felt it. The disconnect in this family. Everyone was scattered, emotionally. Minutes ago, I heard the matriarch being disrespected by her lover. Last night, my sister-in-law having a lover was confirmed. Taaliba was busy sneaking off to create a life with a drug lord she didn't know if she wanted forever with. My nemesis of a brother-in-law had just awakened from a coma and was likely a shell of himself. All the while, the head of the family had been busy trying to keep his lair of lovers secured as he recovered from complications of a heart attack.

And finally, my husband, their golden child, had emotionally parted from his entire family it seemed, only interested in his new nuclear brood. Where was the ironclad unit that intimidated and terrified me less than a year ago? Times had indeed changed. Gone was the lineage Sadik boasted about when trying to gain my attention at *Michelle's* last spring.

16

"*Rain down on me!*" Several high-pitch women belted.

"*Re-Re-Re-Re-Rain down on me,*" a second set of women with slightly deeper vocals sang.

They repeated the series over a track and the hand-drumming on the metal worktop performed by David, the new pastry chef I interviewed when told the kitchen was in need of one. I clapped my hands and swayed along with them. This kitchen choir thing had grown on me. I was in love with them and looked forward to the days I was in charge of planning dinner for the family.

As I bobbed and mouthed along with the catchy lyrics, it dawned on me it had been a whole month since I nervously came in here, meekly asking to help out. And now I was here, at least, twice a week organizing meals. It had been a wonderful distraction. This morning, after a conference call for work, I started my lemon meringue pie and had to refrigerate the filling for a few hours. Next was an even more significant meeting I'd been looking forward to. However, before leaving, I'd gotten caught up in the chorus of the kitchen and couldn't resist rocking out with them.

I'd been managing my two summer courses easily, and even conquered my workload at *Ellis Academy* in record timing while bonding with my baby. S.Q.E., II was approaching four months now. He'd been developing nicely. He was such a sweet, interactive baby and had practically been sleeping through the night for the past couple of weeks. Once in a while, I brought him down here to say hello to the kitchen family. That's what they were to me at his point, and relatively quickly.

"*Rain down on me!*
Re-Re-Re-Re-Rain down on me!
Rain down on me!
Re-Re-Re-Re... Rain—"

The abrupt halt had me blinking hard. My head whipped left to right to see what I'd missed and what, *clearly*, most had caught. That's when I smelled him. I could detect the *John Varvatose's Artisan* mixed with his natural body oil a mile away. I must have been too caught up in the music to have been aware.

I peered over my right shoulder while leaning on the metal island countertop and found Sadik's hard frame golden and suited. His felines were trained on me, full lips with a slight gloss parted. The bespoke custom suit draped around his taut body was tailored to the specifications of each inch of him. He stood urbane in the kitchen with reckless elegance, commanding the attention of several of the women in the room. I was used to it. The topic of Sadik's superior features had been hinted around the kitchen in my presence.

Blinking excessively again, I swallowed hard. "Hey..." I breathed, trying to collect myself. "You leaving for the day?"

He'd been on a conference call all morning in Earl's office. That had been my husband all month: engrossed in work and Julius' policy implementations. By day, Sadik ran his conglomerates, and by night —and in between, at times—he was Julius' brainchild for the city of Paterson. It wasn't until late at night when he'd creep into our room, shower, and oftentimes sleep under our son's crib that I shared the same space as him. I'd have to awaken him to come to bed.

"Yes. My call is done." He affectionately yanked at the *Ase Garb* scarf I had ornamentally wrapped around my head. It was his. "You mentioned something about a hair appointment while I was in the shower."

"Oh..." I called the reminder out to him from the door of the bathroom this morning. That was the last time I'd seen him. "Yeah. The appointment is at two. Just thought you wanted to know."

"I do. Thanks. I can call to see if Imani can squeeze you in for a massage before dinner."

I sucked in a breath. "You can?"

He lifted a brow. "I'd like to." Then his hand was on me again, tracing a line down my jaw with his thumb. "I need for you to be relaxed and as stress-free as possible with this one." His hand was on my belly. "You heard what Dr. Clifford said."

A belly that had made its presence known over the past few weeks. I was larger this time around than I was when carrying Sadik, but that was to be expected with a second pregnancy.

A smile opened on my face. "Okay. I guess I'll have to fish for a driver for this afternoon."

"Rory will be happy to take you." He smiled mischievously.

My face tightened. "So would Robert, one of the drivers here. In fact, I'm sure of it. I'll text him right away."

Sadik's smooth head fell back as he chortled. The dark velvety sound of it caused my belly to flutter.

His unexpected kiss to my lips was too short lived. "I'm out. Enjoy your day." He held my chin.

My hands went to my head. "Yeah. Getting this mop done. I'm looking forward to it." I giggled.

His lips brushed over mine again and we remained nose to nose. "My happiness is predicated on your satisfaction."

Effortlessly stunned, I couldn't speak. Sadik kissed me again before backing away and taking off.

"You okay, Bilan?" Tahlia, one of the cooks, asked.

"Yeah," I breathed. "...now that I've gotten you to call me that instead of Ms. Bilan." I smiled, playing off the obvious: I was perversely smitten by my husband.

Still.

She laughed it off, exposing the beautiful gap between her two front teeth. "Well, that's how Mrs. Ellis referenced you when she told us about her son's 'girlfriend.'" She chortled even harder.

I rolled my eyes at that story. They shared it with me the first week I'd begun spending time in here. Apparently, Sadik bringing home a woman wasn't just a big deal amongst his family. The Ellis staff had thought it surprising, too.

"Speaking of which, I have to go if I want to stay on schedule." I checked the time on my phone. "I'll be back before dinner to finish the pie!"

I dashed out of the kitchen and journeyed the tall halls, even took a set of steps. This trip was a hike for sure, feeling like I was returning to the suite the Sadiks and I shared. It took a few minutes, but I arrived on the east veranda. When I ambled through the opened doors, the sun kissed my face. Already, there was the tea and light refreshments beautifully on display. David and Tahlia did a wonderful job.

"Whew!" I blew out air, taking a seat. "Am I ever going to get used to the commute around here?"

My eyes were cast to the lovely garden. The trees in bloom were full and healthy, those out of season were manicured and kept neat over the picture green lawn sprawled out for miles.

A soft giggle had me turning my attention toward Irene. She sat in the padded lounge chair with a knitted blanket draped around her shoulders. Her legs were crossed as they bounced to a rhythm for comfort.

"I take the elevators now." Her smile was demure, reserved from the lack of excitement.

I turned to her, not wanting to dance around the obvious. It had taken weeks to work up my nerve for this conversation. Endless days of spending time with Ivana and Iesha, listening to their talks and honesty about staying at *Elliswoods Palace* for a month now in virtual isolation. So many experiences of Monica being completely absent, even when she was in the room with us for our weekly dinners.

And my husband...

My lord, Sadik had been so detached. He'd been so engrossed in work and Julius' policy cabinet, these blatant signs of the family being in breakdown hadn't come up. He worked long days, coming in exhausted. At most, I'd get developments on the home we were having built and often nights of quick and hard passion before he reached the baby's crib to succumb to siesta.

It had been a surreal time with the Ellises over the past month. So many glaring telltale signs of dissension, like how Sadik hadn't gone to visit Iban once in the hospital. When I asked about it, his short replies of rebuff would end the attempt at conversation. It was sad. Just sad what this family had been spiraling to.

"The Fourth of July is coming. I was hoping to find out what your plans are for the family."

"I don't have any, my love." She sighed. "I've been so tired and overwhelmed with everything."

My lips pouted and brows met. "Like what?"

She scoffed too spiritedly. "Well, you know. Earl has been down, and so has Iban. The house is a lot to keep up, I have work...my grands have been over..." She quieted for a moment. "It's been a lot on me."

Lies. She sat and lied as though I hadn't been privy to all the family's woes this year, much less living with her this past month. And she spoke it so boldly, demonstrating the disconnect I'd detected over a month ago. I'd arranged the grandchildren's photoshoot, something her photographer had been on a regular schedule for. Stacy informed he called for a date and time, and she asked me to do it seeing Irene had been a fraction of herself.

I sat up in my seat, tossing my left leg over the arm to gain a better view of her. "Can I be candid for a minute?"

Her gaze swept over to mine. "Sure, dear."

"You're being dishonest."

"About what?"

"About everything: you, your marriage, children, work, and family in general."

"How do you mean?"

"I know a little about psychology." I scoffed. "Hey... I don't declare to know you as well as Sadik and even Taaliba do, but I've seen you at a different pace. You were not too long ago the backbone of this family, and now you're a scary wimp."

"Wimp?" Her head snapped back. "Excuse me?"

"How often are you downstairs seeing about Earl?"

"I don't have to live down there with him. He has the medical staff."

"And his companions?"

"Bilan, *wha*—" Her brows furrowed. "What about them?"

"Are you okay with them spending more time with him while he's down than you?"

"I spend time with Earl."

"Likely as much as a friend, but not a wife—with all due respect, Irene."

"I don't just have Earl to be concerned about. You forget I have children and a whole staff to tend to?"

"When was the last time Taaliba stayed here at night?"

"She's here every night, like we're all supposed to be." I shook my head to dismiss that claim. I was no snitch. *Shoot!* I'd been sneaking out for gym sessions with my old trainer, Dimitri, something I knew Sadik would blow a gasket over if he knew. But the Irene I knew would have a better pulse on what's going on in her home, especially because we'd been on lockdown. "I just saw her this morning when I had my coffee, Bilan."

I shook my head; Irene was missing the point.

"How have the girls been since the near-kidnapping of Iesha?" I tried again.

Irene pulled in a deep breath with closed eyes, turning her head.

"Listen, Irene, I swear, I'm not belittling or judging you. I'm simply holding a mirror to you. Do you realize I've been here a month and this is my sixth time seeing you?" My head tilted for emphasis. "I'm trying to make a plea to you."

"For what?" she shouted, lively for the first time.

There was bite in that one question, a side of the matriarch I'd never seen.

"For you to wake up out of the funk you've been wading in for months now."

"It takes time!" she cried, no longer looking at me.

"It's taken too much time. Your family is out of sorts. Your staff has been held together by Stacy...more than usual. I've been asked to take on a few of your responsibilities at work because *Ellis Academy* is a full-fledged institution that needs dedication, too."

I stood from my chair and scooted it closer to her. "I heard your executive assistants are going to the board to ask that they remove you."

"The board?" she spat the words. "I'm the head of the board!"

"A board with enough members to vote you out should they see need."

Her palm slammed to her chest. "What need?"

"Your disengagement to...life!" I swung my arms into the air. "You're not yourself. You're not whole, Irene. Even I, the newcomer in your family—" I pointed to her. "—know this. This family isn't ordinary. You have jets, own an island—your home is an entire zip code, and not to mention, you have a freakin' army brigade in your back yard!" I pointed over the balcony. I'd seen men run circuits with guns out near the gun range on several occasions. It would have been frightening last year as his anxious girlfriend and lover. This year, I understood that type of discovery was par for the course in this family. "What happened to Earl and Iban is called life. It comes in ebbs and flows...valley lows and mountain peaks. You can't throw the whole thing away and succumb to the blues—or whatever you're stuck in—when a double portion comes your way."

"And Palmer," she murmured, sucking her teeth sulkily.

Still sensing a wall between us, tears tugged from my eyes. Had I imagined the cape she wore when helping me with my brother last fall? Perhaps Irene wasn't a superwoman after all.

"Palmer's gone and never coming back," I made clear. "If his presence in your husband's world gave you peace of mind, that luxury is over," I croaked, heart breaking each time Irene spoke.

She had been a shell of herself, and I feared her inability to return. The matriarch had fallen from her throne. If this woman was no longer sound, available, and hands on, I feared for my husband. Sadik worshipped his mother, relied on her sharp wisdom and maternal resolve. She was his rock, shoes I could never fill.

"You have no right to judge me, Bilan!" She shouted. "Is that why you brought me out here? Have I not done enough to prove to you I'm a kind woman? Have I not given and given to my family enough to be shown compassion for this major cataclysm in my damn life?"

I shot to my feet, mouth balled.

She leaned back in her chair in horror of my reaction. "*What*—" She stammered. "Why are you crying?"

I wiped my face with too much speed and force. "The woman I thought to be the quintessential, lionized, Black matriarch all this time has possibly been the overwhelmed, privileged princess unworthy of the spoils provided for you." I turned for the doors.

"Spoils?" She chirped. "Where do you see spoils, young lady?"

"In your husband downstairs in recovery. In Iban, who's still alive. In Sadik, who after all these years is finally walking deeper into his manhood and creating his own family. In Taaliba, whose wings have yet to grow in full bloom so she can develop emotionally and be confident enough to fly. Your unavailability has become an albatross, preventing her from growing into an independent adult.

"In Ivana and Iesha, who are so discombobulated with the absence of their father. And even though they grew up in this house, they feel the place to be foreign because a huge element of *your* home is missing." I tilted my head. "Your spoil is also the business you've cultivated. It's a girl's dream, fully thriving after more than a quarter of a century." I wiped my face again. "Your fortune is in your faith. You're clear on your spirituality, right? Where is the application of that belief?"

Heartbroken, I stepped inside and headed to my suite.

"Next on the agenda," Julius asked, tapping his pencil over the legal pad he carried impatiently.

His eyes were red, shirt undone at the collar and sleeves rolled up. At this hour and only one month into his term, I could understand his exhausted state.

"Yeah, because this community partnering with the *Bronze Heat* group from the fire department is getting played out." Sofia, seated across the table, fingered through a stack of papers. "We've only been visible at schools and senior facilities—oh, and at *Eastside Park*. The next is obviously a policy deliverable from the campaign trail."

"Like corrupt policing?" His excitement was abrupt.

"No," she returned just as quickly. "I was thinking one of the bigger promises like cleaning the city. There are several businesses vying for real estate here. It's time to let them in."

"Begin gentrification?" I noted with clear mockery.

Sofia's long lashes batted as she visibly decided on a tone for me. Her lips pursed before forming a coerced smile. "You know me well enough to know I'm not a proponent for gentrification. The city of Paterson deserves the right to retain its heart and soul even through cabinet changes." She tapped the head of her *Tiffany & Co.* pen against the legal pad beneath her breasts. I was familiar with the writing implement because I'd purchased it for her mother to gift to Sofia when she graduated with her master's degree. "Let's be civil here."

Her tone softened considerably when addressing me. Sofia and I were able to move past her drunken meltdown after the victory party last month. Not only did Julius rip into her ass before I addressed it myself, but when I did get to her, by the time I was done, Sofia was visibly shaking. She apologized profusely and offered to do the same to my wife, something I wouldn't permit. There was no fathomable reason for those two to engage in discourse. Besides, my Nalib was unpredictable when rattled. She was pregnant and I couldn't trust my wife to think of the safety of our unborn child during a violent episode.

Taking a deep breath, I sat back in my seat, casually perusing Julius' new digs in City Hall. There were pictures of him with Keisha, others with her and their children. I spotted one of his mother. Another image posted on the alder wainscoted walls with a walnut finish was of him and a former professor at *Blakewood University*. His degrees were on display, too. These were all the hallmarks of an accomplished man achieving his dreams, which was why I was utterly stunned at the sight of a framed picture of the two of us on graduation day, fully uniformed in hood and gowns.

Abandoning the sentiment, I returned my regard to Sofia. "Which business that you're aware of has expressed interest?"

The tapping of the pen increased as her eyes rolled across the room. "Several. A few local grocery stores, bodegas, a couple of car shops, and hair salons."

Each type of enterprise she named was likely belonging to Hispanic entrepreneurs. There were only a handful of grocery stores still left in Paterson. Major grocers like *Pathmark* and *Acme* had packed up and left years ago, opening the opportunity for smaller ones to start up.

"The only Black-owned grocery store in the city would be my father's."

She readjusted herself in her seat. "What are you saying?"

"Simply that those potential businesses you've mentioned are all likely of Hispanic heritage," I made clear.

"Yeah, Sofee," Julius added. "None are Black, I bet," he groaned, hands reaching to brush frustratingly down his face.

She shrugged, virtually confirming it. "Those are the ones expressing interest!" Sofia argued.

"To a fellow-Latina," I had to indicate.

Her chest fell, as did her eyes. "Are we about to make this about Black versus brown again, Ellis?" Sofia forewent the eye contact necessary to make a sound argument.

I guessed she was still stingy my wrath regarding the victory party check.

"I have no desire to." I plucked a vibrating phone of mine from the table, quickly scanning a text message. "I will, however, state for the record my only condition for accepting this role was to advance the development and agenda for Black men and women in the city. The moment that possibility deviates, I have no interest here."

Sofia chewed the inside of her jaw, peering away.

"What do you propose we tackle next, Ellis?" Julius inquired. "I have a young and motivated staff locked, loaded, and ready to take flight."

I shifted my regard to the blonde with dark roots, which is what I saw more of than her actual face at the moment. "I was actually thinking along the same lines as Sofia, however, on a leveled playing field." She finally returned her gaze my way. "Returning the community, in an ownership manner, to the residents who were here first."

Her brows pinched. "Whites were here first."

"And they left, yielding the city to Blacks." I tossed my chin to Julius. "It's time to engage in cooperative economics."

"Co-op?" Sofia chirped, narrow shoulders lifting. "Of what kind, specifically?" She raised a palm. "And please be comprehensive because lots of those ideas sound great *in theory* but can't be implemented for shit. Low-income people will remain poor while owning their homes. That's not great economics. That's putting more weight on their shoulders and increasing the likelihood of deeper poverty."

Julius' head bounced left and right like a ping pong ball.

When it landed my way, I added, "Community land trusts. Low-income families are afforded the opportunity to own property, equity is formed while it all remains affordable to the owner."

"How?" Julius asked.

"Joint control. With community land trusts, property is purchased by the trust. Then forthcoming, low or middle-income homeowners agree to a long-term, renewable lease instead of a conventional sale of said property. When the homeowner sells the property, he, she, or they earn a portion of the increased value of the property. Ideally, they'll invest in their wealth with what was earned. The balance of the added property value stays with the trust, for the next set of low or moderate-income families. And this goes on for generations, retaining the residence and giving them the opportunity at wealth."

"Really?" Sofia's chin dipped. "Does that really work, though? Long-term leasing?"

I nodded. "The rate of land trusts home foreclosures, in some communities, has been as high as ninety percent less than traditional mortgages. It works."

"That's an astounding stat," Julius breathed, dazed.

"I can have the data sent to you tonight." I tapped the table with my index finger.

"Yeah." He scratched his head, incredulously stuck. "Please do. I'll be pulling another all-nighter with Keisha huffing and twisting until the morning." Jules rubbed his eyes again.

I couldn't feel compassion, however. This was it. It was the role he'd been speaking into existence since I'd known him. This was the big leagues.

I followed Julius' eyes to Sofia.

She was scrolling down her laptop. "A grassroots startup for land co-ops? You've got to be *fuck*—" She swallowed back her comment, governing herself wisely. "It's not as easy as it seems. Have you read the research on it? It usually consists of faith-based organizations. They're difficult to cultivate..." Her head shook in between reading. "The studies will tell you it creates a competition for other grass-roots organizations that have existed prior to said community land trust. People are fallible and can use arbitrary specifications in its selectivity. And finally..." She dropped her face again, her voluminous blonde-dyed mane bouncing over her shoulders. "...it requires either governmental backing or private, neither of which we have time for this term. It could take years to garner the endorsement and funding."

"Shit!" Julius swore, tossing his pen across the table in a tantrum.

His eyes skirted back to me almost immediately, silently asking for a solution.

I sat back in my seat, brows lifting and chin dipping. In direct response, Richards' eyes burst wide, recognizing the gesture of confidence.

"You motherfucker!" he croaked. "What did you do?" A smile crested.

"What I always fuckin' do," I replied with ease. "What Earl Ellis has taught me to do."

Sofia's chest caved, those double Ds she loved sandwiching around my cock resting on either side of her boney sternum still pronounced in appearance. Her lips, I found a familiar experience, pursed. "And what's that?" she breathed, lids lowering in exhaustion from defeat.

"Never to show to a meeting unprepared. I've been meeting with faith-based organizations for months now—nearly a year—beginning with my own. Over the past month, a board has been established with one church."

Her head shot up. "Who?"

"*Olivet Good Shephard* on 14th Ave, a small family-run organization with long-standing roots in the community. Unlike my personal church, they're more humble and modest standing, making them a better visual for the crusade. They'll take the lead in the grassroots effort with several other faith-based and non-profits on the board," I answered.

"And funding?" Jules asked. "Who will we get the backing from?"

"Are you fucking kidding me?" she hissed, head cocked to the side as she peered at Julius.

"Financing has been secured by a private organization from the home state." I announced.

It seemed like the blood had drained from Sofia's face when she uttered at the same time as Julius, "Who?"

I shrugged with my brows. "*McKinnon & Baker*, a large development firm. Mostly commercial."

"Hold up! You mean..." Sofia couldn't speak as fast as her brain moved, it seemed. "Ragee?"

My head dipped in affirmation. "I have a meeting with Marshall Johnson tomorrow to finalize our agreement for funding."

"I know her!" Sofia snapped her fingers, fighting to recall. "She's in finance in the *Kings* organization!"

"The *Connecticut Kings?*" Julius' jaw dropped.

I explained, "Mrs. Johnson grew up in *Riverview Towers*. She's 'Paterson' and has pledged her commitment to seeing the vision of community land funding in her hometown through."

"Fuck!" Julius barked, leaping from his chair and tossed his palm my way. "My fuckin' guy right here! You see that?" I met his palm just in time, understanding what this first implementation of a real policy deliverable meant to my friend's seat as mayor. He began packing up his things. At that prompting, I did the same, hoping to catch Bilan before she fell asleep. I hadn't been keeping up with her eating, which was critical now that she was expecting again. "Not so fast, my extra credit-owner." I glanced up to find him peering down on me.

"Pardon?" I asked, ready to leave the table.

Julius shook his head. "This is an equitable deal. Remember? That means what one policy advisor knows, so must the other." His leer was lethal. "I'll await your data via email while I rub down my wife's feet before she knocks the hell out tonight." With his things in his hands and tucked beneath his arms, he turned back to the table. "Besides, I think you two have had long enough to defrost from last month's quandary." He winked. "Now make it up to me."

The motherfucker took off, leaving us in his office. I sat back and sighed furiously into a balled fist.

"He's right, you know." I glanced over to Sofia wearing a reticent grin. "I totally fumbled over myself—" She rolled her eyes. "—*majorly* fucked up. I could have blown the opportunity of working with one of the brightest, most astute minds I've ever come across." Her expression turned desolate. "I have lots of work to do on myself, I know."

My phone buzzing over the table captured both our attention. I lifted it to find Bilan texted a picture of her and Sadik out in the east garden. The shrubs were perfectly stark, bold colors and the night-lights from the poles illuminated the freckles on her sculpted cheekbones. Those supple lips pouted as she blew a kiss. Her hair an even sheen of fresh jet black curls. My chest tightened at the image.

All mine...

I blackened the phone, placing it back on the table. Reclining in my seat, I sighed, "So, community land trust in Paterson..."

17

I knew the moment he'd awakened because the twitching began. As he lay out in the narrow bed beneath several sheets, he faced the door to his hospital room. His neck twitched like a mechanical device when he slowly turned his head my way. I watched him struggle to focus his one remaining eye. The one damaged by the bullet couldn't be saved.

His body steeled when he registered my presence. Then, for a moment, his entire frame vibrated. Having known him for thirty-nine years, I understood it wasn't from fear, rather contempt.

"Who..." He swallowed, voice so graveled. "Who sent you?" A few difficult breaths dispelled. "Ma ain't...been up much. Pops?"

I lifted my chin. "My wife, actually."

His lone eye circled, brain seemed to be computing. After a moment, he wheezed. "You ain't...have to do me no favors." He tried lifting himself.

"Trust me, I won't," I mumbled, sitting up in my seat. "And now that I'm here, I can let you know you'll be transported to a new facility for the next phase of your recovery."

He didn't respond, though I knew he understood. His fists were clenched at his side, bandaged head awkwardly tilted over his pillow with his one eye patched. Iban looked a gory, weakened sight. I couldn't believe the damage he inflicted on himself and the vulnerable and precarious position he put the family in. News had spread about his near-tragic injury, and it was only a matter of time before the sharks would begin to circle the Ellis dynasty. Unless my father's own revival fast-forwarded, he could be forced out of the game.

I stood to leave, unable to continue to see the imbecile laid before me.

"Hold up..." he choked out. I turned to find the ticks had returned as he searched for a corded remote in his bed. With better mechanical speed than his own motor skills, the bed inclined. The next process was for his head to turn to the opposite side facing me. "You finally got what you want: pop's only gun."

"Nah." I shook my head. "I got a healthy son...in spite of his uncle's selfishness and attention-seeking ass ways. What I've always wanted was what my big brother's had. A bad ass loyal wife and healthy kids. By the grace of God, I still have that after your biggest fuckup to date."

His fists curled again, jaw tightening. "I fucked...up."

"Majorly." I opened the door. "Good luck on that recovery process."

"Last one! One, two, three!" he called the combo, and I implemented it rhythmically and just as fast with burned arms. "That's it."

When done, I barreled over with gloved hands going to my knees, trying to catch my breath. A shower and cheese fries from *B-Way Burger* was the goal for the evening. At after eight-thirty at night, it was late, but I still had another stop before returning to Hunterdon County.

"You come only when you're baking now," Dimitri scolded and teased in his rich Russian brogue, pointing to his stomach.

Out of breath, I stood straight and peeled the gloves off with an unapologetic beam. Dropping them to the floor, my hands went to my small yet expanded belly. "It seems so, doesn't it?"

"I think you know what I mean, Bilan." My stunned regard shot up to him. "I know Sadik Ellis, and I know you know him, too." His lips pouted as he gestured to the belly I was cupping.

I tried to maintain my smile. "Very well."

"I know his family is being heavily guarded and why. You must be coming without his knowledge. It's not safe for you to be here without him knowing."

"I'm coming because I need the sessions. Last year, I missed months of training." *Spellbound and seduced by said Ellis!* "I got pregnant and just had that baby. Months later, I'm pregnant again. I don't want to lose stamina or strength. I may not be the scared damsel I was before taking a hiatus, but I still need the training, Dimi, and you know it."

He stood back, resting on the heels of his feet, expression challenging me. "Ellis does not want me training his lady."

"And why is that?" I was dreadfully curious.

How did they even know each other? When Sadik mentioned Dimitri's name so conversantly last fall, I was too stunned by his patent jealously and possessiveness to consider their acquaintances. That was until three weeks ago when I decided to resume my workouts with my former trainer. Sadik had been too busy to honor his commitment to training me, and my body needed the strengthening. Now, Dimitri's mention of Sadik with a level of familiarity had riled my interest...and concern.

"Because he knew the Dimitri you do not." His blue irises flashed with muted warning.

I switched weight on my legs, hands landing on my hip. "And what does that mean?"

"I don't need any trouble from the Ellises, Bilan. My world is different now. I'm a family man. If he doesn't want you here, I don't think you should be here. You're having his baby again."

"Two weeks after I've come back?" Dimitri didn't respond to my questioning eyes. "Are you dropping me as a client?"

"Only if I see it is making trouble." And just that quickly, there was kindness in his eyes. "Dimitri makes no trouble, no more."

I took a deep breath, recognizing a wall in communication when I saw one. Dimitri repeated the existence of a formal life where he knew the Ellises. That was all the information I needed to infer the obvious. My former trainer was in the illegal trade business once upon a time. I would have never guessed that about him.

Another example of my naïveté...

Breaking my deep gaze at him, I ambled over to my bag and dug into my wallet for his weekly payment. It was almost triple of what I'd paid when I signed up years ago. He'd always been generous with his pricing, but now I didn't need his charity. I needed his knowledge. I'd pay handsomely and what he deserved for his services, and hopefully earn his trust. It could possibly come in handy soon.

Dimitri was right; I had been sneaking under Sadik's nose. I'd been paying an unsuspecting driver and tenured security guard of Earl's to cart me around instead of Sadik's men. My husband had been so consumed with work and public policy, he hadn't asked detailed questions about my time off the compound and I didn't volunteer them either. I simply timed my travel around his leaving and returning to *Elliswoods Palace*. Tonight was even easier to escape because Sadik had ascended on his jet for Atlanta a few hours ago for work. He wouldn't be back for two days.

I tossed my bag over my shoulder and handed the money to Dimitri. "This is for this past week. I'll see you tomorrow afternoon." I smiled, leaving the studio and hopping down the stairs.

Robert was at the foot of the steps waiting on me. As we promenaded to the car, he was visibly on alert with his head swinging and hand at the holster on his hip.

Once inside, I reminded him, "Just one more short stop before *B-Way Burger.*"

"You got it, ma'am."

She yawned again, stretching her chocolate toned thighs in front of her.

Leaning further back in my seat, I laughed at her. "My bad! I'm going to let you go. I know you have to get ready for work. You look miserable."

"Nah. Shit, you good!" She rubbed her eyes, avoiding her long individual lashes. "A bitch woulda probably overslept anyway." I'd called Tasche asking her to come down to say hello, wanting to catch her before her shift. We'd been in front of her place for over twenty minutes now. A smile lifted on her face as she gazed around the car. "Pulling up on a bitch in the Big B! Hahn!" She extended her tongue toward her chin as she fake twerked in her seat. "This bitch is fiyah! I ain't see this shit before."

"It's Earl's...Sadik's father," I explained. Since one of his drivers had been taxiing me around, this *Bentley* had been the chosen vehicle. I heard from Stacy it was bulletproof. A detail I couldn't share with Tasche. "Nice, huhn?" My eyes circled, appreciating the interior lighting.

"Boss level shit," she agreed.

A thought crossed my mind. "Before you go: what are you doing for your birthday? I know we've been hit or miss lately, but trust me; it's been the pace of my life. Some days, I look at my baby and wonder where I've been when I notice a new milestone he reaches. This year is half gone and it feels like a complete blur."

"Don't sweat it, shortie." Tasche waved me off with her hand. "I know how that mother shit consumes you, ya heard. Don't forget my girl, Lex, got three of them now. They so fuckin' cute, and so goddamn busy. I get it." Her head bobbed as she peered out of the window. "But for my birthday?" Tasche shrugged. "I 'on't even know. I know my dude wanna do something special."

My face lit up with wonder like a Christmas tree. "Like what?"

"Get a room or some shit. I 'on't really give a fuck. Maybe fix my room up with them damn rose petals you see at the *Budget Dollar* and candles, cop some *Henny*, and play some Luther." She shrugged again. "I 'on't know. Long as we doing some shit to build something between us, it don't matter. You feel me?"

I nodded with lifting lips. "I thought you'd say a VIP section at a club with your girls." I rubbed my belly. "That may have left me out, though." I pouted ruefully.

"Nah. Fuck them clubs. Since that war in the streets last year with them fuckin' Italians and then the Dominicans, I ain't been wanting to be out like that. But we could do something together. I'll think of something."

"I'm just surprised."

"B, a bitch get tired of the same old fast lane. I'm tryna be like you and Lex: laid the fuck up with my pussy out, smoking a L with my shortie. You feel me?"

"You want a family?" I flinched at that, hands clenching with fistfuls of the hem of my wet shirt. "I'm sorry. I know that's a—I forget sometimes—*most* times." I couldn't stop tripping over my words.

"It's all good, shortie. I'm good with my bones. My princess is living her best life with her father. She good with them on her dad side. Maybe it all worked out for the best." She shrugged while yawning.

I couldn't see how that was possible. A couple of years ago before she moved to Paterson, Tasche's daughter's father filed for sole custody of their daughter after learning she'd gotten beat up pretty bad by a John after work. He waited for her in the parking lot and attacked her. Luckily some guys, cutting through the lot at four in the morning, saw it or she could have been raped or killed. She was hospitalized and kept for two nights. Her daughter's father apparently had enough of Tasche's lifestyle. When he filed, she was in the process of moving to Jersey and thought her daughter was coming with her. She even rented a two-bedroom apartment. The father won full custody. Tasche can only see her daughter when her father grants it. She's only talked about it twice with me, which led me to believe it was a painful loss for her. It understandably should have been.

"I shouldn't have asked that question, though," I murmured.

"It's a legit question, though, Bilan. And my answer is hell fuckin' no!" She laughed. "I'm too old for that shit now, B! It's time for me to grow the fuck up, though. Settle the hell down. I'm getting too old to be turning up with my girls. It's time for some grown-up shit."

My face folded. "You ain't that old, Tasche." Then I thought. "Right?"

"Yeah, girl."

My head remained ahead, still trying to get past my blunder, but my eyes rolled her way. "How old?"

"Shit!" She dropped her foot. "Thirty-seven."

I leaped in my seat, rocking the car. "Thirty-seven?" I parroted. *Tasche's almost Sadik's age? Noooooo way...*

She nodded with an unapologetic smile. "You been fuckin' with a O.G. and ain't even know it, yo."

Her demeanor was casual while I was still in unqualified shock. My eyes roved up her long, strapping mahogany legs to her ever-flat belly, up to her naturally bountiful breasts, and finally up to her smooth, lineless face. Tasche's body appeared as a woman younger than me. She didn't exercise as much as I did and was unfairly muscular.

"You're joking," I choked out. "How old is Lex?"

Completely ignoring my aghast, Tasche chuckled. "She young like you—'bout...three years older than you. She a baby, too, yo."

"How did you two meet?"

"Around the way. She Harlem world. We was in the same schools, but I was a little ahead of her. *Shit!* I shoulda been way ahead of her, but got left back a couple of times, fuckin' wit my moms. She had me missing too many days one year then it got to the point I couldn't keep up the next year. But yeah; me and Lex go way the fuck back, since kids. Then she started working at *Rusty's*. I was dancing and she was waiting tables, and shit. But we went to the same schools—different grades, though."

"Why am I just learning this?"

She shrugged again. "It ain't important 'till you wake up one day and see you been running so fuckin' hard, blowing fuckin' money, fuckin' with no good-ass niggas, and just...wasting mad time, yo." She peered over to me. "I'm tired. Need me a shortie to finish this shit with. Hopefully, somebody that ain't with the shits."

I nodded, still incredibly stunned. "Well, this has been more enlightening than I planned."

Tasche belted a chortle, her palm in the air awaiting mine. "I'm out, yo. I need to call shortie before I get ready for this shift."

"Okay." I ignored her manly dab offering and pulled her into a hug. "I love you too much for hand-smacks." Raw emotion cut through my chords. I knew I smelled of dried perspiration from the gym in the June temperature, but didn't care. "I love you, woman. Grateful to call you friend."

When we withdrew, Tasche mumbled, "Don't start that sappy shit, yo. We good."

I rolled my eyes at that. "Have you heard from Randi?"

"Not really." She yawned again. "My peoples told me she was at *Pulse*. Heard she be there and at *Energy* hard. She prolly at *Pulse* tonight. I think their anniversary's poppin' off." Abruptly, as though struck with a thought, Tasche snapped her fingers. "I meant to tell you some shit, yo!"

"What?" I panicked.

"Ya peoples be at my job!"

"Who?"

"Ya lil' cousin. The one that came to the party you threw me at ya moms' place when I ended up doing that pole class..." I thought for a minute. My face hardening. I recalled no one, likely intoxicated at the party. Tasche sucked her teeth. "The one with the braids! I think you said she a damn trash lady."

My eyes bloomed in realization. "Oh! Brenda?"

"Yeah!" she spat animatedly. "Her. She be at my spot hard. The girls said she be throwing a bundle and shit, yo!"

Brenda?

She was strange, but... Brenda? Aunt Astur would have a conniption if she knew one of my best friends was employed there, much less her daughter patronizing the place. That piece of information thunderstruck me. Poor Brenda had always been strange. Different in more ways than one.

Stunned again, my gaze got stuck at the back of the driver's seat and I nodded. In the recesses of my mind, I knew I had to be urgent with my time.

"That's crazy. Make sure they don't take advantage of my little cousin," I requested. Without waiting for a reply, I groaned, "I need to get going, too."

"A'ight, yo. I'll hit you." She slapped my thigh as a parting acknowledgment.

I shifted down in my seat, still stuck on Tasche's announcement. I tried not giving that my focus. I missed my baby. Too much space and time were between him snuggling into my breasts.

Besides that, I hoped to be settled before Sadik *FaceTime*'d us.

Sadik

"She said they ready," Jamil announced from the front seat.

I was finishing up on an email to my *Ellis International* staff and giving Rory marching orders. My schedule had been derailed by hours, and hours when you're flying with a large number of people on a private aircraft equates to major dollars.

"Now?" I asked, acknowledging him. "Okay." As I finished up on the email, a thought hit. I turned to Rory. "And reach out to Jeffery at the gun range on the compound. Ask him to clear some time for Bilan. I want her in there at least twice a week."

I'd been falling off with my new wife in too many areas lately. After she had Sadik, I pledged to teach her how to shoot various guns. We'd gone to the range at *Elliswoods Palace* until we returned with our new family to the penthouse. Now was a critical time for our security and while she was at the estate so much during this lockdown, she should make good usage of the amenities there. Bilan needed to know how to use a gun, and several types.

Once I hit send on the email, I closed the laptop and tossed it in the seat next to me.

"Rory, hit Mel up and be sure she's got some of Taaliba's tea in stock. Ask her to have it ready."

"Gotchu." Rory typed rapidly in her phone.

"Alright," I sighed, rubbing my eyes. "Let's do this shit."

Seconds later, the door to the limo opened and Rory hopped out first, communicating with Johnson, who'd been waiting on us outside. When given the cue, I slid out and stood to straighten my suit and tie. The cameras flashed on the red carpet a few feet away.

"This way." Johnson pointed as he took off. I followed him and Rory trailed behind me. The moment our feet hit the carpet, all senses intensified. The glaring flashes of cameras, the music from the club when the door opened, the shouting of my name. Tiffany was in the center being primed by her team: fluffing her hair, smoothing down her skin-tight knee-length dress, and one quickly brushing her cheeks. She waved me on with excitement.

"Mr. Ellis, here!" One photographer shouted.

"Sadik! Hey!" Another tried gaining my attention.

It was clear Tiffany made a big deal out of the anniversary of her clubs. This was more activity than I anticipated.

Knowing my role, I assumed the pose when arriving to her. My arm extended, welcoming her to me. She hastily curled into my side.

"I thought you were gonna blow me off again," her tone as petite as a child.

It was a mark of her vulnerability, confirming my need to be here.

"Why would I do that?" I beamed rotely, knowing we were being captured on film.

"I've been calling you for days to confirm you were coming. I thought your lil' wife shut it down, forgetting we had history before her that wasn't sexual."

Before turning to the photog, my grin didn't falter when I warned, "Be careful. Your fangs aren't as attractive as your lips."

Her grip on my back loosened. It was a locution I knew she was familiar with. My father often used it to temper his lovers when infighting. It meant being quiet, for a woman, was more attractive to him than the one who was combative or overly-complained. For Earl Ellis, a woman unnamed Irene with too much mouth didn't get fed his spoils.

I may not have been my father with multiple lovers, but I'd been generous with Tiffany for this event. I'd played nice and made a beeline on the way to the airport to satisfy her request of me attending tonight. I had other reasons, but as far as she was concerned, my father was down, and I understood her inherent need for support when she didn't have much family to speak of. I was aware of what having the Ellis brand represented at her affair meant for her marketing value.

It had been a tough call to make when I'd received a text from her assistant with the question. Not only had I hired extra security for this trip to Atlanta, thanks to the bullshit with Popov, but I had to pay my flight crew overtime for this pit stop. What made the decision easy was the message I received from Tiffany's security. So, I was able to kill two birds with one stone.

"I know Rory said you have a flight to catch." Tiff turned to me once we'd satisfied the press junket. "Please stay longer," she begged.

I shot her a wink dropping my hand from the small of her back and took her at the hand. "I'll see what I can do."

The doors were opened when we arrived at the entrance. Rory had been waiting just inside, her big ass eyes scouring all over.

"This way," she tossed her head and led the way inside.

Simultaneously, Tiffany was being pulled in a different direction. Our hands slipped apart with natural ease, and just as a sea of bodies was being parted for me by Johnson and Rory, Jamil was at my shoulder and J-Dot was behind me. Jamil refused to sit this one out and even requested J-Dot's escort. He hadn't forgotten the shooting here that could have ended my family before it began.

We ended up in a secluded seated area again, this time one closer to the emergency exit.

After I sat on a velvet bench, Rory stopped in front of me with her arm to her chest as she peered into her watch. "The subject's here. Timer's on...now." She nodded and stepped off.

My eyes scanned the club, recounting the magnetic atmosphere. A waitress entered the section, asking to take our order. The men shared their desires, which were bottles of champagne, and Rory ordered me a bottle of *Mauve*, none of which we had time to consume. It would just be a four-thousand-dollar tab for bottles that would be reused on patrons once we left.

Less than five minutes later, the drinks arrived. Just as my brandy was poured into a tulip glass, a hiked volume of voices at the opening of the section caught my attention. I craned my neck to peer around the waitress' hyper-extended ass. Squinting, I caught a familiar face Rory was giving love to, shoulder-to-shoulder. I left the bench and sauntered over to the railing to confirm my assumption.

"LeRoy?" I shouted over the music.

The lanky frame, draped in expensive ass Italian garb too festive for my modest taste, gaze reached mine.

"I just told Rory I didn't know your light-skinned, pretty ass would be here," he beamed with implanted high cheeks and an old-fashioned good spirit.

"Just supporting fam." I offered with a nod. "The hell you doing here?"

"Scratch's here," he shouted.

My head traveled toward the deejay booth across the vast room and found D.J. Scratch elevated in a glass encasement with headphones halfway on as he bobbed hard to the beat.

"Keeping it in the family, I see," I noted when he moved close enough to shake my hand over the rail.

"Raj thought it would be nice, seeing the deal you two just entered into," he clarified.

That struck me particularly. I'd never disclosed my relationship with Tiffany to R&B and Hollywood phenomenon, Ragee. He'd recently become a business ally because of the community land trust agreement. I guessed Mr. McKinnon had done his research. And that would confirm the research my team had done on his passion for the upward mobility of the community.

I nodded. "How's my guy?" I tossed my chin toward him.

LeRoy, the widely known flamboyant best friend of Ragee, rolled his eyes dramatically. "In fucking love." His head rounded, only the whites of his eyes could be seen. "They're in 'common' Dubai. Too commercial for my taste, but they'd been inviting him for years on their dime for patriotic claims." His head shook, cheeks hiked, and eyes rolled dismissively again. "But Raj being..." He nodded. "Raj. He's declined until his recent wife expressed interest, and bam! They're there." LeRoy shrugged.

Moved by the notion, I added, "I can appreciate newlywed bliss. I'm happy for my man."

"Oh, me, too." He shrugged with the rolling of the eyes again. "I would prefer more exclusivity like *Marye Island*, *St. Justin*, or *Karsyn Cove*. Hell, even *Mt. Kamryn* hasn't been over-populated by the commoners. That's where I'd go if I had the millions he did."

His attention was captured by a dame with a short, tapered haircut and a devilishly low cut, purple leather tube top. The combination was eerily seductive to me. My dick leaped in my pants as my mind reeled. There was an imbalance, however. The two not connecting.

LeRoy's arched brows lifted in delight at her. In response, she turned her back to him and faced me. Dazed, my head pushed back.

"You got something for me to sip on up there?"

I paid her a long gaze before I tossed my chin over to Rory to let her up.

As she strutted her loose ass over to the opening, LeRoy followed it. He then reached up over his hand. "Good luck with that, Ellis." His strength was present in his masculine grip.

He took off as I observed Randi coming into the V.I.P. area. I turned to find Jamil, and when I did, he responded with a wink and simultaneous nod while pulling out his phone.

On approach, I asked Randi, "Would you like a drink?"

"A shot of *Henny* and glass of Moscato," she requested.

I repeated her order to Johnson, who relayed it to Rory before I took a seat a few feet from her. "*Pulse* is your speed?"

"It's the last place I recall seeing my man happy." She shrugged. "Plus, there's lots of connected people who come here." She tossed her chin my way. "Like you."

"I'm just a man supporting family."

"Family you used to fuck," she made clear.

I nodded, accepting the blunt passed to me from Jamil. Her eyes ignited with anticipation at the mere sight of it. I took a short draw from it and held it in a moment while she watched, fascinated.

"How've you been making out?"

That question broke her gaze, and too quickly even for Randi. She blinked, head rearing as she looked away. Quickly, she recuperated. "I'm a scavenger, you know that. A savage ass one, too. I'm gonna always land something." Once again, her attention locked onto my mouth when I took another pull of the blunt, and as magical as I knew my lips were, it wasn't them that had her captivated. It was the cannabis, the allure of the immoral and prohibited substance in the environment. My wife's best friend was addictively seduced by the nature of the forbidden.

It was that precise observation I'd had when I learned the woman I'd grown wildly obsessed with before she knew I'd even existed was friends with the savage scavenger. As I sat there covertly taking in Randi's energy, I recalled the first conversation I had with my closest confidant about my intent regarding Bilan.

Rory's glass froze at her mouth while her big ass eyes pinned me to my seat stunned. "Bird ass Randi from Triangle Village?"

I chuckled. "She's not from Triangle Village. She grew up on Belmont Ave—"

Her head shook and left hand whipped the air dismissing my point. "Hoe ass Randi from every gutter in Paterson." *I couldn't argue that.* "She fucked every fuck ass block boy from the old Barnert Hospital to The Pound to Corrado's to fuckin'...Preakness Ave. Anybody that run with that bitch gotta be a bird from the same goddamn feather."

"Easy, Bean." *I chuckled.* "I'm not trying to wife her." *I straightened in my seat at the bar in Montclair, uneasy with her truth about the obvious.* "but I would like to explore her. I don't think she shares the same pastimes as Randi."

"The fuck." *Her head bounced according to her buzzed state.* "You know how these bitches roll. Her pussy may not have the same amount of body tags as Randi, but I bet she on her way."

I took a minute to consider the possibility. Rory had a point. As much as I tried seeing Ab's sister in that lane, I couldn't. I'd had her monitored for months and hadn't seen evidence of her being as acquainted with the streets as her girl. Randi, the city knew; the girl, Bilan's, name hadn't had near the same frequency. The little who knew her identified her as Ab's sister or the daughter of the African who had the restaurant back in the day.

"Can you trust me on this, Bean?"

"Oh, I trust you with my life. It's Randi's whore ass I don't trust sharing a fuckin' blunt with."

I held out the blunt to Randi. Her eyes bounced all over as she readjusted herself on the bench, clearing her throat.

"It's only a matter of time before security comes over and asks you to put it out," I goaded.

She licked her glossed lips, eyes circling uncomfortably again. I'd had it too long. Blowing trees wasn't exactly an indulgence of mine at my age. Two pulls were too many for my preference.

Randi reached over, snatching the rolled cigar from my hand. She put it to her lips and inhaled to the point of her chest rising in the familiar purple leather tube top. Her drink order was handed over from the waitress and Rory brought them up, placing the tray on the table. I pushed it directly in front of Randi and in a friendly gesture, handed her the *Hennessy*.

My phone vibrated against my chest in my inner suit jacket pocket. Bilan texted a picture of her feeding Sadik his nighttime bottle. She wore no makeup apart from a clear lip gloss, and her hair was wrapped in a silk scarf. He lay with his back against her chest, covered by an open silk robe exposing her sternum and the curve of her right breast. The sight of her in such a natural state of femininity reminded me of the power of a woman. She didn't need ornaments to make her beautiful. Her beauty was in her assigned divine gender and especial superpower of motherhood.

My Nalib: *I love you too much xoxo*

My chest tightened as I typed back.

Me: Yet not more than I you and not enough.

"She's sweet." My eyes wandered over to Randi. She took a deep pull of the blunt and held it in her lungs. "Bilan a good one."

"Tell me something I don't know."

"Like about your money she be giving me?"

"You mean the money she gave you last month that was all hers?" With a crooked grin, I shook my head. "Bilan doesn't need my money."

Randi blew the dro out on a chuckle. "*Shiiiiit*. What real bitch don't need your money?"

"Your bestie."

"Bilan ain't got shit. If you think she do, she fuckin' with your head. Her mother and father ain't have shit to leave her but debt. That's how she lost that house."

I nodded, then reached for my brandy. After a satisfying taste, I explained, "She didn't need money to capture my attention."

"Then what the fuck did it?" Randi snorted. "Not her dried up ass pussy. I love my girl, but know she a boring fuck." She made sure to trail the bottom of her glass down her cleavage for my attention."

A smile curled my lips before I took another sip. "That's what this is about?"

Randi giggled, weed clearly fuzzing her head. She placed the wine glass down and drained half of the *Hennessy*.

Her eyes were low when she turned to face me, giving me full view of her tube top, and that's when I realized where the fond memory of it derived from.

"Nah. What I'm saying is I'm a scavenger." Her lips expanded seductively when making her point.

I gave her my full attention when asking, "And what are you hunting for, sweetheart?"

"You know me, Deek. You know the jungle I live in. It cost to survive. I ain't a college-degreed, nine-to-five type of bitch. I'm the type that feeds the fantasies in ya head while your lil' wife make you look good for your friends and family." She inched closer. "I take the nightshift."

I poured the last of the *Mauve* into my mouth, enjoying the way it stimulated my throat.

"Ah, come the fuck on, Sadik," she cried impatiently, masking her vulnerability with laughter. "You know I'm good. You know my head game."

I nodded, affirming her claim with drawn lips. She waited with more patience this time, her gaze burning the side of my face.

Finally, I returned, "You're forgetting one thing, though."

"What?"

"She's your friend. Your best friend," I qualified.

Randi snorted, big pretty teeth exposed as she laughed. "Okay. First of all, my ass too old to be having a fuckin' best friend. And I'm too smart to let friendships fuck with my money. I love my girl, Bilan, for real. A lil' too fuckin' naïve, but got a heart of gold, and she smart as shit. But even she did what she had to do and got with a playboy when she was fuckin' starving. She knew the bottom was 'bout to fall out for her. It ain't matter that she was finishing up school. Bilan knew that degree wasn't gone get her no real money right away. She had shit due, so she did what she had to do."

"And that was fuck with me?"

A scoff rented the air over the music. "Fuck, yeah. You think ol' girl ya speed? You think she fuck with niggas like that? Mad mutha-fuckas tried that snatch and she blocked them. Only nigga that came close was the freckled-face fuck from her school. He used to spend the night at her place, and when the lights went out, his ass was on the couch. I felt bad for the geeky-ass." She turned away with a hard eye roll. "I even let him eat my pussy one night. That bitch ain't even know."

The mention of Jason spending the night at Bilan's disrupted my ability to breathe smoothly. I'd survived her blow about me not being Bilan's type, an insecurity I thought I'd extinguished months ago.

"What?" Randi's brows were hiked when she sensed the sudden spiral in my mood. "I felt sorry for that young fucker, all sniffing up Bilan's weird ass all that time. She knew she liked him. She was just too high strung to know what to do. Shit, she probably fucked him and just ain't say shit—"

"Twenty-five minutes up, chief," Rory appeared over us on the other side of the coffee table.

"Grown folks is talking, Rory," Randi snapped. "Scram, grandma."

"Yo, suck my ass, bitch," Rory snapped.

Randi sucked in a breath, her hand clasping my thigh. "You gonna let her talk to me like that?"

My eyes roved from her shocked eyes to her grinning mouth, down her arm, and finally to where we connected. I stood, effectively dropping her repulsive claw from me.

"Well," I buttoned my jacket. "this has been enlightening."

"What?" She dropped the blunt into her empty *Hennessy* glass. "I thought we was making a deal!"

"Neither this life nor the next will ever yield an opportunity for you to fuck me, Randi. I'm not sure what you thought us sharing a blunt was about, but it damn sure wasn't about the future of us fuckin'."

"Oh, really?" she scoffed. "I 'on't know who you putting on for. Ain't no naïve bitches around here. I know the game. I know what you Ellises like. You need variety pussy. I know how to keep my mouth shut to keep ya family happy. I know Bilan. She won't find out."

I bent over in her direction to reach eye level with her. "I'm an Ellis, but not that Ellis, Randi. I wouldn't let you close enough to my dick to sniff it."

A sleek grin stretched her face, her tongue circling the rim of her lips. "You already did. Remember?" She winked. "I bet Bilan don't know that, just like I bet you don't know if she fucked freckle boy." Suddenly, her expression fell and Randi rolled her eyes. "Fuck you, Sadik!"

A raucous laugh shot from the back of my throat, and I gave in to it. "You want to, huhn, sweetie?" My eyes scanned the section. "Enjoy the free bottles of top shelf. Invite a fuck boy up and trick his ass out. I only turn 'em for Africans."

Rotating, I followed my detail's line out of the section, and then the club. I had business to tend to.

∞18∞

Iban Ellis
Iban Wesley Ellis
Iban W Ellis

I huffed, frustrated by the lack of yields when *Google*'ing each name combo.

Iban Ellis Arrest
Iban Ellis Sentencing

They all produced the same results; articles I'd seen last spring and summer when I *Google*-stalked the entire family. Frustrated, I sat back in my seat, peering out of the oversized diamond grille windows of Irene's office. I didn't have much time this morning and was hoping to capture something new to chew on.

The door opened, causing my spine to leap straight, and I slammed my laptop closed. Monica, so beautiful and charmed, craned inside, arresting my investigative mind.

"Hey, girl." Her smile was deep, deceptively reminding me of the wholesome woman I met a year ago. The one I found to be the standard in this family. "Heard you were looking for me."

My eyes blinked in an attempt to switch lanes in my brain. "Ye-yeah," I stuttered, bringing my elbows onto the desk casually. "Have a seat."

Monica closed the door, her blunt cut, bone-straight shoulder-length, chocolate mane moving like a sheet over her shoulders. My sister-in-law was an undeniable fox. "I haven't seen Sadik around in a few days. He's been busy with his gazillion businesses?" she asked when seated.

"He's been down in Atlanta since Friday afternoon." That mention made my heart flop from craving him so. "I've been trying to supplement his presence with his son, but they are very much two different Sadiks."

Monica's feathery laughter drifted into the air. "Oh, of course, they are. He may look just like his dad, but his father he isn't." I shook my head dramatically in agreement, hating how much I'd been missing that man. Continuing to laugh, she asked, "What's up, girl?"

I took a deep breath, fortifying myself. "This isn't an easy subject to broach, but I've been working on being straight forward around here."

"That's the way you *must* be," she made clear. "Trust me. No one survives around here by swallowing back their concerns." She gave a nod of encouragement. "Speak your heart, sister."

I smiled, wondering if she was truly prepared. My eyes rolled away as my knees began to rock back and forth under the desk, my torso swaying.

"Your husband was incarcerated for murder. There was a year-long trial with media coverage."

She blinked hard several times, startled. "Yes."

"He was convicted of a gruesome murder." I leaned over the desk. "He tortured Hubert Jackson before killing him. Iban carved out his lips and pushed them around Jackson's penis." My breakfast nearly came up at the visual. I swallowed hard. "Iban still got off on passion as a result of reasonable provocation manslaughter, but was originally charged with first degree murder. How did that reduction in charges happen?"

Monica's head shook, eyes fell, as she visibly found it difficult to swallow. Her hand went to her neck in a delicate touch as she cleared her throat. "You're asking me about legal savvy. I'm the wrong person. The family still uses the same law firm."

"You know that's not an inquiry I can put in casually. I was hoping you could help me out."

"Bilan..." Her hand brushed down her arm while turning her gaze away from me. "That was so many years ago, not the best time for this family. I can't possibly recount the details of it."

"Your husband could have spent the rest of his life in prison. Times like that you never forget."

Her chin dipped. "He could have. But with so many years between then and now *and* his many...blunders—"

"Fuckups," slipped from my lips. Monica's surprised gaze hit me, and it was me dropping my eyes this time. "I'm sorry."

"It's okay. It's been my life for over thirteen years." She rolled her eyes, that quickly incensed.

There was a delayed pause as she took a few cleansing breaths, struggling through thoughts I was sure were dark. I delivered patience, seeing it was only reasonable after my slip up.

"I don't hate him," I wanted to make clear. "Am I angry? Yes—absolutely. My child is my only close blood living relative. He honestly feels like the only." I bit my lip to stop its quivering. "But I'm more than in love with my husband; I'm committed to him and his family. All of them. They're all fallible, including Sadik; I get it." I shook my head. "But I don't understand Iban. He's the most surfaced diabolical of all the men. He kills for sport—has threatened me several times. I need to know what I'm working with here," I partially lied. "He'll rejoin us at some point."

Monica stood, drawing in a deep breath. "I think you should speak to Sadik about this. He likely recalls all the details you're curious about."

As she waited at the door for my responses, I realized the conversation was done. Monica had decided. I nodded, dismissing her.

When she pulled the door open, Robert was on the other side, pushing through.

"Pardon me," he addressed Monica, realizing he'd nearly hit her with the door.

"It's okay, Rob," she replied. "I was just leaving."

Monica skirted out without a final glance.

"Ms. Bilan, I'm ready when you are."

I'd already began grabbing my things. "Okay. I'm ready. Glad you found the keys."

"Yes. Whenever car keys are missing around here, I forget as security, I have access to the backup ones. There's a big, backup room with spare keys to every lock on the grounds."

When an odd visual came to mind, my body steeled. I turned to Robert still in the doorway.

"Like a repository..." I breathed with wild eyes.

A memory flashed in my mind.

"How were you able to find this?" I asked, shocked as I thumbed through the print outs.

Jason took a seat across from me in the private library room. I'd been in there for hours trying to collect relevant documentation on Corey Booker's first mayoral campaign. His opponent was a tenured politician using dirty tricks to ensure his incumbency. There were no relevant articles coming up via Google, and the school's library was no better.

Earlier in the day, Jason texted to invite me to lunch and I declined, explaining my grief. Hours later, he entered the private room with an accomplished grin and a stack of papers warm from the printer. He'd given me countless articles on all the alleged claims of political intimidation.

"I'm the information and technology guy." He beamed. "You forget."

Dazed, I breathed, "I guess I did."

"But I bet you won't forget who came through in a clutch." He winked, flirting again.

"How did you get this?"

Jason shrugged. "The school's technology program has a relationship with the state. Whenever there's reporting on local matters, the state collects all media coverage—in each medium. Anything you want on events in New Jersey, there's a database housing it. It's like a repository for media information."

"But how are we supposed to have access to it as students?" Then I thought. "Or is it only available to students in certain departments?"

He clicked his teeth with his tongue as he shot the gun he formed with his hand. "Bingo," he sang. I rolled my eyes. "Don't sweat it. You can have my sign in. The login is my first initial and last name. My password is that backward."

"That's a weak password."

Jason shrugged with his brows, sitting back in his seat. "I've got way too many damn passwords to remember. Besides, I know how to Google."

I gasped. "Is that a jab?"

"The true jab would be you falling asleep on me last night at your place. That was cold."

"It was late!"

"And you had company."

I shook my head, gaping at him with an imperceptible smile in my eyes.

Robert's soft chuckle broke my reverie. "Yeah. I guess you can call it that."

I blinked his way. "Thank you, Robert."

"For finding the keys?"

"No. For giving me the best idea I've had in a long time." I was headed his way with my laptop wedged beneath my arm. "I'm going to kiss my baby goodbye and grab my purse."

I had work to do while we traveled to Paterson to pick up Tasche, then on to Harlem.

"We give You praise...

We give You praise.
We give You glory...
We give You glory.
You have all power...
You have all power.
You give us mercy...
You give us mercy," the small group of singers at the microphone led, and the massive choir behind them emphasized.

There were dancers in ballet-like costumes twirling around in unison on the stage with the singers and below on the main floor. The place was ginormous and spirited.

"We worship You, our Strong tower!" the choir belted.

The music and presentation was like a Broadway production. Live, it was magical and engaging. This was nothing like the streaming experience. Inside the walls of *Redeeming Souls for Abundant Living in Christ* was as theatrically moving as I imagined *Disney* to be, even more. Everyone on stage radiated joy or was with an expression of glee. Even the woman who showed Tasche and me to our seats in the center column row carried a cherubic countenance. The smiles, nods, and warm gestures couldn't have been for simple show. This all —from the engaging singers to the expressive dancers, warm greeters, to the musicians who were clearly gifted–had to be studied and practiced. It had to be believed by the people administering moving energy.

Tasche and I looked like agents, being the only two in our row not swaying rhythmically like everyone else in the house. She sat and I stood to have a better vantage point of the production. My hungry eyes swept around the two-story sanctuary. I couldn't get this overwhelming feeling online. Everyone I could see was on their feet, dancing and singing.

The up-tempo song ended and the start of another, a more slow, dramatic piece began. A few shouted their praise almost in anticipation of the mood-switch that was taking place. Again, magical. This vibe was a human experience of divine unity I'd never seen before. Growing up under the Muslim faith, at most, my father would emphasize Islamic platitudes repetitively and expect us to abide by them without the benefit of enforcement by way of congregating with fellow-believers and religious leaders. This was—

A thwack to the side of my knees had my head jerking down. Tasche waved me closer.

I bent to give her my attention and she shared directly in my ear, "You see Trent Bailey and StentRo up there?" She pointed to the balcony. I couldn't make either out right away and felt self-conscious for gaping, so I resumed my seat to continue to peruse. "There's a section up there for celebrities only, so don't stare too hard, yo. Lex said it's for their privacy. If you try to take one pic, you get taken outta here. Ezra don't play when it come down to his peoples."

Surreptitiously, I shared, "I can see Trent. Doesn't Ragee come here, too?"

"Yeah, he do," she replied. "Young Lord be stopping through once in a blue, too. His lady into this shi—" She coughed into her hand. "Into all this."

I nodded. That's when I finally spotted Stenton Rogers. His lanky frame shouldn't have been that difficult to identify amongst mostly average height people, but he was in the front row on the balcony, which blended with those behind him. He wore yellow-lensed glasses and a fedora as he two-stepped with a little girl in his arm.

Another whack to my shoulder had me yanking my head to Tasche again. She appeared cool and collected in her seat as she jerked her chin toward the stage. The first new attraction from the last time I'd gazed that way was a large coat of wooly hair, bouncing in the air. Only one woman I'd met had possessed such an interest. She was tall with a commanding presence and held a servant posture.

I stood quickly to my feet as all those around me had been so I could get a better view of the elaborate stage. Lex sauntered out onto the stage without pomp, holding a device portfolio. She moved ahead of her equally arresting husband with the thick beard and hypnotizing aura. Both their heads were toward the floor and their pace was one to not attract more attention than they naturally would, being the leaders of this influential organization.

The husband and wife split with Bishop Carmichael going to a wooden, high-winged clergy seat on the stage behind the six-people singing directly into the microphones. I watched as Lex continued to the glass lectern and lay the portfolio on top. She then journeyed over to her husband and leaned over him with closed eyes as her palms lay over his broad shoulders. His head was bowed, eyes squeezed closed as Lex mouthed over him. As she spoke, her hand traveled from his shoulders to his head, then his forehead. Ezra's body jerked abruptly and his hands shot into the air as he mouthed something inaudible, too. This strange transaction didn't go on long enough for me to figure out exactly what had taken place. Before I knew it, Lex stood to full height and calmly left the stage as quietly as she'd appeared. She ended up on the floor in a special section with mostly collared men and women.

As I stood, I wondered how much of the behavior was taught versus organic for Lex. It had to be a trained procedure. Any friend that close to Tasche had to have some level of ratchetness in them. Hell, even I had a measure in me: I threatened the biggest, Black drug lord in the state of New Jersey with turning his son against him.

A few minutes later, the emotion-provoking song created a heightened atmosphere. Bishop Carmichael rose from his seat, traversing to the lectern. A wireless microphone was placed on his robe as he observed the short man, leading the choir and the musicians. Ezra strolled toward them singing along, though his voice couldn't be distinguished among the choir. He clapped his hands in praise. He also lifted a hand of orchestration for the musicians a couple of times. The parishioners were all caught up with the moment of joint worship, something I'd never experienced live.

The music quieted and Bishop Carmichael had returned to the lectern. "Good morning, tabernacle." I recognized those deep raspy vocals. The audience cheered in reply as he opened his portfolio. "Welcome to *Family and Friends Day* at *Redeeming Souls for Abundant Living in Christ Family Worship Center*. It is an unqualified privilege to gather amongst the people of God." A charming grin curved his lips. The room reacted to that small yet intimate gesture from him. "I know I declare this every week now, but I won't be before you long. My wife has laid hands on me a few minutes ago for covering, and the sooner I'm done—" An abrupt chorus of laughter ripped through the air. The Bishop nodded this time, sharing a full beam. "You know the rest."

Even I had to chuckle, taken by his intimate gesture and affection for the woman seated to my right, who cracked a modest smile.

"Okay." He took in a deep breath. "While you're on your feet, let us petition Jehovah Shammah..."

They were flocking to the stage in droves. I'd seen this countless times online. People were screaming and shouting praise. Some even expressing raw emotion I was sure had to do with their circumstances rather than praise. The entire building, it felt, was caught up by the stimulating message Bishop Carmichael shared. He'd closed the homily but was still fired up, declaring God's power and willingness to heal and correct. The only people in my peripheral unmoved were Tasche and men and women I was now convinced served as security for the church. They stood motionless like secret service officers.

Like my husband and father-in-law's bodyguards...

Being in the sanctuary was a moving experience. This was the height of the production, but it was far from simulated. This was a transferring spiritual occurrence if I'd ever imagined one before. I wasn't accustomed to this liturgical order of service, but I was definitely affected by it. How could I not be? I actually felt an unusual and contagious wave move over my body that, mixed with his words, inspired a flame of hope.

I, too, was inspired to go to the stage—provoked, it felt, by an unnamed energy. The only two things preventing me from acting on my emotional inclination was I didn't know what to do or request if I got up there and was received. Secondly, and most terrifying was I was still aware of the Ellis family being under guard, and I'd breached the orders of my own husband even being here.

So, I remained in place, fighting to contain my emotions. My palms were clasped and eyes squeezed shut as I silently voiced my fears, desires, and gratitude, something heavily addressed in the homily earlier. In between, I watched as Bishop Carmichael prayed over flopping bodies until he peacefully closed the service with rasped words of encouragement.

Two hours later, we were in the church's dining room. That area was massive, too, impossibly outfitted for thousands of attendees. While there weren't as many present in here as there were in the sanctuary, because of the *Family and Friends Day* themed service, this place was packed. It was tastefully decorated and filled with rectangular and round-shaped tables to give that family feel. As guests of the first family, Tasche and I were assigned seats at the Carmichaels' table with their associates. Notably, none of the celebrity members attended this part of the service. I couldn't wait to debrief with Tasche later about why. I was sure it was the obvious reason. Not that it mattered: the only one I would have been thrilled to see was Ragee, and he hadn't attended service today.

The food provided was pretty good and in generous portions. My nerves were frayed from being this close to a man who, too accurately, predicted my future so far. He was rather intense, not addressing the table much and patiently attending to each person interrupting his meal with a question or greeting. He assisted Lex with feeding their newest baby—another girl—whom I learned was named Christ Harmony, pronounced *Chris* with the "T" silent. Their middle child, Mia Grace, seemed glued to him the whole dinner, only going to her mother when baby Christ needed to be fed and burped by dad.

The site of this family's dynamic had my belly fluttering. They were functional, balancing leadership and partnership in the public's eye. Tasche, while enjoying her girlfriend's children, didn't want to be there. She asked that we leave after the service. Lex and I insisted that we stay for food since we'd traveled such a distance. After eating, when Tasche wasn't tending to the kids, she sat stiffly, appearing grossly awkward. It was comical. I was grateful for her agreeing to stay. More than for the Carmichaels, I felt like I belonged here, in this atmosphere of clarity.

"Mommy," an adorable mocha princess called out so sweetly. The Carmichaels' oldest daughter, Lisa-Mare, patted her mother on the arm across from me. "I gotta potty."

"Oh, sweat!" Tasche leaped to her feet and raced toward the girl's side. "C'mon, lil' buggy. Auntie TT gotta potty, too. I'll take you." They began to take off. "I'm just like mommy, 'member. You can't sit on the seat. You gotta hold on to TT like you did before."

I watched them thread through the sea of chairs moving about the restaurant-sized dining room with an expanded heart. Tasche looked no older than twenty-five; she'd preserved herself well.

"Aren't they adorable?" The voice startled me, forcing me to whip my head in the opposite direction. Lex had somehow landed in the seat next to me.

I pulled in a relieved and pleasantly surprised breath. "Completely."

"I've been dying for a moment alone with you. Thank God T's in love with that little girl. She treats her like they're the same age sometimes." My brows lifted, reacting to that knowledge. "My husband believes Tasche lives vicariously through our daughter." Lex tossed her head in a shrug, long thick locks of hair bouncing about. "I'm just grateful my friend didn't run the moment I began pushing out babies now that I have one on each tit, as Ms. Remah would say."

"To say she wants no more kids, Tasche's excellent with them," I noted.

Lex nodded, eyes avoiding me when she shouldered me. "Soooo..."

I scoffed, amused by her horrible act of clandestineness. "Pardon me?" I giggled.

"The last time I saw you, you were fleeing for your life. Now, you're here and seem very much at peace, spirit calm and open."

"And very pregnant," I added, eyes elsewhere as I threw that fact out there. "Again." I nodded.

Her entire lengthy body swung to face me. I turned to find Lex's face lit up like the Fourth of July sky in suburban town, USA. "You've got to be kidding me!" Her eyes flew to my mid-section, which was hidden behind my opened, sleeveless duster.

"Nope." My hands brushed down my tapered nape, fighting to control my smile of elation.

I loved being pregnant. Was thrilled to give Sadik another baby.

"Is that another thing we have in common?"

I leaned in to hear amongst the chatter of the room. "How do you mean?"

"You mentioned not fitting into his world, but apparently you can't protect your uterus, like me. You have a back-to-back pregnancy like me." She rolled her eyes while beaming.

"Not just pregnant, but married." I lifted my left hand, wiggling my fingers. That's when I recalled I didn't have a wedding band, only an engagement ring. "It happened so out of the blue, and things are moving *so* fast, as you can see." My hands moved to cup my small belly. "I don't even have a wedding band." I took in a deep breath. "But yup." I popped the "P" on that word. "We sent the clergy with the signed paperwork for filing."

"Wow!" she breathed.

I nodded while going for my purse. "That's why I have to give you this." I discreetly handed her an envelope practically under the table. "You were so generous to me last summer, you have no idea. I feel foolish in retrospect, but I needed you more then than I needed water. I have to reimburse what you gave me."

Lex's eyes lit wide once she realized my actions. Her gaze shifted over the area, I guessed, to see if anyone was watching. "We don't accept reimbursements, Mrs..." she prompted me for my new surname.

"Ellis," I returned. "Mrs. Sadik Ellis, *which* is why I have to do this. This is the money you loaned me with interest. At the very least, consider it a donation to your organization. I can't explain the terror I felt those weeks your donation kept me afloat. There's no way I cannot address it. Sadik would be insulted if he knew." I tried containing my amusement with a hand over my mouth. "He'd have my head if he knew the extremes I went through to run from him."

"Are you safe?"

That reasonable question brought Bishop Carmichael's homily earlier to mind. He shared how when Jesus encountered an unsuspecting Peter and asked to use his boat, Peter permitted him, not thinking much of it. Jesus used it to go and minister, and once he returned, he offered to take Peter fishing...at night. *At night*. Jesus told him to go cast his net for a great, massive catch. *At night*. The Peter guy had to wonder how smart it was to go out that night when he'd previously been unsuccessful. But he went, in an "act of faith" as Bishop Carmichael put it.

When Peter went out and caught such a great multitude of fish, the net couldn't hold them. Several things happened. The first was Peter was generously loaning his boat. The second was his obedience even when things were not looking good for him. He and his brother had been out fishing earlier, which yielded nothing.

In using this biblical story, Bishop Carmichael wanted us to understand how God can bless us even in the least desirable circumstances. More than that, He gives us the tools we need to achieve our desires. A discouraged Peter had a boat. He had a faulty net, but he also had a crew to repair it with, and faith to walk in. That faith allowed him to achieve his need. Sometimes you have to utilize what you have to be used to create what you need.

It made me consider my own circumstances. For years, even before my father passed, I desired a family. Once my parents passed away, that yearning intensified. Abshir never satisfied the definition of family. Losing them left me broken. Then, entered Sadik. I'd been fearing being connected to The Ellis family because of their legal illegitimacy. Even more recently, fissures had been found in their remarkable bond. The family had been painfully breaking down.

After experiencing the message today, I'd walked away with a revelation. Maybe I'd been given the family I desired for so many years. Perhaps I'd been given that through this flawed dynasty. I'd seen them strong and functioning. I'd witnessed the Ellises whole, glued, and at their best. So, yeah. Maybe things had been awry as of late, but if I viewed their strength as a tool and worked from there, I could see the gift in what they were to me. What if God had been working in my favor all this time?

"But the Lord will be with you. The Stranger you've never known knows each strand of hair on your body, has covered you since your conception, and will continue to during this next phase of your life." Ezra's words from over a year ago flooded my mind.

I decided I needed to view, not just Sadik, but the Ellises as a blessing instead of a crime family I should distance myself from. I'd been sensing that over the past few months, but today solidified my resolve. Just like Peter was fishing at night, the least likely time most would think fish could be caught, I had to believe in this family at a time when they were wounded. And especially the man in question because he'd been out already—

I turned to Lex. "After experiencing your husband's spin on 'nighttime blessings,' I think I'm going to be okay."

"A'ight, yo." My head whipped to my left to find Tasche had returned with little Miss Lisa-Mare. "I gotta go. I need to sleep before my shift tonight."

My phone vibrating on the table caught my attention. Seeing his profile name reminded me it was outdated. I'd have to think on how I'd change it.

My Lover: *Change of plans. This afternoon's meeting got delayed until tomorrow afternoon. Sorry Nalib. I won't be back until late tomorrow. I'll call tonight.*

Disappointment settled in my belly. I'd been looking forward to seeing those kaleidoscopic irises and to running my hands over his smooth golden scalp. I'd been missing Sadik, unable to recall the last time we'd spent so much time apart.

With a throbbing heart, I turned back toward Lex to find her roll her faux angry regard from Tasche above us down to me.

"I can take that, Bilan," Candy offered over my head.

I hadn't noticed she was standing over me.

"I see you still can't eat without my son feeding you," Earl announced from the head of the table.

His glare over his reading glasses caused my belly to flutter, it was such a welcomed sight. I handed over my plate of cherry pie to Candy, realizing how bad I'd messed over it. It was the same with my dinner, but all with purpose.

I pulled my elbows over the table and a smile to my face as I regarded Earl. "I'm satisfied looking at the man of the house, who so happens to be the man of the hour, too." I didn't try to control my beam. "What did you think of your first dinner back at Irene's table?"

I'd arranged this meal just as I had over the past month in Irene's absence. Tonight, for Earl's first meal with the family since his heart attack two months ago, I had a special meal prepared for him with his dietary restrictions in mind.

"Love," he answered. "This was all love."

Most were present tonight, but not all. It was Monday evening, the day after my revival visit to *Redeeming Souls for Abundant Living in Christ*. It was the closest to old times as we'd had but with Iban, Irene, and Sadik missing. Ironically, Irene's absence was the second most obvious, my husband's being the first. The room wasn't as charged, the dynamic was somewhat off. Sadik was supposed to have returned last night, but his business was pushed back another day. This disappointment of his absence was reminiscent of loneliness.

"Because we love you, PaPa!" Ivana shouted over the table.

We all snickered at that show of affection from her.

"Not more than I love you two, though." He gave a faux frown, a sign of a sad heart.

The girls giggled feverishly at that.

"And Sadik, too," Iesha reminded him.

"Oh, of course, my number one grandson." Earl pouted more, playing the role of emotionally needy PaPa. "I wish he would have hung out with us longer tonight, but I'll give him a pow-wow for it when I see him in the morning."

That made me laugh. The baby began dinner with us but got fussy and Camille took him upstairs for a good burping and an early bath. Thank goodness for her. I didn't want to miss Earl's night back as the head of the table. It was enough Irene was missing. The reminder of that tore at me.

I pulled my phone from my pocket under the table, needing the time. Standing to my feet, I marched over to Earl.

"Alright, young man. I told the nurses I'd make sure you'd eat responsibly and would have you back in time for your meds." I grabbed the handles of his wheelchair and made the sound of a motor to entertain the girls.

They fell for it, leaping from their seats. As Monica typed into her phone, *something she'd done a lot during dinner*, Ivana and Iesha raced over to their PaPa cheerily.

"Daddy, I'll be in tonight to talk to you after my video chat with my mentor," Taaliba reminded him after snapping a picture of us taking off for the entrance to the dining room.

I tried maintaining an expression of contentment all the way to the door. The girls raced aside us as we eventually met the colossal *Harlem Renaissance* artwork framed in gold cases, boasting the walls of the gallery'esque halls.

When we arrived at the opening of Earl's study, a nurse I recognized so happened to be there waiting.

"Girls!" Monica shouted behind us before I could speak. "Let's get bath time going. Mommy doesn't want to miss her show."

"Awwww!" Iesha groaned.

"Night, PaPa." Ivana kissed her grandfather on the cheek.

Iesha followed up with blowing a raspberry kiss into his hairy cheek. "Night, PaPa. Tomorrow we play cards."

"Sho you right, princess," Earl agreed. "I'm gonna beat your little hind, too!"

"You'll have to catch me first!" Iesha shouted as she took off behind her mom and sister.

I turned to him. "You're a lucky man."

Earl shook his head, removing the glasses I didn't see much of until after his heart attack. "Baby, fools run on luck. Successful men are blessed." He gestured his seated body. "This here is from blessings, sweetheart—"

"Bilan," I corrected quickly with a smile.

"Daughter," he countered. "Hate it or love it, you're my daughter, young lady."

I reached over to kiss the side of his head. "I don't think I've heard a more beautiful ultra-alpha command from anyone but your son," I murmured. "Thank you."

Earl winked before the nurse wheeled him into his primary living quarters. I waited, following them with my eyes until they were out of sight. When I turned to leave, I bumped into Nena, Earl's girlfriend.

"Excuse me," I breathed, startled with a polite smile. "I was..." my words halted.

Nena scoffed in a friendly manner, her tapered hair cut in one of its usual jazzy and meticulous styles, full lips stained red, and a look of one-way humor in her dark eyes. This one had always worn an expression of self-assurance and private humor while Diane, her counterpart, was straightforward with her thoughts and words. But tonight, Nena appeared subdued. I'd never been comfortable with the two women's roles in this family to speak much to them. I wanted to ask her about the sadness clear in her eyes, but thought against it.

"Night, Bilan," she murmured with a dry smile, almost as if to say *'it's okay to speak to me.'*

Nonetheless, I was taken by her addressing me with familiarity.

I ducked my head in submission. "Goodnight."

Without breaking my stride, I moved down the hall. My mind ran with so many thoughts, those including Nena's strange countenance and kissing my baby once more goodnight.

That was before I stumbled over my feet into a hard, capable arm.

I blinked successively to clear my vision.

Under those dense, unruly brows I'd come to appreciate were a dark brown perimeter enclosing a hue of green, then yellow, and an impossible orange before a speck of black at the mecca of the irises. My breaths were ragged and gaze heated on his cool veneer. I could feel the swelling between my legs at the sight and scent of him alone.

"You ready for me, Nalib?"

∞19∞

Utterly stunned, I steeled in that awkward position in his arm. When had Sadik arrived? No one made me aware of it, including him.

Sadik pulled me up at the shoulder with his one free hand. When I straightened, I turned to face him, taking in his urban sophistication. He wore deep blue denim jeans, a stark white V-neck tee, and thong sandals. According to the color combo in the material of the straps and the design, I could tell they were *Ase Garb*. Just a few moments ago, I was subconsciously planning my night without Sadik and now, here he was, alive and in the flesh.

"You seem in deep thought."

"Of my baby and snuggling with him tonight."

"Is that all?" Those recusant brows lifted, irises gleamed in challenge.

I swallowed back my concerns regarding Nena and pulled in a deep breath to reveal my truth.

"I thought I'd be without you again tonight."

His hand gripped my side with proprietary, his thumb strumming my belly. "You're never without me, Nalib. I've made sure of it."

I swallowed hard, nipples ringing. "How was your trip?"

"Dull," he shared rapidly and unequivocally. "I've recently learned my disrelish to lengthy time away from you."

My breath hiked and eyelashes smacked together as I processed that claim.

"Sadik would appreciate a kiss."

His shoulder pushed against the wall. "I've been with my heir for over an hour now. He was gassy, pooting against my chest until he sighed of relief." He snorted, lips curling from light humor. "I gave him a bath and put him down." My eyes swept down his body. Why they locked onto his thickly-corded forearms was beyond me. "I asked Camille to lay him down in our suite for the night. We'll relieve her when we're done reacquainting." He stood to his full height, nearing me again. "If you like, we can go up to say goodnight again."

Trembling with need for the man before me, my husband, I nodded. "I'd like that very much."

It was dark out on the compound, a beautiful summer night. The air was kind and the outdoor lighting created a warm glow along the garden as we traveled in a mini motor cart across the grounds. This trip was better than the one I'd taken with Monica during my first visit here.

"How's school?" Sadik's velvety chords awakened me from my musing.

He had one hand on the wheel, the other resting against his thigh as he drove us.

I blinked hard, considering that. "It's been a balancing act for sure. Mostly papers in both classes. I've spent more time in the library here than I care to."

"And that's the weight of it?" he asked. "The papers? That's been filling lots of your time?"

I shrugged. "That's grad school: research and papers. All of the classes are pre-recorded and mostly filled with resources for our assignments. So between that and the *Ellis Academy* reports, I've been busy."

"Hmmmmm..." he hummed, turning into a dirt road leading to a modest-sized building.

Odd...

"Have you heard from the developers?"

"Yes." He pulled the cart in front of the building where I saw the marquee.

LOVE IN RHYTHM & BLUES

I pulled in a sharp breath, recognizing the name of the film I'd been wanting to see. It'd been out for a couple of days, and the latest hottest ticket around for Black cinema.

"The lot has been approved and all the permits are squared away." He keyed off the motor and faced me, hand draping over the head-rest behind me. "The construction starts next week."

A relieved breath left my lungs. "That was fast."

He nodded, hand tapping the headrest. "It's taking a lot of lever-aging at the township level, but we made it happen." Sadik reached over and fingered a curl on top of my head. "Were you and Kimmy able to settle on the kitchen design?"

I nodded. "Two weeks ago. She came up to meet with me and the rep from the developer's firm. We were able to put together what's going to be a gorgeous and functional kitchen space. She was also happy to see a mockup of her room on the lower level."

His head bobbed slowly, back and forth as he processed, it seemed. Then he leaned over and planted his supple lips on the side of my neck. I leaped in my seat.

"Why are you being skittish?" he whispered, lips still against me.

"I'm not."

"Your pulse is audible."

"You please all of my senses." I was all breaths and pants.

He withdrew, a wicked smile playing at his sensual lips.

A moment had passed before his expression sobered. "Did you wait on me to eat?" I nodded. He asked me not to eat with the family so we could have dinner together. I'd just began to regret my obedience. "Let's go, Nalib."

I trailed behind him with laced fingers as he led me into the building. From the vestibule, it was clear this was the Ellis cinema theater. There was a popcorn machine spurting cooked kernels, a counter display with various candies, a hot dog roller, and pretzel stand. Along the dark walls were cinematically framed pictures of classic movies like *Coming to America*, *Home Alone*, *The Color Purple*, *Jaws*, and *Malcolm X*.

I'd never been inside, only had it pointed out to me during my first tour. The marquee couldn't be seen from the main road, so I didn't pick up theater vibes from there.

"Mr. Ellis, Ms. Bilan," the attendant greeted us from behind the counter. "Welcome to the Ellis theater. Your things are all set up in there for you. I'll be here if you want a snack during the show."

"Thanks, Devin," Sadik replied then opened one of the large double doors for me to enter.

The theater was outfitted identically to the smaller ones in standard venues. The rows were tiered in height. The carpet was a rich burgundy and the oversized leather seats matched the motif. Against a high wall was the standard size projector screen. The seating was more plentiful than that of the main house. This place could seat about a couple of dozen people.

In the center of the room, David, the new pastry chef, was delivering plates covered in metal dome cloches to a candlelit table set for two. He offered a neck bow before disappearing into a back door.

"Let's eat, Mrs. Ellis." He lifted my hand in the air for prompting. "I hate when your salutation doesn't reflect that."

"Not everyone knows we're married, Sadik," I reminded him as I took the stairs in my heels.

"Let's repair that."

He held the chair out for me to sit. As he traveled across the table for his seat, I took note of the Muzak flowing softly above us.

"This is nice," I breathed, contented.

"You're more than nice," he returned almost too quickly. "Besides, as I've stated pathetically, I've missed you."

I felt my eyes sparkle his way. Those sentiments were music to my ears. "I've missed you, too, baby."

He offered me the hand sanitizer on the table. I accepted it and rubbed the gel over my hands, watching him do the same. He then poured himself a glass of brandy. My water had been prepared for me.

"You like beets, Nalib?"

My face tightened in disgust. "Ewww, no. They reek."

He removed a cloche, revealing a salad of sorts. "Not glazed beets. They go well with goat cheese, walnuts, arugula, tangerine slices, and a delectable balsamic vinaigrette dressing." He forked a combination of the ingredients, managing a walnut on there, and brought it to my mouth.

I dithered, sniffing the food. Sadik lifted an admonitory brow and I opened for him. My eyes were on him as he licked his thumb and waited for my reaction. I moved the food around in my mouth, tasting the different textures. Similar to our sexual dynamic, I rarely found a problem letting him lead. And for the act of obedience, I was rewarded with a delicious culinary experience. I nodded my head.

"Mmmhmmm," he gloated. "Sometimes you just have to trust me." His lips curved into a grin.

"I do. Too much," I shared honestly. "but I do."

His eyes lowered into a lascivious slit before he forked salad for himself this time. I relaxed into contentment as my husband went about feeding me tasty foods. After the salad was a delicious plank of Chilean seabass, juicy baked chicken breast, the best roasted sweet

potatoes I'd ever had, steamed asparagus, and creamy mashed potatoes. Best of all, I didn't have to lift a finger to fill my belly.

"What?" he asked while stacking our plates.

"You're fahn!" I joked, intoxicated by satiation.

Sadik snorted a laugh, eyes rolled adorably. "I'm pleased to know
I 'please' *all* your senses."

He sent a text on his phone then pulled his elbows up to the
clothed table, his inescapable gaze fixed on me.

This time I asked, "What?"

"Your hand."

My regard fell to the table, where I wiggled my fingers. "You
don't like the neon orange?"

"I'm not referring to your nail color, baby. It's your ring finger on
your left hand."

Once again, I glanced at my hand, specifically the glistening
diamond of my engagement ring. "I'm so lost, Sadik."

"I've had you out here illlegitimized."

My faced tightened more with curiosity. "How so?"

He tossed his chin my way. "Under your seat. Take a look."

Hesitantly, my gaze dropped to the floor. Gripping the end of the
table with my right hand, I leaned over to reach beneath my chair.
Sure enough, there was a small box there I managed not to kick over
during the meal. When I pulled the small ring box up to the table,
Sadik had his left hand splayed in the air.

I frowned.

On his ring finger was a thick platinum band fitting him
perfectly, making Sadik appear lusciously owned. Next to his ring, on
his pinky, there was another one significantly smaller in size, but the
same design.

My mouth opened just to close. "Is...that..."

Sadik took a deep pull of his *Mauve* before removing the ring on
his pinky and grabbing my hand. In the center of the table, he
removed my engagement ring then slid the new band on. Next, he
returned the engagement ring, pushing it into the band until they
both rested at the base of my finger. The set was beautifully
matched.

"Thank you," I murmured, adorning the symbols of what we'd been building since I decided to let go of my fears last summer and embrace this reckless need of him.

"Thank *you*," he corrected. "It's something I should have done a month ago, but as you know—"

"Yeah," I sighed nervously. "Life can get ahead of you."

"You just make sure you don't, Nalib." He traced an infinity ring inside the palm of my hand, spiking my blood.

Sounds of the door effectively broke my trance. David had returned to collect the plates.

"The movie is ready when you guys are," he informed us before exiting out with the rolling tray table.

Sadik stood and reached for my hand. "Let's see how your favorite R&B artist flexes his acting skills in a drama."

I sat in the seat, scooting back. "You say it as though he's my crush or something." That was my way of denying something that was somewhat true.

Out of all the R&B artists over the past ten years, Raj had been the only one keeping my attention. There was something wholesome about his aura and his musical talent was out of this world soulful. It was no surprise to me he could act years ago when I watched the first major motion film he was featured in. This was his second lead in a dramatic film. So far, the movie critics had been mixed, nothing too bad. But those of us who championed the passion Ragee exuded in every aspect of art he pursued had high hopes for this venture. The previews had been compelling.

Sadik lifted my foot and unbuckled the strap to my sandal. "I would never say something untrue, baby. Ragee can't possibly be your crush when it's me, alone, crushing your ass on a regular." He shook his head, hard eyes on me. "I'm your one and only. Those rings solidify it, sweetheart—"

I issued a swift kick to his leg that was caught mid-air. Sadik chuckled at my brazen act before removing my other sandal. Suddenly, I was irritated, sex pulsing. Sexual frustration could do that to you. Maybe it was the pregnancy, but my body, mind, and soul craved him. Sitting through a movie with my favorite artist, *or not*, couldn't cure the ache in my core and the longing in my heart to be one with him again.

Sadik settled in the theater seat beside me, causing a pang of loneliness far worse than what I felt when he was in Georgia. The lights dimmed for the start of the main attraction. Ten minutes into the film, I was crawling aside him, wrapping my arms around his tapered waist. His body heat warmed me, his scent thrilled me, and the feel of his skin against mine tortured me well into the movie.

My hands moved around him subconsciously. I started beneath his shirt with just my hand resting on his abdomen. That led to a light caress from side to side, enjoying the hilliness of it. Midway through, Sadik ran out to get us candy from the concession stand. When he returned, he fed me *Raisinets* and *Mike and Ikes*. At some point, my hand returned beneath his t-shirt, brushing north, feeling the wiry hairs of his chest.

When the movie was over, and the credits ran, I was left with a miscellany of feelings. Sadik hit a button on a remote and muted the room.

"So," he pulled in a deep breath, his eyes low from exhaustion. "what do you think?"

"About his performance?" I turned to him. "Raj did well. I knew he'd be able to pull this one off."

"No. About the state of my skin," Sadik quipped. I didn't get it. "Your damn hands have been examining me the whole movie."

I glanced down and my hand stilled at the same time I realized my thumb was circling around his peaked nipple. When my eyes reached his again, Sadik's brows shot up. He was effortlessly gorgeous, impossibly cursed with exotic features. And he was mine, the father of my children. My spouse. Without a second thought, I reached for the side of his face and pulled him toward me. I pecked his lips reverentially before leaning in again, swiping my tongue in his mouth.

I tasted his candy almost as much as I did his powerful countenance. I had to remind myself frequently how Sadik wasn't an average man. He didn't carry a fair amount of responsibilities; he had that over several men. He didn't earn like the average man, didn't stress like the average man. And I could guess he didn't make love like a common man either.

"Sadik," I whispered, desperately needing him inside of me.

His eyes were low and groan feral, "It was my plan to complete this date before taking you back to our suite and ridding you of this dress."

My dress. Thankfully, the Ellises had a dress code for family dinners. Hard bottom shoes were preferred. Today, I decided on an asymmetrical midi wrap dress. One shoulder of the satin piece was exposed as well as a thigh. I found the hook at the side of my waist and detached the fabric, exposing myself to him. Those irises darkened to a green as his regard swept me from my chest down to my crossed feet. I lifted a leg to perverse the visual.

Sadik's eyes rolled to the back of his head on a squeeze as he inhaled deeply. "Shit," he swore. "The scent of your pussy will haunt me well into a senile mind. I've missed how pretty it is."

My eyes rolled around the theater, noting the closed doors.

Sadik pushed a button to lower the footrest. As he slipped to the floor, he murmured, "I can't wait until we get back to the suite."

With a few tugs and me lifting my hips, my panties were being pulled down my leg. Without much prompting, my thighs opened to him, releasing my feminine odor into the air. Sadik's face drew to my sex and he pulled in a deep breath, causing my hips to flex. His soft lips met my own and my lungs shuddered. The deep rise and falls of my full breasts in lace obstructed the view of his shiny golden head.

Warmth cradled my body from the strokes of his magical tongue. Against the lightning zaps flashing in my feet and back, I widened to him, wanting nothing discouraging this closeness I now craved with Sadik: my husband, my lover. My spine bowed at the sounds of his nimble tongue battering my clit. He sucked, licked, teased, and kissed in a sequence to control the speed of my orgasm.

The build began and I pushed into it, holding onto his smooth scalp, harnessing the control center of my pleasure. My suppressed breasts felt heavy in my bra. So badly, I wished I was completely naked for him, had the caress of his hands everywhere. Almost as though he'd read my mind, his big hands pushed up my hips and planted on my curved belly. The sight of them there was so damn erotic to me.

A quickening began in my core. So overtaken by sensations heightening in nearly each corner of my body, I couldn't decide where to focus and eased into the growing pleasure. I didn't want it to end. I was so wet, I could hear it. Feel it. Sadik's mastering of my body felt like total world peace. It was happening too fast. I wanted to savor the bliss of his return.

I scooted back, hands gripping the armrests aside me to break his cadence and relieve the tipping pleasure. Sadik growled, roughly yanking my hips to his face. His mouth was on me again, tough —*firmer* hands plastered over my round abdomen. My resistance waned and I knew my orgasm was imminent.

Slouching even more with helplessness, my lazy eyes began to float above my lover's shiny head and landed on a large set of dark curls. In a haze, I blinked once then twice before I recognized Tiffany's aghast expression. But it was too late. I felt the thin capsule of bliss break and my orgasm flooded my groin with fury. My hands shot to his head again, orchestrating his efforts, yet my eyes never closed. They locked onto her, heightening my ascension until a cry ripped from my lungs and I screamed out my husband's name in helpless pleasure.

"One more," his command was graveled as he repositioned himself before me.

Sadik lifted my legs even higher above his shoulders. When his mouth hit me again, I understood why. From this angle, I felt new sensations, his swipes reached lower, sparking crackles of decadent pleasure. He didn't caress my swollen clitoris right away, but when he did, it didn't take long at all before my second orgasm began to brew in my groin. The lewd sounds of his tireless lapping pushed me over the edge and I came again. This time, my husband's former lover and bastardized relative was nowhere in sight. It made my second orgasm no less ravishing.

When I was done, pelvis still shaking, Sadik lowered my legs and pulled me to the edge of the seat, wrapping my legs around his waist. He stood with me clung to his upper torso. I felt him unbuckle his pants beneath me as I toured his mouth with my hungry tongue. So lost to him orally, I didn't feel being turned around and lowered into the seat until I was straddling him. Sadik hit the remote to the seat to recline his body. Then from behind me, I felt his smooth bulbous head swiping along my slit. So sensitive at the nub, I leaped. I didn't need the preamble. Lifting, I reached between my thighs for his thick, heavy appendage and pulled it to my opening where I immediately sat on him.

"Oh," I squealed, emptying my lungs.

Sadik was dense, hot, and throbbing inside of me. I bit my bottom lip as I peered down on him.

"Go slow," he could barely speak, his head thrown back and cords on his throat protruding.

His breaths were harsh, teeth pushing through his tight lips. I began to move, slowly reacquainting with his size. Sadik's hands lifted to the top of my dress, pushing the one shoulder down. Next was my bra being unclipped, releasing my heavy globular breasts I didn't recognize.

Gosh...

The sight of them in the same frame as Sadik's lazy eyes sparkling with unadulterated excitement had my head tossing back. My hips strained, taking him all the way in from the thick root. Sadik overwhelmed, in the literal and figurative manner, my mental and physical senses. If enduring his absence for a couple of days would be rewarded with rabid pleasure like this, perhaps the tradeoff was fair.

Sadik was a physical wonder; experiencing him beneath me was something I didn't want to miss a moment of. Seeing him mist at the forehead. His rolling abs moving from under his t-shirt that was flipped up at some point. The entire scene so intoxicating, my groin imploded again. I managed my cries through tightened lips and wide nostrils. My torso jerked dangerously as I rode out my orgasm, my walls clutching his throbbing stiffness.

When I was able to see again, Sadik's eyes were dark and the muscles around them strained. "Come here, Nalib."

I reached over, capturing his mouth, enjoying the aftershocks from my explosion. Sadik grabbed my hips, manipulating my strokes.

My clit was stimulated at this angle, maintaining my excitement. Just when I thought I couldn't sustain more pleasure, Sadik's thrusts into me from below grew rocky, his clasp on my hips would bruise me for days from his intensity.

"Fuck, Bilan!" he groaned unabashed while slamming into me with ferocity.

That sequence of movement and pressure against my clit caused my third orgasm to barrel through. I mewled helplessly, grasping his shoulders.

So good...

Those two words carouseled in my mind until our desperate movements slowed to a stop.

"My belly," I grunted urgently.

Too weak to hold myself at a distance to his chest, I needed to be pushed up. Quickly, Sadik pushed the button on the chair and we inclined.

"Better?" he breathed roughly.

With closed eyes, I nodded, trying to catch my breath, too.

I was in love. Helplessly. Who maintained all of this combustible energy in a relationship, much less a marriage? My blessing. Bishop Carmichael was right: Sadik was my fortune. He's given me more than a life of worldly spoils. Sadik's given me an identity in life.

I kissed his soft lips, nibbling as my fingertips massaged his head. The moment was perfect and just for us. I felt so sheltered in his arms. So protected and adorned. That was confirmed when he reached up and swiped his thumb beneath my left eye.

"How do you feel?" His tight eyes beamed.

A sheepish grin lifted on my face. "Like a kept woman."

He snorted a chortle. "You're my woman. You'll always be kept, Nalib."

My eyes rolled to the side as I thought. "Then I feel...nasty." I wiggled over his cock that was still hard. "Real nasty and so good."

He nodded, tracing the contour of my face with his thumb. I melted into his touch. My lashes fluttered as I leaned into him. "I've missed you."

After a beat, he murmured, "Oh, yeah?" I nodded, biting my bottom lip to hide my beam.

God, just a few hours ago, when we pulled up to the theater, I felt an unnamed tension between us, working against the euphoria I was now feeling. It amazed me how much Sadik influenced my mood.

"Yeah."

"So how did you pass the time while I was away?" My body tensed unfairly, eyes rolled to the right. Sucking in a deep breath, Sadik lifted to nuzzle the side of his face to mine. "And before you decide on which truth to share, just know I've been aware of your arrangement with Robert."

Air vacuumed into my lungs. I leaned away from him, capturing his eyes. Sadik rested back against the seat again. My heart began to beat out of my chest, limbs trembling.

"I..."

"You just had to go to that church in Harlem, didn't you?"

Swallowing hard, I blinked several times. "*I—* Well, you know I've been..."

"And my family's church couldn't do until I returned home?"

I didn't know if I should feel relieved or afraid of being found out. "What's the difference?" I asked confused. "Why would you going with me be any better? I'm not a child."

With lifted brows, his head shifted back. "What would be the difference?" he echoed. "Do you understand the security risk you and Robert took by going there?"

"I didn't go alone. Robert isn't just a driver: he's security, too. He's armed and trained."

"One trained security," he spat from his belly. "One armed man in a facility housing nearly eight thousand people."

"But nothing happened. I'm fine. I'm here!" I argued, reminded of Sadik's swift and severe mood swings.

"You're here by the grace of God. But you also put all those people at risk for someone wanting to hurt my father and this family by killing you. It was a stupid and goddamn foolish call. How fuckin' reckless could you be?"

I shuffled off of him with a quickness I never had to employ. Frantically, I searched for the top of my dress to slip back into, no longer wanting to be bared to him.

"I'm sorry I'm not well versed with the Mafioso manuscript of this family."

Sadik scoffed, standing to his feet to retrieve his pants from the floor. "Please tell me you at least know if cornered by law enforcement, unless read your Miranda rights, you're free to go."

"Fuck you!" I turned to leave.

The minute I grabbed my sandals from the floor, I felt his hand at my arm. Sadik pulled me into his chest, my face against his hardness. I hated breathing in the mixture of his natural scent, cologne, and our sex in that moment.

"You forgot something," his velvety alto murmured over my head.

"What?" I cried, the barrage of pending tears heated my cheeks.

"That this thing is forever. We can fight, but we don't run from each other, Nalib. Not ever."

"And you can't be rude to me."

"I adore you," he countered.

"Not with that tone, you don't." I backed away from him, chin in the air and lips trembling. God, I wouldn't have felt so raw if wasn't for the love we'd just made. It completely obliterated my defenses. How did I have a chance to defend myself if he led with sex and not what had been on his mind? "I'm not your employee!"

Sadik stepped forward and pulled me into his chest again. He kissed the top of my head. "You're the love of my life. The mother of my children. My world." With my face buried into his white t-shirt, I trembled from tears. "I'm sorry, Nalib. We'll get better at this."

The battery on my iPad would soon die. I told myself then was when I'd call it a night—or a morning. I'd just finished going over the latest cannabis regulations and moved on to Julius' approval predictions for meeting the mark on his proposed policies. It was still early in his mayoral seat, but I wanted to stay connected to his constituency.

My focus faded while reading and I used my other hand to rub it away until I heard one of my phones vibrate near me. The clock next to them on the nightstand read one-fifty-three in the morning. After picking up both phones to see which one vibrated, I saw the alert of a text message from Sofia.

S. Cruz: *Please excuse my lack of formality, but where was your ass tonight? You said you'd be back today and I've been left alone to sort through the talking points for the land trust pamphlets.*

She ended it with the crying emoji face icon. I chuckled.

Me: I did return tonight. Had a pressing matter to attend. We'll settle those in the morning.

I placed the iPad on the nightstand, officially calling it a night.

The phone vibrated again.

S. Cruz: *There's no time like the present. Hop on your jet and head over to P-town. We can knock it out tonight and have tomorrow off.*

My head rolled over the pillow and I scoffed softly.

Me: *As much as I would love to have tomorrow off I no longer have the lifestyle to avail myself to work engagements at crazy hours.*

S. Cruz: *Oh! Disculpe, hombre de familia. I have to remember moving forward. Night.*

I questioned whether my explanation was harsh. It wasn't my intent to shit on old friends because of my new life. I wasn't that type of guy. I also didn't want to set the wrong expectations of my availability.

After placing the phone down, I gazed down my chest to Sadik's chubby face. His long lashes curled and little lips parted, breaths so soft I could hardly hear them. I lifted my head looking farther down on my belly where his mother's head rested. Her face was now washed of running mascara and sculpted cheeks peppered with cinnamon as she slept like an angel on me. She had one hand on his small foot and the other splayed on my thigh.

As I reached over to turn off the lamp, I thought more of my new world. This was it. I fell asleep feeling like a king, and woke up each morning with the mentality of a hunter. I had a family. Responsibility to cover. Having my wife creep around beneath my nose spoke more to my irresponsibility rather than her disobedience. I had to do better at balancing the blessing.

∞20∞

I was over the bathroom sink shaving my head in the mirror when Rory's face craned inside.

"Yo..."

I met her eyes in the mirror. "You guys haven't left yet?"

"'Bout to now. Just wanted to put you *D* on the latest."

"What's that?" I carefully guided the blade around my ear.

"That beach house Popov keep his sister and them?" My eyes widened to her. "That shit a mountain of ashes."

I lowered the blade. "Who?"

"Danny Lopez." Her expression was a mixture of shock-humor. "Look like that nigga, Danny, ain't forget his pop's restaurant. He waited it out."

It had been a little over a month since Popov burned down *La Cocina*, one of Lopez's restaurants. I'd heard Danny, the son and current inheritor of his father, Luis', estate, took it hard. He'd lost family in the fire.

"I guess no one can fault him." I tossed my chin to her. "What now?"

Rory scoffed. "Obviously, a muthafuckin' war popped off with that."

I shook my head, meeting her gaze in the mirror. "Lopez's crew ain't long enough for that. Plus, they're heavily reliant on relatives and not employees. When one of their men drop, the L is different."

"No cap."

I took a minute to think about that. Under normal circumstances, I wouldn't advise my father to get involved, but in this case, there were several compelling factors beckoning my attention. Taaliba had seemed to be...involved with him lately. Per Popov, they'd developed a disgusting sexual relationship. I could give a shit about a kiddie kissing game, however, she'd spent time with him. Leaving Danny Lopez alone in this battle assured the end of the Lopez name. They didn't have the resources to go against Popov. Also, my father and I were at war with Popov, too. My father for dropping Popov as a weapons supplier, and me for his foot soldier using my wife as a pawn to get to my father. Bilan could have easily been killed that day if Popov's plan was to do more than rattle my father.

"Hit up, Double E Bags' new right hand, Daz. Tell him I said it may be wise to send a few good men to war aside the Lopez's. Keep an eye on the situation in case they need more before we have to pull in fully under Double E's behalf against Popov."

She nodded, but Rory's eyes were to the floor.

"What is it, Bean?" I knew that look.

"I just..." She changed position, swiping her nose. "Going to war... I'm good with wherever the shit goes. You know that; I'm built for this shit."

"Say it."

"You never wanted it." Rory shrugged. "Whenever we got our hands dirty, it was underneath Double E. This shit with Popov and you is personal. Going to war put you on the fight line next to your pops. That some shit you ain't never want." She shook her head, her eyes unable to meet mine. "You busted ya ass for all the shit you got. You bust ya ass to build a legit dynasty, and you just filled ya seeds and a wifey in it. Now that some nigga stepped on ya shoes—meaning wifey—you ready to shoot the park up in daylight. I just 'on't want that for you. I want you to have that happily ever after, my nigga."

Quickly, she left the doorway. My gaze shifted to myself in the mirror. After her words of heeding, I saw something there. It was something that had been present for over a month, but I'd been too busy moving to recognize it.

I saw Earl Ellis.

On my way to the waiting car, I texted Randi.

Me: I got us a hotel suite. Ask Brenda if she wants to come. I can't drink but I can turn up somehow.

Rolling my eyes at my comment, I glanced up to open the back door of Sadik's sleek ruby-black *Mercedes-Maybach*. My truck was undergoing maintenance repairs and he told me I'd have to "settle" for his car today. That tickled me as I slipped inside, scooting over to center myself in my seat. My gaze lifted to the front of the car and I steeled.

Rory's small frame twisted around to face me as she sported the widest most disingenuous grin.

I rolled my eyes, letting out a deep sigh of disappointment and annoyance.

"Out of all the drivers on this 'plantation,' why are you here?" I grated.

"Because my sire asked me to drive his royal highness to the mall today."

"Don't do me any favors." My face was tight with unbridled anger.

She pushed her phone out to me.

On instinct—*and foolishly*—I took it. Rory had a *Droid*, but through the annoying curvy, colored font, I was able to make out a message between her and a "Jawbreaker." At least, that was the profile name. The person asked her when would they be able to hang out now that they were related. Rory asked how were they related. Jawbreaker said through her cousin...

Bilan?

Rory asked, "*Who is you, my nigga?*" That ebonics made me dizzy. But seeing the next entry was my cousin, Brenda, blew my mind. She sent a picture of herself. In this image, Brenda didn't appear as the asexual, nondescript person I knew her to be. Here, she was a clear lesbian. Full-on butch with her pose and hairstyle. I almost didn't recognize her.

Rory replied, "*I 'ont no wut type a party u think this is but it ain't this sus.*" I blinked before reading it again. Brenda replied, "*A'ight. I'll see you at the fam reunion. LMFAO*"

My stomach rippled. Brenda was strong-arming my husband's security and assistant. I had no idea she was gay, much less capable of such boldness. It brought to mind Tasche telling me about Brenda frequenting her job. This was too much. Taking a deep breath, I handed the phone back to Rory.

Her smile slipped when she accepted it. "Tell ya people's I 'on't get down like that."

"Tell your boss you don't want to drive me to the mall today," I countered.

"It's my job, B."

"Don't do me any favors. It's not too late to arrange for a new driver."

"I 'on't want you to. I wanna take you to the mall." The letter "V" formed between her large eyes. "Chill. I wanna be cool again."

"Again?" I snorted. "We were never cool. We learned to live with the fact you don't like me, never did. But since then I've seen the truth in how you feel about me."

Rory rolled her eyes, mumbling incoherent words through tight lips, resembling a teenaged urban boy. Then she tried calming herself as a new approach. "How I feel about you, B?"

"Oh, let's not act like you don't know. You never liked me, Rory. Since day one, you've been so cold, unlike how you are with Sadik's exes. I've never been given a chance, only tolerated because your boss fell for me!"

"That ain't exactly true." Her eyes rolled again. "And don't act like you ain't slip and tell me what you really been thinking about me at Richards' victory party. I peeped that shit."

My head swung to the side. "What are you talking about?"

"When you called me the employee, or some shit. That shit was foul as hell!"

I recalled that. It was the first thing that came to mind that night when I was in a fit of anger, because it was what Earl referred to her as last fall when he popped up at my job for the first time. I hated that he used that term. I guessed it stuck because I said it at the victory party to hurt her, just the way she hurt me that night.

I turned away from her, lifting my chin dramatically, something I noticed I'd been doing for the first time in my life to Sadik. "You've made it clear that's the relationship we've had all this time."

"Fuck!" Her little body jerked as she shouted. "The fuck more you want from me, Bilan? I ain't one of ya girls."

"You're damn right, you're not! You're far too cold and...mannish to ever be."

She nodded at my words, eyes traveling away. "Nice. Now I'mma fuckin' man," she mumbled.

Embarrassed by that claim, I made clear, "I didn't say that!" I was out of breath. "It's just... Since I met him, you've made it clear I don't fit into his world."

"Maybe 'cause you fuckin' didn't!" she shouted. "You ever think about that?"

"Of course, I have. Almost every day, I question whether I'm good enough for him! But it's not up to you to make me feel I don't!

It's not your fucking business, Rory! I hope he doesn't interfere in your personal life like—"

"That muthafucka *is* my personal life!" she spat back, leaping around. "That's the part you can't see. That man *is* my responsibility! Who the fuck you think go out to get you fuckin'..." she stalled quickly to think. "*Chanel*, *La Perla*, fresh fuckin'...polypropylene braided ropes, and shit? Who you think do that man's research for *Ellis International*, his damn dispensaries, and the house he building for you? How you think luxury vacations get booked while he seduce ya ass like some pussy-fiend Romeo, or some shit? Who the fuck you think been quarterbackin' shit in his life before he got a wife?" She pounded her chest. "Me!"

I rolled my eyes outside of the window, gazing over other parked fleet of luxury cars, trucks, buses, vans, and limos in the massive garage house.

"I'm sure you're paid well," I mumbled loud enough for her to hear.

"You think this shit about money?"

My head whipped, facing her again. "I'm sure I'm not far off! I know who I married."

"And that's my fuckin' point, B! You married a complicated ass fuckin' man. Nobody know that more than me. Maybe you right." She nodded. "Maybe I ain't think you was a good look for that man when you started coming around last year."

Allowing my emotions a momentary slip, I asked, "And why not?"

"Because of how you is right now. You wanna cry, B, and I see that shit!" She neared me over the seat. "I'm fuckin' paid well *because* I see that shit right in ya face."

A tear slipped. "Fuck you, Rory! I'm a woman...with real feelings. You don't know how it feels to love a man who's beyond you!"

"And that's my fuckin' point, B!" Her hand shot out expressively. "Y'all wasn't on the same page last year. You wasn't thorough enough to handle the real Sadik Ellis. I was scared as shit that the man was pulling you in without a fuckin' life vest. You know him now. You know his fuckin' pops and how he move. I ain't like that some girlie, jumpy ass bitch was getting so fuckin' close to my 'employer.' Somebody that was scared of her own fuckin' shadow. Him going to jail for some fuck shit don't just fuck with his livelihood; it fucks with my life. That nigga is *my* life! I would die for that man to have freedom, fuck millions." Her face tightened something ugly like a hardened criminal. Maybe Rory was and I didn't know. "I may as well put a bullet to my own fuckin' head if that man ain't good, yo! And you was just that type to run to the fuckin' pigs at the first sight of some of his gray shit."

"I didn't!" I argued. "I may have run, but I never talked to anyone!"

"Yeah, but you fuckin' ran with the nigga's heart!" her shout was louder. "I ain't never see my mans so fuckin'...hurt. *Urgh!*" she growled as though trying to contain her blooming rage. "I hate even speakin' that weak shit!" Rory shook her head viciously, like a crazed woman. "You did shit to the man I ain't even think was possible."

At this point, my arms were crossed beneath my chest, effectively slipping into shutdown mode.

"Well, that doesn't explain why you're so nice to the ones before me."

"I ain't nice to nobody—"

"You called her *Sofee!*" I screamed at the top of my lungs. "Tiffany calls you to ask about my lover's...*my* husband's whereabouts while you're carting me around. You don't give them short, snippy responses like you do me. You don't think that gives me the impression of intimacy between you and them?"

"I ain't saying what it be givin' you, but I damn sure know what I 'on't be giving them, what my boss 'on't give them bitches."

My lips trembled as I ripped my gaze away from her. I swiped the tears from my face. "That still doesn't explain why you're so distant with me. I don't even know your real name. You tried to give me the name of a wealthy woman in Paterson out in *St. Justin*." It had taken a few days, but it had dawned on me out of nowhere that Rahdeah Smith was a well-known woman in Paterson. She was highly noted as a celebrity event planner who never left her roots. She had bought a home in The Manor's section and was rumored to have armed security to prevent robberies. I felt foolish for not catching her lie that day. "You think I wouldn't have figured—"

"Rokema Watkins!" she shouted again, flashing that short temper again. "You got my fuckin' government. You happy now?" Rory snatched her small frame away, facing forward.

I ignored her mumbled string of expletives as she roared the engine. She'd upset me, and I needed a moment to collect myself. The ride to the mall was done with no words exchanged. Rory played her usual underground hip hop while I logged into my old school's email.

Sunday night, after church, I'd used Jason's credentials and gained access to the database he mentioned. It was a fruitless lead. Yes, there were more hits per word search combo, but all were pretty much the same I'd found via *Google*. The one interesting piece of information I did come across was about Hubert Jackson, the man Iban murdered, was the director of an alternative youth program for *NJ Department of Corrections*. Apparently, he was a tenured, tough warden of sorts.

When my undergrad inbox loaded on my phone, I was surprised to see I'd had over one hundred messages. When Sadik purchased this phone for me last spring, I never downloaded the school's app, which would have given me quicker access as well as alerts for emails.

My jaw collapsed and I gasped. I slapped my hand to my mouth and glanced up to Rory to see if she'd caught my expression.

Half the emails were from Jason.

I'm emailing you because you haven't answered my texts or calls. Hopefully you'll see this.

Have you had the baby yet? Call me.

What's going on over there? It's past your due date. Please contact me.

Bilan, call me. It's important.

I'd like to see you and the baby. Hit me up.

Please call me. Here's my new number. I had to get it changed.

I saw the baby on Ellis' sister's IG. He's beautiful like his mother. Please, please call me Bilan!

Still reaching out. Here's my number again.

I've been trying to reach out to you. I went to Ellis' place but they wouldn't let me up. I need to see you.

My parents were in an accident. There's something I need to talk to you about.

Sadik Ellis is dangerous. I need to talk to you. I'm concerned about you and the baby.

I shuddered a breath. Who knew Jason was this persistent? My heart broke for him. He had no idea the type of man whose life he was trying to infringe upon. I shook my head, eyes rolling out the window to passing, blurred trees. This had to stop. As much as I'd succumbed to my illness of accepting I was in love with a murderous man with a violent family, Jason didn't know the half. He had no idea of how much of a risk he was putting himself at contacting me. I had to do something to put an end to this. I had to save Jason's life without him knowing exactly what I was doing. I'd have to meet with him. Where and when was the question. Sadik would never be okay with it.

By the time we'd pulled up to the mall, I'd searched Rory's real name in the database and learned a few new details on her. She was forty-five years old and had been in and out of correctional facilities from eleven years old until the last robbery stint just over fifteen years ago. It was my assumption her employment with Sadik began sometime after. The biggest kicker—other than her advanced age—was that one of the facilities Rory had visited was the same as Iban when they were underaged. It was the one Hubert Jackson ran until his death.

We pulled into a parking space and Rory cut the engine.

"Rory..."

She let go of the door handle and sat back, bracing herself. "Yeah, B."

"You said you met Iban in a probation program." She didn't move to speak. "You two were locked up together in a juvenile program." When she still wouldn't reply, it angered me. "I guess you think I'm stupid along with jumpy and scary, huhn?"

Rory sucked her teeth, shouldering the door open with force. I left the car, too.

"The fuck!" she screamed like a teenaged quarterback. "What do you want from me, Bilan?"

"Why are you here?" I asked. "Why do I need you—no!" My hand shot into the air. "More specifically, who is attacking the family?"

Her eyes swept across the parking lot. "You know I can't answer that?"

"Yeah. Right." I snapped my fingers in a revelatory manner. "You're just an employee."

"Don't fuckin' try me, B!" She started my way.

"How did Iban only get four years for killing Hubert, and how did the law team the Ellises hired pull it off?"

She froze instantly, one leg ahead of the other, and Rory's eyes enlarged impossibly. "That's some shit between Sadik and Iban." *Huhn?* Then her head cocked to the side. "You really tryna get me fired? You hate me that fuckin' much, B? Word?" She seemed genuinely betrayed before taking off.

My eyes closed to a squeeze before I followed her toward the entrance. On the way, my phone pinged in my hand.

My Lover: *How's it going? You aren't killing her are you?*

I snorted before typing back.

Me: Not yet, but don't be surprised if only one of us returns. BTW it was sneaky of you to not tell me she'd be my driver today.

That was mean. How in the world did I end up in a lifestyle that required drivers and personal security? It was an ungrateful comment I immediately regretted. It didn't matter that Rory scanned around me again to make sure I was okay and *that* annoyed me...again. By the time I made it to the curb of the entrance, Sadik was texting back.

My Lover: *Take it easy on my girl. She's my top employee. And while you're at it, I need a pack of Ase Garb trouser socks. Neiman carries them.*

Me: I guess that means I'll have to secure this victory and slay the turtle to ensure I return home tonight.

I dropped the phone to my hip after hitting send. Rory was holding the door open for me. Seconds later, my phone pinged again.

My Lover: *Knock it the hell off Nalib.*

I rolled my eyes as I hissed through gritted teeth to Rory. "Your boss needs something from *Neiman Marcus*. I guess we can head there first."

And that's what we did. We walked a considerable distance to the luxury department store. I found cute trousers socks for Sadik and collected several pairs. On the way out of the *Ase Garb* section, my eyes latched onto boxer briefs. There were a few design patterns I found attractive and complementary to his hard, golden skin. I grabbed a couple of those, too. Ten minutes later, we were out of the store and traversing the large mall.

On the way to my intended pace, I stopped at a baby store. It had cute clothes for my growing baby. Rory was quiet and observing as I purchased Sadik clothes and onesies. Camille recently commented on how snug the current ones had become. When I was done there, we continued our stroll. I decided on this particular mall because it had an array of stores ranging from high end to modest and budget-friendly merchants. At the other end of the mall, we finally made it to an urban clothing store. This was my primary reason for coming here.

Tasche's birthday was quickly approaching and I wanted to get her something she'd like. She'd been talking about this spot for some time. Apparently, they have clothing and designs not found downtown Paterson, Passaic, or Newark, where she shopped. Randi called the store hood. One day, she told us about a fight that broke out in one part of the store while security was shaking down patrons in another area for shoplifting. I hoped neither would happen as I browsed the store for a few things that Tasche may like.

I saw a few mannequins modeling dresses I could see fitting her style. Grabbing the tag on one and reading $17.99, I knew I'd landed in the right place. Then I began grabbing dresses in her size, and even a few tops and leggings. The more I scrolled through, the more I understood why Tasche blew this place up. The clothes were a little too raunchy and the material skimpy for everyday wear for me, but the goal was her happiness. I still couldn't believe Tasche was so close to forty.

Shoot! Rory's forty-five!

These people around me were in the best shape of their lives! Rory looked all of fourteen and Tasche in her early twenties. Such was my life, it seemed: full of mind-blowing discoveries.

Whispering sounds caught my attention while I was at a table tray of leggings searching for the size medium. I turned toward the direction of the sound and saw three women looking my way. I rotated to see if I'd missed something or if someone was there who had their attention behind me. The only person I saw was Rory backing into an aisle, sporting a strange expression. I didn't think much of it, believing Rory wanted nothing to do with cattiness among women. I went back to browsing, knowing whatever had those girls' attention couldn't have anything to do with me. I'd never seen them before.

I found two pairs of leggings in medium; one a neon pink and the other an orange. I smiled to myself and mumbled, "*Hot girl summer.*"

"Say something!" My head shot over to find the girls closer. "I'mma say something."

"I see your punk ass, bitch!" another of the three stepped out of the narrow aisle and shouted my way, but over me. My head whipped the opposite way, and again, I saw nothing. "Oh, you open them lil' legs when my nigga around, but run them lil' legs when his bitch see you."

The women crossed me, going into the same direction I'd just seen Rory. I rolled my eyes, grabbed up the clothes I laid down to do my search, and went into the opposite direction. I stopped at the hosiery section when I spotted red fishnet stockings. Thinking about her line of work, I grabbed three packs for Tasche; red, white, and black.

When I moved on from there, I ran into Rory. She appeared abruptly, startling me.

"You ready?" she nearly whispered.

I glanced down and saw my hands were full from the Sadiks'

things, and my arms were small mountains for Tasche. It was time to call it quits.

"Yeah. I guess I am," I finally replied.

"Gucci." She gave a hard nod. "Go 'head to the register and I'll meet you by the door."

I regretted nodding my understanding the moment I did it. Rory didn't deserve anything from me. But I put that out of my head as I headed to the register. I saw two of the girls again as my things were being rung up. They were moving fast as though in search of someone. I rolled my eyes hard.

Oh, god...

I needed out of there. It had seemed Randi wasn't off on her description of this place. It was busy, but not overwhelmingly so. Maybe after being in isolation on expansive, palatial grounds for over a month, I grew sensitive to crowds. Again, I felt guilty instantly. I was being pompous just as I had coming in here. Maybe it was the pregnancy that had me feeling so irritable lately. As soon as I had paid and was handed my bags, I began toward the front of the store.

"You see her?" One of the three hood girls came running my way with her phone to her ear. "She in a suit, looking like my fuckin' nephew be going to school on picture day." She laughed. "I'm 'bout to drag her lil' ass!"

That hiked my heart rate. The description was eerily close to my current nemesis and escort today. I began taking deeper strides, moving down racks of clothes.

"B!" I heard barked and I almost toppled over, trying to stop.

I backed up to find Rory on the other side, along the wall. Her small frame waved me her way. Quickly, I obeyed, but not before I was seen moving too frantically.

"I think she over here, y'all!" someone shouted. The tallest of the three was on my trail. "Hold the fuck up!" she yelled behind. "Oh, shit! Y'all she right here!" she screamed at the top of her lungs. "Rory, I'mma fuck you up!"

I moved so fast the bags began to smack up against my legs.

"You got 'em?" Rory asked once I neared her. I nodded. "C'mon!"

We continued to the front of the store where, luckily, we glided out without a problem. But we were barely to the store next door when I heard the riotous shouts behind us.

"Shit! There they go!" I heard a series of voices.

"I'm fuckin' you up, Rory! I told you and Blockboy Jay it was on sight!"

"I got her!" Another yelped.

Rory stopped with apparent reluctance.

When I followed her actions, I asked, "Why are they after you?" I was out of breath, but not exhausted.

These girls' pursuit was like that of a scorned woman. What would Rory have to do with that...

"Is this about Sadik?" I screamed with wild eyes, adrenaline shot wildly through my veins.

Rory ignored me and addressed the girl running up on us. "Look, I'm fuckin' workin—"

It was too late. The girl swung on Rory once up on her. Rory ducked, grabbed the tall woman by her legs and flipped her over her shoulder. The girl—because that's precisely what they were acting like—flew into the air landing on her back. When I thought the girl could have been broken into two, she jumped to her feet, dazed.

"Get her!" The thickest girl screamed a yard away.

Rory's palms flashed defensively. "Yo! I 'on't want no trouble Mook! I'm workin', man!"

"Nah, hoe!" She threw her fists in the air on approach. "You wanna fuck my man and tell me to go kill myself? I told you, you was on suicide watch, bitch!"

"Mook, he played me, too! I ain't no he was fuckin' witchu until you came at me!" Rory tried pleading with the girl. "I swear to gawd, yo, I want no troubles. Fuck that nigga. He 'on't know how ta eat pussy no ways."

I felt lightheaded. What matrix was I caught in where Rory was begging a girl, who had to be in her early twenties to leave her alone? *Rory!* The same woman whose rap sheet I'd just read on my way here. The one who wore sports bras on island getaways and not bikini tops, which meant she had to wear them every day. The same lethal executioner I'd seen in action was afraid of hood girls whose only knowledge of self-defense was the fights they'd been in around the hood. This woman who'd been so cold to me, so *'you're a corny girl and I'm so cool, I run with big boys'* was afraid.

"Fuck you, hoe!" The girl's punch missed Rory, but before either of us realized it, the third one had descended and they were both swinging.

On little Rory...

My body steeled at first, then jutted violently at the sight. Rory turned to the last woman who jumped in and punched her once, winding her. While enduring thwacks from the second woman who accosted her—the one whose man Rory apparently slept with—she positioned herself and knocked the last woman to the floor with an even harder blow. Without warning, the first, tall woman had finally regained her wits and was back in the ring as Rory was choking her friend, Rory's nemesis. I knew Rory couldn't survive her. Physically, Rory was limited compared to the short, stout woman who had to be well over two-hundred-fifty pounds and the tall one, who likely weighed the same but was close to six feet tall. There was no way I could let them attack my husband's right hand in this fashion. There was something humbling happening here with Rory. Something I could feel, but couldn't quite understand.

My eyes swung around wildly. Something. I needed something blunt. Luckily, across the walkway was a *TJ Max* with shopping carts. *Didn't I say how much I appreciated the diversity in this mall?* I dropped my bags and darted over there, threading through the traffic of people who'd stopped to watch the melee. Racing across the way with the cart in lead, I returned to the two women pounding on Rory's small frame. She was down on the floor, curled over.

The tall girl was the biggest and clearest sight of them all, and no one was helping Rory. I yanked the cart to a stop. When I had control of it, I bent my knees, taking a deep breath, and used all my strength to swing and lift it in the air. I let it go in her direction. Thankfully, it hit my target, knocking the giant in the head and back. The giant hit the stubby girl, causing her to wobble and almost hit the floor, too.

I raced to Rory, grabbing her. "Come on!"

She shuffled to her feet, glancing around. "Get ya shit, Bilan." She pointed to my bags on the floor.

"Oh, shit!" a bystander trilled. "She's got a gun!"

My eyes shot over to Rory. The hem of her suit jacket was somehow tucked above the holster of her jacket.

"Rory!" I shouted. "Fix your jacket!"

Quickly glancing down, she did what I said. "Come the fuck on!"

We sped off once all the bags were secured. I had no idea what had just happened; my mind drew a blank as I trailed after her. We entered a store, traveling toward the opposite end until it led us outside.

"Sit right here," she ordered over her shoulder, gesturing a bench. "I'mma bring the car around."

I shook my head first, feeling a shooting pain from my lower back. "No." I shook my head. "No attention by bringing the car back up here." I was out of breath again, this time tired.

Still, I followed her through the heated parking lot. We walked nearly five minutes until we were at the car. Rory popped the trunk as soon as it was in sight. Before heading to the backseat, I dropped the bags at her feet as she dumped my others in there. Once inside, my eyes closed in exhaustion. A cry bubbled from my belly unexpectedly as the car shook from her slamming the trunk.

Rory slid quickly inside and locked the doors before pushing the engine button. "Why you cryin', yo?"

I tried controlling my breathing. "I forgot all about my baby." I juddered with my palms over my small belly. "My...back hurts."

"*Fuuuuuuuuuuck!*" Rory slammed her hands over the steering wheel, once again causing the car to tremble.

"Just go, Rory!" I yelled through my tears.

Obediently, she backed out of the parking space and eventually out of the mall's lot. My breathing didn't even out until we were well into our travel and trees appeared in a blur. No underground rap played during our long commute. Rory's thoughts were so loud as she drove silently, they kept me awake. My eyes were closed as I tried to breathe through the ache.

"B, I'm so fuckin' sorry for this. I ain't mean to get you involved in my personal shit. Fuck!" she grated. "S.Q.E.'s gonna kill my ass. One to the dome and toss me in the fuckin' minefield!" she muttered, mostly to herself. Her big eyes appeared in the rearview mirror. "The baby okay? I need to take you to the doctor or the hospital?"

We were minutes away from the compound. Was she serious?

Thick laughter pushed from my belly through my nostrils. "You're someone's side piece." I snorted like a pig, laughing so hard. "And by the looks of it, it's a block-hugging thug. Is that your type, Rory?"

"You'da preferred my type to have a slit between the legs?"

My head rolled over the headrest. "I couldn't care what your sexual orientation is." I couldn't stop laughing no matter how much it cost me in pain. "You think my beef with you would have been any different?" I leaned over to relieve one side, but couldn't kill my amusement. "But now that I know more about you, maybe I should pay more attention to you around my man. I wouldn't want to be the next chick running down on you. If I wasn't pregnant, I would do way more damage to you than those hoodrats. And I can shoot guns, too. Sadik's made sure of it." That raised my howl up a notch.

"I see yo ass *is* good." She rustled. I laughed while eyeing her in the mirror. Rory appeared more feminine than I'd ever imagined. "Name ya price."

It took a minute, but I sobered.

"What price?"

"I don't want the big homie to find out I had you out there like that today. What you want from me?"

That clarification sobered me. My mind raced until it settled on one thing. "You know what I want: information."

I watched her big eyes and head roll to the side. "That's fuckin' double jeopardy. I'm running my fuckin' mouth and tryna save my ass." Her head began to nod successively. "I get it now. You hate my ass."

The solemnness in her words wrapped around my throat, choking me. I wasn't trying to manipulate her. I was just desperate for insight on the family I'd married into.

"You don't know me at all," I hissed.

"Evidently, you 'on't know me either, baby girl." She turned onto the road of the estate with practiced familiarity. The over an hour trip felt like minutes. "Talking about my boss'll never be a deal between me and no fuckin' body."

Rory stopped at the guard's booth, expressing our identity. Then she drove into the designated parking space for Sadik's *Mercedes-Maybach*. Wordlessly, I exited the car. The trunk was unlatched by the time I closed the door and, quickly, I grabbed all my bags, not waiting on her assistance.

As I marched into the corridor leading to the house, I realized I'd been wearing heels. They were modest, three and a half-inch heels, but not a factor I considered before hauling that full-sized cart into the air. I knew it was only because of my recent workout sessions that I wasn't in bad shape. If it were not for the absence of abdominal pain, I would be concerned. I'd have to monitor my body's response to my reckless act for, at least, the next twelve hours. Right now, I needed to rest in bed, and I wanted to do it with my baby.

First, I'd get an ice pack for my back from Stacy. At this point,

Rory was in the rearview mirror of my mind. I had bigger fish to fry: I could feel a dark cloud descending over me. It was something I didn't want Sadik to see. I didn't want to have another episode in front of him. It had been weeks since the last.

Icepack, baby...

That's what I'd pursue to hopefully calm the brewing. I didn't break my stride down the wide and tall, warm-hued hallways. That was until I heard a commotion sounding to be in my path. I maintained my stride toward the butler's parlor, too tired to make out voices. I turned a corner then quickly another before the chaos heightened. Then finally bodies—spirited bodies—were congregated near one of the kitchen entrances. Nena, Diane, Tom, and Stacy were in a circle. The only person visibly calm was Nena. Her arms were crossed while in a silk kimono wrap and deep red lips pursed, applying that knowing smirk. Diane, who could be no more than five feet, one inch and just as short as Stacy, spoke with her hands, arms, and head. Stacy, in her apron uniform, had her arms stretched the length of Diane and Tom. Tom, the tallest of the group, alternated between folded arms across his chest and his hands at his waist.

"Please. Please!" Stacy begged. "If you would just give me a moment to get her on the phone."

"You said that five minutes ago." Diane's head rolled as she spoke. "I don't see why we have to wait on her anyway!"

"Because it's what Mr. Ellis and Deek wants," Stacy explained.

"Man," Tom sang, arms wrapping around his chest again. "This is some bullshit. Earl ain't the boss of me."

"And Irene ain't mine either," Diane made clear. "So what the hell are you saying? You don't get priority around here."

"There she is," Nena's deep, raspy vocals floated above the party's.

All eyes turned my way, but only Stacy started toward me. She was visibly shaken, her hand going to her forehead.

"Ms. Bilan, oh my goodness," she breathed. "I tried having the girls call you several times. Finally, I had them call Rory."

In a panic, I dropped the bags aside my feet in search of my cell. It was dead. That discovery had me swaying on my feet a bit. What if Camille tried calling me about the baby? After the fight at the mall, my last thought was my phone.

"It must have died while I was in the mall," I tried explaining and breathing through the slight dizzy spell. "What's going on?"

"We have an impasse happening," she tried to explain.

"About what?"

"Mr. Ellis' jet."

My eyes brushed over the trio behind her. I was wholly confused. "What about it?"

"Well," Stacy tried. "Tom wants to use the *Bombardier 7500* to fly to *Ellis Island* in Antigua with friends this weekend." My brows flew toward the ceiling as my eyes shot over to Tom. "That would create a scheduling conflict."

"Of what type?" I asked with my eyes still glued to Tom, standing with crossed arms, a posture of righteous indignation.

"Well, it's already been arranged for Ms. Nena to fly home this weekend."

"By whom?"

"Mr. Ellis."

"And when are you returning, Nena?" I asked.

"I'm not." Her head shifted left to right over her narrowed shoulders. A cool arrogance exuding from that act along with those two words.

"Not?"

She shook her head. "I'm staying home."

My chin dipped. "Forever."

That's when there was a break in her cocky resolve. A slight eye shift, breaking our contact told me Nena was hurt.

"Did he..." I cleared my throat, not knowing how to ask a simple question regarding my father-in-law. "Did he ask you to leave?"

"No." Her chin lifted. "*I* told him it's over."

My eyes blossomed.

"Tell her the rest!" Diane demanded.

Nena readjusted her silk wrap, once again appearing uncomfortable. I saw her throat move as she swallowed. "I'm pregnant."

This time, the wall broke my fall. The dizzy spell lasted longer. "By whom?" I asked, fighting through it.

"That's none of your business, sweetheart," her throaty vocals hissed.

Miraculously, that crossness sobered me. "It is if it's an Ellis baby, don't you think?"

"No, but to answer your question..." Nena shook her head. "It's not Earl's."

"That shit better not have been." Diane huffed, rolling her eyes. "Earl would've had another heart attack when I was through with his ass."

Stacy shook her head.

"What have Earl and Irene said about this dilemma?" I asked.

"It gets more complicated." Stacy's hand rested on my shoulder, a warning for me to brace myself.

"Okay..."

"See, Ms. Diane wants the jet, too, this weekend."

"For what?" My eyes swept over to Diane.

"For a trip to *Marye Island* for a few days. I need to get away," Diane explained, arms wrapping beneath her breasts. "Too much has been happening around here. I need an escape."

"A trip to an exclusive Florida Key? Why?" My face folded.

"What do you mean why? You've been around here, too." Diane's head began its rolling again. "Even Irene's taking one. *Shit*. Earl's been sick, Nena's pregnant, Palmer's dead, the family's on lockdown, you and Sadik staying here with a brand new baby, the girls are here every damn day, Iban's...gone. It's too damn much. I need a damn break."

Taking a deep breath, I tried offering an affable smile. "And what did Earl say to that?"

Diane swung her arm toward me. I looked to Stacy.

"*Maaaaaan*," Tom sang again, displaying irritation.

"Again, Mr. Ellis asked me to have you and Deek handle it," Stacy tried explaining.

"Where is Earl?"

"He's back at the hospital—just for tonight." Stacy's hand went into the air. "They're running tests on him that can only be done there. He'll be back tomorrow afternoon."

"And Irene?"

Stacy's regard met Diane. "Like she said, Mrs. Ellis has left town for a few days." Then she stepped closer to me and whispered. "I think your talk with her did some good." My eyes widened again. I had no idea Stacy knew I'd spoken to Irene. Stacy stepped back. "She is unavailable to deal with this. I called Deek, who asked me to have you deal with this."

Deal with his *parents' lovers fighting over the appurtenances of the Ellis name?*

I addressed Tom. "Do you know where Irene is?"

"No." His nostrils flared.

"So she's not on *Ellis Island*, in Antigua?"

His nostrils flared. "No, Bilan."

"Then why are you going there?"

His head reared as he scoffed. "I don't think that concerns you."

"Stacy, you're saying Earl and Sadik are deferring this call to me?"

"Yes, Ms. Bilan."

It was my turn to snort as I neared the three of them. "Earl has a heart attack two months ago, and you're pregnant by another man and leaving him." I pointed to Nena. "He's had complications from the heart attack, and *you* need a break?" I then pointed to Diane. When she began her rebuttal, I spoke over her, addressing Tom. "Your lover's husband almost died. You stay at their home, vacation with and without their family. Her son almost died from shooting himself in the head. She's so beyond her capacity, she's slipped into an emotional shell where she's hardly present for herself, much less her husband and their family. And *you* choose this time to want to grab up your buddies, take her husband's private luxury jet to an exclusive island he owns, eat his food, and labor his staff."

My eyes swept over the three of them. "You guys get to escape the heat happening on this twenty-acre estate, but still cool your-selves with the accouterments of the family. All the while, we're left back here trying to put the fire out—*if* we survive."

I backed away to grab my bags, once again, gathering them into my hands. Then I glanced over to Stacy. "The jet is unavailable until Earl or Irene says otherwise." My eyes cast over the trio. "Indefinitely."

"Whoa!" Nena barked out. "Earl already said I could go home on the jet."

I nodded. "Oh, you're going back home this weekend. I'll see to it myself you'll have a first-class, one-way ticket there on a commercial plane. In fact, Tom and Diane, you two can find some place to escape to that isn't on the Ellis' dime, nor with the use of any of their properties."

"The fuck does that mean?" Diane trilled.

"It means your getaway has been granted, just not the way you wanted. You need an escape from the Ellis Titanic? That's fine. You just don't get to use any of their lifeboats for a reprieve. You also don't get to stay on. Until Earl and Irene are present and able to call and invite you back, all three of you are out of here by Friday at ten a.m."

"Who the hell do you think you are, Bilan?" Diane demanded. "You weren't even around last year this time. You think you can make calls like that?"

"I wasn't here this time last year, Diane, you're right. But I married into this, unlike you. There's no cheating when it comes to family. You don't hopscotch your way through it. For better or worse, you stick around. This isn't a clubhouse you hang out in to have fun. It's these people's real lives."

"I ain't about to sit here and let somebody who just learned how to spell *Ellis* judge me." Nena waved me off, positioned to walk off. "I've got better things to do, and it don't include you telling me when I have to be off my ex's property."

"Don't wait on me." I warned. "Wait on security." I walked off, needing to distance myself from them. "Feel free to leave before Friday...on your own dimes."

"I'll send dinner up, Ms. Bilan." I couldn't deny hearing the triumph in Stacy's chords.

"With an icepack, please." I continued my stride to the elevator.

I turned two corners and was stepping on before I knew it. The back of my head rested against the metallic gold walls and I closed my eyes. My feet began to throb and belly toil from hunger. That's when it occurred to me I hadn't eaten since breakfast.

When the elevator tolled, I cringed. I bent over to remove my shoes; it was a great task. By the time I was done, my entire frame was vibrating of exhaustion. I had half a mind to leave the bags in the elevator, but knew it would be rude. God, I wished I could soak in the tub. I had quite a few months in between me and total body submersion in hot water. With fleeting energy, I gathered the bags and the straps of my sandals and left the elevator.

Sadik's suite still felt a hike away. The endless marble floors, Grecian column banisters overlooking the atrium on the first level. The three-story trees and water fountain made this side of the home's architect feel like a mall. My trek faltered again when I heard soft hums of pleasure. Immediately, my brain went there. The beat of my heart increased to violent levels and my mouth dried. I was on the floor of the suite, on my way to our wing. Why would I hear soft, rushed pants?

Slowly, I turned around, but that end of the house was empty, darkened. It was typically vacant. Then my eyes rotated across the atrium. It took a few seconds to adjust my eyes, but two slender, feminine bodies could be seen grinding seductively against each other. One was more aggressive and agile than the other. I leaped behind a column and tried not to breathe. Then I craned my neck to look again. Taaliba was tonguing down a woman I'd never seen before. Both their eyes were closed, but the woman's hands were all over Taaliba's breasts then waist before finally pushing between her thighs.

My face tightened with confusion so bad it hurt. Last I knew, Taaliba was protesting Sadik about her not being able to support Danny after one of his family's restaurants was burned down. Who was this woman she was making out with?

Taaliba pushed the woman back marginally with the palms of her hands. She looked uncomfortable, but not helpless or victimized. The woman, understanding, lifted from her.

"Are we going to do this again, Leeb?" I could make out.

Taaliba licked her lips, taking heavy breaths. "I told you I wanted to take it slow. This isn't slow."

"Then what is? You called me, and I came running right after my last class." The woman's hands swept in the air in questioning.

"I told you I needed a friend. I want to be friends again."

"You told me you were ready," the woman with the deep vocals argued.

Taaliba attempted a cleansing breath. I wasn't convinced it worked. She appeared incredibly edgy. "I called because I need a friend, not the bullshit,"

"And I've been needing you all these years." The woman's voice was crystal clear at this point. "I've waited and watched, and have been ignored, and chosen over—"

"Who said I've chosen?" Taaliba questioned.

Maybe that's the problem...

I turned and toed off to our suite, not caring if I was found out or not. This family—the one I once found so tightly woven and fiercely intimidating—had officially worn my soul. When I finally made it to the doors of the suite, I closed them behind me, dropped my bags and shoes, and sank to the floor in submission to a level of exhaustion I'd never experienced.

"I didn't ask for—" Danny blinked successively. "I don't expect...because..."

"Because you're fuckin' my little sister, you don't expect Double E Bags to offer assistance?" I lifted a cynical brow.

He let go of a breath of discomfort while combing his fingers through his hair. "Look, Ellis." We were at another one of the Lopez's restaurants in Bloomfield. This place wasn't as vast in size as *La Cocina* in Newark, but it was more contemporary in décor. We sat in the back of the restaurant partitioned by his men from the larger dining area. He turned back to face me. "I don't know what you think is going on between Leeb and me."

My chin dipped. "Taaliba." I corrected. "It's of no consequence to me, honestly. So long as she's safe and happy, I don't need the details of her contentment."

"Then why are you giving me—" He glanced around the room, lowering his voice. "—shit about it? What's wrong with Taaliba being mine?"

Shaking my head, I stood from my seat. "I didn't drive all the way out to Bloomfield to discuss my baby girl. I came—" My attention shifted to my vibrating phone in my inner suit jacket pocket.

S. Cruz: *If you cause me to miss my red-eye, you're going to have to send me to Miami on the Ellis II with your flight crew on YOUR dime.*

I snorted, reminded of her impatience. My meeting with Sofia was due to begin soon to go over Jules' speech for the housing coalition. Just when I'd adjusted to the moods and temperament of my wife, it seemed I had to with Sofia again now that we'd been spending so much time together in Julius' cabinet.

"You were saying?" Danny's brown eyes expressed a mixture of curiosity and annoyance.

I tucked my phone away. "I came to inform you of my father's loan of twelve street soldiers. Nine are new recruits, recently trained on his turf for long term battle. The other three are vets who will provide guidance and fight alongside them. They're totally at your disposal." I took a deep breath, feeling the weight of this. I knew the Lopezes were not a formidable opponent of Popov's. Their strength was street level. Popov was a patient thinker...like me. He had technology Danny's men couldn't begin to grasp. Hell, neither did my father. The only difference between my father's army and Lopez's was Double E Bags' was the largest in the state, and my father had...me. "He may not permit more, so use them prudently. Keep him in the loop." I moved to take off. "Be safe, Lopez."

"You don't seem to have much faith in me," he called to my back.

I peered over my shoulder. "Faith in you is for my sister. Respect is what you should be vying for from me." Then I turned to him. "You got my attention when you killed your father. Earn my respect by moving with ration and not the emotion from losing your family in the *La Cocina* fire. This is how the men are separated from the boys."

Finally, I continued to the door.

In the car, we were minutes into our commute, about to hit the Parkway when my phone rang. I glanced at the caller's ID.

"Hey, Stacy..."

"Deek, I deferred the issue to Bilan as you and Mr. Ellis asked."

"And?" I opened a file on my other phone to prepare for the meeting.

"And they're all leaving."

"Come again."

"They've been told they all have to leave...by Friday." I could have sworn Stacy snickered. *She would never.* "Ms. Bilan told them if they aren't out by ten am on Friday, they'll be escorted off the premises."

My hands stilled midair.

"Did something happen? Someone threatened her? Upset her?"

"No. Tempers were ablaze before she came into the discussion. Bilan said no one will be using the family jet or visiting *Ellis Island*, or utilizing—*and I quote*—any of the family's accouterments." Again, I heard smothered giggling.

I blinked hard.

"What about Nena's flight out on Friday?" She mentioned that when she called me with the dilemma earlier.

"I just left from serving Bilan dinner in your suite. She asked me for Nena's cell number. Ms. Bilan called while I was there setting up and booked her a flight out for Friday morning."

"Really?" My question echoed in the car.

Rory, sitting next to me, jerked her head to face me.

"Really."

"Is she okay?"

"Bilan or Nena?"

"My wife."

"Other than being irritated, she seemed just fine to me. She had Sadik with her in bed. She gave Camille the night off. I can check on her in a few, if you'd like me to."

"Yeah." I needed to make sure she was eating something. "I'll be in late again tonight."

The frustrating thing about my long scheduling now was not beating her to sleep when I got in and making sure she ate something. My chest tightened at the prospect.

"Consider it done."

"Thanks, Stacy."

"Goodnight, Deek."

I took a deep breath after ending the call. My eyes rolled over to Rory. "What the hell happened to my wife today?"

Her big ass eyes shot wide and head reared slightly. "Fuck you mean?"

Tilting my head to pinch between my eyes, I shook my head.

"Sire," Rory croaked.

"What?"

"I gotta put you *D* on some shit."

I cracked one lid, then two when I saw the unusual fear on my girl's face.

Sofia was packing her briefcase, her back to me in cropped leggings, a *YSL* tank, and her hair in a ponytail over her head. The ensemble reminded me of the ones she wore after working out in my gym at the high-rise when she made herself at home there as a broke graduate student.

She peered at me from over her arm. "I'm surprised you're still sitting here. I know you always have a fire to run to." Her smile was teasing.

I lifted my wrist for the time as I sat reclined in a hard ass, old fashioned wooden rolling chair. It was after ten at night.

"You're right: there's always a fire to put out in 'Ellis-land'," I joked wryly.

Then I took a deep breath, stretching my arms. She was right, I needed to act as though I had a long commute ahead.

Sofia stood straight, facing me with her little fists on her slender yet curvy hips. "Dude, you look...fatigued. I'm not sure I've ever seen you like this—other than that time you got shit-faced at my cousin, Roberto's, wedding when uncle Alonso made you his prosperity juice. That shit had you floating."

That memory caused me to chuckle. Two glasses of that concoction in Monte Plata put me on my ass until I landed on American soil the next day. "I'm old. It's official," I murmured with amusement.

Sofia's smile faded. "Don't say that, papi."

My brows pinched, though I found humor in her sudden mood change. "Why?"

"Because..." She shifted on her feet and shrugged her shoulders. "Because."

I stood from my seat. "There's nothing wrong with aging, sweetheart." My movements faltered on the way up. That pet name was regrettable although it held no sentiment. Bilan didn't like it, and I was now conscious of casting it. I recovered quickly with a smile as I reached for my phones on the conference table. "It's a blessing to age, even if you begin to feel it after thirty-five," I jeered.

It wasn't lost upon me that her eyes were on me from my shoes to my face as I slipped on my jacket. "You still look as vibrant as the day I met you." She spoke slowly, considerately. "Just more reserved, or maybe that's because of..." She scratched the back of her neck before taking a deep breath. "You're a new man...family man."

I nodded with hiked lips. "You may be on to something."

"But having the American dream doesn't make you old. It makes you happy, right?"

I leaned over my chair to give it thought. "It makes you cautious, constantly aware of people other than yourself. Every decision I make will affect those closest to me. I want the best for them and to protect them until my dying breath." I felt the subtle nod of my head. "It's the best overwhelming state to be in for a man my age."

"You're smiling," she whispered breathlessly.

Gazing at Sofia's stiff, petite frame, a feather-stroke of arousal waved over me. It was her. Bilan. She did shit to me. How could I look into the eyes of another woman and still be aroused by my wife who was several counties away?

She made them leave. My wife ordered my parents' lovers out of our home.

Her audacity stunned and impressed me. It relieved and comforted those concerns I'd wrestled with and embarrassment I'd always carried since those relationships were established.

Sofia's sniffle had my attention return to her. She swiped tears from her cheek as she turned to grab her things. "I'm happy for you. I really am."

But she couldn't look me in the eye to corroborate the sentiment.

I rubbed my bottom lip with my thumb, suddenly uncomfortable about the trance I found myself in. One that involved my wife and a former lover.

I collected the rest of my things, too. "It's late. You going to be okay getting out of the city?"

She cleared her throat. "Of course." Then Sofia forged a fortifying smile, quite a clever one. "I'm familiar with the place."

I was referring to her safety, but was sure she knew that. Heading to the door first, I held it open for her. She dipped under my arm and strode mutedly to the elevator. When it arrived, she stepped on first.

My head dropped and my mind ran with thoughts of the following day as the car dinged each floor we descended.

"When I told my mother I've been working with you a couple of weeks ago, she told me you were the one I was supposed to marry." Her words were so soft, I wouldn't have known if she was really speaking if Sofia's sad eyes weren't locked onto me. "She said you slipped through my fingers because I'm too 'community' and not enough family." She scoffed, her head shaking.

There was a balance at the end of her sharing. Sofia wanted a response from me, and I was wordless. We didn't speak again until the doors parted and we stepped into the lobby.

"Enjoy your time away, *sweethea—*Sofia."

Even in her absence, Bilan corrected me.

Sofia's small shoulders wiggled slightly as a superficial grin lifted on her face. "A destination wedding. Once again, I'm the professional bridesmaid." She winked before taking off.

By the time I made it up to the suite, it was late. All but two lights were on: the open bathroom and the nightstand lamp on my side of the bed. Bilan left one of the balcony doors open. I strode over to close and lock them. Then I removed my jacket and tie as I kicked off my shoes before traveling over to my boy. He was asleep in his portable woven wooden bassinet on the bed. We agreed to cutting back on putting him in here now that he was sleeping, almost, through the night.

However, tonight, as I carried his warm body over to his crib in the sitting area, I understood why. Bilan had a long day and sometimes, at the end of a trying one, you needed the comfort of a familiar body.

"At least that's what I need of your mother tonight," I whispered to him before kissing his cheek and nose.

I lay him on his side, straightened his gown and placed a thin blanket at his waist. As I stood over him, I struggled to leave. Parental paranoia is what my mother explained I'd been feeling since Iban robbed my family of the peace I provided. Most nights, I couldn't leave his side and opted to sleep beneath him on the floor. My wanting to give him consistency and peace won over my comfort, so I slept on the hard floor, but near him.

My flat palm held his delicate back as I mumbled a few words of prayer over him. *Shit*, he was beautiful. The ultimate gift from God. I just didn't want to fuck it up. Fuck him up with what I knew to be the culture of this family; the makings of me. Sadik coming into my life when he did caused a cataclysmic shifting of sorts. It highlighted all the evils and dilated my views of purity and consequence at the same damn time.

Regrettably, I left him to fulfill a silent, yet histrionic yearning deep within. As I approached the bed with animalistic need, I peeled off my shirt and tank and doused my pants and dress socks. My engorged dick caught at the elastic of my boxers when I pulled them off. Seconds later, I slipped beneath the comforter, revealing her naked body. After burying my hungry mouth between her thick, toned thighs, Bilan's hands roved over my head in her subconscious. It wasn't until she was climaxing that it felt she'd fully awakened.

I urged Bilan to her knees, loathing the need to be gentle because of her expectant condition. I fucked her balls deep. Bilan's curls stood shapeless on top of her head from my occasional fisting of them to hold her head to the mattress. Her pulsing walls swallowed me so deep, my balls slapped against her pussy. The arch in her back and the vibration of her ass cheeks when I pounded into them all worked against my stamina. When her spine bowed and wobbled and I felt her coming around me, my fucking balls drew up, body warmed, and feet curled before I exploded inside of her. My mind went blank for a moment, body feeling, smelling, and hearing only Bilan.

She cured me of every insecurity, worry, and question in my mind regarding me being able to keep her near. The biggest risk for a man of my stature isn't losing your wealth when you fall for a woman. It's losing the vital tentacles she helped you grow when your worlds collided. Bilan didn't gain just money when I lost myself to her, she owned parts of me I could never get back. After her day of regulating in my parents' home, I was sure she was close to the edge of a meltdown or had possibly had one. I should have been here to catch her and spur on her authoritative actions as a rightful Ellis.

As I stood behind her, swaying on my knees with my eyes squeezed closed, chest misted with sweat and head reclined behind my shoulders, I felt exponentially lighter and a renewed purpose.

Slowly, I released her, feeling my sensitive cock pulling gently out of her. Bilan rolled over onto her side.

"Sadik," she whispered.

Still out of breath, my lids parted and I answered, "Yes, Nalib."

"What do the Russians have to do with us being on lockdown here?" She panted audibly. "And why do I feel there's...some...hidden information about Iban's conviction and imprisonment for murder?"

My eyes burst wide.

Shit...

∞22∞

"One-Two-Three-Two!" he commanded and I shot four jabs.

Rhythmically, he shouted the combo again "One-Two-Three-Two!"

And again, with rapid succession, I jabbed his padded mitts twice with each fist. We moved circularly as I dripped with sweat and my feet felt like boulders and arms numb.

Dimi's thick tongue projected even louder. "Damnit, Bilan, jab-cross-hook-cross!"

As if I didn't understand, I continued with simple yet hard jabs. I'd decided my punch combinations minutes ago, and I'd stick with it until my arms fell off. I was in a beautiful zone where pain couldn't disrupt my determination.

"Stop!" I heard him yell, but didn't process until he dropped his mitted hands and my next powerful jab sent me careening into the air. Dimi broke my flight with his arm at my chest. "The hell's wrong with you?" His cool breath pushed over my head; he was such a tall man.

And it happened. I stopped repetition and my muscles began to fatigue and lungs burned. My body swayed as I tried to regain my balance. Dimi helped steady me even with the impediment of the mitts.

"Can you stand alone just...few seconds?" His language was broken, but I understood and nodded.

He jogged over to the other side of the gym, tossing off the mitts, and grabbed a giant exercise ball. "On your ass and lay on your back!" He pointing toward the floor en route to me.

Slowly, I obeyed, but boy was it a task of trying to go south while struggling to breathe. I was lightheaded, so I swayed and dropped a bit.

"Can you lift your legs?" he asked.

When I didn't get them in the air fast enough, he bent over and swept my legs up, arranging my feet on the ball. Dimi organized them until my toes were pointed toward the ceiling. My chest heaved something mean as I squeezed my eyes.

"We have to get blood back to your head for the dizziness to stop," he explained. "Shit!" he swore again, and I realized I'd never heard Dimi curse as much as I had tonight. He was also more anxious this session than I'd ever seen of him. Then he began a string of words in his native tongue as he shuffled around me. I watched as his big, pink body swung back to me. "Is it better?"

I nodded, heaving hard.

He began slapping the back of his right hand into his left palm. "You didn't follow directions and you pushed too hard. This is not like you, Bilan!"

I closed my eyes again. "I'm sorry." I panted. "Got a lot on my mind."

And boy, did I ever.

Last night, when going to get the baby from Camille in the staff's wing of the house, I overheard a few of the girls talking as I approached the room.

"I can't wait until Sadik or Mr. Ellis says this mess is over," one groaned, causing me to stop in my tracks. Any mention of either of the Sadiks would

catch my attention. They were the salt of my world. "I'm sick of this house restriction. I can't move like I want."

"Yeah." *Another, more mature, tenor replied.* "It's been years since we've had this happen."

"Not really. Remember last summer? Mr. Ellis had a beef with those Italians—"

"Yeah!" *A new voice chimed in.* "Remember, I found out it was with baby Liza's family?"

"Oh, yeah!"

"But I heard this one is more serious." *I recognized that voice as Camille's.* "When I took baby Sadik to see his grandfather a few weeks back, I overheard Mr. Ellis mention Russians."

"Russians?" *the most mature tone of the group mocked.* "What in the hell's gotten to this family? Trump?"

The women snickered.

"I think we should take this seriously. Anytime Sadik addresses the house, it's usually serious. Mr. Ellis is getting up there in age, and I see him talking more and more to Sadik. If the beef is with Russians, they probably have all of our information."

"Jesus!" *one whispered hard as though in panic.*

"Yup. I'm good," *Camille spoke with confidence.* "I don't have classes this summer, so I hope it's all cleared up by the fall." *There was a slight pause before she continued.* "I've been meaning to ask if you still had the books for that Clinical Inquiry for Evidence-Based Practice class?"

I tuned out after the subject changed to school then Stacy's new schedule for them. To not make my timing awkward, I made a beeline to the kitchen and warmed up a bottle for Sadik, something I was going to do after I got him anyway.

As my lungs began to slow, I peered over the ball at my feet and asked, "Dimi, what do the Russians have to do with the Ellis family?"

Dimi froze, bending over while putting away dumbbells for the night. It was similar to Sadik's reaction when I asked him last night after making love. My husband's answer was the biggest blow-off known to a wife. I vaguely recalled a Russian being mentioned in *The Commission* Sadik told me Earl once belonged to, but not much beyond that. And because of that, I thought he'd be willing to provide an honest answer. I was wrong. Sadik kissed me sweetly on the forehead and told me to trust him to be my protector. It was bullshit. Maybe a better answer could be provided by someone with a distance from the madness.

Slowly, he lifted and turned toward me. His jaw was collapsed and eyes wild with...fear?

"Bilan..." he pronounced his usual *Beelon*. "If your husband doesn't want you here, you shouldn't come."

My head lifted from the floor. That annoyed me. "You know, I've lost count of how many times you've basically asked me to stop coming to your gym since I told you who the father of my child is."

"He's not just a partner of passion anymore. He married you. He told you to stop coming."

I kicked the ball from beneath my legs and leaned to my side, sitting up. "And I'm a twenty-nine year old woman, wife, and mother who makes her own decisions, Dimi. If I want to come to a reputable trainer where I feel safe, I can and most certainly will!"

Dimi's eyes closed and neck gave out as he grunted. It was clear to me he was torn, but between what? What was bothering this man to the point of being so irritated by my presence?

Then I knew it for sure.

"You know my...Sadik and Earl Ellis." My heart tripled its pace as I stared him directly in the eyes.

"I know Double E Bags," he made clear.

I considered that for a minute. Suddenly, I was desperate, though I tried concealing my excitement.

"Dimi, who are the Russians?" His face rotated away from me. "I swear, I won't tell Sadik. I'm just tired of feeling like I'm living in a bubble. I have a child now to be concerned about."

"That is why you shouldn't be out during times like this." He was curt.

"Times like what, Dimi?" He did that long pause thing again, looking away. I waited until I couldn't anymore. "What?" I demanded.

Dimi took two steps closer to me, his splayed hand leading him. "I'm going to say this, but before I do, I need you to know you can't come back here unless Ellis says to my face you can. I have a family to protect and provide for, Bilan. I left that bad life so I can do this."

"I don't get it."

"You don't!" he shouted again, his deep chords vibrating across the empty room. Again, Dimi regained himself, shaking his head. "I'm in danger every time you come."

"By who?"

"Your husband, his father, and Popov." His tongue curled around that last name. "The last two are from my old world."

He kept referencing that. "What world is that, Dimi?"

His voice was perceptibly low when he shared, "I used to work for Feodor Popov, a Russian like me with the biggest arms trade in the state, and one of the biggest sex trafficking web on this side of the country. He has a very big organization...probably billion-dollar company by now. I was one of his guns...like..." He paused to think. "The little Black woman your husband keeps around."

I breathed, "Rory?"

Dimi nodded. "Popov has got lots of guns. That was me. I saw deplorable things—women, girls...dead babies from abortions in a basement—that will give you nightmares. I was okay with it. I did my job well."

"But you left."

"When I met my Nadia at one of his receiving houses." My eyes bulged wide. "She's from my hometown, back home. I knew her family as a boy. When she showed up off the container from the big boat, it shook my soul. I did not know Popov was taking Russian girls. It was sickening." He spat and uttered words from his native tongue. "Out of all the girls in the world, Popov started taking our own. Disgusting!" Severe anger creased his face as he shared.

"So you left with her?"

He snorted. "It's not your American love story. I had to pay for her freedom and mine. It took years—taking years. I'm still paying each month. I'm almost paid off."

"You still owe?"

"We had the baby before I was done with our payment. Then I owe again."

Guilt wrapped around my throat, squeezing me to a choke. "I'm sorry, Dimi."

"This is why I say you should not be here. Your husband knows me. I don't want him to..."

I swallowed. "You don't want him to think you're a threat to me because of your old association with Popov."

He nodded, eyes sparkling with the need of mercy. "Popov is a very dangerous man. Your husband's father is a dangerous man. Dimi need no trouble. I have a family to protect. The Ellis family are brutal savages." He lifted his hand to demonstrate with his finger. "They devour anything...everything in their way, from the top of the state to the bottom."

I nodded, licked my lips, and swallowed hard as I stood to my feet. "Again, I'm sorry, Dimi." I couldn't look him in the eyes. "I won't bother you again."

Broken. My heart was shattered in several pieces over the rejection and implication of me putting him in danger. Dimi was a six-foot, five-inch tall man with biceps I couldn't wrap both hands around. His chest and abs were one thick armor plate. He never showed much emotion, and never fear. If he was asking me to not return, perhaps I should be fearful, too.

I ambled over to the wall and collected my bag and bottle of water. Crestfallen, I headed out with my head hung. When I made it to the door, a thought struck.

"Who do you think will win?"

I waited for Dimi to turn my way. When he did, his response was as delayed as expected.

"I don't know. The Ellis family has outsmarted the law...even have some on their payroll. But Popov..." His eyes fell and nostrils widened with emotion. "He doesn't fear the government."

"He fears someone. We all do." I bit my lip, suddenly feeling bad-ass.

"The only one I've seen him back down to is a Polish man. Jankowski. But he disappeared from the U.S. over ten years ago." I nodded my understanding and opened the door to leave. "Bilan," he called out to me. "Popov doesn't fear death. He fears losing power."

It was countless seconds later when he explained, "He has power over me, even now."

It was why he didn't want me coming back to his gym. I understood it completely. I was a threat to Dimi's welfare. That wasn't what I wanted for him or me. This time, I passed through the door with tears pooling in my eyes.

"*We give yoooooooooou,*" the kitchen choir sang. Candy directed them to hold the note flapping her fingers. Then she pumped her fist in the air and simultaneously they belted. "*Praaaaaaaa-aise!*"

I joined them in clapping my hands. Not only were their voices beautiful, but the loving and welcoming atmosphere was a direct effect of this comradery they practiced by way of song. Being in here with them several times a week was good for me. Calming and soul-soothing.

The crowd resumed their duties of cleaning after another family meal, one Irene joined us for, for the first time since her return. Earl asked us to meet in the family room, and that would be happening soon. Sadik was on his way to make the family conference. If he could have come to dinner earlier, it would have felt like old times.

Minus Iban, of course...

I didn't exactly miss him, but had been concerned about how no one brought him up but the girls. No one seemed to talk about Iban. That could have been because the family didn't convene much lately, only for these dinners twice a week.

As I dried the salad bowl I'd finished washing, I knew it was time. My eyes gazed over to David, who stood over the leftovers, wrapping them up. I glanced around to be sure no one was watching then sauntered over to him.

"Hey, you," I whispered teasingly.

"Hey, BB!" His big bear of a body shouldered me, rendering a giggle from my belly.

My eyes circled around again. "I have a proposition for you."

"Oh, yeah?" His focus was on measuring and cutting saran wrap. "Then go off, sis."

I rolled my eyes at his silliness. "You still have that opportunity to observe the kitchen at *DiFillippo's*, right?"

"Yeah." He hummed. "I hope. It was like a week ago when he made the offer."

That "him" was the master chef of the *DiFillippo's* restaurant chain. The restaurants were all owned by one man but his executive chef, a world-renowned master, circulated the country, supervising each one, according to David last week. He shared with us how the guy created new dishes, changed the menu along with the owner, and tweaked older recipes. He was at an event a week ago in Jersey where David so happened to know a friend, who knew a friend that got him in. As luck would have it, David got face time with the Italian chef and was offered time to observe in his kitchen at the location in Hackensack. However, the men's hours clashed. David worked here most days and evenings.

"I can make that happen for you by taking over your duties all next week." I waggled my brows.

Finally, David's ebony eyes were on me. I had his attention. "If I didn't walk in on you molesting that husband of yours in the pool last week, I would think you're crushing on me." His face neared mine. "What are you up to, BB?"

A silly smirk crested my face. Memories of me tonguing Sadik down while I stroked him inside his swimming trunks in the pool last week began to flood my mind. It was the day after I was asked to leave my gym and trainer. I was horribly blue about it and think he sensed it that day. Sadik invited me to go for an indoor swim with him that morning before he left for the day. What began as quiet laps around the L-shaped pool turned into me having Sadik accidentally bump into me. He apologized profusely for the painless collision, of course, concerned for the baby in my oven. And I took advantage of his remorseful state and seduced him. That's when David walked in, looking for a place to nap in secret while his mousse settled.

"I did look kinda hot, didn't I?" I winked with the goofiest grin.

"I think if we asked Sadik, he'd say smoking."

It was me bumping my shoulder into him this time before I left the kitchen for the family meeting.

I'd arrived a few minutes earlier than the requested time to *Elliswoods Palace*. However, not in enough to see Sadik before the meeting my father called. In the halls, I greeted the passing staff while answering text messages. I made it into the family room and found my mother was the first there. With an easy smile, I stowed my phones away and addressed her.

"Hey, baby?" she greeted with a soft murmur as I leaned over to kiss her on the cheek.

"How are you feeling?" I asked, standing back inspecting her. "You look a hell of a lot better."

She cracked a wry smile, but it still soothed me as it always did when shown it. "A lot better. I'm not one hundred percent, but that retreat was necessary." She squeezed my hand. "Thanks, baby."

My face folded. "For what?"

"For recommending the place and for your patience with me."

This smile was warmer, filled with the admiration I was accustomed to receiving from her. "My one therapist told me if you do a good job at totally committing yourself to raising your children, when they become responsible adults and have to step in and help you, you shouldn't be ashamed."

My chest tightened. "I hope you aren't."

"I am, but I'm grateful, too."

"I'm grateful to have you back. I know the girls are, too."

Her eyes rolled away. "And Bilan..."

"She's tough...long-suffering. As long as you're restored, she'll forget about those few days when your back hit the wall. You're a matriarch; I'm sure it's not uncommon."

"I'm also an example. I feel so embarrassed." She shook her head, eyes rolling close. "I couldn't get up in the mornings some days, Sadik. I've experienced horrible post-partum depression with your brother, but this bout of darkness was worse than that."

"And you're facing it," I tried assuring her. "Fighting it every day."

She nodded. "But I'm not out of the woods yet."

"You'll get there, queen." My confidence was strong yet unfounded. I'd never seen my mother so disengaged in my life. She'd always been my superheroine, battling the obstacles of life for our family. Even when my father was incarcerated while awaiting his trial and sentencing and she was left with a newborn Iban, she did it with dignity and strength. Those were the words of my father. "You were built to carry this family."

There was a breath of silence before she murmured, "Tom and I are over."

I straightened to full height, though she didn't release my hand. "Is it?" I posed as a statement rather than a question.

She nodded again, and in that split second, her motherly air of confidence had dissipated, revealing an insecure girl. "Stacy told me what Bilan told them. She was right and, at the same time, Tom wasn't wrong. Neither were the girls. I can only speak for Tom in saying he only acted according to the parameters I gave him. It's something I learned in those intense therapy sessions on the retreat. Relationships in life are relatively about parameters. Parameters in friendships, marriage, with relatives, and even with your children. They're key in defining who you are as a person and how you govern yourself while functioning within them."

I listened intently, trying to follow where she was going.

"It all started when I enlarged your father's parameters as my husband. When I allowed him to continue with his affairs, I opened the opportunity for dangerous relationships and people to enter our marriage, our lives, and our children's lives. More people in the confines of that sacred place made for just two corrodes the marriage. Then I added more people; men for me, thinking I could survive the marriage if I could play the game using your father's rules."

She shook her head. "It's been years, but it hasn't worked. Tom wasn't a partner or a loved one to me on any significant level. He's been a comfort against your father's inability to commit fully and exclusively to me. But it's never been about Tom. I've never demanded much from him other than his exclusive attention when he was with me. That's it." She shrugged. "I'm already married, what more do I need? A husband? That's what I have, and that's where I should place all of my eggs until we're no longer married. So, just as I've been doing with my marriage, I'd done to Tom. I didn't demand enough outside of what he did in my presence. That's only half a commitment. I didn't require much more from him. But I do my husband." She took a deep breath. "And that's the next phase of my healing. That man," she whispered, her forehead pointed ahead.

My father was being wheeled into the room by a nurse I'd been seeing around the house. She rolled him straight to my mother, where he kissed her gently on the lips. That vision of the young, insecure girl was still there as her eyes closed with submission as he did. A small smile lifted on her face when she finally gazed him in the eyes.

I was thrilled she'd come to this place of understanding and rich revelation in her life. I just wished it didn't cost me upward of twenty grand for a two-week intense therapy retreat in the mountains. I could have told her the same shit. There was no way I'd send my wife up there. I'd have to figure out another route for her. She'd get her help without leaving my bed at night.

Fuck that...

My parents held in that position for a few seconds before his chair was situated next to the sofa my mother was sitting on. I moved away to give room.

"Sir," I greeted with a head bow.

He returned the gesture, though in his usual aristocratic manner. "Good to see you, son." However, his voice and delivery to me were humble.

"It's good to be seen," was all I had in return.

I backed away for the corresponding single sofa in the room, wondering where Bilan was. The start of the meeting time had passed. Taaliba promenaded into the room with Monica. They both greeted our parents with hugs and kisses, then me before taking their seats. Finally, my Nalib entered. She looked delectable in silk floral print, loose cropped pants, a matching blouse with gold strappy heels. Her tapered hair was freshly cut and curled. Her full lips a tan gloss, highlighting those freckles I worshipped.

Bilan smiled at the room. She sauntered over to me first, her eyes narrowing as though pleased with what she saw. I stood and greedily took her at the sides of her face to kiss her soft lips.

When I released her, Bilan's lashes fluttered as she smiled. "Hey, Sadik," she murmured.

"Hey, baby."

She left me to greet my mother, then my father with hugs before returning to me. I gestured for her to sit on the cushioned arm of my sofa. She did with silent obedience then wrapped an arm around my shoulder. A satisfied breath left my lungs. Bilan was acclimating. She'd just left dinner with my parents, yet greeted them as though it was her first time seeing them today. Could she please me any less?

I clutched her hand as we waited.

My father cleared his throat and swiped the tip of his nose with his thumb. "Monica received a phone call from the rehab center. Iban's ready to move up in his therapy."

"What does that mean?" Taaliba sat up on the sofa anxiously

awaiting. Her thighs were spread wide as she lay her elbows on top of them. It struck me as such a tomboyish posture and reminded me of her occasional androgynous mannerisms.

"It means, he's finally been on the mend," Monica explained, biting her lips. "His progress has been excelling since May."

"Praise God," my mother mumbled with a fist clutched to her chest.

"About damn time," Taaliba sighed.

"So that creates a dilemma," my father continued. "They're saying he don't need the facility no more. He can come home and get his therapy a few days a week."

"Intensive rehabilitation is needed to help restore some of his functions and help him adapt to his permanent handicaps," Monica emphasized as she peered over at me. "And we're not talking just one type of therapy; it's several he'll need for possibly a few years. That's how they say improvement for his level of injury is measured; by the year, not weeks or months. He'll need round-the-clock care for months, at least."

"Damn." Taaliba blew out a dramatic breath. "I'm surprised he survived shooting himself in the head." I felt Bilan tense above me.

"Believe it or not," my father addressed her. "The doctors is calling the shot a *superficial* injury." He used his hand as a gun to illustrate. "You see, what happened was the bullet only hit one hemisphere and only one lobe of the brain."

"The one neurosurgeon working with him said if you're shot in the head, this is the way you want it to happen." Monica scoffed bitterly, and I couldn't begin to understand the complexities of her sentiment.

"Okay." Taaliba clapped her hands together, elbows still on her knees. "But he's doing well. He's going home. What's the problem?"

My father's eyes swept from Taaliba to Monica, then to me, and finally above me to Bilan. "Location," he croaked the word. "We discuss everything as a family. And because we had a lot of tragedies hit us this year, it's even *more* important for us to move as a tight ass unit."

I readjusted my chin on my hand as I listened, sensing the bull-shit coming.

"Okay?" Taaliba's hands swung out as she sat inclined over her knees.

"Monica's saying it'll be too much on her to quarterback his homecare," my father continued to explain. "She still got the liquor stores, the baby...the girls. She saying it won't be ideal to send him home."

"She can't take him home," Bilan spoke up.

"Yeah," Taaliba added, rolling her eyes. "We've all been marshaled here."

My mother shifted in her seat. Her eyes squinted and worry was etched into every corner of her face.

Slowly, my father's head descended in a long nod. "That's why we're discussing this, baby. We wanna be sure everybody's good with where he'll be."

"He can come here, I guess," Taaliba announced, nodding obliviously. "Hell, your family has a whole wing." She reminded Monica.

I felt my father's eyes burning the side of my face. When I turned to face him, I was right. He was regarding me communicatively, expecting I'd respond in his favor.

"I was hoping the sequestering would be over soon so the girls and I can resume our lives." Monica mainly addressed my father and me. "It's been quite stuffy here lately."

"Well," Taaliba sat back and snorted. "You ain't lie about that."

"We're not telling Iban he cannot stay in his family home because of his nephew and me," Bilan insisted. "At this point, he's more vulnerable than my baby. If Sadik and I are so inclined, we can leave *Elliswoods Palace* and be just as fine."

My father shook his head. "There is no safer place for us than here. We have full armed security, twenty-four hours a day by men trained with my specifications. The staff here is carefully investigated and uniquely coached for invasions of any kind. Even that David you hired. You was a part of the hiring process, but not the interview and training. Just about every employee here has two skills. The one that we needed in our insulated community and one to protect it." He shook his head, heated regard shooting into her. "My son got resources, but not like his daddy."

"He's right, Bilan," my mother chimed in, voice soft with compromise. "We have this place with top-notch security. You all are safe here. I don't want to see any of you go."

"Stay and be bored out your mind like the rest of us," Monica offered.

"Another one claustrophobic in over thirty-thousand square feet," Bilan mumbled imperceptibly over me.

"Speak up, dear?" my father requested.

"Didn't catch that," Monica made clear at the same time.

Bilan didn't respond right away. I glanced up at her, measuring that glib comment. She shrugged casually with her lip. I smiled with my eyes, impressed.

"I said," Bilan sighed. "I see we have another person complaining about being bored on this massive estate."

Monica's mouth dropped. "What do you mean?"

"I guess I'm tired of hearing people's complaints about having to stay here. Is it your primary home? No. But let's not act as though great moments and memories didn't happen here. Taaliba, let's not act as though you didn't grow up here. You get bored in one wing, try another. You want to venture out of this museum of a home, go bowling a mile down on the property. Monica, go have a muffin at the coffee shop on the estate. There's enough room and resources for us not to bump into each other unless we want to."

Taaliba's face fell and hand paused from pretending to push back her cuticles.

"I'm glad you feel that way, sweethear—" Double E Bags stumbled over his words and his proud smile faded. "Bilan."

"It's not that I'm ungrateful," Monica explained. "It's just been a rough time for all of us." She pointed my and Bilan's way. "Even for you and the baby. It's been a tough adjustment period. I'm sure you want your normal routine back, Bilan."

"I do." Bilan agreed, her palms flexing over my shoulders as she spoke. "I'm just not rushing a circumstance I have no control over.

I'm choosing to trust Earl if he believes we need to stay here until he works out issues he has in the street."

"Bilan, I've been in this family for thirteen years," Monica hissed, seemingly offended. "I know the protocol."

My father raised a hand of finale. "We all know that, baby girl," he placated Monica. "And Bilan, I appreciate your obedience. Matter of fact, I appreciate everybody's obedience over the last couple of months." A derisive and abrupt hum left Bilan. The whole room suspended at that. She pretended to smooth down my dress shirt, likely a nervous response. "What we need to figure out is the matter at hand. What are we going to do about Iban?"

"I'd like to hear what Sadik and Bilan's thoughts are, considering his cause of injury." Monica's brows hiked and her eyes locked into us as Bilan remained over me.

"Iban is your husband, Monica." I finally spoke. "This will be your call. I'll support you either way."

"It can't just be my call. I need his family to help with this," Monica argued. "This is the most precarious situation I've had to deal with as his wife." Her eyes swept back over to my father.

His met mine. Bilan's hands continued to work over my shoulder and arm again.

"Irene," Bilan's small voice was constricted. "What do you suggest?"

My queen blinked several times, her mouth ajar. "I—I..." she hesitated. "I don't want to be rude to you or Sadik. I don't want to compromise your feelings or your safety."

"He needs therapy. How much of a danger could he be to me or my son?" Bilan asked.

No one answered right away.

I reached back to cover Bilan's hand with mine. "Baby, I think my parents are acknowledging how reckless my brother was with your life and that of our son. They don't want to lack consideration of our tragedy."

"But there's an even deeper one at this point. Iban is incapacitated, possibly for life. The threat has been removed."

"Have you forgotten he could have killed your newborn child?"

Monica's voice was disembodied as she patronized Bilan. "Have you forgiven him that easily? He could have killed that precious little baby as soon as he got here."

My chest tightened and nostrils spread at that truth. It was why I wouldn't advocate for my brother. He'd crossed the line to the point of no return with that selfish act.

"No, but what I am saying is we can't discard him from the pack while we're doubling down as a family for safety," she made clear. "He's out there alone and vulnerable. That's what got him into this 'precarious' situation in the first place."

Monica's face screwed. "Are you mocking me now, Bilan?"

"Never. I've only known this family for just over a year—"

"I'm glad you realize that!" Monica shouted.

"And in that little time," Bilan continued determinately. "it's become clear to me you've endured unreasonably as his wife."

"I damn sure have!"

"But you're still his wife. Are you not prepared to oversee his healthcare? You don't have any concerns about his welfare?"

Monica shot to her feet. "What are you saying?"

"I'm saying your answer is your decision." Bilan's voice was one of compassion. "I'm saying make a call. Don't leave it up to his family to say if he'll be under your supervision. I don't think anyone in this room will judge you if you said you're done. But you can't say 'hot potato'."

Something passed between the two women, something unspoken. For a moment, I feared having to interject. But Monica backed down. Rolling her eyes, she stormed out of the room. Taaliba jumped to her feet, frantic and with confusion in her eyes as her gaze fell upon Bilan. She then ran after Monica.

A perceptively painful groan left my mother's lungs.

"I wish things ain't have to go down like this." My father rubbed his forehead. "The last thing we need is a breakdown in the family. We should try to see it from her point of view."

"And what about yours?" Bilan challenged.

My father's brows raised. "Pardon me?"

"What about your perspective on your son being an invalid and needing a safe environment to heal, and your making the family believe him not being welcomed into your home is an option."

His hand went into the air expressively, eyes bounced between her and me for help. I wouldn't dare. "Now, Bilan, I ain't say all that."

"But you—or you, Irene—aren't saying he's coming to stay here with us. How could you manage to make me feel at home here but your firstborn isn't welcome back?"

"Iban has issues, Bilan. Mental issues he's battled for years," my mother tried to explain. "I was sick when he did that to you and the baby."

"And so was I," my father agreed with a note of righteous indignation. "He could've killed my legacy."

"He *is* your legacy." Bilan stood to her feet. "He was ostracized... banished from the family he takes pride in, just like all of you. You knew about his mental issues when you allowed it."

"No. He had a pity party and took it out on you." My father looked my way. "Tell her, Sadik."

"We will not ignore and create a new storyline of lies for Iban, Earl." Bilan's voice was low, but I could tell she was teeming with wild energy as she moved to the center of the room. "It seems to be what this family does: create an alternate view of the mess it's made.

"It's just like when you and Iban killed my brother and Sadik smoothly jumped in, took him to a hospital where he was spared a month to live, forcing me to create lies to my friends, family, and even the authorities as to what happened to him. Seamlessly, I jumped in and became a liar I never knew I was capable of being, all to survive the Ellis way. No more, and not with Iban. We deal with his issue head-on. He does not go to the editing room where you guys send other mess. And he certainly doesn't go to the executioner because you feel he betrayed you. He will be loved and forgiven. End of story!"

That final shout of hers was the benediction in this production. I stood to my feet and placed a firm hand on Bilan's shoulder. I could feel the frenetic energy vibrating from her.

Slowly, I leaned down toward her ear and whispered, "That's enough."

Then I took her at the waist and gently pulled to prompt her movements. Bilan turned to leave first.

"Goodnight," I bade my parents before I took her at the hand before there was much of a distance created between us.

I walked my wife out of the room with an air of satisfaction. What I'd sensed about her since the first conversation we had back at *Michelle's Diner* was Bilan was a fierce lioness: gorgeous, mesmerizingly disarming, and lethal. You could easily get so caught up in her surface timid nature that you're completely caught off guard when she unpredictably pounces on you for the kill, if necessary.

My father knew what he was doing when he called this meeting. Through the family, he tried to play on our vulnerability of the trauma Iban brought to our household. It didn't work. Bilan's a proponent of family. She respected the sanctity of the Ellis family, and even to my displeasure, that included Iban as a functional member.

∞23∞

My eyes somehow focused on the same mole beneath her right bouncing breast until my sight blurred and they closed. Bilan sucking in a deep breath while, simultaneously, her pussy clenched around my cock forced my eyes open again. Above me was the oscillating ceiling fan and Bilan's curls neatly designed at the top of her head, her tight eyes, and bouncing tits. My regard lowered past her slightly protruded belly and landed where we connected. The opening of her slit around the root of my dick covered in a translucent gel dizzied me. Her pretty clit was there, swollen and glistening.

"Come again with me, Nalib," I groaned, lifting my arm to circle the pearl of her treasure with my thumb.

That propelled her thrusts and began her mewled cries of pleasure. With my other hand, I slapped her jiggling ass. Bilan kept at a beautiful cadence, stroking me. When it quickened, I knew my time was coming to an end. Her hips locked, though she tried to continue with her thrusts. I could feel her gripping me like a vice now.

"*Uh*..." she began, and that's when my first spurt shot into her. "*Uh! Uh!*" Her spine straightened and she let the pleasure overtake her.

I gave in to it, ass cheeks squeezing and my abdomen convulsing helplessly. Her palms reached my chest, splayed and clasped for anchoring. With both hands, I pulled her into me by the ass until we both sang our last cry of bliss. Wheezing, my head spun and balls throbbed. Bilan's lids were low as her shoulders caved from exhaustion.

I collected all the strength available in my condition and swiftly flipped us over.

"Deek, wait!" she squealed, giggling. "The baby!"

"I know where my child is, girl."

I settled between her thick thighs, making sure my chest met her tits without putting weight on her belly. Bilan's head pushed back into the mattress as she pealed in laughter. I bit her chin then used my tongue to swipe my teeth marks. Her eyes were closed, breathing just as rapid as my own.

"When are we going to find out what's in here anyway?"

"I think at the..." She hesitated with pinched brows, considering it. "next visit in a couple of weeks. Are you anxious to find out if it's a girl or boy?"

I kissed the center of her chest. "No."

"You're lying." I didn't acknowledge the accusation. My hands found their way to her full breasts in caress. The tips of Bilan's nails softly scraped my back, causing me to flinch in several places. "It's okay. I want to know myself."

"Why?"

"I'm curious to see if we can have more estrogen under the S.Q.E. umbrella. Then maybe I won't be out-voted."

I kissed her nose. "Doesn't seem like you need much backing to me. I saw how you handled the senior Ellises last night."

Bilan rolled her eyes away. "Was that too much?"

"What do you think?"

"That they need 'too much' right now."

"Then okay."

"But did I step out of line, even with Monica?"

"You're an Ellis now, Nalib: the line for you has been erased."

She took a deep breath, clearly preoccupied with this now. I pulled out of her and lay on the mattress. Bilan closed her legs and turned to me. "I love your family—now. I'm wondering if I loved them too fast...like I did you."

My brows lifted in amusement. "First," I swiped the tip of her nose. "You didn't love me fast enough. Secondly, I would hope you loved my family. I knew you were capable. There was no other way this could work."

"Then why do I feel like I'm constantly fighting with them?"

"Because like you said: we're not at our best. And when we're not, chaos happens. There are so many things happening now over our heads; we're wounded. But I don't want you to feel guilty because you see the fissures."

"Oh, my god!" She gasped. "I used that same phrase when describing the family." She slapped her forehead. "It's frustrating feeling like I'm the only one who sees it. Sometimes it's lonely. You're gone all the time and Taaliba has her hands full with...life." She sighed and I could feel the weight of stress. "And I always thought I'd have Monica's wise counsel."

I tightened my lips apologetically. "Monica's been too busy fuckin' a guy she went to high school with." Bilan's mouth fell open and panic alarmed her eyes.

"You know—" She swallowed, blinking hard several times. "How do you know that?"

I smiled at my wife's naivety. "I know everything concerning my family..." I thought to amend that claim. "eventually." I kissed her stunned lips.

Like I knew Bilan had seen the man in my father's home and didn't breathe a word to me. I knew more than she could imagine.

"She's with someone from her past?" Bilan could barely breathe and, at this point, it wasn't due to exhaustion from the last orgasm I gave her.

I nodded. "She ran into him at a Christmas party last year. I think it was her first class reunion—the first she's gone to, I mean."

"Did they date?"

"A little, but I don't think Monica's had a serious boyfriend before Iban. She was young when they encountered. Maybe this guy is someone who she felt got away." I shrugged. "I honestly don't give a damn. Monica's out of line with this one."

"Are you sure she's...cheating?" Bilan seemed afraid to say the word.

"I can show you videos, but I respect my sister-in-law too much." I kissed her temple. "And I don't think you'd recover well afterward."

"Videos? She's been here for the past two months."

"Monica hired him as her personal security, which was her second mistake. She gave him first level access to *Elliswoods Palace*, so he's here often. He was even in *Macen Beach* when we were down for Palmer's funeral. She hired him as her security right before."

"She can just hire anyone? Anybody can be a part of Ellis security?"

I kissed her again. "Don't you get any ideas." I shook my head. "The answer is no. Because of who she is, she was able to request first level access and the head of our security didn't question her. But what she didn't know was when she submitted the necessary information, it's protocol for us to run a background check. We found he has a record. Did eight years for armed robbery."

Bilan sucked in a breath. "And he still has access to the grounds?"

"Limited. He's been followed the two times he's gone further than the community room, but monitored all over the property. He's no danger to anyone and will soon be handled."

My hand pushed between her legs until my fingers landed in the puddle we made. I rubbed her clit, enjoying seeing her squirm this time from the aftermath of an orgasm.

Bilan slammed her legs closed and moaned. "Now it's going to start leaking." She scooted until she made it to the edge of the bed. "If he wakes up, change him before you feed him," she called behind to me.

As I licked my fingers, I sat up, eyeing across the suite to Sadik's crib. I didn't hear or see much of him, which meant he was still asleep. He woke me up at five, wanting to talk about nothing. Exhausted out of my mind, I sat on the sofa with him, listening to the most captivating talk of my life. That went on for over thirty minutes. When he crashed, I had to keep myself from laughing out loud.

Now, it was after nine in the morning and felt damn good to sleep in with my family. I wished every Saturday could be this way and wondered if I should fashion them to be considering my growing family. The thought of another child still didn't seem like a reality. Last year, I was underwhelmed with my personal life and now, in a matter of months, I'd have a family of four.

My phone vibrating snapped my thoughts. Rory texted about our schedule today. It would be another late night, thanks to Jules' work in the city of Paterson. As I texted Rory back, my other phone rang. I checked the caller ID and answered.

"Yeah."

"Sadik," Sofia sounded throaty in a dejected manner.

"What's going on?" When I didn't hear a response, I lowered the phone I'd been texting Rory on. "Sofia?"

She sniffled. "Yeah, I'm here. Just wanted to tell you I'll be at the townhall meeting this evening, and at the debriefing afterward."

"Are you sure? I know this is a rough time for you and your family."

"Mi papá querría que lo hiciera," she murmured, and I could tell she'd been crying.

I nodded then brushed my palm down my face. "Of course, your father would want you to. He knew you were strong and kick-ass at what you do."

"Thanks, papi." My body steeled. "You still there, Sadik?" That let me know I must have gone quiet for a spell.

I cleared my throat. "Yeah... I'm here." Soft, familiar sniffles rang out from across the suite. "It'll be good to have you at the table for this one. I'll see you this evening."

I stood to leave the bed, in search of my boxers.

"Okay," I could hear her breathe, her mouth had to be that close to the receiver. "See you then."

I pulled up my boxer briefs. "Sofia?"

"Yeah?"

"I'm sorry about your father."

"I know. You said so already."

Maybe I had. I truly sympathized with her. My father was one of the herculean figures in my mind, too strong and formidable for demise. That included death, though I understood the prospect to be impossible. I couldn't imagine the pain she'd been dealing with over the past week.

The sound of the toilet flushing amplified Sadik's sniffles.

"Okay. See you later." I grabbed the bottle from the table near his crib.

"Bye," she murmured, and I disconnected the call.

"Hey, I'm here, Mr. Ellis," I greeted my son, wondering in the back of my mind how much alcohol had Sofia consumed since learning her father died in a car crash.

I opened one of the doors to the suite, rolling my suitcase out. It wasn't until after I closed it that I glanced up to find Monica standing across the hall. Her toned mocha arms were crossed and face set like a hard stone. If she wasn't dressed in a black sleeveless blouse, checkered capri pants, and slide-in heels I'd think she was as much of a threat as her husband was when he accosted me here.

The moment I opened my mouth to speak, her eyes roved down the hall where Taaliba stood, resting the bottom of her foot against the wall as her fingers drummed next to her hips. Her expression was implacable, resembling her younger brother when he was upset. In spite of that familiarity, my eyes blinked as my brain processed me being accosted.

"Well, if we don't have the Ellis-femme fatale here in action." I dropped my head to the side, focusing my gaze onto Monica. "You know, this reminds me of my first morning here when Iban stood just a few feet from where you are right now and tried to intimidate me by threatening my life?"

"I'm not Iban, Bilan," Monica hissed.

"Good to know." I began to move away from the door, not wanting to alert the Sadiks of my company. "Is the queen B awaiting me on the veranda facing the gardens, too, to complete the trilogy?"

"No, but how about we take this tête-à-tête out there," Monica suggested.

"Seems like it'll be more of a colloquy, not to mention there are more than two people present," I noted loud enough for them to hear.

After turning a few corners, the opening to the balcony appeared. I left my bags inside and stepped out, halfway prepared to see Irene. However, the balcony was empty. I ambled over to the balustrade and crossed my arms and ankles.

"Bilan, I can see how defensive you are already," Monica began. "I just want you to know I don't mean to alarm you—"

"Because waiting for me outside of my bedroom with crossed arms and a grimace shouldn't give me a reason to be alarmed," I posed sarcastically.

"We didn't want to give you an opportunity to avoid this conversation," Monica tried to explain.

"I know you haven't known me for long, but I have no reason to run from confrontation, especially from those who I care about."

"I'm glad you mentioned that," Taaliba finally chimed in. "It didn't seem like you cared much for Monica last night, considering the tone you took with her."

"I took the same tone with her that I took with you and my husband's much-adored mother. I have no reason to single Monica out. I feel like you two haven't taken these restrictions serious enough, and you're too old to be complaining about being bored. Not even Ivana and Iesha have reasons to complain of boredom here."

"I'm talking about what you said regarding my commitment to Iban," Monica clarified.

My head reared and eyes blinked. "No. I think you covered the extent of your commitment to him, Monica."

"And I think you're judging her when it's not your place to?" Taaliba switched weight on her hips.

Again, my head shifted backward. This morning wasn't the best one to try me on, and especially tag team me. Just like with Sadik and his father—because Iban, I never got the opportunity to level— I needed to settle my footing or my sisters-in-law would lose respect for me.

"I think she put the obvious out there all by herself. I also believe they were depending on Sadik and me to give the convenient 'hell no, he can't come' to make them feel better about their decisions. That's not cool on any front."

"It's not like that." Monica turned her head away.

"Then what is it really, Monica? I'm no angel. I don't like your husband very much, but I am human and realistic about his condition. The man is powerless—pitiful is more like it. He can't be a part of this powerful, insulated family one day and isolated the next because of a decision you all knew he was capable of making." My eyes brushed against both women. "You all loved and claimed Iban when he was a deviant, intimidating me; so why not continue to love him through him being him? I don't have to, but one thing I believed about family, until this incident, is they stick together through correction, too."

"And that's where I think you're overstepping," Monica interjected. "Who are you to tell me, as a wife who has suffered through those years that man acted as a tyrant, how to react when I'm finally fed up?"

"Exactly!" Taaliba's arms flayed in the air.

"Then make a call," I urged her. "It honestly doesn't matter to me which one you make; I won't judge you and will still respect you! But you doing what you've been doing around here will make more important people than me lose respect for you."

"What are you saying?" Taaliba charged.

Monica's entire frame whipped away from me, shame coating her before my eyes.

And apparently, Taaliba's, too. I saw when revelation hit her and Taaliba's face fell.

"Monica," Taaliba called out to her. "What in the hell is she talking about?" Her glower hit me. "What are you talking about, B?"

"About the Ellis cheating curse that you, who claims to hate how your parents and Iban conduct their marriages, are clearly repeating."

Her eyes blossomed wide and palm met her chest. "Me?"

"Yes, you." I cocked my head to the side again. "You think that alpha brown man of yours who loves for you to suck on his dick, increasing his obsession for you, is going to be okay when he finds out you're entertaining a woman?"

Taaliba's forehead creased. "Who told you that lie?"

I began toward the house. "I can't do this," I mumbled, but loud enough for them to hear. "Listen, before you guys decide to rally against me, make sure you show up with strategy and ammunition." I turned toward them. "Oh, and honesty. I get keeping some things to the chest, but you can't come for me when you're sloppy about your dirt."

"You have dirt, too, B!" Taaliba warned.

"And what dirt is that?" I braved. "Me sneaking off the compound for church?"

"Yes!" Taaliba shouted. We now had Monica's attention. "And that one time to go to the gym. You don't think anyone knows you did it two weeks ago? You left out in workout clothes, and came back with messy curls and a stained shirt."

My heart dropped to my throat, but not totally from fear of being found out; from relief of her possibly believing it was a one-time occurrence, something I didn't have any reason to believe Sadik knew about.

"Me sneaking out to church—something your brother knows about now—and one session at the gym doesn't damage this family." I hoped she wouldn't say different. "Yes, it puts us and others at risk." My eyes fell in shame. Sadik's rebuke still stung. "But I've not been disloyal to my husband, or boyfriend for that matter." My eyes swept between the two. "All I'm saying is if I know this, Monica, don't you think the family does, too, or will soon?"

I pivoted to my other sister-in-law. "And Taaliba, I couldn't give a shit if you're gay or straight. It doesn't change who you are as a person. But it matters to Danny. And while I know there's no other alpha on this earth like Sadik—not even his father, contrary to what most believe—I don't doubt there will be hell to pay once Danny finds out. So figure it out instead of tag-teaming little ol' me with Monica. She's a big girl: she needs no help compartmentalizing her guilt. She sure didn't have any getting into her mess."

At that, I took off.

"Damn, her glow up is real!" Brenda gushed over Randi's shoulder into her phone.

"You know my cousin went to school with her. Right?" Randi shared.

"For real?" Missy, Tasche's colleague and friend, asked.

Randi nodded while scrolling down an IG page. "Yeah. Well..." She rolled her eyes and head. "We grew up like cousins. She lived down in the fuckin' woods in South Jersey, but came up in the summers and on spring breaks, and shit. When my best friend, who I *call* my cousin, went to get ol' girl one time, she said it was mad trailer parks down there." Her hearty laughter was contagious. "I thought them shits was made the fuck up. She was like, nah. That bitch really lived in one, too!"

"Who?" Tasche asked. "Tori McNabb?"

"Nah," Randi answered. "My bestie who was cousins with the one that went to school with ol' girl. Keep the fuck up with the story!"

We belted in laughter. Randi was on one tonight. We'd been at the hotel suite I'd reserved for us. I had the Ellis kitchen whip us up pans of foods, including sweets to help the girls absorb the alcohol and weed I knew they'd be consuming. I only asked that they were discrete with the pot and kept it away from me. That meant them going out on the balcony for thirty minutes earlier and leaving me alone in wait. Everyone's eyes were low, pink, and tight. Missy's were even pink from the indo.

"Well, bitch," Tasche started, her arms in the air defensively with a plastic cup in one hand. "You on Tori's page, I thought you had some insider shit!"

We laughed at that, too.

"Oh, shit!" Randi shouted, snapping the fingers of her available hand. "Y'all shut the fuck up. You remember this?"

I leaned in so I could hear, but didn't recognize the song.

"The fuck is that?" Brenda asked before draining the last of her cup.

"That's that shit, yo!" Tasche exclaimed, rocking side to side on the sofa. "Yo, B, rock that shit on ya *Tidal*. Gimme ya phone." She stood, taking my cell from the coffee table. "Put ya code in." She handed the phone to me.

I laughed and tapped for it to recognize my face then handed it back to her. She went to the Tidal app and typed in a song.

"This bitch sangin' this shit!" Brenda croaked, still peering over Randi's shoulder. "I remember now. That's that old school right there!"

I caught her tap Randi with her shoulder then toss her chin over to me. Randi glanced my way and snickered. I'd lie if I said it didn't annoy me. Once again, Randi had been acting shady toward me. It started when I offered to pick her up. She said Brenda was with her and they'd get here how they could unless I wanted to get them and ride them around to get a few things. I was no cab. No way would I have Sadik's driver chauffeuring them around Paterson. So I declined.

Then when she arrived, Randi didn't hug me. When I opened the door to let them in, she offered a drily hello as she carried in a box of liquor and beverages. I knew then what type of night this would be and decided to make the best of it for the sake of Tasche.

A song began to pour from the portable speaker I brought.

"That's that shit!" Brenda stood and began swaying to the intro, which was just music.

Then she and Tasche began singing with the woman on the track. Missy laughed while snapping her fingers in a conversant manner. Randi stood and began dancing.

My nose turned up, not recognizing the tune. "What's this?"

"It ain't Somalian!" Randi blurted, being silly.

Or facetious?

"You mean '*Somali*'?" I lifted a tight smile to my face.

Brenda and Tasche both sang at the same time, "*You're that lady's husband!*"

That's when I began to pay attention to the lyrics. A woman was torn over cheating with someone's husband. She still wanted him, but knew it was wrong.

Again, I asked, "Who is this?"

"That's that bitch, Shirley, yo!" Tasche finally answered.

"Shirley." I nodded with sarcasm.

"Shirley Murdock," Brenda expounded. "Your momma ain't never blast Ms. Shirley on Saturday mornings?"

"Or after she got fucked over by another fuck boy!" Tasche added. The two women laughed as they slapped hands.

Randi dropped onto the sofa across the coffee table from me. "Shit. It ain't have to be your mother that get down like that. It could be you." She huffed. "I know my ass been the other woman. I was ready to do it again recently, too. Right, Brenda?" She laughed alone.

That wouldn't have struck me as odd if Brenda's expression didn't drop from warm nostalgia to pure shock. Her eyes moved between the side of Randi's face to mine. Randi's regard was a daring one as it shot bullets to me. Quickly deciding to let it go, I rolled my eyes away and hopped up to get my phone from the coffee table, where Tasche placed it after selecting the song.

"I'm not doing this tonight," I mumbled to myself.

People grieve in their own way. Lord knows I had my fair share of mourning and wanted grace with it each time.

"You got something to say, say it?" My eyes rolled up to find Randi's head bobbing while her eyes were now red and wide on me.

My face tightened. "You drunk, Randi?"

"No, I ain't drunk. I just don't like people whispering shit under they breath. You got something to say, fuckin' say it."

"I said I'm not doing this with you tonight!" I made sure my words were clear.

"Do what? Judge me?"

Why was I being accused of that again today?

"Judge you for what?"

"For fuckin' somebody else husband," she answered.

"Randi, so long as it ain't my husband, I couldn't give two shits who you sleep with. I've never judged you."

"Oh, you would care if only you knew!" She laughed.

Laughed. In my face. My friend attempted to torment me by being suggestive and laughing in my face. My patience waned by the minute.

"Just chill the fuck out, yo!" Tasche begged, pouring herself another drink.

"Yeah," Brenda agreed, looking at Randi and communicating something strange with her eyes.

Why?

"What have I ever done wrong to you?" I finally asked. "You've been extra shady with me for over a year now. As a matter of fact, since I met Sadik. Are you the crab type of bitch, trying to claw me down, Randi? The woman who can't see another have her happily ever after, even if she's your friend?"

"I ain't never hate on a bitch in my life." She kissed her fingertips and shot her open palm into the air. "That's on my uncle! That's why I 'on't get why you bring him up like you better than me. Is it because my nigga got killed? Ask Sadik who did it."

My eyes leaped over to Tasche, whose expression was a hybrid of shock and confusion. I took a deep breath, feeling my body heat all over with uncontrollable anger. I didn't want to go there with Randi. I didn't come here with that type of energy. Right now, I wanted nothing more than to be at *Elliswoods Palace* in the bed with my son, not here with a drunk and nasty Randi.

"I never said I was better than you in any way, and I would never speak against Ricky, Randi. You know that. But what I would like to know is why haven't you shown the same respect? What is your problem with Sadik? Tell me!" I screamed. "Once and for all! What?"

"Nah." She laughed. "The right question is who husband I was gonna fuck last month—"

"Oh, hell no!" Tasche yelped, taking a defensive posture.

Brenda appeared so panicked, she could cry. "Chill, Randi."

When my gaze met Randi's again, I saw the devil in her eyes. In an instant, I knew she was referring to Sadik.

"I think it's time for you to say whatever it is you've got to say," I advised calmly, welcoming her to it. "And if it's that you were gonna fuck my husband, you should try again."

The room hushed to a silence. It became so quiet, I could hear my pulse race.

"How much of his bread you wanna put up?" Randi's grin was pure evil. She tapped into her phone. I swallowed involuntarily, uncannily nervous. I went for my bag, pulling it to my hip as I waited. Randi turned the face of her phone my way. "I'll let you see it for ya damn self."

It was blurred and a bit smoky, but I recognized a VIP section of Tiffany's club, *Pulse*. Then a familiarly suited man was clear, sitting next to Randi. They were close, but also exchanging words in a club I could assumed played loud music, explaining their proximity. But when Randi turned the phone to swipe to the next picture, I saw her hand inappropriately on his thigh. She turned the phone to swipe again. The third photo was of Sadik blowing out smoke while passing her a blunt. Randi snatched her phone wearing the biggest *cat that ate the canary* grin.

"When was that?" I asked helplessly, steeping in fury.

"I told you a month ago. It was at the *Pulse* anniversary joint," she answered casually. "See." Randi reached over the coffee table again, showing me another photo.

It was an IG post of Tiffany in Sadik's arm on a red carpet. Her smile was priceless, eyes filled with palpable joy. This time, I thought to catch the date before Randi pulled the phone away again. Per the timestamp, it was the night Sadik should have been in Atlanta. The time his return home was delayed. A gamut of deceitful motives raced through my mind.

"Why are you doing this to me?" I wanted to cry.

Betrayal was as physical as a gut blow.

She couldn't stop giggling, but I suddenly got the impression that more than Randi found this situation funny, she was nervous about dropping the bomb. Yet, that revelation eased nothing. She'd still betrayed me.

"All I'm saying is Sadik a nigga like the rest of them." She pointed at me from head to toe. "He done got bored already. You knocked up and married and the honeymoon's over. I tried to warn you."

"The fuck?" I could hear Tasche hiss, but then I couldn't.

"And you had to prove it?"

"Nah. This was a little more about survival," she explained. "I woulda fucked Sadik, but he's an arrogant asshole and said no. I had Brenda take the flicks 'cause I know your naïve ass wouldn't believe me when I told you."

"But he said no." I noted.

She shrugged, choosing to gaze into her phone. "He's a ass. It is what it is."

"He's an ass because you're not his type?" I grated, fighting back the stinging tears. My throat burned viciously, stomach toiled. "And he wouldn't touch you with a ten-foot pole?"

Tasche and Brenda were shooting words of letting it go over us, but I couldn't pay that any attention as my hand clutched inside of my bag.

"Don't go there, Bilan." She shook her head hard left to right. "Don't do it."

"Do what? Speak the truth, which is that a man like Sadik would never find a chick like you attractive enough to take to *B-Way Burger*, you whore?"

Explosively, Randi jumped to her feet, leaned over the table, and pointed her finger directly to my face. "I was attractive enough to let that nigga put his dick in my mouth. I was attractive to him for him to nut the fuck down my throat, bitch! Sadik killed Ricky because of me. Bet ya dumb ass ain't know that." I didn't, and it caused my head to swirl, kicking up nausea. "Ricky kept fuckin' with him 'cause he never got over what me and Sadik did! I'm *that* type of bitch. Don't you ever try to put me in the gutter. I will slap the living shit out of you!"

Her lime green, coffin-shaped index fingernail was inches from my face.

I was lightheaded when I whispered, "When was this, Randi?"

"Way before he met your dumb ass. And I bet you still don't believe that I did it," she sneered. "Why the fuck you think Ricky ain't never want me around him like at his birthday party? Ricky was about to body that nigga when he found out."

"Why didn't he?" My voice was so soft; I felt like I was having an out of body experience.

"What?"

"Why didn't Haitian Ricky kill Sadik?"

"I 'on't know." Her face tightened. "Why would you ask some bullshit like that?"

I jumped to my feet and palmed her face, pushing her backward into the sofa. The girls gasped, yelped, and squealed, leaping into action. I swiftly shot around the table, pulling my gun from my purse, and pointed it centimeters from her nose.

"Because that's what I feel I need to do to you after learning this."

With a pounding chest and wounded heart, I stood in front of my friend for many years, talking myself off the cliff. The barrel of my gun was centimeters from her face, and my decided hands didn't tremble. Pulling the trigger would take the effort of a blink of an eye.

"You're a gutter bitch, you know that?" I grated, facial muscles tightened, top lip hiked. I peered a shaken Randi directly in the eye, enjoying the shock and fear I supplied. "I have no idea what took me so long to see it. Was it my naiveté?" I shrugged. "You've played on that weakness of mine long enough to know. But this time, you toyed with my heart."

"Bilan, don't do it, girl!" Tasche begged. "I done seen this shit go down too many fuckin' times around my way. That baby boy need you, and the one in ya belly don't deserve to be born in no goddamn prison then shipped off in two hours to the Ellises, yo!"

"She right, B!" Brenda's voice was shaky and squealy. "She ain't mean nothing by it. It wasn't personal."

With my eyes set on Randi, my head shot back at that one. "It wasn't personal?" I asked Randi. "Because it felt damn personal when I see you rubbing on my husband's thigh while you were in my damn clothes!" She wore the purple leather halter top I loaned her last fall. "You wore the top you borrowed while I was too big and pregnant to wear it. Did you think wearing my clothes would attract him to your dingy ass? You think it's that simple?" I snorted. "You were wrong. I'm his dirty habit, nasty addiction, and his inspiration. What the hell is he going to do with you after having me?"

"B, let's just put the gun away, yo," Tasche pleaded. "It's late and people do stupid shit like this when they been drinking."

That was claptrap and Tasche knew it. I hadn't been drinking and Randi had receipts for her story, so it wasn't just about what she said. It was what she had been doing and for some time, apparently. But Tasche was right about the hour. Time was a factor for me tonight. That reminded me I had to keep someone from the fate Randi had almost faced.

Finally, one side of Randi's face lifted. No matter how forced it appeared, she muttered, "Bilan ain't doing shit stupid tonight. She know it's bitches over these niggas every day."

I hawked up all the phlegm and saliva I could and spit it in Randi's face. It landed between her eyes and flopped down her nose. When she reflectively moved to leap up, the ladies shouted fearfully. That's when I knocked the barrel into her forehead, pushing her back onto the sofa.

"Don't speak to me or Sadik again in your life, or I'll show you just how authentic an Ellis I am." I snatched my body away, grabbed my things from the sofa across from her, and took off to the bedroom where I slammed the door.

Then I lunged into the closet and slid on my sandals. Next, I went to the door in the bedroom adjoining the standard room next door to the suite. I reserved that, too. It let out to a different hallway than the suite. Johnson and the other new guy Sadik assigned to me for tonight wouldn't likely be in that hallway. With a racing heart, I opened the door to the room and thankfully, no one was around. I crept to the exit door and dropped down three levels of stairs until I came out of the stairwell and crossed the hallway for the exit at the other end of the floor. This helped me catch my breath and get to the side of the building where the car was parked.

Getting down five flights of stairs took effort because I had to be sure not to stomp too hard. Doing that caused an ache from my belly button to my pelvis. By the time I made it to the first floor, my lower abdomen ached, but my adrenaline ran so high, it wasn't a focal point. I let myself outside, into the parking lot as I fished for the keys in my pocketbook. I had to walk up one level to get to where I was told the car would be. Once there, I clicked the fob, locating the car.

Out of breath, I open the door to the *Ford Fusion* and slipped inside.

"Ewwwww!" I cringed and my face tightened. "David, you smoke weed?"

He didn't mention that when I arranged for him to park his car here this morning before checking in at *DiFillippo's*, and to pick it back up later tonight. The scent permeated the upholstery. I didn't have time to dwell on that. I needed to get to campus.

After locking the doors, I adjusted the seats and pulled out of the parking lot. About thirty minutes later, I was stepping out of the car on my old campus. As I checked my phone again for any signs of Sadik or his security contacting me, my feet moved faster toward the science and technology building. The campus held a peaceful vibe at night. Not many were around at this hour, but the manicured lawns and trees were illuminated beautifully under the pole lighting.

My mind continued to race with the words I'd use to persuade Jason to stay away. Words and phrases that wouldn't incriminate Sadik or his family, but would confirm what he claimed he already knew. I couldn't just say *My husband will kill you then have dinner with his family and me and discuss our next vacation destination while your body is being disposed of by his tactically trained men.* That would be too implicit. Jason had been annoying since I left him in *Macen Beach* last summer, but I cared about him enough to sacrifice upsetting Sadik by warning him.

Although Sadik didn't deserve my consideration after the stunt he pulled with sneaking off to Tiffany's "little" celebration and having a whole ass "set up" conversation with a "friend" of mine. That palpable betrayal lanced through my belly. But it was something I had to deal with later. For now, Jason's life had to be saved. He was not built for my husband and in-laws' world.

The building was still open, inside lit brightly. I was familiar with it, though I had very few classes here. I went to my right, where we planned to meet. There were small private media rooms along this hall. On this side, there were five in total. All but two were open. I knocked on the first closed door. A young woman opened it immediately, eyes wild from exhaustion, it seemed.

"Sorry." I smiled with mild embarrassment. "Wrong room."

Then the other door opened. I saw Jason's tightly coiled hair that had grown longer. He waved me in. My nerves roiled unnecessarily. This was only Jason. What could be hard about telling him to back off?

He opened the door to welcome me in and the moment I crossed the threshold, I understood my body's apprehensive state to tonight.

One white male pushed off the sound booth, standing erect. "Ms. Asad-Yasin. Did I get that right?"

I shook my head, feeling flushed. "No."

Jason closed the door behind me, the clicking sound made me suddenly claustrophobic.

"I'm sorry," he provided. "My pronunciation of African surnames may be a little off. I don't mean to offend you, and apologize if I did." He offered a bow of humility, though his green irises sparkled with manipulative charm. "My name is Joshua Parks, an agent from the *Federal Bureau of Investigations*." His hand lifted to the right of him. "This is my colleague, Agent Lawrence Pierce, and next to him, Agent Michael Jefferson. We're here tonight because your friend, Jason, has expressed concern about your well-being as well as your child's."

Two of the agents were white and one was Black, but they were all males. My eyes shot over to Jason. His chest heaved and eyes were wild with anxiousness, similar to mine, only I refused to show it.

"Please have a seat." The Black agent pulled out a chair at the small round table.

Too overwhelmed to think of a method of refusal, I took a seat.

The third agent moved into my peripheral. "We understand you're romantically involved with the son of the man at the helm of the most profitable drug organization in the state of New Jersey. We also know you don't have the background to be involved in this type of business. It's understood that Sadik Ellis is a man of a wealth of resources.

"He, himself, is worth millions, and from his personal and business tax records, we can see he's earned it mostly legitimately and without his father's assistance. But we have reason to believe Sadik's the mastermind of Double E Bags' empire." I wanted to laugh at that. Earl needing a mastermind? That was ridiculous. "When we received the complaint of concern for you from your friend, Jason, here, we hoped to gain an ally out of you."

That time, I did react. I scoffed, "And why would I do that?"

The Pierce agent grabbed a chair from the corner and took a seat across from me at the table. "Simple. We're familiar with Sadik just as much as we are Double E Bags and Iban. You're the first woman he's gone these lengths to claim, but he's been quite a philanderer, and that hasn't stopped; only slowed."

"Excuse me?" Anger snaked up my spine like a wild vine ascending to my tongue.

He shrugged. "You've managed to get him to fall in love, but he's still an Ellis."

My forehead lifted. "And what's an Ellis?"

Pierce lifted an expectant hand over his shoulder. Without words, the Parks agent handed him an envelope. Pierce dropped it on the table, causing me to leap. He then opened it and pulled out an 8x10 color photo of Sadik with Tiffany at *Pulse*'s anniversary event. My belly did a freefall at the sight of that image again. I'd just seen it for the first time, thanks to my supposed best friend. I still couldn't believe he'd been with her while having me think he was on a flight to Georgia.

Dismissively, I replied, "She's a family-friend. She's Earl's god-daughter."

Pierce cracked a cunning smirk. "I'm sorry to have to remind you, Ms. Asad-Yasin, but Tiffany and Sadik have been and are more than family."

Could my stomach drop anymore? I felt nauseous.

Swallowing hard, I asked, "Who are you to say what they are? What proof do you have that there's something going on between them? A picture they took at her place of business where it would benefit her to be seen in public with an Ellis?"

He pulled out another photo, same size. "Not necessarily, but this could contribute to what we believe. It was taken in Rome last August. They'd just left the restaurant, *Imàgo*."

It was a photograph of Tiffany and Sadik with his arm snaked around her waist as they smiled, walking down broad concrete stairs. They were close—intimately close. Sadik's smile appeared so pure, evidentiary peace.

He had peace while I was losing my mind in fear and morning sickness in a foreign place...

I glanced back at Jason, suddenly grateful that I had run into him in *Macen Beach*. That seemed to be when things lightened up for me. He leaned against the wall, gnawing at his fingers. Jason appeared uneasy about this ordeal, rightfully so, considering he'd set me up. Even still, I now wondered if all of his insistence to keep in touch with me was for my good.

I turned back to the table and murmured, "Again, she's a family-friend. They've known each other since childhood, and—as you explosively put it—they were lovers once upon a time. I was aware of Sadik being in Europe with Tiffany. She needed a flight out to have a gown done by a designer there." My voice so heavy from despair, my throat hurt.

That was the weakest excuse to give in the matter of infidelity, but it was the one Sadik gave me. The part I left out was that he too had business there. I didn't want to share that because I didn't know what type of business it was and if it should be mentioned at all in the company of the *Federal Bureau of Investigations*. It would seem safer an excuse for him to be out there cavorting with an old flame than him being there on business. So, I decided to go with the dumb, naïve girlfriend role. It was one I seemed to have played best, according to many. What was evident to me was these agents, who swore to know so much about Sadik, didn't know everything.

Even still, this hurt. Badly.

"And what about this?" Pierce pulled out another photo. It was the same night of *Pulse*'s anniversary. "Isn't she your friend?"

The pain didn't dull the second time I'd seen Sadik and Randi so close. She touched his leg as they gaped fondly at each other—in my clothes.

"No news here. Just a jealous friend," I provided dispiritedly.

Joshua Parks leaned over the table, placing two palms to keep him upright. "So, you don't care that he's sharing a blunt with your best friend, whom he had intimate relations with previously?" He pulled out two more photos of the same type. One was of Sadik pulling from the blunt and the other was him passing it to Randi.

What stung the most was how I was able to identify Sadik's sexual past with Tiffany, Ameerah, and Sofia the moment I met them. And now it was clear why. Those three women gave their hearts to Sadik to some measure. They were in love with the man who owned my soul. However, this wasn't the case with Randi. I couldn't sense their sexual past because it was just physical. Randi was heartless and couldn't give Sadik more than what she did: a simple emotionless blowjob.

"Again. I'm aware of this night." I fingered the top of my hair as I rolled my neck uncomfortably.

"And you're okay with him being with all of those women, but being photographed like this with you?" Pierce pulled out yet another photo.

My breath caught audibly in my throat at the sight of me being hauled behind Sadik to his limo with my wrists tied together and mouth gagged as we left Julius' victory party at *Wilson's*. My face was stained with tears and running mascara, and I looked frightened.

Because I was. I was also violently roused and disturbingly horny. I was betrayed and uncharacteristically territorial. Sadik had a talent at making me feel that way. He rendered me dizzy with a dangerous mix of emotions.

An itch on my top lip made me wipe my mouth. That's when I realized it was snot running from my nose. I'd been crying.

My eyes swung from agent to agent to agent. "Why am I here?" I turned to Jason. "Why did you do this to me?"

When Jason opened his mouth to speak, Parks cut him off at the path. "Sadik isn't an innocent man. We have reason to believe he's been involved with embezzlement, murder, and a host of other charges subject to federal indictment. We figured if you are in a dangerous, unwanted, and violent relationship with Sadik, we can help you out."

"And in turn," Pierce interjected. "you can help us connect a few dots, ensuring an indictment or ten. We know you've seen him violent or make a call that led to violence. You've been inside. I mean..." He scoffed. "You've seen here he can't even be trusted to be faithful to you: I'm sure he's been immoral in other ways you've seen. Do you not see this?"

Too pained to speak, I shook my head, refusing to look at the pictures he tried bringing to my attention again.

"A woman who doesn't value fidelity." Pierce blew out an exasperating breath. "Okay. Then how about a woman of humanity." I bit into my lip to the point of breaking skin when his hand went for the envelope again. Pierce lay out several pictures of a car wreckage. "Sadik did this to your friend—" He tossed his chin to a cowardice Jason behind me. "—Jason's, parents back on May 22nd."

There were images of busted glass windows, blown tires, and deflated airbags of a minivan of sorts. There were also pictures of wounded body parts, some bloodied. A man had a black, swollen eye.

"This was done to them as a threat tactic for Jason. Sadik has been wanting him to stay away from you. He called him moments before their accident. We found the crossover vehicle had been tampered with before the Andersons left for Delaware."

"We weren't in the country on May 22nd," I struggled for my voice then cleared my throat, lifting my chin. "Try again."

"We know," Pierce made clear. "Sadik sicced his goons in his wake. Now, do you believe us?" He pushed his hands to the waist of his pants, exposing his gun.

That reminded me of the one I had on me. I didn't have a license to carry, something that would change after today. I needed to go. While I didn't feel a meltdown episode coming on, I did feel an impending explosion.

"I'm ready to go," I made clear.

"We'd rather you not." That Pierce guy was quite nasty, typical of law enforcement.

He wanted to intimidate me, hurt me with these photos. He didn't care about me. He wanted Sadik.

"Am I under arrest, Agent Pierce?"

Pierce blinked. "No." His jaw churned. "You're not."

"Then I'm free to go." I stood and headed for the door. When I laid eyes on Jason, he looked reduced to a spooked child. "If I had an ounce of trust left for you, you just spent it on this 'intervention for the abused heart' bullshit. Don't ever contact me again."

I went for the doorknob.

"Ms. Asad-Yasin," I turned to Pierce behind me. He flashed a wicked smile. "Or did I pronounce that wrong again?" The question was insincere. "We—"

"You're wrong about the pronunciation of my name."

Pierce bounced back on his feet, eyes brushed over his partners as he snickered. "My apologies. Please feel free to correct me."

"It's Ellis. E, L, L, I, S, as in Bilan Ellis. Or better yet, Mrs. Sadik Ellis. Why no pictures of my nuptials or a copy of my marriage certificate?" I snorted and suddenly caught the winking of an eye of the Black agent, who hadn't whispered a word since I'd been in here. "Next time you want to speak with me, my attorney will be present. Goodnight, agents."

When I yanked the door open, Johnson was there, appearing as though he was about to open it himself. His narrowed eyes toured the small media room, then they hit me questioning.

"I'm fine." I assured him and at the same time, surrendering to the obvious.

My life was no longer my own. It belonged, in part, to Sadik.

"We gotta go, Mrs. Ellis," Johnson urged.

His reference of my title couldn't be more apropos. I turned to the room, paying one last gaze of false confidence before walking out.

After slamming the door behind me, I took off. "Are you alone?"

"No," Johnson answered.

"Good. Take me straight to him."

"A hunned-twelve pounds, dripping wet!" Jules teased.

Sofia gasped, tossing a piece of popcorn over the table at him. "No, I was not, Richards!"

Keisha and I laughed at his assessment.

"You damn sure were," Jules asserted. "I remember that time I crashed at Ellis' high-rise after my brother-in-law's birthday party." He pointed to his wife. "Remember that, Key?" Keisha hummed while nodding her head. "And it was at this spot closer to the high-rise than Paterson. I couldn't drive back, so I had his friend drop me off at like...four in the morning. I woke up around eight to reggaeton blasting. I jumped the fuck up, still drunk, and wobbled my ass toward his room." We laughed as acted it out in his chair. "I was about to cuss your Prince of Bel Air ass clean the fuck out! When I stepped into your room, I see this bean pole of a caramel stick whipping her head back and forth. I thought the big ass thing was gonna roll off that little frame."

"Whatever!" Sofia laughed, blushing like crazy.

"You only had on a towel, Soph!" He sat up in his chair. "I remember blinking like..." He demonstrated. "Who the fuck is this Ellis got up in here! You *know* he's never been known to have women in his home like that."

My humor slowed; Keisha's continued. We'd all had a couple of glasses of *Mauve* I had brought here to City Hall, where we debriefed after the successful townhall meeting. Now, at close to midnight, we were going the long route at saying goodnight. The Richards had to relieve their sitter, and I had to do the same for mine—or, at least, that should have been the plan.

"But we all know I wasn't just any woman," Sofia announced in her Cardi B. impersonation. "And I was like a buck fifty back then!"

She issued a fake smile that had the three of us cracking the fuck up. Even Sofia had to laugh.

"How much did she weigh?" Keisha asked.

"It wasn't no damn one-fifty!" Julius shot back the last of his brandy.

My eyes met Sofia's low lidded ones. She was definitely nice off the *Mauve*. I just hoped she hadn't overdone it. With her, you never knew when she'd tip over to the total inebriation side of the line.

"She was well over one hundred pounds," I snickered good-heartedly. "Otherwise, she wouldn't have seen the high-rise—exterior or interior." My brows lifted.

"Man, those were the good days," Jules breathed out. "When I decided to grow some balls and run for councilman. I had the right people around me, the resources, the hype..." He scratched his head. "Now that I'm doing the math, I had all that because of you, Ellis. You helped form the team for that, too. We strategized, ate well, rubbed elbows with key constituents to get my name out there. Had Sofia, here, writing compelling speeches and proposals. I had a dope ass cabinet even for that role."

Keisha and I nodded, taken by the memory.

"Yup," his wife agreed while taking from her chair. "And now that you made it here, we have to practice balance." She placed her hand on his shoulder. "Let's do that by getting home to our babies." Keisha rolled her neck, expressing exhaustion.

Jules stood. "The wife has spoken, guys. I'm gonna go shut down my office and get home to these snot-nosed babies of mine."

Keisha smacked his arm. "Richards!"

"What? It ain't like I'm gonna get that good-good when I get there," he whined like a damn baby.

Keisha sucked her teeth as she turned for the door. "Boy, if you don't get your narrow tail ass on!"

He grumbled behind her out the door.

Sofia turned to me and giggled. "Is that what married life is like?" She pointed behind them.

Amused, I asked, "Which part?"

Her eyes fell and smile broadened as she swept her head away. "I'm sure you have nannies."

"One."

She faced me again. "She's okay with that?"

I shrugged with my mouth. "She's a busy woman with a demanding life."

Her eyes danced and smile dimmed. "What does she do?"

I considered her question for a few moments then placed my chin on my fist as my elbow rested on the table. Taking a deep breath from my own tiredness, I answered, "She has me, for one. I'm a full-time job alone."

She spat a laughter. "Oh, I can only imagine." I nodded with humility as she cackled. "Go on."

"She also has a key role at *Ellis Academy*, maintaining the funding."

"Is that her field?"

My brows lifted again. "I'm her field. Found out she had a master's in S.Q.E."

"Stop!" She laughed again, throwing popcorn at me this time. "Really. What's her field?"

"Education. It's what her degree is in, and the one she's currently pursuing."

With poked lips, Sofia shook her head. "I remember those days."

Her eyes hit me as she giggled. "Me coming home late nights from class and study groups at *Columbia*. You coming in around the same time from your gazillion jobs, and Kimmy having something for us to eat although she'd be gone for the day." I nodded. "Damn, she hated me!" Sofia chuckled.

I knew that was coming. Kimmy never verbalized it, but she didn't like Sofia. Kimmy believed she was too bossy and territorial—and messy. Sofia was very disorganized and left chaos in whichever room she was in, even though she didn't live with me.

"I remember fantasizing about living with you when you'd be out of town and okayed me to stay at your place so I could have privacy and quiet to study and work." She winked my way, elbows to the table as she leaned over it. That position pushed her breasts out, making them appear incitingly ample.

Sofia must have caught my line of sight because her face dropped down to her chest. Then only her eyes returned to me and she bit her lip. Her next move was predictable. She stood and catwalked mere feet over to me and planted her ass on the table. Sofia turned to me, her fingertips brushed against the back of my hand.

"Are you in love?"

My eyes raked from her caressing hand to her face. "Every hour of the day." I returned my attention to our point of touch. "Obsessively."

"I'm familiar with the preoccupation." She nodded.

My head reared. "Really?"

She hummed her affirmation then giggled. I knew this Sofia. She was the precursor to a long night of erotic acts. Visions of her sweaty torso between my legs until my spine shivered circled in my mind.

She moved even closer to me. "And sex?"

"What are you asking, Sofia?" Slowly, my eyes climbed to meet hers.

"You're demanding in bed," her voice breathy. "Does she please you? What does she know that we didn't?"

"She knows only what I've taught her, and what I taught her—"

"More than satisfies you at your age," she surmised in a low murmur. "It drives you wild." I didn't respond to confirm what she'd already known to be true. There was a time where Sofia was under my tutelage also, but I hadn't been her first teacher. The culmination of a list of experiences was hers. Sofia came to me with a tenured past, but it had been an erogenous benefit to our chemistry.

"What makes her different from the rest of us?" she breathed. "I mean...I know you've always had side relationships when we were together. I couldn't expect for you to be faithful." But I *was* faithful to Sofia. After the third time I'd fucked her, I saw something satisfying in her for some time. It was enough to only give her that part of me. "But what did you see in her to choose her over the rest?" The sadness in her voice was affective.

"My mother."

Her eyes fell away. "It's because of my race, isn't it?"

I couldn't deny that. Irene would have never made nice with Sofia's political views. But it was more.

"My mother is my axis; she centers me. She's always been the gatherer, the server of encouragement, correction, discernment, and navigation. Irene has held the banner of 'family.' When I encountered my wife, I saw a long-sufferer, a sharp mind, a blinding resilience, and a legacy-bearer." I nodded, decidedly firm on my summary. It was my weakness. My truth. "I saw my future when I encountered my wife—I *see* my future, and it becomes my reality each morning I awake with her in my bed."

"And if you want to continue to have that bed, you'd tell your little drunken mamacita goodnight, and to have a nice life." I leaned my head to the right with casual speed and found Bilan in the doorway with a terrified Julius to the right of her. A troubled Keisha stood to her left, and Rory and Johnson were behind her. A segment of my family postured as though I'd been caught with my hand in the cookie jar. It was so comical, I struggled to not laugh.

Standing straight, Sofia turned to face the door. "Now, now, Bilan. We don't have to play nasty to clear this up. Sadik was just telling me how you—"

"We don't have to play at all." Bilan's head cocked to the side. "And that's 'Mrs. Ellis' to you, Ms. Cruz."

I stood to my feet internally amused, collected my devices, and grabbed my jacket. Then I sauntered over to my perturbed wife and kissed her sweetly on the cheek, an act of affection she didn't respond to. Bilan's eyes remained locked to a flummoxed Sofia.

"Jules," shot from Bilan's gut.

"Yeah?" His scary eyes reached me, almost asking for help.

"Sadik or Ms. Cruz: choose one. My husband will no longer work in tandem with her." She turned to face him, finally releasing Sofia from her deathly glare. "I won't ask you to make this call right here or right now, but what I will share is if my husband decides to carry on with your current arrangement, it will be without me as his future and/or the reality he awakes to in his bed each morning. I hope I'm clear." In response, Jules hung his head. "Goodnight, Keisha." She bade before taking me by the hand and leaving the conference room.

∞25∞

The ride home was a game of quieted patience. Bilan's manufactured steely veneer had been melting from the time we got into the car. She didn't emit a word the entire ride and I hadn't cared to either, afraid of losing my cool. I felt my tolerance fading the moment we crossed the security barrack.

Once we were at a stop in front of *Elliswoods Palace*, I hopped out of the car and messaged Rory to not open Bilan's door. With long lunges, I made it there and did it myself. She barely looked my way when she stepped out. Bilan continued up the stairs toward the entrance. The doors were opened for her by a staff member, and I was on her heels. When greeted, Bilan mumbled something in response, yet maintained her speed.

When the foyer opened in my peripheral, people began to move into our pathway. Bilan and I slowed at the sight of Daz, my father's deputy. Then came a red-faced and nosed Taaliba. Monica and my mother were behind her.

"You're home?" my mother noted with thick emotional cords. "Thank God."

"Yo, Deek, man," Daz began. "We got some shit poppin' off."

"We're under attack!" Taaliba cried, getting straight to the point.

"By whom?" I was finally able to speak.

Taaliba shrugged. "You know who. Those damn Russians!"

My eyes shot over to Daz, who confirmed with a slight nod. *How does she know?* That answer came to mind quickly. "Where's Lopez?"

"He's at the hospital. Their estate was bombed, Sadik." Taaliba began to sob. "His home! So far, possibly eleven people dead, and five injured."

"And the rehabilitation facility where Iban is was seized," Monica's voice was shaky as she shared, her arms protectively crossed over her small frame. "Their electrical system went out of whack with alarms going off, doors opening and closing...sprinklers going off."

That stirred a panic in me immediately. "Where's Iban?"

"That security team you assigned to him was able to get him out of there after the first two minutes of it. The nurses thought it was premature and fought for him to go to a secluded place in the building instead of leaving, but the security guards took no chances and slipped him out." Monica began to tremble. "Sadik, the nurse said minutes after that, white masked men descended on his room with machine guns. They shot his bed up! The nurse would have died if she didn't dive into the bathroom. She said they shot first then searched the room for him!"

That's when I knew we were at the end of Popov's grace. He'd been laying low, entertaining Danny Lopez's war. Tonight was when he decided to strike, and hard. He was looking to kill, not just rattle like he did when he infiltrated my father's hospital nonviolently.

I turned to Rory. "Amp up the security around here and add another layer at a ten-mile radius." She nodded, pulling out her phone. Then I asked Monica, "Where's Iban now?"

"They're on their way to the warehouse," she supplied.

I shook my head, annoyed at that prospect. The warehouse

would be an easier target than *Elliswoods Palace*. It was in an inner city. I turned to Daz. "Call Jamil and fill him in. Tell him to have the "IB" team bring Iban here. Tell him they may have a trail, so send another armed vehicle." He took off after a gesture of understanding. Then I asked Taaliba, "What's the status on Lopez himself?"

She shrugged dismissively, more out of frustration. "I haven't spoken to him, but he's unharmed. He was coming in from Atlantic City when it all happened."

I nodded. "Offer an invitation for him and no more than five of his men to come here to regroup for a few days. I need to speak with him anyway." I needed to find out if any of the men I loaned to him were injured. I moved closer to my sister, leveling her with an intentional glare. "But make no mistake: you are not to step a goddamn toe off this estate. Is that understood?"

With an agape mouth, Taaliba nodded, a new light in her eyes I could only assume the nature of. She turned while pulling out her phone, too.

"Oh, Sadik!" my mother cried, falling into me. I caught her with my arms and held her to my chest.

"It's going to be okay, queen," I assured without the benefit of a solution, but with strong confidence. "I swear, you can sleep restfully tonight once Iban arrives."

"This is happening too fast!" she cried. "We heard all the news at the same time it seemed, just a few minutes ago. I told Daz not to worry Earl about this until you said so. He's been doing so well at recovering. I can't afford for a setback. He could've died, Sadik! This business is killing him year by year!"

Taaliba returned, calmer but her face was still swollen as she watched me console our mother, along with Monica.

In my peripheral, I could sense Bilan taking off toward the kitchen.

"Where are you going, Nalib?"

She turned on her heel to face me; the levy of tears had broken in her eyes. "To get my child for the night."

"No the fuck you aren't." Her body tensed visibly. "You're going upstairs and will see Sadik in the morning."

Her chest lifted. "I think after the night we've had, you can understand my need of—"

"I don't give a fuck about understanding shit!" I shouted, at the end of my fucking patience.

"Sadik!" My mother trembled against me.

"Sadik, please!" Taaliba cried simultaneously.

Monica went to comfort her, but Bilan shot her palm in the air, turned, and made a beeline for the grand staircase. We watched as she ran the first level and turned for the next.

"What is going on?" my mother demanded.

I kissed her head. "Nothing that won't be resolved momentarily." I motioned for Taaliba to take our mother's side.

Monica faced the staircase, apparently tempted to follow my wife.

"Don't worry about her, Monica. Stay here and wait on Iban. Make sure he's comfortable and relaxing." I dipped my chin, fighting for humility. "Please."

Once Taaliba was paired with my mother, I raised an index finger to Rory, who was awaiting my next move. Swiftly, I traveled to the staircase, leaping up two steps at a time until I made it to the second level. Once there, I did it all over again until I made it to the third. From there, I took powerful lunges, hearing a door-slam reverberating on the floor. I knew it was Bilan having made it to the suite. Moments later, I was there, pushing through the door.

"Don't you ever speak to me like that in front of anyone, much less your family and staff!" She screamed at the top of her lungs, one index finger toward me. "If I want my baby, I can have him anytime I damn well please, Sadik!"

My head fell to the side. "Does the same apply to Jason?"

Her eyes blossomed into big saucers. "Oh, your watchdogs ran and told you that fast?"

"No." I shook my head. "I knew it the moment you booked a suite and a room at the fuckin' hotel!"

She sucked in a breath. "How did you—"

I was on her ass in one spring. *"I'M A FUCKIN' ELLIS! THIS GODDAMN STATE BELONGS TO MY FAMILY!"* Eyes still wild, now with necessary fear, Bilan's chest heaved beneath me. "When are you going to fuckin' learn who I am and the power at my goddamn hand, Bilan?"

"The power to what?" Her lips quivered. "Woo women into some helpless web of fascination with you, only for you to dispose of their hearts the way you do your son's soiled diapers? If so, I've got news for you: I'm not Irene or Monica. I've got the power!"

"You've got my protection. And I've got the goddamn serried rope to bind your control. You're a hypocrite, Nalib." It pained me to say. "You can't call me an infidel of troth when you're sneaking out to meet a man who, by all measures, wants to fuck you."

"And what did Sofia want to do with you tonight?"

"I've already fucked her. I've moved on and married!"

"Moved on from her and Tiffany, huhn?"

"Where's the fuckin' lie?"

"It was in your claims when you told me you were en route to Atlanta, omitting you were making a pit stop at *Pulse* to encourage that woman's obsession of you!"

I took a deep breath, stepping back. She had it all wrong. "I didn't go to *Pulse* to be a support to Tiff."

"But you sure took lots of happy flicks with her on the red carpet. I'm sure she would argue different."

"She would because I made her feel I went to support her."

"What was the real reason? To enjoy some weird ass fetish of smoking weed with my best friend while she played dress-up in my clothes?"

So Randi did take the opportunity tonight to spill the beans...

I shook my head, pulling out my phone. "No and...yes." I tapped my way into my saved videos. "Tiff's head of security there is a friend of Jamil's. He'd been sending word that Randi had been showing up at both clubs asking for me."

"For what?" she asked animatedly. "Why?"

"I don't know. Just as I told you last spring: I don't hang out at clubs, which is why you didn't find me there when you went with Randi last year." I issued her a leveling gaze. "Your friend is toxic, and apparently dumb as fuck. She doesn't understand my world—yours, too—is bigger than fuckin' Paterson."

I found the video and faced the phone her way explaining, "She'd been asking for me, so when I got the call that night saying she was there *and* Tiffany had been begging me to come, I used it as an opportunity to capture this."

"If it's the pictures of you two, you can save yourself the time." Bilan was being dismissive. "I don't want to see them again."

"Actually, it's video of your 'best friend' showing her true colors." I hit play, fast-forwarded to a specific point, and turned up the volume.

"She's sweet. Bilan a good one." Randi's voice was moderately clear in the recording, considering the blasting music.

"Tell me something I don't know."

"Like about your money she be giving me?"

"You mean the money she gave you last month that was all hers? Bilan doesn't need my money."

Randi's laughter was hard to pick up because she was blowing out smoke from the blunt at the same time. *"Shiiiiiit. What real bitch don't need your money."*

"Your bestie."

"Bilan ain't got shit. If you think she do, she fuckin' with your head. Her mother and father ain't have shit to leave her but debt. That's how she lost that house."

"She didn't need money to capture my attention."

"Then what the fuck did it? Not her dried up ass pussy. I love my girl, but know she a boring fuck."

"That's what this is about?"

Randi's giggle was clear and then there was a period of silence between us when only the music could be heard. *"Nah. What I'm saying is I'm a scavenger."*

"And what are you hunting, sweetheart?"

"You know me, Deek. You know the jungle I live in. It cost to survive. I ain't a college-degree, nine-to-five type of bitch. I'm the type that feed the fantasies in ya head while your lil' wife make you look good for your friends and family. I take the nightshift." There was a break of music before she

cried, *"Ah, come the fuck on, Sadik. You know I'm good. You know my head game."*

There was another spell of silence on my part until finally, I returned, *"You're forgetting one thing, though."*

"What?"

"She's your friend. Your best friend."

Randi's snort was clear. *"Okay. First of all, my ass too old to be having a fuckin' best friend. And I'm too smart to let friendships fuck with my money. I love my girl, Bilan, for real. A lil' too fuckin' naïve, but got a heart of gold, and she smart as shit. But even she did what she had to do and got with a playboy when she was fuckin' starving. She knew the bottom was 'bout to fall out for her. It ain't matter that she was finishing up school. Bilan knew that degree wasn't gone get her no real money right away. She had shit due, so she did what she had to do."*

"And that was fuck with me?"

She scoffed hard. *"Fuck, yeah. You think ol' girl ya speed? You think she fuck with niggas like that? Mad muthafuckas tried that snatch and she blocked them. Only nigga that came close was the freckled-face fuck from her school. He used to spend the night at her place, and when the lights went out, his ass was on the couch. I felt bad for the geeky-ass. I even let him eat my pussy one night. That bitch ain't even know."*

Bilan gasped, her hand flew to her mouth in shock. My happiness for her reaction was petty of me, but I couldn't give a single fuck. She needed to trust me on this. Jason had no good intentions for pursuing her. I'd been questioning his sanity lately.

"What? I felt sorry for that young fucker, all sniffing up Bilan's weird ass all that time. She knew she liked him. She was just too high strung to know what to do. Shit, she probably fucked him and just ain't say shit—"

"Twenty-five minutes up, chief!" That was when Rory appeared.

At first, I thought to not have her listening to Rory on tape with another woman pursing me, given their recent history. But Bilan needed no filters on Randi's toxicity.

"Grown folks is talking, Rory," Randi was heard barking at Rory. *"Scram, grandma."*

"Yo, suck my ass, bitch," Rory barked back.

"You gonna let her talk to me like that?" There was a pause after

Randi asked me that question, expecting me to pull the leash on Rory.

I watched Bilan's eyes circle in their sockets as she processed that.

"Well, this has been enlightening," I told Randi.

"What? I thought we was making a deal!"

"Neither this life nor the next will ever yield an opportunity for you to fuck me, Randi. I'm not sure what you thought us sharing a blunt was about, but it damn sure wasn't about the future of us fuckin'."

"Oh, really? I 'on't know who you putting on for. Ain't no naïve bitches around here. I know the game. I know what you Ellises like. You need variety pussy. I know how to keep my mouth shut to keep ya family happy. I know Bilan. She won't find out."

"I'm an Ellis, but not that Ellis, Randi. I wouldn't let you close enough to my dick to sniff it."

"You already did. Remember? I bet Bilan don't know that, just like I bet you don't know if she fucked freckle boy. Fuck you, Sadik!"

My laughter was clear on the recording. *"You want to, huhn, sweetie? Enjoy the free bottles of top shelf. Invite a fuck boy up and trick his ass out. I only turn 'em for Africans."*

When I pulled the phone back, my chest filled with a strong emotion of satisfaction.

"That was why I went to *Pulse*. To finally put this shit to bed," I explained.

Bilan's eyes closed to a squeeze as a fresh round of tears raced down her cheeks. She shook her head. "How do I always find myself in this predicament?"

"What predicament?"

"People holding knowledge over my head and secretly feeling superior to me." Her shoulders trembled.

"I'm sorry to have to be the one to break the news about your frie—"

"You do it, too!" she shouted. "You just did it again. You only had that video recorded to end my relationship with a friend I had for years before you!"

"Because she's fuckin' toxic!"

"An attribute *you* had to be the one to illuminate to me...like this?"

"What was I supposed to do? Let her keep you in the dark about this shit?"

"You've kept me in the dark, Sadik! And at this point, you're more at fault than she is!"

"How?"

"Because when you met me, I was her friend. When you recorded this, I was *your* wife. That title and bond trumps all. You kept pertinent information from me all this time. Why wouldn't you share this before begging to be my 'friend'? And definitely before we became lovers? Why?"

My head reared and eyes widened. "You think I was going to risk not having a chance with you over someone like Randi? Fuck that. I would've taken it to my grave before risking it all."

Bilan continued to cry, but this time, she didn't close her eyes. She didn't hide it from me.

"You keeping significant information from me is no different from lying. Do you not understand that?" Her delivery was breathless.

"What substantial information do I keep from you? I've unlocked my entire world to welcome you in."

Bilan's frame stiffened as she peered up at me. "Why didn't Iban get a long sentence for murder?" she whispered.

Shit...

I swallowed a gulp of air.

I snatched away from her. "I'm not going to answer shit that ain't got nothing to do with us."

"Then your proverbial world isn't unlocked to me after all, is it?"

She turned and walked off dejectedly. I watched as she headed for the bathroom.

"Bilan," I called out for her with pain replacing the pride in my chest. This woman weakened me to ruins.

"Don't worry, Sadik." She turned to me. "I can't go too far with a belly pumped full of you. You have me exactly where you want me." She nodded as if to try to soothe me. "Trusting, naïve, emotionally dependent on you, attached to your family, the employee of your mother, the mother of your children, and your wife. You have every ounce of me—saved me from a lonely world of loss and paranoia." She continued nodding. "I've gained under your arm. I have a family, but apparently, I also have a place in it."

"What are you talking about?" I begged, roughly raking my scalp with my fingers. "You're my everything, Bilan!"

"But I'm no longer that spice I used to be before you conquered me. You no longer have to work to appease me." Her head shook. "I'm not that spark of inspiration for you when you lay your head at night because I'm there with you. There comfortable, naïve, and pregnant."

"That's not true and you know it." I couldn't speak fast enough, my damn head was spinning so fast. "That's bullshit, baby. You can't even prove that."

She scoffed. "You haven't roped me once since I've given birth. I can't even inspire an act performed on animals."

The room had finally stopped rotating. I blinked a few times, appalled by her words.

"And after exposing you to my wilds, I can't seem to stop you from sneaking out and engaging with other men." It was weak, but exactly how I felt in the moment.

Weakened.

"I went out to try to convince Jason to leave me alone *one time*, and now I'm the male Ellis type? Really, Sadik?"

"I'm talking about Dimitri." Her mouth closed and eyes blinked successively. "You don't think I knew you continued to seek out his services?"

"Only because you haven't had the time to train me anymore. You've been out early each morning and late every night. It's almost like you don't want to be here."

"Maybe I don't! Maybe I wanted my family away from this?"

"But *I'm* wrong for carrying on with my life while you do that with yours?" Then with swift speed, her deep, suspecting eyes hit me again, face tight. "Did you tell Dimi to cut me off?" *You're damn right I did.* Dimitri Sokolov valued his life and that of his family over his clients. He'd made the right decision. When I didn't respond, Bilan took in a deep breath, rolling her eyes. "Don't worry. After he told me how he was connected to the other Russian, Popov, and how *he's* connected to the friggin...Polish man, he kicked me out of the gym." She turned for the bathroom again.

"Wait!" I called out. "What was that?"

Bilan faced me again, shrugging. I could tell she'd reached her limit. "He told me he didn't want any trouble with you and your family or the Popov guy!" she yelped.

I shook my head. "You mentioned a Polish man."

Bilan's eyes bounced around then rolled. "Yeah. He said the Popov guy only feared one man; a Polish guy."

"Do you recall his name?"

She shook her head. "No."

"Does Kolwaski ring a bell?"

"Yes, but that wasn't it. It had a different beginning, a J..." Her eyes danced again in concentration. "Jankowski." Dispiritedly, Bilan turned back for the bathroom.

This time, she slammed the door behind her. Regrettably, I needed to get to my father's office and convene my team. I felt a shredding in my chest with each step I took toward the door.

I felt my body roll over, though lost in a deep sleep. I was on my back. Relieved from the misted heat from being under the thick comforter, I felt the cool air against my torso. I tried to slip back into the subconscious, chasing the last memories of a dream. That was until I felt a slither up my inner thigh. Once it was inches away from my apex, I tried to swat it with my hand until my wrist was caught in the air. My head jerked and eyes swung open to the middle of the night.

He lifted, standing on his knees. Parts of his golden torso were illuminated from the exterior lights shining through the open terrace door. His face couldn't be made out from its angle. Behind him were dozens of tea lights with glimmering flames.

Using both hands, he lifted my feet, kneading into the instep arches. So dangerous for a woman in my condition, but so good. Pleasure shot straight to my core with rapid speed. How could I be aroused that quickly by a simple maneuver?

We'd fought just a few hours ago. The battle was brutal. It broke my heart. My lover made nasty accusations, things I was incapable of doing simply because of how masterful he was at predicting and satisfying my needs. His tongue caressed my left thigh before moving to my right, dizzying me with shooting pleasure. He stretched my legs, spreading my thighs lewdly until they were astride my torso. My breathing quickened. Sadik plucked my clit and my body spasmed.

An enduring breath pushed from my lungs, my head hung to the left and my eyes rolled to the back of my head. I needed his mouth on me now. And as though reading my mind, his mouth nibbled its way to my sex. His tongue and lips were unrushed as they toured me. My head thrashed left and right, pelvis lifted to be closer to his hungry mouth. When he began to concentrate on my clit, my hands rushed toward his head again and were yanked back at the wrists. I was roped to the bed, rendered helpless to his ministrations.

His tongue pushed into that tender spot with heavy pressure, and licked and licked and licked. I felt my body and mind yielding with each stroke. Emotions I struggled with internally surfaced as my groin churned. I moaned, feeling myself crest until I exploded. A fierce orgasm ripped through me. Reactively, my hands reached up for the cord of the ropes and held on, as my body quaked. In between my moans, a cry broke but I quickly swallowed it, not wanting to leave eroticism.

It was the ropes. They forced me to forfeit my expectations and personal agenda and suspend my will to allow Sadik's to pleasure me.

I had to trust him while bound. I had to submit my control, and even mistrust.

My thoughts were broken when Sadik pushed one leg flat on the bed and kept the other arched in the air. He shifted so he straddled my leg on the bed and shuffled closer until the head of his erection met my sex. He plunged into me with impatient force. His hard thrust resounded in my core. Those sparks of collision turned into bites of pleasure. As he thrust into me scissor-style, Sadik flicked my nipple and circled my clit. In under two minutes, another orgasm was rippling through me.

"*Mmmmmmm!*" I cried, trying to fight the puppeteer of my emotions.

Instead, I slammed my sex into him, moving against his thumb impressions and his long thrusts. I hummed and pumped into him until I tapped out and dropped down to the mattress. Sadik leaned over me, taking me with his mouth. He pulled my lip back with a deep suck then released it, rimming it with his tongue. With my hands above my head, he strummed my nipples unfairly, keeping me roused. His tongue swiped the roof of my mouth before finding my own. He swiped fluidly, seducing me. Beneath his hot frame, my body hummed with satisfaction from my last orgasm and, at the same time, brewed with need of more from him. His thick cock throbbed inside of me, still strong and with sensual promise.

His tongue made love to mine. His hands adored my needy body. I was lost to him in desire and submission. Around us was a halo of protection to guard our cohesion. How could I be enthralled with a man I didn't understand, one who kept things from me? Except pleasure. Sadik was never short on doling out physical bliss.

"I love you so much," he croaked, peppering my mouth with sloppy kisses. "There is no other being above you, Nalib, not even my queen." A wet kiss. "I'm new at this relationship thing, too." More sloppy kisses. "Please be patient with me, Nalib. I can't go back to life without you and Sadik." He pushed his tongue into my mouth and my heart ruptured.

It was a mixture of his vulnerability and mine in trusting him.

Sadik withdrew from my aching core. Within seconds, I was

flipped over and secured on all fours with my wrists still bound, the movement so fast and protective of my growing belly. His mouth was behind me, between my cheeks. When his tongue rimmed me, I finally cried out unrepentantly.

"*Ohhhhhhhh!*"

I leaned into him with intentional perversion, recalling the first time he'd put his mouth there and I was so incredibly insecure, it took some time to release myself to the pleasure. Then he thrusted into me with blunt force, the ridge of his mushroom head swollen and reckless at my opening. My hips wobbled upon entry, my pussy swallowing him deep, my sick need for him begging his intrusion.

His angry cock rammed into my assuaged core. With each whack into me, my eyes saw stars and flashes surfaced in my mind. Times from my childhood, like when my father had to go to the hospital after being assaulted by Abshir. I worried about him until he returned home. Those times when my mother worked late and I couldn't sleep until she came in because my father's drug addiction had progressed to a degree that made him forget his role as a protector of the family. The time Abshir was jumped so badly by a neighborhood gang over drug turf.

Despite these terrible memories, my body trembled with pleasure each plunge he toured inside of me. Memories of the first night I spent in my bedroom after my mother's passing. My father had been long gone and my brother was incarcerated. There was no one to provide comfort to me. I didn't want to sound weak to Randi, and Tasche worked that night. It was tragic. I didn't fall asleep until after five in the morning, and had only slept a solid two hours before getting up to start my day.

"Oh!" I croaked when my groin quickened.

Sadik's fingertips dug into me with uncompromising pressure to keep me in place. The sound of Dog barking in the yard while I tried to sleep one night rolled to the front of my brain. I shivered under my blanket that night, struggling to go out and see about his safety versus staying in bed relishing mine. I used that animal to protect me, all to have him shot for simply doing his job.

I began pelting back into him, meeting his vicious plunges. Then the memory of sitting in that old *B-Way Burger*, tied to that chair and regaining my consciousness surfaced. The recollection of his velvety alto when I heard him declare, "*Shhh, baby. It's me, Nalib.*"

My nipples tightened even more over the mattress. My roped wrists made the memory more crisp. I recalled being heavily aroused when I came through that day. His scent and formidable presence spoke to my subconsciousness. Just like that day, last August, my body responded to his commanding and capable presence without the benefit of seeing him.

Tears fell from my eyes as our thrusts collided over the mattress. That day was the first time I'd been rescued in my life. So many missed opportunities of capturing me until I encountered Sadik Qadir Ellis, the first. He was sure of me in spite of my insecurities and meltdowns. He may have been imperfect, but he'd always been clear. On me.

"Come, Nalib," ripped from the bowels of him, awakening me from my haunted thoughts.

I felt my sex pulsing, my groin spasming around his stiffness and I released myself to the inundating pleasure.

"Sadik!" I cried with urgency rippling all around him.

My knees and trunk were lifted from the mattress, and he plummeted into me with brute dynamism. And I gave into it all, receiving his imposing ultra-alpha until I broke. The pleasure became so intense I cried. Hard. Sex isn't always about physical connection. With the right partner, it's very much spiritual and self-awakening.

Sadik sensed my sobbing and kissed my back as he freed me from the rope. When he pulled out of me, it didn't improve my feeling of being broken.

"Why are you crying, Nalib?" I'd never heard his voice so gentle.

"*I*—I'm feeling...everything." Including those words of declaration he'd shared with Sofia earlier tonight. Sadik had reciprocated my feelings for him.

My body trembled. He gathered me into his arms, being sure to lay off my belly. For a while, Sadik said nothing. My crying slowed and my body began to relax into the silence. I'd just have to figure it out on my own, as usual.

"Iban was a...troubled kid." His velvety chords were so smooth, though his delivery seemed hesitant. "Although my father's income had improved our environment by upgrading our neighborhoods a couple of times, he was addicted to the thrill of the streets. He idolized my father's work. My mother was too busy establishing *Ellis Academy* to tend to him. And my father made her believe he'd been putting in the time with him. It wasn't true. Iban got arrested more times than I can recall. He spent lots of time in juvenile detention centers." There was a pause for an extended time, leaving me too afraid to breathe.

Then he continued, "He spent months at a time in juvie, a few times missing holidays my queen deemed important for family. But we dealt with it, supporting and loving him. My father had me believe his behavior was a symptom of his idolization of our patriarch. My mother always warned it was something more.

"Years later, when he was well into his adulthood, we noticed strange behavior. Violent bouts with the men we were training. Monica complained of him getting physical with her. She said he'd go on these rage binges for days at a time. Once, he was arrested for practice shooting in their suburban back yard. They didn't want to let him go so easily, so bail wasn't an option for a couple of days. While in there, Iban got into fights with inmates unprovoked. He had...episodes of rage again in there."

I felt him tense all around me. "Our lawyers got him out. But I was livid. I felt he was, once again, out of control for no reason. So I picked him up one day and took him to a secluded field...to bust his ass if I had to. I just needed to get him back to himself. We went out there, and he resisted. I whooped his ass. It was pretty bad. We were both bloody. He banged up my eye, and I had a busted lip. I'd done far worse to him. But when it was over, it was over."

I heard him swallow deep. "While we were laying out in the dirt, soiled and breathless, he told me something that broke me like nothing else before it." This time, my body went rigid. I stilled, tried controlling and muting my breathing. "When he was being... detained in juvie all those years ago..." Sadik's breathing turned harsh. "He was assaulted by the warden, a man named Hubert

Jackson who was twice his size. It was, apparently, the culture for the center. The kids with the biggest personalities and sharpest tempers were disciplined by the head."

My heart rented at the sound of Sadik's croak. "He made my brother go down on him." I felt his body tremble next to me. "I'd seen my brother humbled at the physical hand of our father, but never had I seen him weakened outside of our parents. Iban could hardly repeat the stories of terror that day in the field. And he shared there were more who faced assault under that sick mutha-fucka. Rory was one. They were locked up together once and when she fought off one of the officers, Jackson tried to humiliate her by fuckin' her in a room full of men and boys. The fucker personified evil, and I couldn't live in a world where the Ellis name didn't provide protection for its own."

I felt the same way. The Ellises doled out their own justice.

So that was Rory's connection to Iban...

"I hugged him—hard. I felt him cry in my arms, almost not recognizing the hardest man I knew outside of my father. That night I couldn't sleep. The following week, I couldn't focus at work. It wasn't until I'd come up with an airtight plan that I rested soundly. I used my scant resource, at that time, to gain information on Jackson. I shared the plan with Iban and we executed it. We found Jackson at a sex club of sorts for kids. Incidentally, Popov ran it.

"We were able to isolate Jackson one late night in a warehouse room. He was drunk with his pants down when we accosted him, but he recognized my brother. He begged for his life, sobering quickly enough. Iban and I beat the man until he was unrecognizable. It was so emotional for my brother; it consumed me to the point of strip-ping down to my pants to relish his revenge. I knew it would be a bloody pursuit, but actually wanted it all over me. I had him tied up to the ceiling, hanging from a rope. I beat Jackson's ass to point of cutting into my own skin, busting my knuckles."

Sadik's chest heaved. "At some point, Jackson was still alive, but his body barely reacted to the blows. Iban fell into an episode of sorts, sobbing and collapsing into a fetal position against the brick wall. I had a job to finish. I wouldn't be satisfied until Hubert

Jackson was dead." He paused again. "He needed to be humiliated—even in his wake—as he'd done my brother, an Ellis man. I stripped him, pulled out my machete and carved out his lips."

His body trembled again. "I placed his lips around his dick, pinning the soft tissue to his belly. Then I shot him in the head. When I was done, I grabbed my tools, my brother and my discarded clothes, and we got the hell out of dodge."

I spent the next few minutes in silence, creating a visual of the event. My entire frame had chilled, too. Sadik must have felt it because he began rubbing down my arm and leg exposed to him, creating heat.

"Two days later, Jackson's body was found. Iban began telling his former juvie mates what he'd done, leaving my name out of it. A week later, my brother was arrested for the murder. He'd told too much for the cops to ignore. My father rounded up the most competent legal team in the region. The state threw every charge they could at Iban, making him pay for my father's reign as a drug lord. It didn't look good for a while. It wasn't until they found another blood type on Jackson's corpse other than Iban's.

"On top of that, adults and children once incarcerated in juvenile facilities he ran in the state came forward with compelling complaints of sexual assault. I'd seen to that when plotting to kill Jackson. Apparently, for some reason, even more survivors were willing to come forward after proof he was dead. The prosecutors ran the blood samples found on Jackson against Iban's to find it was an inconclusive match, at least not enough to convict. My father and I had airtight alibis for that night and were never considered to have involvement. Those two factors: the new and overwhelming allegations of Jackson's previous assaults and the faulty blood match, provided victory to my brother's legal team."

"While Iban was being held after he was charged, he'd gotten into a bad fight in the county jail. He fucked up two correctional officers. The state wanted to be petty and hold him to those offenses. Our attorneys conceded, seeing how one of them would never be able to work to the capacity of a C.O. again. Iban had done that much of a number on him. With that happening, the prosecutors pushed for the lesser charge. They wouldn't let him walk scot-free. So, he did the four years."

It all made sense now, even though, once again, I'd totally overlooked a major detail. When I *Google*'d the case last summer in *Macen Beach*, I'd been struck by the usage of a rope. It was a detail too glaring, seeing I'd just witnessed Sadik use one on Damien in the old *B-Way Burger*. *That* was the sight that had aroused me to sick degrees.

"Why couldn't you share this before?"

"Because it's something we don't discuss—not me, Iban, my parents, Monica...Rory. No one. There's no statute of limitations on murder. The case could be reopened at any time, putting me at risk. The only reason the prosecutors didn't target me was because of the countless people who came forward with claims of assault by Jackson. It wouldn't have been a good look for them attempting to prosecute the victim's brother for killing the predator. That would have opened a can of worms the state didn't want on their plate. It's been a weight I've carried for years and didn't want to share with you."

My head shook.

"I've scared you," he murmured, fear crackling through his vocals.

I pushed my hand down to his dried cock. It swelled in my hand immediately.

I squealed lowly, "I'm sick, Sadik."

I was. Had to be. How else could I be aroused after hearing about my lover—my protector—gruesomely murdering a man?

I fisted him several times before his face dropped to mine and he covered me in an impassioned kiss before taking me all over again.

∞**26**∞

I felt vacuumed into consciousness. A very pleasant and virile scent crept up my nostrils and infiltrated my brain. Heavily, my eyes rolled open and just a few feet away, the Sadiks sat at the side of the bed expectantly and unmoving. The senior's face opened to a warm smile. Too disoriented, I couldn't return the courtesy. My baby began to wobble in his father's arm. If my brain wasn't so fuzzy, I'd think he was happy to see me.

That was confirmed when Sadik let him down on his belly next to me. My baby boy's breathing hiked, his eyes widened, and he began to babble in excitement.

Finally, I smiled. "Morning, Sadik."

I pulled him over my chest and kissed his cherub cheek. He pulled his fist to his mouth and began to suck. Then his eyes landed on his father across from us and the sucking stopped. He studied his father then traveled his gaze over to me. My son appeared stumped at first. His dad and I exchanged a look of confusion. When the baby began to laugh, it was contagious. As if a switch was flipped, the baby's laughter stopped and his fist was the main attraction again. That caused me to chuckle, too.

"Morning, beautiful," Sadik's velvety alto greeted.

My smile was involuntarily. "Good morning."

Visions of last night into this morning began to flood my mind. Positions of eroticism, declarations of forever, and my equivocating emotional response all flashed in living color before me. I reached to clear the crust from my eyes; I'd cried so much up until just hours ago. Embarrassment blanketed me. Last night had been an event of more lows than highs.

"Are you mad at me?" my voice cracked from shame.

"For what?"

"For showing up to your meeting at City Hall unannounced." I sat up, reclining against the headboard. "For the things I said."

Sadik shook his head, a peace settled over him I couldn't explain, but could feel. "My time in Julius' cabinet isn't long-term. He and I always knew this would be. It was only to lay a firm foundation for his work in office. Much of that was done before he was elected. Most of it has been completed." He thumbed his bottom lip as he considered his next words. "It wasn't a good idea for Sofia and I to work together at this point. The problem was, we'd planned so much of this before March of last year, when I finally decided to get to know you." Sadik playfully tried to pry the baby's fist from his mouth. "And you weren't unexpected last night. No one runs up on Sadik Ellis, you know that. My security escorted you over and brought you in."

I nodded, biting my lip, considering that. "So Johnson told you where he found me?"

Sadik nodded, his eyes fixed on the baby. "I knew about your plans to see Jason, and I knew the *FBI* would be there to ambush you. I found out late, but was still able to have my *FBI* connect, Jefferson, be there in case things got too overwhelming for you." My heart stopped. *The Black guy.* He was Sadik's associate! "But before I learned Jason invited them there, I did know you were up to something, booking that room. It was just a matter of waiting you out to see what you'd do with it." An alluring smirk cracked his golden face. "I thought you bonding with the kitchen staff was you diggin' into your Irene Ellis bag, but now, I'm not so trusting."

I smiled, rolling my eyes. "Getting to know them was born out of boredom and simply returning to my roots. I know kitchen staff. My parents had one, and I was a part of one professionally at *Michelle's*. The group Irene's put together here is soulful and family-like." Then a thought struck. "Please don't punish David. He had no idea what I needed his car for."

"Which is the only reason he's still allowed on this estate." Sadik's eyes were on his son when he advised. "But I will be having a sit-down with him."

"For what?"

"To give him an official orientation, something that hasn't been provided because when he was hired, my parents were on mental retreats. Stacy's been inundated with managing almost the entire domesticated staff. He slipped by her. David needs to learn the chain of command."

"And what does that mean?"

"That my wife is the boss of me, but not him. And if he's going to be friends with you, he needs to know how unreasonable of a husband I am."

I rolled my eyes again. "Did he get his car back? I was supposed to park it again by midnight last night. It's what I told Johnson when I gave him the keys before we left campus for Paterson."

"Rory was sure to arrange for his car to be delivered to his home at a fair hour last night.

My eyes fell. "I pulled out my gun on Randi," I muttered.

Why did I feel a morsel of guilt when in greater measure, I still felt rage at her betrayal?

Sadik held the baby in the air. "You should have. She looked horrid in your purple leather top. She made a mockery of it." He shrugged with his lips.

"She said you killed Ricky because of her." I held my breath.

Those feline eyes were upon me. "I've only killed for one woman." His regard returned to our son. "Ricky's death had nothing to do with Randi, Nalib. It had nothing to do with me either. That was your father-in-law's business."

It was clear he didn't want to talk about it in great detail. I didn't care. As long as the reason didn't involve Randi, I wouldn't concern myself with it. I came so close to being a murderer. The thin line was so chillingly frightening.

"I spit in her face, too," I felt the need to share.

"That couldn't have been more gangster than throwing a shopping cart at a woman fighting Rory." My eyes blossomed. Without looking at me, he hummed. "I told you, I know everything, Bilan. I've been waiting for you to tell me. Then I had to tell Rory I may have to fire her."

I gasped. She said I'd be the reason he'd let her go. "Why?"

"Because apparently, your loyalty to her compromises yours for me. You haven't mentioned a word to me. That's very unsettling."

Not expecting that response, I covered my mouth as I sputtered a howl. "Sadik."

"I'm sorry." His kaleidoscopic irises were on me regretfully. The quick change of mood took my breath away. "I shouldn't have interfered in your relationship with your friend. More than that, I should have thought long and hard—after"—his volume increased for emphasis—"—I became your lover. That would have been my only hope at keeping you. You gave me such a hard fuckin' time just to be your friend." His forehead wrinkled as his face morphed into an expression of grief.

All I could do was shake my head. "And just to think, I went along with your every unreasonable command at each turn."

"What do you mean?"

"You wanted to be my friend, I went along with it." I counted off on my fingers. "You wanted to be my lover, I went along with it again—"

"You were more than interested in that prospect." He lifted a brow, as though daring me to disagree.

"My point is, I've done everything you've asked of me, including fall in love with you. And still, I feel like I'm not where you want me to be. Do you think we've moved too fast? Maybe that's why you've never been satisfied with my pace. Maybe if we'd just dated longer, used condoms..." I pushed my bottom lip into my teeth and chewed on it *and* that thought with doubt.

"Nalib, there's no goddamn way I would have moved slowly with you. And there's no fuckin' regret in the world about not using condoms. Using them with you felt unnatural even before I'd been inside you." His eyes went to the baby admiringly. "I've only been obsessed with two things in my life. The first was power. This is the result of my second obsession." Sadik's regard landed on me. "You're that obsession, Bilan." His tone was suddenly regretful.

"Obsessed? With me? I mean, how can you be so obsessed with a woman who has emotional meltdowns when violent occurrences happen as they though it's natural in a world like yours?" I'd been getting better with the breakdowns, but the anxiety was still there. My worst nightmare lately had been having my children witness it. "I'm now beyond sick, I'm desensitized to human life and complicit. I almost killed my best friend last night."

After a few wordless seconds, Sadik nodded and gathered the baby into his chest as he stood. "I came to wake you up. There's someone waiting on you in the garden." His attention dropped to Sadik, who tried grabbing a fistful of his father's beard. "This curious tike wanted to say good morning after I told him his old man denied his mother of his presence last night." My heart smiled at the sight of them together. Sadik wore dark blue trousers, a stark white dress shirt, tie, and brown brogues. The baby's *Connecticut Kings* onesie with matching socks didn't fit his father's motif at all, yet swelled my heart. "Get showered and dressed for the day, baby. Time is of the essence."

I scooted out of the bed, feeling sore at every corner of my body. Unease washed over me as I padded toward the bathroom wearing nothing but dried soil from my time with Sadik ending just short hours ago.

I glanced over my shoulder at the two Sadiks. The elder held an ultra-alpha expression of impatience as he peered my way. For that reason, I continued into the bathroom without further delay.

A little more than twenty minutes later, I was finishing my hair. I flipped my wrist using a flat iron on my last curl when I heard the door of the suite open and close. I fingered my mohawk into a pattern then quickly applied lip glass. When I sauntered into the bedroom, Sadik was there without the baby. He held a tea mug and saucer in his hands.

"It's for you. You ready?"

I nodded, dread stirring in my belly. Then I grabbed my phone from the charger and slipped it into the pocket of my duster before heading to him.

Sadik handed me the tea. "Candy has breakfast waiting for you. Do you have an appetite?"

We crossed into the hall and he closed the door behind us.

"I don't know now," I answered. Anxiety had overtaken my senses.

Sadik provided muted support by laying a hand at the small of my back while he directed me to the elevator. Minutes later, we crossed into the garden. It was still early in the day and the heat hadn't hit sweltering temperatures yet. The month of July had brought with it unbearable heat. No matter how nervous I was about my husband's enigmatic behavior, the sight of the *Elliswoods* garden transfixed me.

The colors, leaf and petal shapes varied, but created a summery theme. There was a mild breeze pulling my sleeveless duster behind. I drank the delicious tea as we strolled a moderate pace. At this point, all I could think of in terms of who I'd be "meeting" with was Iban. He'd arrived last night. I figured there was no need to prolong the inevitable. There were a few things I needed to clear my heart of concerning him. After learning about his struggles last night from Sadik, I'd decided on an approach.

My attention locked onto the leaves of the smoke bush, a shrub that appeared as tall as a tree. It was one Earl schooled me on during one of our many talks in the garden last spring. Those memories would remain some of the fondest. The shrub had only budded back then and he described what it would bloom into. The visual was better than the expectation.

My feet halted at the sight of suited men wandering the court-yard set up with food. It wasn't them, per se, that seized my attention. It was the tall, broad-suited figure with his back to me. His hands were interlinked behind his back as he studied what looked to me as galaxy blooms on a particular shrub. They were big white balls, some with yellow spikes all over.

"Pastor Carmichael," Sadik called out to him. The Bishop swiveled an unhurried 180-degree angle. His men moved a lot faster. "Or is Bishop the appropriate title?"

Bishop Carmichael traversed the courtyard our way. "That is an interesting shrub your parents have there," he rasped casually. "It's called a Buttonbush, but formally its name is cephalanthus occiden-talis, and it's from the coffee family. Buttonbushes reach the peak of flowering around early July. Its rotund-shaped flowers which resemble exploding Fourth of July fireworks make it a spectacular bloom."

My eyes blinked then bounced between the shrub and Bishop Carmichael. I had no idea how to respond to that tidbit of random knowledge. It was remarkable and totally unexpected. A smile curved his lips. Next, he offered a nod to Sadik then addressed me. "Let us forego the formalities of titles for this venture. Convention-ally, I'd refer to you as Mrs. Ellis. However, due to this crash course in our engagement, we don't have the time for the stiff introduc-tions. Ezra is far more appropriate."

"Nalib," Sadik called to me while studying Bishop Carmichael. "I reached out to the man of God after seeing how captivated you've been by his messages, *and* how haste you were in visiting his church last month." He finally turned to me, eyes melting with familiar sensitivity, bravado lost in his voice. "When I learned of his background in counseling and therapy, I thought you'd feel comfortable speaking with him."

"About?" I was so nervous, I couldn't recognize my own voice.

Ezra took a step toward me, disarming me with a soft smile and closer proximity. "Which era of the saga are we in now? Or chapter?"

"Excuse me?"

"The cinematic experience we spoke of the night I met you in Paterson," he rasped. "The one found in a fiction novel." There was a knowing flip in his eyes.

My chest exploded so fitfully, I almost lost my balance. Breathless, I asked, "I thought you didn't remember me."

"I didn't." He took a deep breath, expression filled with humility. "After your husband pushed his way into my office..." He cleared his throat, and Sadik was readjusting the waist of his pants when my neck snapped toward him. "I spoke with my beloved—my wife, Alexis—and Tasche. I had to include her because Alexis mentioned how I'd run into you two at *DiFillippo's* a few months back, before you attended our *Family and Friends Day* at church. As they both recalled things I'd mentioned to you, details began to return. I've been praying about this since I agreed to see you. I'm looking forward to getting to know you and seeing what I can do to assist on this journey."

"So, you're going to counsel me?" I was confused.

"Just for a short while. I'm no longer practicing. My personal and pastoral worlds are far too demanding at this point. Therefore, I'd like to think of it as gaining your confidence. Maybe I can help point you in the right direction for an appropriate solution," Bishop Carmichael tried to clarify.

"He's going to diagnose you, Nalib." I flinched at Sadik's blunt words. In an instant, he was in my face, hands clasping mine for comfort, his eyes pleading. "It's not you. It's me. You're not crazy or unstable. I've been considering this for while now, especially after your time alone in *Macen Beach*. You're perfect for me—perfect for Sadik and our unborn baby—I swear. It's just my life," he whispered. "This world of mine that I'm changing, but didn't in enough time to offer peace to you. There's nothing wrong with guarding your mental health while you're still adjusting to this family." Sadik's eyes fell. "To me, your ultra-alpha."

Still reeling, I nodded, honestly not knowing how I felt.

"Thank you, Bilan." Sadik leaned into my ear. "No one needs you more than me, but your well-being will always come before my selfish needs of you." He pulled back to study my reaction. I had none. His last words to Ezra were "Fix it to where she can't live without me, because I'm damn sure no good on this earth without her." Sadik's jaw flexed.

Bishop Carmichael replied, "I don't believe I've ever met a man so eager to tend to his wife. I can learn a lesson from you. However, my endeavor is to awaken in her a godly purpose. If that includes you, then no one will be happier for you than me."

Sadik paid a few moments of gaping to Bishop Carmichael. I was witnessing my S.Q.E. silently sizing up another alpha male. Maybe Sadik could sense the dominance in Ezra's personality, but I had a strong inclination Bishop Carmichael was aware of my husband's before stepping foot on *Elliswoods Palace*. Why else would a man of his stature go out of his way to see me when he no longer tended to clients? The reassuring factor in this tense moment was Bishop Carmichael's unflappable demeanor. He wasn't folding to the Ellis in my husband, and for that, I knew Sadik would respect him.

Demonstrating just that, Sadik returned to me and planted the sweetest kiss on my forehead. Without further flexing, he gaited out of the garden. I followed him with my eyes until I could no longer see him. Still confused, yet extra curious, I turned back to the pastor, still not believing he was here.

Bishop Carmichael beamed; his chocolate eyes combed the colorful garden and the beautifully set table topped with a bountiful spread. "So," he sighed. "*He's* been with you, I see."

Sadik

"Mr. Ellis," Kolwaski greeted after sauntering into my conference room with his men at *Ellis International*. He shook my hand and I directed him to take a seat at the table. "I was surprised and, to be honest..." His hands danced in the air as he fished for the correct English phrasing. "...anxious when your woman said you wanted to talk."

That woman was Rory and I was quite sure that was a dig on his part. She sat at the other end of the table with Jamil, unaffected and accustomed to these types of jokes. My personal assistant dressed like a male and had all the mannerisms of one, but would quickly correct you if you accused her of being anything but a woman. Until recently, when my pregnant wife aided her in a physical altercation over a lovers' quarrel, I wasn't sure who Rory fucked.

I waited until Kolwaski was seated before speaking. "The purpose of this meeting is actually two-fold," I shared, leaning over the table. "A few months ago, I lost a warehouse receiver due to your account. This overzealous employee discovered the contents of your containers were in violation of the *Ellis International* policies, and that of federal regulations. It escalated to the point the tenured team member had to be let go. The employee in question made strong statements of suspicion and refused to back down. He threatened to go to the authorities, which made him disposable."

Kolwaski didn't react, instead wearing an impassive mask.

I continued, "You know, when I accepted you as a client, there were stipulations. I don't run illegal contraband through my warehouse, neither am I in the business of transporting it. I'm one hundred percent legit in my business. I may be Earl Ellis' son, but I'm my own man. In doing work with you, I'm compromising my broker's license."

"That sounds like an assumption of an overzealous employee."

Kolwaski shrugged. "You don't know what was in there. Has what's been accused of being in there been proven?"

"Yes." I issued an affirmative nod. "According to the terms of our signed contract, I retain the right to open any vessel for inspection when there is suspicion. That was in May and we've been observing your containers since, several of which hold contraband."

"Are you threatening to terminate our contract?"

"Oh, if I've not made myself clear, that's exactly what I'm doing."

Kolwaski snickered. "I'm confused. I'm sure you're aware of the relationship I have with your father."

I paced away from the head of the table, hands stowed into the pocket of my pants. "And that's what you don't understand. I am not my father, Kolwaski. I never took you on as a client with any consideration of my father. This is *my* enterprise. He's Earl Ellis: I'm Sadik Ellis."

Kolwaski and his men chirped laughter in unison. I guessed I hadn't been convincing at this point. Or maybe it was cultural misunderstanding. Either way, I'd wait. He still had my patience. I stood and waited out their amusement.

His smile faded first. Next, his men quieted.

"You're serious." Kolwaski noted.

"Gravely." I paid him a leveling glare. "There's not much you can do to make me complicit to any dealings you have with my father. Trust me: the government has tried since I began *Ellis International.*"

Kolwaski glanced over to his men, all of whose eyes were more spirited than I'd ever seen of them. When he'd gotten nothing from them, his regard fell. His face turned hard as stone as his last thoughts circled, it seemed. He knocked softly on the table. "Name your price."

"I know your largest shipment to date since you signed on with me last summer is coming in from Russia in three weeks. It's virtually impossible in my business—and trust me, I know my business—to arrange to have a shipment, particularly one of that size, cleared by another broker."

"Okay." His palm lifted with impatience. "Give me news of fortune, Ellis."

I nodded, patience paying off. "You and I both know we have a common enemy."

"Who is that?"

"Don't play with me." I shook my head, disappointed. "I may be a Black man, but ain't no nigga shit going on here. I'm extremely versed at this game." I pointed toward the floor. "I know this business very well, and I so happen to know my father's just the same. But *you* likely know the men in my father's industry better than I do, just like you know Feodor Popov." His eyes lit with recognition. I wanted to gloat, but decided to stick to the point. I now had his attention. "Apparently, you two are so acquainted he knows you're in the States under an alias, Aleksy Jankowski."

Kolwaski showed his hand just slightly when his head whipped to his second in command. He tried to move then froze as though rendered thunderstruck. With a red face, Kolwaski turned back to me.

I noted, "You were right the day we closed this deal; you do need me more than I need you."

Kolwaski smiled. "And why do you say that?"

"For the reason you danced around, and the one you actually copped to that day. You need a broker who's unafraid to assume your risk. You knew you'd be passing contraband into the States and assumed, because of my father's line of work, I was that broker."

At first, Kolwaski forced a smile. That was quickly replaced by a flash of anger. "Like you, I come from a lineage of illegal money. But I wanted to be different. I wanted to make a change and provide for my family in earnest." His nostrils flared.

"Not that I give a single fuck, but..." I stood straight folding my arms over my chest. "What happened?"

"Life doesn't favor the good man, only the wicked. I do what I have to do for my family, just like Double E Bags!"

Jamil snorted at his pronunciation of my father's street moniker. It was quite comical. However, unlike Kolwaski, I wouldn't show arrogance to another man when I believed I had him by the balls.

"I'm sure you're familiar with Popov, you jacked my father as a client from him. But what I didn't know at the time was you have a history with him, and evidently, it's one where you're the victor."

"Feodor's men attempted to kidnap my niece and her friends while they were coming out of a movie theater three years ago back in my homeland. He didn't know who they were, but it doesn't matter. He should not have had men in my neighborhood. Let's say Feodor Popov will never *forget my name as* long as he lives. Had they harmed my niece and her friends, your father would have needed a distributor long ago because Feodor would have been a dead man."

I was glad Kawolski was at least honest in sharing. I wouldn't ask him about his name change. It was of no consequence to me.

"Switching distributors has given you and my father a common enemy. And from your words moments ago, you know you can alleviate this enemy as a problem for my father and Danny Lopez. Trust me, my father would never crumble under Popov's regime. However, you can obliterate him easier than my father because of how proficient you are at evading the federal government and knowing his weaknesses better than they do." I stood straight again. "As you know, with my father's physical recovery, it'll be easier for you to annihilate Popov than having to find a new broker for this incoming shipment."

The room went silent again. This time, Kolwaski didn't look to his men for input as he considered the corner he had been backed into.

"I feel like I'm being puppeteered here. That's not wise to do to a man like me."

"I would call it me manipulating the pieces on the board to work in my father's favor."

Kolwaski stood to his feet and aired out his suit jacket, straightening himself. "Although I don't like feeling threatened, I have to agree: you do have me by the balls. I do need that shipment to happen in three weeks." He crossed the room, his men around him. "Double E Bags can consider his issues with Feodor expired as early as tomorrow afternoon. You get my fucking shipment in, Ellis." He continued to the door.

"Kolwaski," I called out to him. My hands gripping the chair in front of me, head hung toward the floor. I heard their heavy stomps halt. "I may not cut you off before this next shipment, but you only have ninety days before I do. I can't allow the business I've built legitimately be compromised by the same illegal possibilities that have the federal government up my ass for each year, trying to catch me with my pants down." I lifted my head. "We're done in ninety days, whether you've found another customs broker or not."

Kolwaski laughed as he continued out.

∞27∞

The door to his room was open when I entered. The doors to the veranda was open, too, and I could see a body dressed in blue scrubs moving about. I headed for the doors and when I arrived, it could be deduced Iban had just finished lunch. Viewing him from his profile, I wasn't expecting the sight I encountered. It was clear he'd lost a lot of weight and a scoop of his shaved head was carved out and covered in stitches. He sat inclined in a motorized chair with a high headrest and guards to hold him upright. A mobile IV pole was next to his chair, the bag fueling a tube linked to his arm as he faced the outdoor pool from this wing of the house. And based on his slight and awkward lean to the side, I could tell Iban had no control over his body.

"Hi!" the young Asian woman greeted. "I'm Tawny, Iban's nurse. You here to visit him?" Having lost my voice, I nodded. She collected his breakfast accessories, loading them onto a tray. "Okay, cool! I'm going to take this over to the kitchen and grab his meds. You can keep him company in the meantime. I'll be right back." Her smile was bright. Before I could answer, she took off.

Nervously, I moved toward the chair closest to him and took a seat. When Iban's regard hit me, I noticed one of his amber hued eyes was gone. Unpatched, the lid was just about closed. He gaped at me expressionless as his hand twitched, possibly in reaction to my presence. I shifted my eyes away uncomfortably. Backing down could not be an option. I had to push myself to see this through.

At this point during the day, I should have been tired of talking about painful stuff. Bishop Carmichael, who I had to now call Ezra, had left a little over an hour ago. Over breakfast and for some time after, I had to share my story, which meant telling events of my childhood up until now. He was a patient listener. Picking up on the smallest details and asking me to expound on them. Some things were easy to share, others were not. When he ended our chat, we synced calendars for our next talk, which was the following week. After seeing him out, I was drained, but went to check on Earl in his study. Irene was with him and we talked for a while before I did the inevitable.

Faced Iban.

I swallowed hard, trying to fortify myself. "Do you know who I am?"

Almost with the pace of a robot, his head jerked and mouth barely moved when he cawed, "Yeah." I could assume Iban had no control over his voice box. That was likely one of many therapies he had to undergo.

"Do you remember what you did to me—to my baby?" Iban didn't answer, but both his arms jolted over the armrests. I took a deep breath, not understanding what that meant, but knowing he'd just shown how incapacitated he now was. "I won't ask you for an apology. Earl and Irene just told me you've had memory loss but during your care, you've been constantly reminded of how you landed in this condition."

Iban's one eye gazed above me to the pool. He was closing me out. I took another deep breath.

"I want to hate you so bad. Most days, I can't fathom forgiveness. What does it even mean? Then, there are those days where I'm feeling violent about you." I felt my lips constrict. "They're usually the ones when I think my son missed a milestone, believing he's been traumatized in some way because of what you did. And sometimes, it happens when I finally recognize the milestone, and I want to hurt you for my unnecessary panic. Too many times when I look at him, I think of you undeservingly. You've become a part of my life in a way I hate."

I needed to be honest with him, and for so many reasons. "I fought for you to be here. I'm sure a lot of people, including your family, think I'm out of my mind." I scoffed. "They probably think I'm too naïve and weak-hearted to feel the hate for you I should. But I can treat you no different than my own cold-hearted brother. Family is family." I shrugged. "And I believe we should avoid, at all cost, cutting them off. What Sadik did to you last fall was wrong. You should have never been ostracized. Your parents and brother should have worked with you to resolve the issues you had with me. I could've worked with—" I choked on my words when I saw a single tear leave his one surviving eye.

His face was stiff and Iban still refused to look at me. I continued on, "I've learned so much since encountering your family. I learned to never put so much on one child or sibling. Your parents planted a crown on Sadik's head, never thinking of him sharing responsibilities with you and Taaliba. As the oldest, you should have been highlighted more." Taaliba couldn't settle on a romantic relationship because her parents were so lost in their own affairs and building separate enterprises. They didn't give the girl the attention she needed; the seeds she needed to grow.

"I learned that being the head of the family should, in no way, be shared with your children. Leaders are imperfect, but they should be held to a higher standard. Your father makes Sadik his equal too much. It's unfair to all. And your parents' infidelity issues should have never been exposed to you guys. The message of family and the structure of it gets lost when the 'leaders' aren't respecting their vows to each other." What Earl and Irene had done with having their lovers being residents here—albeit, second class—was disgusting and damaging to the fiber of their family's unity.

"The last thing I'll share with you is I'm learning about your brother's protection. It's his natural role, it seems. He protects this family as though the job is his alone. I hate the weight it bears on his shoulders, but he's damn good at it."

Sadik had demonstrated protection in many ways. One was the obvious of gathering his family here at *Elliswoods Palace* in June when the family was under attack. He'd even scared Dimi enough for him to cut me as a client. He'd made sure his own brother was a distant threat to me by keeping him away. Not only had he hired a special security team for Iban while he was hospitalized, Sadik made sure when Iban needed to be removed for protection that he'd come where we would be: his family.

My friend and lover's protection wasn't just from violence. Sadik arranged for counseling for me. At first, I panicked over what he must have thought of me to go to such lengths, but after settling into my time with Ezra this morning, I realized Sadik did it because he wanted me whole. Just as he did for his own mother. Some men would have been turned off at the prospect of a woman having meltdowns and aversions to eating. Sadik was sticking by my side, as he'd done his brother through his mental health bouts.

I was crying. The tears came without warning. I held such a fountain of love and admiration for Sadik. Because of my fears, I struggled with being free with my feelings for him. Even as I sat and tried to make peace with his brother, I didn't recognize myself. I was pregnant, in fancy clothes, and on a palatial estate. I didn't even recognize my very real problems; my life had changed so much since one man.

Quickly, I wiped my face and sniffled back the tears. "I can't promise you forgiveness. That part, I'll have to work on. But what I will pledge to you is to treat you like family. I promise to humanize you as you go into this next phase of your life." My brother-in-law was an invalid. He'd never know life as he once did. Iban could never reclaim his place in this family as the enforcer. He'd now need protecting. "I've got the power, but I won't abuse it."

I flew from the chair, needing to get away from him. I'd done what I needed to do. Right now, I needed my baby and bed. As I skittered off the veranda and through the room wiping my eyes, I told myself I'd have to wait for Sadik. He may not be in until later on in the night. Monica standing just inside the bedroom startled me. With my face being to the floor, I didn't see her.

Monica's eyes were sad. I couldn't muster the words to ask if she was okay.

"I heard what you said to him," she murmured, letting her tears go. "To say you've only been in this family a year, you've sure pegged us right."

"So, there's still an us?" I asked then glanced behind me and lowered my voice. "You're staying with Iban?"

More tears spilled down her cheeks as Monica forged a smile. She shook her head. "I don't think so. I'm not making a move anytime soon, though. I think it's best for the girls and the family that I stay on for his first few months of recovery." Her eyes fell away as she dabbed them with a burping cloth belonging to baby Irene.

"Does that make you sad?"

She shook her head again. "No. The thought of losing my family does." Her tears came uncontrollably. "This is the only family I've known. I don't know who I'd be without them."

"But you've been keeping in touch with your own family." At least, I thought she had been.

"It's not the same. The Ellises are a tight unit," she cried. "We do everything together. Everything. It would take years to build that type of bond with my family—and that's if they were the cohesive type. And besides..." She wiped her eyes. "I feel like I've gained a sister since you've been here."

I rolled my eyes, balling my mouth. "I can't tell. It's been pretty lonely since I had Sadik. You've been running around here getting your freak on." Then a thought struck. "Are you leaving Iban for him?"

Somberly, Monica shook her head again. "I haven't heard from Leon in days. I think the Ellis men got to him." My heart fell to the floor. "Something happened with his access to the estate. He can't step a foot onto the property. When I called the head of security, they said I have to talk to Earl or Sadik. If I have to do that..." Her head shook and eyes closed as she sobbed. "I decided to drop it. But I've been calling Leon for days and he hasn't returned my calls. Hasn't been on social media either. I called the one friend who knew about us and he said he'd call me back when he's heard from him. That was three days ago. I haven't heard back from him."

I took a cleansing breath, closing my eyes. "You're not the average woman, Monica. We're not married to average men. Their rules are different in this family. Their respect for life and ability to kill the ego doesn't exist here. No matter how much Iban upset Sadik and Earl by shooting himself in my son's nursery, he's still one of them and will be looked out for."

Monica's tears fell fresh. "I know. It was stupid. I decided last night to drop it. I'll focus on the girls and getting Iban to a better and more independent place. But after that, I'm divorcing him. I want better. I deserve better."

Nodding, I offered her my fist. "I support you on that."

She met my knuckles with teary eyes. "Thanks so much for being you, Bilan."

I kissed Sadik's cheek before laying him in his crib. For the first time in months, I wasn't inclined to lay beneath him to sleep. Tonight, I'd let it go and resume a peaceful state of mind. After paying a lasting gaze, I ambled over to the bed, slipping beneath the comforter and shifted inward until I found her body curled onto her side. I molded over Bilan, inhaling the perfumed scent of her hair.

My hand brushed down to her round and solid belly. Her naked body, its natural aroma and heat lulling me away immediately.

"Deek..."

My eyes shot open after one cheek lifted in amusement at that nickname. "Hmm?"

"As soon as this travel restriction lifts, I want to go visit my family."

My brows met. "Any particular reason?"

She didn't answer right away, and that raised red flags about her meeting with Pastor Carmichael. What had he said to her?

He's only supposed to provide a diagnosis and recommend a practitioner based on that, not start meddling...

"I want Sadik to know both sides of his family. He's obviously going to be an Ellis." I heard the eye roll in that comment, "but, having another culture in there would be great for him—for both the kids."

That mention of children warmed me. My hand circled her belly. I couldn't wait to feel the baby kick. At this point, we were only fifteen weeks out and had a few weeks to go for that. Bilan told me that would be coming soon.

"When's the next doctor's visit?"

"Next week." She yawned. "You coming?"

"Don't I always?"

"You missed one."

My chest tightened. "Won't happen again. I'm ready to find out what we're having."

"Me, too."

My mind began to race with thoughts of preparation. When would the house be ready? If this was another boy, would he and Sadik share rooms for bonding purposes? If it were a girl, would she have her mother's freckles? Would we home school?

Would queen go for that?

"Sadik..."

"Hmmm?"

"Whatever happened to Monica's...friend? He hasn't been heard from—" She cleared her throat. "—from what I hear."

My Nalib didn't want to dry snitch on her sister-in-law.

Cute.

The sounds of Leon's whines of fear and wails of pain coursed my mind. It was pleasantly surprising to see Double E Bags throw hard bows without becoming too winded. *Fun*. It was a great time with the old man. A time preceding a much needed chat between the two of us.

I kissed the back of her head. "What do you think happened?"

Her body tensed. "You hurt him."

I snuggled into her soft frame more. "Then you've been paying attention all this time."

My face stretched into a smile in the dark.

"Sadik..." she groaned.

"Go see your family whenever you want, Nalib."

Bilan flipped over to face me. "Really?"

"Yes. The restriction's been lifted. I plan on informing the compound in the morning. You want me to come with you and Sadik to see your fam—"

Bilan's warm mouth covered mine. Her tongue pushed through my lips, causing my dick to lurch in my boxers. She swept my mouth with a gratitude and exuberant contentment that spoke to my groin. I held onto the fat of her hip while she blew my mind, sucking on my tongue and lip.

When she pulled back, Bilan breathed, "Thanks, Sadik. I'll call Aunt Franzel to see if they're available this week."

Regaining my wits, my face lifted in a smirk. "Does that mean you want me to go with you guys?"

"No. Not this time. If this visit goes well, I'll invite them over again. We didn't celebrate the Fourth of July. Maybe we can do a barbeque in the courtyard and have my family and Monica's over."

My dick began to pulse, not ready to end the passion. I grabbed Bilan's hand and pulled it to my growing erection. "I think you should do that. But right now, you have something else to take care of."

"Thanks, Candy." I gave a neck bow as she collected my plate in case she didn't hear me over the clamor in the room.

I glanced down to Sadik on my mother's lap at her dining room table. He stuck his finger in a bowl of her homemade apple sauce and sucked the puree off, all just to do it over and over again. He didn't want her to feed him with his spoon anymore. I guessed he wanted to do it himself. My boy was exerting his independence already at five months.

Ivy sat next to them, now with her attention fastened to the cake she was finishing up on. Iesha was on the other side of my mother, playing some hand game with her mother while Monica held a conversation with Taaliba directly across the table from her. Next to Taaliba was Danny Lopez. He appeared as awkward and out of place as he did last week when Bilan invited him for the first time. Well, it actually wasn't the first time. It was the first time he'd obliged her. I had a feeling it was the first time Taaliba passed on the message. Her immature ass was all over the damn place with Lopez, a glaring reason why she shouldn't be dating.

My father was at the far end of the table cleaning up baby Nene's high chair table. She ate with him tonight, giving Monica a break. A beat of pride rang out in my heart at seeing him here without any wheelchair or health care personnel assisting him. Also, having no women flanking him made him look younger and more present to the table.

I glanced down at Bilan next to me. She was texting under the table. From what I could make out, Tasche was sending her pictures of her and her guy at an amusement park.

Tasche: *He said ain't no ride better than the one this pussy give.*

I shook my head at that entry.

Bilan: Aye! And how 'bout I'm about to break my joy stick tAnOight!

Yes, I stalked my wife with no shame. I'd just picked up my wine glass when I saw she ended the text with the emoji face with one eye closed and the tongue hanging. I almost choked on Malbec.

"Nalib!" I grunted.

Unsuspecting, she peered up to me. When she realized I'd been watching, Bilan made an expression to mimic the emoji. I shook my head, not believing her level of crass. Is that what women discussed?

Before I could reply, my queen called for our attention at the end of the table. Ivy and Iesha shushed the room to assist her, making me snort. Damn, I missed this. My family was finally back to business, dining together at least twice a week.

"Excuse me," Irene Ellis pulled out her false soprano as though timid. "I know dessert concludes our dinner, but it's that time of the year again. Next week, leave time after to discuss our holiday excursions. So far, Bilan has recommended we stay home for Christmas."

"Why?" Taaliba asked, sincerely perplexed.

Her eyes met Bilan's. Bilan's freckled contoured cheeks lifted bashfully.

"You want to tell them?" Queen offered her.

"What, Aunt Lani?" Iesha gasped.

Bilan's face spread into an extraordinary beam. "I'll let Sadik do it."

As I stood, I invited Bilan to come along. I caught the expression of surprise on my father's face as we waited for her.

"We've been waiting for an appropriate time to share this. I know you've been asking the sex of the baby." Goddamn. Every day, it seemed, someone asked. Stacy, Jamil, Taaliba, my assistant at *Ellis International*, Julius—my goddamn dentist last week when I went in for a routine checkup. "We found out early last month."

"Aw, c'mon! Don't be one of those snobby couples who want to time sharing every detail about the incoming baby!" Monica tossed her cloth napkin.

"I think it's a girl!" Ivy shouted.

"I hope so," Danny added. "The Ellises don't need another man. The ones they tend to make are unbearable."

I shot him a warning glare, to which Taaliba shooed me with her hand.

"It's another boy," my father informed with confidence. "My loins reach that damn far." He winked at my mother, then went back to cleaning NeNe's face.

When my eyes returned to Bilan, she shoulder-bumped me, gesturing that I share.

"Well, you're both right. Apparently, I'm double-barreled." I raised my wine glass and pulled a cheesing Bilan into me with the other hand. "A boy and a girl."

"What?" my mother trilled.

"Twins!" Bilan shouted.

There was a mini choir of shouts around the room. Candy and her staff joined in on screeching cries and claps. Taaliba jumped out of her seat and pulled Bilan into her arms, rocking her side to side.

"I'm so happy for you!" she cried.

My mother was the next at our side. She yanked my neck down. "My heart can't take it!" She had me in one arm and Sadik in the other. "Just don't overdo it with her uterus. Give her some time after this one, okay?"

I laughed, watching Sadik trying to grab me. "Who's to say she didn't take the babies from me?"

"He may be on to something there," Bilan chimed in. "There's nothing like baggin' an Ellis!"

"What's begging?" Iesha asked, squeezing between adult bodies to hug Bilan's growing belly. She did this often. "You two don't have to beg. We're gonna share everything," she informed the gestating twins.

Bilan's head tossed back as she hooted. "I have to hit that bathroom now."

Taaliba laughed. "Oh, lawd! Let me see you to the powder room in case you have an accident on the way."

The two found their way out of the circle just formed around our chairs.

"Come on, girls," Monica announced. "Let's spend some time with Daddy before we go home."

The girls didn't take long to obey. Iesha took her mother by the hand and headed for the door. Ivana skipped behind. Monica grabbed NeNe from my father on their way out.

Stacy appeared right behind them. "Deek, your guests were just cleared by security and are approaching the house."

I nodded. "Thanks." Then I finally stopped ignoring my son and pulled him into my arms. I plopped his pacifier into his mouth, and that quickly, he lay his head on my shoulder to relax. "Queen, come to the foyer. I have something for you."

"Ooh!" She breathed playfully. "I love surprises."

My father waited near the door for his wife, his expectant hand extended for her. We all took to the foyer together, my parents fussing over Sadik. He was cranky, only wanting his pops. That could change as his food was digesting.

"That's my hair," queen observed during our stroll.

"But them my damn eyes," my father challenged her. "And he gone thank his PaPa for 'em when them girls start coming around."

I laughed internally at them. Sadik lifted when his grandmother pulled his shirt down to cover his back.

"You think he's running a fever?" queen asked.

"Nah." I lifted Sadik in the air, checking him out. "He probably just wants a nice shit, a bath, bottle, and his mother's chest to fall out on."

"Mmmhmmm." My father agreed. "That food you made him got

him right, baby. He's getting to the big leagues now; putting weight on his belly."

"Mr. and Mrs. Ellis," Stacy called. "The Rizzoes are here."

My mother's head whipped over her shoulder, her mouth hanging open as Catena Rizzo approached the foyer table where we stood. She held Liza in her arms, and my, had she grown in mere months. Marco Rizzo followed behind, hands in the pockets of his shorts. I could see his face healed, minus a few dark marks around his nose. I felt a tinge of guilt. That night, at his home, I'd taken my frustrations out on him. I could have been more diplomatic with my stance.

"Irene," Catena spoke first, smile sincere. "Someone wanted to spend time with their Nana."

My mother's expression hadn't change. "Liza?" Catena handed my niece over to her paternal grandmother. "I've missed you so much, baby." My queen kissed her. "You've gotten so big! Soon, you'll be running around with my big girls." Marco stepped closer and placed a baby bag on the table. Queen asked with her eyes.

"I think it's time for Liza to spend time with her other family, and especially with her father," Catena explained. "Lia wants it, too. She's working tonight or else she'd be here dropping her off."

Yes, Lia had been working. She had to. Now with Salvatore Rizzo dead, there was no substantial income providing for their family. I'd been told when Marco called me asking for a favor that if he didn't get work soon, the money Rizzo had set up in life insurance wouldn't last to keep up with the taxes on the property. He shared that Catena used much of the policy to pay off their home and two cars. There was little left after that.

Marco had been let go by Abram Murphy, the newly appointed chief of operations at the *Port of Paterson*. Murphy had cleaned out a lot of nepotism at the port, specifically Rizzo's family and friends, who held significant positions for decades without earning them. They weren't responsible with them either. Marco was one of those fired. He had a family to provide for. He was forced to sell his home and move his family in with his mother.

So when he called me a couple of weeks ago with his hat in hands,

I cut a deal with him. I gave him, his wife, and Lia modest positions in my warehouse at *Ellis International*. I was fair with their salaries, too, giving them full benefits and paid time off. It was the same deal I'd give to any incoming employee, only they didn't earn it. But as Bilan said, it didn't matter. *"Like it or not, the Rizzoes will forever be connected to the Ellises because of Liza. They should be granted grace until they burn it."*

I kept Marco under my foot, never forgetting his words in that bathroom not quite two years ago.

"Like my father says, 'if Lia likes to fuck niggers and is stupid enough to get pregnant by one, let it be one from a solid standing family. That's what the Ellises are. And if she's gonna do it with any of the Ellis boys, better it be that educated nigger than the crazy one!"

He now needed the educated nigger to make a living.

"Do you have a minute to talk about her care?" Queen asked Catena. "We can meet in the family room this way." I could tell she was still stunned, possibly shaken.

"Sure," Catena replied and began to follow her.

Marco was the last to take off. Stiffly, he paid an acknowledgment of a nod before he followed them.

"You see, baby boy?" My father lifted Sadik from my shoulder. "You always look a man in the face, even when they have you by the balls. Don't do it like that weak muthafucka and have shifty eyes. Keep them straight and unflinching."

Behind them, I saw Tiffany click-clacking against the marble floors toward us. She beamed the moment our eyes met.

"I missed dinner. I'm so fuckin' pissed," she groaned.

My father saw her over his shoulder. As he turned, he greeted, "Hey, baby!"

She kissed his cheek. "Hey, Poppa Earl."

"I was wondering what happened to you."

"I know!" she cried regretfully. "I had a staff meeting that ran over. Some stupid muthafucka is letting bitches and niggas into *Energy* for free. I had to cuss everybody the fuck out tonight and let them know I'll be hiring a new security team by tomorrow. Shit got heated before I kicked them all out."

I stood there, waiting for her to acknowledge my son for the sake of lightening her language. I, myself, hadn't seen or heard from her in months. It was almost as if after that red carpet photo-op, she stopped fucking with me. Tiff gave nothing as she turned to my father. While bouncing Sadik in his arms, his regard swung between her and me.

"You don't see my legacy here, baby girl?"

"I don't see but one." Her tone was cold.

My father scoffed the type of scoff he did when trying to pace his temper. "Baby girl, you can't still be holding onto that."

My face tightened. Tiffany rolled her eyes, her attention finally falling to my son. Again, my father chuckled, sans the humor. We'd had our father to son heart-to-heart around the time we found out about Monica's affair. It was an organic meeting of the hearts. Our reaction to the breach of our home was met with the same passion. Days after, he'd called me down to his study to apologize for conspiring to kill Bilan last summer. The emotion he displayed while doing it would be imprinted in my mind forever. I'd never experienced Double E Bags apologize to anyone but my mother. But when he expressed gratitude for what I'd been doing to preserve him and this family over the years, nothing mattered but the health and well-being of my father.

So when he issued that flick of the single brow, I knew Tiffany had crossed a line with him, forcing my father to clear the lines of boundaries in our triangular connection. "You're crossing a line here, sweetheart."

"I'm not. I'm finally getting the picture." She pouted, profile still to me.

"So you getting that damn picture—or whatever you gone call it —makes you rude to my son?"

"I'm not being rude. I'm staying in my lane," her voice cracked.

I snorted. "Someone gonna tell me what's going on here?"

Tiffany faced my father, eyes on my son's leg. She refused to look at me. My regard went to my father.

"Tiffany got a beef, saying she walked in on you and baby girl in the movie theater a few months ago."

My face folded more. "And?"

"And she saw some shit you only show people if they pay or get off from just watching for free," he expounded.

It took a few seconds for me to recall my time with Bilan that night in the theater house. My goddamn balls and heart were so heavy from missing her that night, I wouldn't have known Tiffany was there if she had hit me over the fucking head.

"Do you think I should apologize to you?" I asked, trying to understand her issue.

I may not have given one single word of apology for what I did with my wife on my family's grounds, but I cared for Tiffany enough to attempt peace.

She didn't answer. So stubborn and emotionally unintelligent in the moment, Tiffany tried to deflect by adjusting Sadik's pant leg as he lay on my father's shoulder. My fucking stomach dropped when she did that. I switched stances.

"Ummm..." I was stumped, not knowing how to say this and not be rude. It was enough that she had the ridiculous beef with me. I was sure this was her first time being this close to the baby. What gave her the balls to touch him? *Shit*. As innocent the act, she wouldn't stop. "Uhhhhh..." My hand lifted in the air.

"Listen, baby," my father began, and I so badly wished he shifted away from her just a foot or three. "You can't do this. It ain't right for you to be beefin' with the man over what he do with his—"

His words were cut short when an object flew past my face and whacked Tiff's head. I saw a small, gold padlock dangling from it and should have known. She stumbled back, trying to gain her equilibrium. When it landed, I recognized the *Tom Ford* sandal I'd just bought for...

"I told you to never lay a fucking hand on my child!" Bilan shouted from behind me, tossing her other heel across the foyer. "*TRY ME AGAIN!*"

Taaliba was behind her, hands covering her mouth as she raced toward us. I grabbed Bilan before she crossed the foyer. Sadik began crying in my father's arm from his mother's alarmed shout.

I turned to my sister. "Get him and meet us up in our suite!" Leeb stumbled, but finally jumped into action.

When my father was relieved of the baby, he went to help Tiffany, who was bleeding somewhere on her face. I knew it was a matter of seconds before Tiffany would try to retaliate. Even Bilan was fighting against me, trying to get to her.

"Rory!" I shouted.

And as though it was unnecessary, Rory and Jamil were rushing toward us, assessing the situation.

"Oh, I'm about to fuck you up!" Tiffany finally came through. She snatched away from my father's grip, something I didn't want him doing to begin with. He didn't need the physical toil. "Bitch! I'm 'bout to drop ya monkey ass—" Tiff was jolted by Rory's choke hold.

Thank you...

Rory's move was precise and decisive, something that would save us lashings from Bilan later. We could both use the break. Rory for her blunder when dealing with Sofia, and me for not asking Tiff to remove her hand sooner.

I was able to hold Bilan into my chest from behind. "If you try and fight me, you're going to hurt the twins," I grounded in her ear. "You hurt them, Tiffany will be the least of your fuckin' problems." Bilan's frame steeled in my hold. I turned her around in the opposite direction. Taaliba could be seen marching Sadik through the house to calm him. "Good choice, Nalib."

I walked her down the hall until we reached the elevator. Bilan's chest heaved, lips tight with venom.

"I told you to never—"

"I fuckin' know!" I shouted. "But you have to trust me to do it."

"You obviously took too long!"

My head swam in chemicals brought about from relief and worry. That could have been so ugly. "I was trying to be sensitive to her feelings because I just found out she saw us having sex."

"Good for her stalking ass! She knew we were in the theater, and I dare her to lie!"

My head flew back. "You know she saw us?"

Heaving, Bilan shot me hard eyes.

The elevator door opened and I moved in closer to her. "Answer me."

When I thought Bilan wouldn't respond, she grated, "One of the best orgasms of my life happened while she watched."

I sucked in a breath. Who was this woman?

Seconds later, Bilan stepped onto the elevator. My mind was so far gone, I halfway paid attention.

That was until I heard a familiar cry. "Sadik…"

She may have concluded her services with Carmichael to learn Bilan suffered from post-traumatic stress disorder with arousal and reactivity symptoms, but he said she was still capable of displaying the signs for a long while. He recommended a therapist for her to see to help with coping mechanisms. Those services wouldn't begin for another two weeks due to scheduling conflicts. But right now, her eyes were heavy lidded, breathing choppy, and one thigh extended out, slightly raised beneath her maxi dress. I knew that look.

Shit…

I had the duty of fucking my wife on the elevator.

"This is going to be nice, Bilan," my Aunt Astur commented as her eyes measured every corner of the unfinished kitchen. It was the final room of the new house I showed. "Big, too!" Her face brightened.

"I know!" Joslyn breathed out.

"Seven bedrooms, five and two half bathrooms, a television room, family room, dining room," my cousin, Angela counted off verbally. "and this big ass kitchen, a full basement that'll be designed for the kids, two offices, and the partridge in a pear tree all on eight acres."

"Yup." I nodded with pursed lips.

I hadn't even shared what Sadik had planned to do with the land. He wanted to build a lake on the far end, a pool with a cabana closer to the house, and basketball and tennis courts. It was a lot, and I was anxious about it all. I'd never had a house built from the ground up, much less an estate.

"Seven bedrooms is a lot," Joslyn noted with an indecipherable expression. "How many more kids y'all plan to have? Me and Teddy said two is enough." Her expectant body language was unfortunate. She was comparing our lives.

Either way, that question caught me off. I laughed nervously, rubbing my belly. "I don't know yet, but I think I can do this again."

With hiked lips, Joslyn nodded, clearly processing that answer more than necessary. Pregnancy hadn't been too unkind to me, considering I was carrying two. It certainly had been different from my first. I was more tired and way heavier. My nose had spread, too. That part hadn't been fun at all.

"Don't have too many," Aunt Astur warned. "You don't wanna lose that Yasin figure now!" She snapped a finger.

"Oh, hooya," Mimi groaned, waving her mother off dismissively. "Sadik's rich. She can pay for a new Yasin body."

Brenda and I laughed.

Aunt Astur rolled her eyes, and mumbled, "You can't pay for no Yasin body, girl."

"So, what's next for the house?" Aunt Franzel asked. "What will they do next?"

It was two days after Thanksgiving. Because the Ellises were still adjusting to Iban's new condition, we decided to spend the holiday at *Elliswoods Palace*. My family was invited, and when it was brought up that the Ellises had been to the building site of Sadik's and my new home, my Aunt Astur claimed to have felt slighted from not being included. Quickly, Sadik offered to have the house fitted for safety the first day my family was available. Today was that day. I was able to show them the main floor, basement, and some of the second level. The construction was behind schedule, something Sadik had been warning me of.

I thought to check my phone for missed texts or calls as it was a weekday, and work could have tried contacting me. I rolled my eyes when I noticed my phone had died. I sighed, noting I'd charge it in the truck. Today, I drove myself here. No security. No Rory. The property was in the middle of nowhere, making my biggest threat animals.

"Next," I sighed again, upset that I didn't think to charge it on my way here. "is finishing the roof and doing the exterior design. We went with a stone veneer. I'm so excited to see it come together."

"Good for you, baby," Aunt Franzel praised.

"All right, we gotta get ready to go," Joslyn informed. "I have to pick up my kids soon."

"Okay," my aunts agreed in unison.

One by one, I hugged both aunts and cousins. Brenda lagged behind as usual. She waited for everyone else before approaching me.

"You mind if we chat for a minute?" I asked her. Everyone's neck whipped to face us. My head cocked to the side. "Is it a crime to speak privately to my younger cousin?"

"Okay. Just making sure she ain't in no trouble." Aunt Astur issued Brenda a warning stare.

A goofy grin lifted on Brenda's face as she bobbed her head, likely out of nervousness. Or maybe she was bouncing to the beat of music; her ears were plugged with *Airpods*.

"She's too old to be in trouble." It was me who waved her off this time. "You ladies go. We'll just be a minute."

Slowly, my family filed out of the kitchen. After speaking to Monica when leaving Iban's room last summer, I decided to make more of an effort at getting to know my family. I had taken the baby to see them several times over the summer. Sadik attended with us twice since. It hadn't been smooth sailing dealing with a competitive cousin like Joslyn or a know-it-all like Angela, but being with family had its rewards. One was Brenda. She and I had gotten to know each other more often, and it had been a pleasant surprise.

After seeing them off, I spun around to Brenda. "Why haven't you told them?"

"Who said I ain't?" Brenda's grin was infectious, but I wouldn't get suckered in.

"They did, because they came today. *All* of them," I emphasized.

She laughed. "That's because I only told my mom."

My shoulders dropped as I considered that. "Hmmm..."

"And guess what..."

"What?"

"She said she knew already."

I sighed dramatically, rolling my eyes to a close. "That relieves me so."

Brenda laughed again. These bouts of giggles was a symptom of her insecure persona, according to her therapist—our therapist. When I gently approached her about the incident with Rory and how I'd heard about her time in the strip club, Brenda told me she was gay. It wasn't something that surprised me. She walked around in loose clothing, body holding no grace in posture, her cornrows was the only style she knew, and she worked with mostly men. Either my younger cousin was gay or asexual as Taaliba—who was an entirely different case—claimed. My concern for Brenda, however, was she didn't have to feel inferior to anyone because she came from a family who didn't agree with her sexuality. I believed she had taken high risks because she wasn't comfortable enough being her out loud and pursuing happiness openly.

"Why?"

"Because it tells me she's been paying attention. There's nothing worse than a parent who doesn't recognize the various elements that make up their children." I learned that from Taaliba's situation. To this very day, no one had a clue she'd been seeing her former professor and Danny Lopez at the same time. With her, being attracted to a man and woman at the same time wasn't a concern, so much as doing it in secret was. Neither party had a clue about the other. That was a dangerous game. "If Aunt Astur claimed to not have known, it would mean she hadn't been paying attention or didn't have the balls to ask. We're a family. It's our job to provide a safe community for you in spite of the non-violent things you do in your personal world."

"Well, she ain't been saying much since I told her. I can tell she's mad, but..." Brenda shrugged, that grin in tow.

"That's not your problem. But you're not trying to pick up random people like strippers anymore, are you?"

She laughed. "What's wrong with strippers?"

"Nothing. The problem is with 'random.' Whether it's a stripper or a mailman, you deserve deliberate and intentional." I winked.

"You right. You right." She extended her hand, offering me a handshake.

I pulled her into a hug. "I think you're my favorite cousin." How could she not be? Brenda was vulnerable and now transparent with me. She was generous. Sometimes when she'd come to see me, she'd bring loaded fries from *B-Way Burger* or delicious chocolates from *Guilty Pleasures*. She was funny, smart, and kind, too.

"Who was before you got all up in my business?" She asked with a hiked brow.

"No one!" Brenda chuckled, causing me to laugh myself. "Now, come on. They're waiting on you. And I need to use the potty before I hit the road."

We started for the entrance of the kitchen. There were supplies all around: saws, hammers, ropes, cords, nail guns and such we had to step over or walk around. I couldn't wait for this process to be done.

"Where you gonna do that?" Brenda asked.

"That porta-potty out there. It's what the builders use; it must be functional." We continued to the vestibule section. "I swear, I've had no water in hours to avoid this very thing."

"Yeah, but you got two of them dancing in there. You good."

When we passed through the entryway, I could see my aunts and cousins had loaded up in two cars.

"Tell them not to wait for me. I don't know how disgusting this 'outhouse' will be."

"You sure?"

"Yeah. Nothing out here but lions, tigers, and bears." I patted her shoulder. "I'm in perfect condition to take them on."

Brenda laughed as she took off for the car. "You crazy, cuzzo."

She went in one direction, and I power-walked in another, passing more supplies, unstained wood, more ropes—which brought just one thing to mind—tiles for flooring, and other equipment I couldn't name. It was just a messy clutter all round. The porta-potty was on the side of the house. Thankfully it was unlocked and other than a slight stench of urine, bearable. How clean could I expect a bathroom used by men only to be?

Right away, I locked the door and did my business. I was surprised to see the liquid soap dispenser full. One could only assume the men building my home didn't wash their hands after using the bathroom.

Just gross...

I rolled my eyes as I pulled at the toilet tissue roll to dry my hands. Despicable! I immediately decided to use my hand sanitizer the moment I stepped outside. After using the tissue to unlock the door, I tossed it into the overflowing trash. Then I shifted my cross-over purse in front of me and pushed the door open with my foot. I stepped outside and glanced down to dig through my purse when I felt the hairs on the back of my neck stand. My head shot up and Jason Anderson appeared.

My heart dropped from my chest and body instantly chilled. He stood about five yards away wearing a dark gray trench coat. His hands were pushed behind his back as he inspected me. I could see his hair had grown out considerably since the summer. Those tightly coiled strands on his head were now grouped in to tiny locs on top of his head. His eyes were darker, skin blemished, and his aura murky. I could feel it emanating from him like a furnace. Jason looked familiar, but this wasn't him.

My pulse galloped in my neck when I attempted to casually speak first. "Really? After all these months, this is where you pop up on me?"

Jason's expression was impassive. "You're not surprised."

My mouth was a citrusy mess I only experience when nervous and afraid. I shrugged. "Of course, I am. You come up here on an Ellis property. I'm surprised." I sniffled back a cry, trying to cover it with a giggle. "You know his security is always around. I'm surprised no one told me you were here."

He snorted, face finally opened into a grin I didn't recognize from him. "You're by yourself, my Somali girl. Don't lie."

"How do you know?" My eyes squinted in curiosity.

"I hacked your phone."

My mask of bravery fell. "*Ho*—how? When?"

He scratched his head contemplatively. "It started when I was alerted of someone signing in to a sensitive, state artifacts database on campus, using my credentials. I wondered who it was and needed to know, because now that I'm an alumnus, I had to answer for it. When I saw what the search characters were, I recalled me being so generous and sharing that resource with one person." The humor in his face disappeared. "You. Who else gives a shit about the Ellises?"

"You still haven't answered how you were able to hack into my phone?"

"It's called technology." His sneer was a new energy of his being introduced to me. "Through a program a friend of mine created. I was able to gain your cell's identification information from the times you accessed the school's database from it. Your computer, too. You're quite boring, by the way. I guess that Ellis guy isn't into nudes or tease vids."

"Why do I suddenly feel you are?"

He scoffed. "The first time you've actually paid attention to me outside of having me as a human pet?" A brow raised skeptically.

I swallowed hard, fighting for a concrete façade. "Don't come up on my property unannounced to talk about something so stupid as that. No. Especially after I learned how sneaky you are—were—having sex with Randi in my parents' house."

Jason laughed. "Oh! She finally opens her eyes!" he shouted into the open, chilled air. When his dark irises met mine again, the promising leer returned. "I only ate her pussy. Let's not make shit up. Damn! How do you go through life for twenty-nine years so fucking blind, Bilan? I'm sure they make them brighter than you in Somalia."

My face folded. "What? There's nothing dumb about me!"

He nodded, chuckling sinisterly in my face. "Oh, there is." Jason finally moved, shifting weight on his hips. His arms fell aside him, revealing a gun. My hands clasped my purse at my round belly. "Your 'husband'"—he used air quotations with his hands, arrogantly brandishing the gun—"is sharp, though. He figured out a lot." Then his eyes narrowed. "He didn't tell you?"

"Tell me what?" Jason sputtered a laugh. Arrogant and loud, he laughed in my face. That familiar sense of betrayal blanketed me. "Tell me what, Jason?"

I waited for him to quiet. He dipped his chin, but his eyes remained on me. "That we had a friend in common."

"Who?"

"My cousin, Damien Brown."

All types of synapses fired in my brain, at first, trying to recall the name. "Damien?" I finally got it. Never would I have connected the two to figure it out. Visions of being accosted and taken to an abandoned building to be killed circled in my mind. What was going on here? First, Damien, then Iban, now...Jason? My phone was dead and the closest neighbor was over two miles away. I was pregnant—high risk at that from the twins. All of that and I was discovering another inconvenient truth. "Was he your friend or cousin?"

"My cousin. We didn't keep in touch much until a few years ago. He hit me up saying he didn't know I was in school. That's when he told me about the girl he wanted me to keep an eye on."

"So you were watching me for Damien?"

"I was having fun, trying to fuck you. He just asked that I made friends with you."

My blood turned cold, and I felt light-headed. "Did he say why?" If he did, it meant Jason knew of my torment the entire time while posing as a friend.

Jason shrugged. "Eventually. I didn't care, though. I thought you were cool...really liked you. And then Ellis happened. Damien thought he wouldn't be trouble. That once he fucked you, he'd be done. That was the part that fucked me up. He did fuck you; fast and easy."

Suddenly, I felt naked. "That's not true, and none of your business."

"Maybe it wasn't. Damien told me to leave it alone, but I couldn't. I called the *FBI* on him figuring they could find something on an Ellis man."

That was how he got in touch with the *FBI*...

He'd reached out to them last summer.

"Because he supposedly had something you wanted, you threaten his livelihood? That's not fair. It wasn't your place either. I'm not your business, Jason."

"You weren't until Ellis killed Damien," he grated. I blinked hard. "And he got away with it. I tried the nice guy route of trying to call, text, and even stopped by Ellis' apartment. You listened to him and ignored me. You've changed, Bilan."

"No, I haven't. I've never owed you anything." He was crazy. "We never dated."

He shrugged noncommittally. "And my cousin didn't live... because of you."

Rustles from the leaves on the ground caught both our attention. Jason glanced to his right and my regard shot into the opposite direction. I didn't see anything. Nothing more was heard.

Cautiously, Jason advised, "Let's move into the house." He waved his gun over his shoulder, demonstrating his command as he walked backward. Then he returned his gaze to me as I followed him with apprehension. I couldn't come up with a plan to run. I couldn't run. Nestled into my third trimester, carrying twins, I didn't possess the stamina. "I know you're up here by yourself. I saw the texts you sent to your family and the one you sent to Ellis saying you'd be fine alone."

Anger wrapped around my neck, choking me. He'd been reading my text messages.

"You look shocked, Bilan." He scoffed. "You're naïve, just like your friend, Randi, and Damien said. You can't see the forest from the trees. And you think you can keep up with the brightest Ellis of the kids. I've done some searching, and learned a lot about the sordid family. I'm sure you know his parents have live-in lovers. They do it out in the open." His face tightened as he stopped several yards from the house almost center of a huge slab of black granite. In the recesses of my mind, I realized it would be cut and used for the countertops Kimmy and I had agreed on. "How do you think that shapes the mind of a rich young man? How many bitches do you think he's fucking right now? I count three, including sexy ass Sofia Cruz, and thickums, Tiffany Jones. She's a boss bitch—Sofia, too. They're sharp minded. Not unsophisticated and gullible like *yo* —eww—"

His words were cut short by a manila rope I didn't see being thrown until the lasso had slipped over his head and was quickly tightened and yanked. Jason's body spasmed, trying to pull the braided lariat from around him. His lips tightened to a squeeze as he twisted against the granite, eyes bulging when panic kicked in at realizing he couldn't escape.

My spine juddered watching him and my hands went to by belly protectively. In my peripheral, Rory was approaching at my right, low with her gun drawn at him. Jason's eyes mushroomed and his gun pushed up above his head. He shot wildly into the air and to his right, clearly having no target in sight.

Finally, my regard ascended and saw Sadik's golden face set into a scowl as he manipulated the rope, pulling it back against the flying bullets. Instinctively, I reached for my purse and pulled out my gun. After paying a few seconds of focus while Jason lashed in the air, I pulled the trigger three times, hitting Jason twice. His body leaped backward into the air, colliding with the black granite slab before falling listlessly onto the ground.

"Fuck!" Sadik yelped from the roof. "Rory could've done it, Nalib!" The arteries in his forehead were pronounced as he scolded me. Simultaneously, Jamil crunching leaves beneath his feet to the right startled me again.

My focus went above the house again. "So could I!" I shouted back past the point of mild tempered. Jason called me naïve in a way that hurt like never before. Expecting people to be how they present didn't make me naïve; it made me optimistic about mankind. It was something I'd been tackling in therapy. The very word raised my hackles. Right now was not the time to challenge me. My head whipped to find Rory over my shoulder. "Somebody had to! He could have shot Sadik!"

"Man, I had him, B." Rory rolled her eyes, pushing her gun into its holster. "I been doing this shit since before you had ya first nut."

A spit of laughter shot out over my head. I pivoted to see Sadik cackling on the roof.

"Oh, that's funny?" I turned back to Rory with my gun pointed. "What do you know about my first nut, Rory?"

"Aye!" Sadik shouted, the authoritarian bark reverberated in my spine. "You're going too far!"

"You go too far!" I kept my gun on her. "You keep things from me and tell your employee about my sexual experiences?"

Rory's big eyes blossomed. "Yo, that's true? I was just fuckin' witchu!" She turned to Jamil with a delighted smile. "Didn't I tell you sire hit it first!" She guffawed, and from the looks of it, Jamil was prepared to join in.

"No, he did not!" I shouted, feeling like a child.

"The fuck I didn't, Nalib!" Sadik yelled. "Don't fuckin' pop off because you got a *Glock* in your hands."

Was he serious? As he disappeared from the roof, I discovered Jamil had been laughing with Rory, only his was apologetic when our eyes met briefly. He couldn't look me in the face, though he tried just as he did to stop laughing. Rory disregarded me as she howled.

When Sadik emerged in the entrance of the house, I asked, "Why are you here?"

"You think I'd let you come up here alone?"

My chilled body began trembling out of nowhere. "This is going to be my home! When do you think I'll be able to come and go alone?"

Out of breath, he sauntered over and pulled me into his chest, holding me fervently. "You're cold and shaking," he noted. A heavy breath left my lungs. It was dangerous how at home I felt in Sadik's arms.

"Did you know he was related to Damien?" When he didn't answer, I knew he had known. "You can't be married to me and continue to keep things like this to yourself."

"It's not what you think. I didn't know until a few months ago when my *FBI* contact made the connection. I wish I knew he was diabolical. He'd been dealt with accordingly a long time ago. I've been trying to call you for an hour now."

"My phone died." My eyes closed the moment the tears fell.

"I was coming up with Rory anyway to surprise you and your family," he explained. "We were running late when I got a call from the sheriff. His officers reported an unknown car we soon realized matched Jason's plates was in the area. He must've gotten lost trying to find this place because the patrols saw him in several places since the first sighting. That's when I called Jamil to try to get here before us or at least meet us."

Sadik withdrew from me sooner than I needed. He walked over and kicked Jason's leg.

"Yeah," Rory observed out loud. "He's a goner. Bilan been puttin' in that work at the range, I see." She pounded her chest. "Respect."

"Yeah, man." Jamil agreed. "Good work, Bilan!"

My shoulders dropped as I paid Jason a thorough inspection for the first time. He looked fitfully sleep but with blood draining from his head. I couldn't believe it. There was a dead man mere yards away. *Again and just like Damien*. More than that, I'd killed him. My teeth began to chatter; I was so cold.

"Sadik!"

"Oh, shit," Rory grumbled. "You need for us to go?"

She and Jamil began backing away immediately. I hated it.

"Oh, fuck you, Rory!" I shouted at the top of my lungs.

I despised the expectation of my weakness. But she was right: my body was humming in inappropriate excitement. It needed assuaging only one man could give. Nipples peaked, panties soaked, my heavy eyes found the target. Those kaleidoscopic-hues irises darkened in an instant. His full lips parted as his tongue swiped the inner lining of his bottom lip, back and forth.

"The best I can give you is the back of the car, Nalib. We have to call the cops."

Ashamed, aroused, loved, and protected, I nodded my ascent.

Epilogue

Sadik

Christmas Day Three Years Later

"Is that the last one?" Bilan asks as I press the adhesive bow on Sadik's motorized toy *Bentley* coupe.

I know he's going to love this one. He asked for a manual toy buggy, but his poppa had something better in mind.

"Yeah." I sigh. "This is the last one."

"You know you made a bad move with getting just one of those things, right?" Bilan stands back with a fist propped on her hip.

I shake my head, not agreeing. "Sadik is the oldest; he's going to get different toys, Nalib. He's about to be four years old."

"But he's also the big brother to a soon to be three-year-old who doesn't understand they're ten months apart. Asad wants whatever Sadik gets. You know this."

I shake my head, not wanting to fight about this on Christmas morning. The kids will be awakening and down any moment now. It only took one, and the others would soon follow. That one is usually Asad Yasin Ellis. He's the most rambunctious of the trio. He and his twin sister, Sadia Idil, have louder personalities than my firstborn. Those two are thick as thieves, though Asad trades in his twin for his big brother often. He admires Sadik...this soon in their lives.

My baby girl allows it, though. She's smart and independent like her mother. We named Sadia after Bilan's mother and me. Her name was Idil, which means perfect and complete, I was told. I thought that was an ideal vibe for our first daughter. It represents Bilan's and my story, or at least how I felt about securing her in my world: perfect and complete.

"If Asad makes a big deal about it, I'll order him one and have it delivered to the house. It'll be there when we get back. We can surprise him with it," I try to placate her concern and quickly move on.

Bilan crouches next to me; her chin is propped on her fist as she smirks. She shoulder bumps me. "You've been a parent long enough to know it's going to be a miserable three days until that happens. There will be lots of screaming, crying, and fighting over this one object until we get home."

She's probably right, but I'm still anxious to see Sadik's face when he opens this baby. We flew in late last night. Bilan and I had the last of our staff's holiday engagements to attend. Julius invited us to the city's holiday party, which was the last one we did before loading our kids and their Christmas toys onto the jet and flying out to Norden, California for the annual Ellis Christmas extravaganza.

We missed the Christmas Eve activities, something the kids complained about. They wanted to bake cookies and enjoy the caroling and storytelling in the sleigh Bilan arranged for the kids in the family. As we boarded, Sadik, Asad, and Sadia griped. Once settled in, they all knocked out right away, stretched out over each other like little logs with their mouths open. Mel, the flight atten-dant, made Bilan and me teas Taaliba has just returned to making. Our plan was to sleep the entire flight and not sleep when we landed until after breakfast. I wanted to celebrate Christmas morning with a twist once we were done with the children and our family.

"Did you decide on what to do with Sadia's kitchen set?" I ask Bilan.

"Yeah. I had Camille set it up. NeNe is going to want to play with her. It's over there." She points across the expansive living room made of all wood with floor-to-ceiling windows giving a view to the snowy grounds outside. "I got NeNe the same one, but hers is boxed and wrapped so Monica can easily ship it back East." She yawns. "I'm so excited to see their little faces."

My brows meet. "You're not getting sleepy on me, are you?"

"Are you kidding me?" She shakes her head. "Awwww, hecks nah! I'm looking forward to my Christmas treat."

We laugh, and hard. The *hecks nah* phrase is one of many authored by Asad. Like I said, his little personality is loud. We never know what's coming out of that little mouth next.

I glance around at our handiwork. The gifts for the children are color-coded. It was something Taaliba came up with a couple of years ago to keep the kids from opening the wrong gifts. And there are a lot of damn gifts.

Bilan hums next to me, checking her phone for the time. "We got it done just in time. You see the sun coming up over there?" She points again. "It's almost showtime!"

I'm lost in her contentment immediately. Small events like the moment we've just shared over our son, something we created together, cast me in a trance. Bilan catches me after she fingers her hair. Her smile reappears and deepens.

She turns for me, pushing her arms to encase my waist. "What are you thinking about, S.Q.E., the first?"

"How so mine you are," I answer honestly.

Bilan has been a series of metamorphoses since the first time I made love to her. After that trip to Costa Rica, her dog died and I forced her to live with me. She ran to *Macen Beach* soon after that and when she returned, Bilan was stronger, though she didn't realize it. She survived my brother putting our son at risk and shooting himself in our home. Even after that, Bilan covered my family during one of our darkest periods in history. She took command when my parents were down and I was selfishly upset and in my feelings. And then, she killed a man; someone she thought to be a friend.

After shooting Jason, Bilan spiraled emotionally. She became so distraught, we endured countless trips to the emergency room and doctor's office for the twins. She was put on bedrest two weeks after he died. We were in the papers for over a year, thanks to our surname. The Ellises weren't new to headlines, and Bilan now being one was treated no differently. The police took their time investigating the incident. They wanted the wait to be painful, and for

Bilan, it had been. She wanted to apologize to his parents, something my mother adamantly opposed.

Jason was wrong. He'd stalked her with the intention of killing Bilan that day. He had three guns in his car on our property. There was an internal campaign to prosecute both of us. However, my team of bad-ass attorneys argued I was well within my right to protect Bilan with the rope because Jason had brandished a gun at that point. And Bilan was well within her rights to shoot him because he'd fired several shots in the air. The only issue was the gun she used was registered to me and not Bilan. My lawyers were able to have that charge dismissed, too, just around Sadik's first birthday. It had truly been a long road.

Bilan's hands snake up to the wings of my back, her tits pushing into my chest. "I better be. I had a dream last night."

My head reclines and eyes close. "Oh, shit."

"What?"

"When you dream, I pay attention. Remember the one you had almost four years ago about the goral?"

Her eyes loll left to right above her head. "Oh, yeah. The goat."

"Mmmhmmmm." I nod. "It was a Russian goat. You said it was circling the family while they held in a tight circle."

She murmurs, eyes now low. "Yeah. I remember the dream started off with Jason leading me somewhere. We were running and when I saw the family, I stopped. He kept going while laughing, or something like that."

That's news to me. Bilan didn't share that detail with me back then. I would recall.

"That's a striking feature of the dream, now that you mention it."

"How so?"

"Well, months after that dream, I came to the conclusion the goral represented Popov."

"Ah..." I can tell she recalls. "Feodor Popov. How can I ever forget him? He was the reason our family was on that travel restriction. Ugh!" Her eyes roll. "I'll never forget that. We were all miserable."

And he's dead. Has been for over three years now. Kolwaski kept his word and Popov was dead the day after our deal was settled. The morning after he was electrocuted in a hot tub at one of his underground sex clubs, my father, Danny, and I were invited to see his body. My father and I shot up his corpse, not leaving a stone unturned. That was the last formidable opponent my father's had. A nightmare ended.

"But for the most part, together. I remember that being the time you showed how Ellis blood ran through your veins. You took control while the family was under siege...with everybody."

It's true. Since that summer, my parents have been together exclusively. Diane ended up in Texas with a new sugar daddy. Tom got engaged to Ebony, the former councilwoman in Paterson, two years ago. They're expecting their first baby soon. And Nena had a son with the guy she left my father for. He's an investment broker who helped her launch a fashion line. She seems to be doing far better than she would have with my father. He wasn't a partner she needed, only a sponsor. I've learned in my own marriage, partnership can take you faster and further than any other dynamic in a romantic relationship. That's what my parents have, and my father's physical health as well as my mother's mental have both improved since.

"You guys made me respect you, then admire you, and left me disappointed," Bilan shares as the sun is dawning. "I was so scared of this piece of concrete called the Ellises being reduced to liquid. I'd just had my first baby and was pregnant again. I needed you guys strong for my kids." She kisses the tip of my nose. "For me."

Bilan has stepped up in a way I didn't know my family needed. She's totally taken a load off my mother's shoulders in keeping the family and business together. Now with a master's degree and the necessary certifications, Bilan is the CEO of *Ellis Academy*, a role she still claims she never wanted. She probably didn't because of how villainized she felt after Jason's murder. The academy has been a long-standing institution in the state. Even the acceptance of that role was highly publicized. Bilan spent months in the paper about that, too. So many argued nepotism and having a murderer working that closely to children. She's stepped up despite it all and has been instrumental in re-wiring the curriculum to include a balanced presence of technology, and she's introduced a solid mentoring program.

She's also been at my mother's side, planning family vacations and gatherings. It was she who found this secluded, eleven-bedroom cabin home with mountain views. She planned the activities for the children, although we wouldn't be here until today.

So when I gaze into her eyes, completely enamored by those freckles on her chiseled cheeks, my chest tightens with gratitude. It's a sensation hard to explain with mere words, so I drop my mouth to hers and try it that way.

"Oh, shit." Taaliba holds my nephew on her hip at the entrance of the room. "Ealy, I thought we'd sneak in a few pictures near the tree before your cousins awake, but your uncle and auntie want to pervert the scenery."

"Not yet," Bilan murmurs with her back to Taaliba so only I can hear.

I chuckle, humored by her annoyance of Taaliba.

"Morning, Leeba. How's my nephew this morning?"

She takes down the step as she sighs. "He may only be fifteen months, but I'm starting to think he gets the Christmas excitement," she explains on her way down to us. "This joker had me up at four-forty, saying he was hungry." She rolls her eyes while passing Ealy off to Bilan's outstretched arms.

She watches as Bilan sings to Ealy and his face lights up. He's our only nephew, so we get to spoil him the way Sadik had been spoiled before the twins. In fact, Sadik still gets spoiled by my father. But I understand the gleam in my sister's eyes as she watches her only child smile. Taaliba has been completely enthralled with motherhood and in love with my nephew. Being a mother has made her more responsible, but she's still as indecisive as she was as a child.

"You're the only person he woke up?" Danny asks from the entryway.

Taaliba's beam falls and she rolls her eyes. "But who got up with him, changed him, and brought him down to the kitchen to eat?"

"Who provided the seed, Leeb?" Danny uses that line often, talking his shit.

I don't mind; it's the same energy I keep about my children. But Danny isn't me and likely will never be.

"Buenos días, señora Ellis," he greets Bilan with a kiss on the cheek.

"Morning, Danny!" Bilan quickly returns her attention to Ealy.

"Good morning, Sadik." Danny proffers his hand for a shake, to which I oblige.

"So you made it?" I ask.

"Yeah. Apparently before you guys did. It was late and everyone was asleep," he answers, taking Taaliba at her side and pulling her into him at the waist. "And I mean everybody," he murmurs close to her ear.

Taaliba rolls her eyes again as she laughs. "Maybe next year you won't be invited."

"Wherever my little Lopez man is invited, so will I," he explains at a higher volume and with a bite of conviction I understood, even if it did annoy the shit out of me.

"Boy, please!" she groans, unable to hide her smile. "I'll go out and make another," she threatens.

"All your babies'll come from me, woman." He pulls her into his side again, kissing her on the neck. "Don't play."

"You all can have your photoshoot," I announce. "We're done in here. Come on, Nalib. Let's get you something to eat." I hold my hand out for her as she's passing Ealy over to his father.

Bilan accepts my hands and we stroll out of the dropdown living room for the hall.

"Another baby?" Bilan whispers. "By whom, Linda the herbalist?"

"Or Professor Porsha," I amend, agreeing.

Bilan snickers, dropping beneath my arm before straightening. "All these years together and a baby, and they're still not married."

"It's Taaliba. She still hasn't grown the fuck up."

"And he's miserable over it."

"He allows it. Some shit I would never go for," I declare, angry just thinking of it.

It was precisely why Danny Lopez could never fully earn my respect. He couldn't walk the path of an "ultra-alpha," a title Bilan still plasters on me. Having just my woman's pussy won't do. She had to be mine; heart, mind, body, and soul. Danny Lopez was sharing my sister's pussy with other women, something I'd never tolerate. It sickens me now just as much as it did when I learned about it right after the twins were born.

"It's deeper than you think, Sadik," Bilan tries once again to defend Taaliba.

"Choose a side, Nalib," I warn her as we turn for the kitchen where the staff is laying out baked goods, fruit, coffee, and tea.

"I don't have to, Sadik, and neither do you." She rubs the side of my abdomen. "I feel your arm tensing around me and don't like for you to be upset over what another adult does with their own life."

I growl as we separate for the buffet table. Bilan makes herself Taaliba's energy tea, something she'll need soon. I settle for grapefruit juice. The moment we head for the table to sit, a series of pitter-patters sound.

Bilan's face opens brightly. "They're up!"

I check my phone for the time. It isn't quite six yet. "And I bet they woke their cousins, too."

I grab her hand to head back to the living room. Bilan's anticipatory giggles are joyous behind me. We're almost knocked over by the herd of little people coming from an adjacent hallway. They're laughing deliriously as they race for the living room. I count six heads. Ivana and Iesha are in the lead. NeNe and Iliza hold hands behind them. And trailing behind the pack is a blond afro and an orange braided head: Asad and Sadia hoot the loudest, ignoring us as they jet past.

So far, Sadik and Asad have their mother's freckles, Sadik and Sadia have light-colored eyes, and Sadik and Asad have my mother's blonde hair. Sadia's hair is more of an orange so far, but Bilan says that can change.

"One's missing," I note.

"Where's Sadik?" Bilan asks a tight-eyed Camille, who lunges behind them. Stacy and Lois, another nanny, are behind her.

Camille sighs exhaustedly. "You know that boy does nothing

without his father and grandfather," she shares in movement. "He's with his Papa."

I snort. That's my boy.

"Ready?" Bilan asks, beaming. She loves this shit as much as I do. "The sooner this is done, the sooner I'll have my candy." She winks, pulling me at the arm down the hall.

The kids are tearing into their respective wrapping papers as soon as Taaliba positions them in front of their spaces.

Monica steps into the room, pouting in her housecoat. "You girls couldn't wake me up?"

"You were too sleepy, Mommy!" NeNe shouts before gasping at the pony she discovers with the last rip of wrapping paper.

"Yeah," Monica murmurs. "Tired from wrapping all these damn gifts last night."

She walks over and greets Bilan. "Hey, sissy!" Bilan hugs her tightly.

Monica approaches me and I hug her with my free arm.

"Glad you two made it in on time. Were you able to wrap everything?" Bilan answers with a nod, her eyes on the kids. "Damn. And how were you able to get the gifts from the plane to the house without them knowing?"

"Rory and Johnson stayed back at the airport after we pulled off with the kids," I share. "They brought the gifts in while we were putting them down for the night."

"You two are the real MVPs!" Monica marvels. "Let me go make sure Iban's up. He went to bed early last night."

I nod, acknowledging her before she takes off. That's when another explosive light gallop catches my attention. Sadik leaps into the family room.

"Merry Christmas, every one of you!" he shouts with outstretched arms. "I'm so happy we made it!"

The room lights up with laughter, including the staff helping the kids keep organized in their bubbling excitement. My parents appear behind him in their robes.

"Did he wake you up, too?" I ask my father.

"You know he did," my mother answers for them both. "That boy wasn't having Christmas without his Papa and Poppa. He tried to go to your room." She winks. "But I told them you guys had already come down for coffee."

I nod then go back to watching these little inspired faces. That's until my attention is beckoned elsewhere. To the left of me, Iban's at the top step looking into the living room. On either side of him are Monica and his home health aide. He looks a little winded as he holds onto his walker. I put my glass on the mantel and go over to him.

"You need help?"

He shakes his head slowly as he glances down to the lower living floor level. His aide murmurs words of instruction and encouragement to him. Iban drops the walker to the living room floor, steps closer to the edge. He lifts and drops the walker again, this time farther from the step. Finally, he drops one leg down, circling the other in the air, then drops that one, too. The speed of his movements and range of motion has improved over the years, and his need for therapy has decreased in frequency. All of that, and my big brother is still a fraction of the convivial spirit he used to be.

"Daddy!" NeNe screams elatedly. "Come. Let me feed you food. I cook!" She smiles, bringing attention to her apron.

Liza runs up to him and lifts her new toy mobile phone to him. "Call Momma, Daddy."

Holding tight to the grips of the walker, Iban smiles brightly. "Okay, baby." His words spill at a low to moderate speed; all of his faculties seem to. "Let daddy get his chair in here, okay?"

From the entrance at the other side with a ramp for accessibility, his chair is being brought down by another home health aide. It's why Bilan chose this particular house—why she chooses all the properties we rent for the family now.

I watch as Iban slowly transitions from the walker to his motorized chair, where he spends most of his day. I'm at his side as always, in the event he needs help. He rarely asks me. He's out of breath by the time he's settled in it. I'm waiting too tensely. I should be used to this by now, but I'm not.

Finally, a smile opens crookedly on his face. "I did it," he utters. "I walked in on Christmas with all my kids."

My chest expands and I nod. "You did, man. I'm proud of you." I really am.

Bilan puts down her tea mug when NeNe asks to open her kitchen. She explains Sadia has one they can play with now. When Sadik makes his way around his stack of gifts and finally unravels the coupe, I watch intently.

"Hey, I want that!" Asad trills as he points.

My regard finds their mother, hoping she has an immediate solution.

But Sadik has an even better one. "It's okay, brudder." He squats in front of Asad as though he's so much taller. "We can share. You can go first. Okay?"

Fighting through a pout, Asad approves. "Okay, Deekie." He quickly goes back to his group of gifts.

A long breath of relief pushes from my lungs. Subconsciously, I peer over at Bilan, who's on her haunches in the girls' kitchen. She winks and blows a kiss of her own approval.

Shit...

This parenting thing causes more stress than staff conflicts. It is a tightrope balancing act to attempt happiness for a family of five. But it fucking thrills me at the same time.

About an hour later, the adults have found our way into the kitchen for breakfast.

"I hope you ain't going back to that shit," my father grounds out with animated eyes, eyes pointing to my wife.

The entire table quiets.

Bilan lifts a brow. "What're you talking about, old-timer?"

"That not eating shit." He peers over to my mother. "Remember she used to do that at your table?"

My queen laughs as she feeds Ealy cheese. "Oh, leave my child alone, Earl."

"Please do," Bilan rotates her head over her shoulder with closed eyes as she groans. She's showing signs of crashing. "I eat and you know it. That was so three-four years ago." She waves him off dismissively. "You just better be up for those slopes. Better hope you can keep up with me."

"Little girl of mine, I will smoke you!" my father playfully challenged.

The table finds humor in their verbal battles. I'm likely the only who doesn't. My eyes are fastened to her profile, trying to measure her mood. For me.

"Bilan," Taaliba calls from across the table as she scrolls through her phone. "We have time for me to show you the designs I'm between for my tea boutique." She pats the empty seat to the left of her as Danny is at her right. "Come. Let's get started."

Before Bilan can answer, I drop my napkin and prepare to stand. "That would be a negative." I reach for my wife's hand.

Without a moment of dither, she reciprocates and stands next to me.

"Why? You guys flew in late," Taaliba notes, cleaning her gums with her tongue as she speaks. "I haven't had any girl time with her."

"Same here, girl." Monica rolls her eyes, holding her coffee to her face.

It's nice to see how, after Bilan dropped Randi as a friend, she grew into healthy friendships with my sister and sister-in-law. Bilan and Tasche have remained friends. Two years ago, Tasche applied for visitation rights for her daughter in New Jersey now that she's a resident. Bilan had Julius put in a word with the judge presiding over the case, and she granted Tasche weekly visitation rights and a review of her ability to parent fulltime. I'm still humored at how Bilan knows to use her "Ellis privilege" when necessary. Bilan hasn't spoken of Randi since years ago when she said Tasche and Randi had a falling out over Randi wanting to stay with Tasche after Tasche's boyfriend moved into her apartment. Selfishly, that delighted me. It put even more of a distance between Randi and my wife.

"And neither have I." I clear the chair from behind Bilan. "I take priority. Sorry, ladies. Hold down the Ellis trio for us."

"For how long? I really need to go over this with her." Taaliba is demanding behind us as we head for the hall.

I shrug, peering at her from over my shoulder. "I'll see what she's got left in her when I'm done."

"My boy!" my father shouts over Bilan's feminine giggles as we turn the corner.

I hum, totally relaxed at his hands and fingers in the jacuzzi. One hand is tightly clasped to my scalp as I sit in front of him, between his hard, hairy legs. His other hand busy strumming my swollen clit beneath the heated water. He's precise with the massages. Pressure on my head necessarily strong, and the one between my spread thighs, locked outside of his, is circling the parameters of my pearl.

I'm relaxed and heated deliciously in the silky water, submerged in white rose petals. Soft, relaxing music plays, deluding the reality of the early morning hour. I need this time alone with him to regroup. These past few weeks between work and preparation for today had me stretched. Sadik, too, has been busy acknowledging his staff and supporting Julius in Paterson. He's finally been seen publicly with his friends since... Jason. I quickly switch my thoughts. It doesn't help that Sadik's rubbing has neared the nucleus of my pleasure house.

My breathing hikes again, pussy pushing into his hand to increase the pressure.

"Don't cum again, Nalib," he cautions in my ear, those velvety chords enticing.

I want to. So badly, I want another orgasm to take the last bit of the edge off. I clutch the rope binding my wrists in the air as my head pushes back into his hard shoulder. He peers down on me, his face fixed into a scowl as he focuses on the varying pressures. I angle my face so my mouth can near his. Thankfully, he takes the hint and brings his lips down to meet mine, taking me ravenously. His tongue strokes my mouth, aggressively licking against my own. His hand on my head pushes me closer to him. The assault drives me wild and I buck my pussy into his hand between my legs...until it disappears.

I'm in love with this man. *Still*. He's powerful, broad-minded, talented, and protective of his family.

"I get it now." I whisper into his lips when I pull back.

"Get what?"

"What you were offering the first time you approached me at *Michelle's*." When his eyes glaze over, I know he needs specificity. "When we discussed Christina C. Jones' stance on Black love. You said you agreed there's been a deficit of Black love and commitment presentation in America." I swallowed, developing my words. "You've been my Black love story. You friended me when I rejected you, made love to my doubts of this...thing existing, and you protected me even when I didn't give you my best."

I think the revelation came full circle last night when I saw Sofia Cruz at the holiday dinner. She couldn't keep her eyes off of Sadik. *When we spoke to people, I caught her gaping. When we ate dinner, I found her staring. And when we danced hard on the dance floor and I endured his hands all over me, at one point, I opened my eyes to her chocolate ones as she clutched a martini glass in her hand.*

When I found my way into the bathroom to relieve myself, Sofia appeared. She told me for the first time since knowing him, she'd seen Sadik in a natural element she never knew existed. Sofia shared how she followed the news reports when Sadik and I were covered for Jason's murder and thought that would be the end of our marriage. She followed each court appointment the media captured us walking into and paid close attention to the coverage. Sofia shared she noted Sadik's hands or arms around me in a protective manner each time we were photographed together. I was shocked to have that much of her attention. I was also reminded of my Google-stalking of the Ellises for Iban's trial.

"His mother pulled me aside one day when visiting his place while I was over." Sofia shared. *"She said, 'When a Black man loves you, he protects you. The prize for a Black man is finding a woman who understands and appreci-*

ates his plight because she, too, has one akin to him.' I thought she was being mean. But when I saw how you two were there for each other through that debacle and stayed together, I saw something I didn't feel when I was with him. Something I didn't know to aspire to. Tonight, I saw it was something so organic, I couldn't replicate it even with the help of his mother." She turned to leave the restroom. *"Congrats for finding that with him."* Wordlessly, I *watched her slip out as quickly as she'd slipped in.*

"That's because you were always mine," he declares effortlessly, spiking my temperature. "And you will forever be."

His lips are full and promising, eyes under those dense, unruly brows, a dark brown perimeter enclosing a hue of green, then yellow and an impossible orange before a speck of black at the mecca of the iris. I look forward to seeing such exoticism every day of the rest of my life.

"Please, Sadik," I beg.

He stands, causing heavy beads of water to fall over my head. When I think he's going to untie the rope from the hook above, he ducks to cross beneath it. The moment his steely rigid erection nears my face, I shift forward, taking him into my mouth without the assistance of my hands. I watch as his eyes darken while watching me bob over him. My tongue lashes on the underside of him against the thick veins. I tighten my lips around him and suck him deep, nipples pebbled, clit throbbing, and sex contracting.

With sudden speed, Sadik withdraws, bends to lift me from the water, and turns me around. Before I catch my breath, he's inside me, thrusting into my hungry sex. I relax into him until those thrusts turn into plunges. My groin spins and hanging wrists go numb at the same time.

"Best lover..." he grunts over me. "My friend."

My ultra-alpha's declarative words take me over the edge and my thighs jerk crudely as I implode over him.

Best friend, my only lover, and protector.

Forever.

SADIK AND BILAN

#PenningWithoutParameters
#ImGonnaMakeYouLoveMe

www.LoveBelvin.com
See visuals from the series here on my website – https://www.
lovebelvin.com/projects/sadik

~LOVE ACKNOWLEDGES

Visuals: **365 Photography** – "Hello, Brooklyn!" Your talent is boundless. Thanks for taking a chance on Black literature. I look forward to more collaborations! **Fierce Faces** – Kaydene, I can't say thanks enough for brokering this deal. As we both learned, what's meant to be will gel seamlessly. Thanks for your artistry and patience (and not cussing me out as you threatened). KNGQ – Q. Williams & Brittney April, thanks so much for serving as visuals for our Sadik and Bilan. May this be another ideal step in the direction of your promising careers. My best to you in all your endeavors!

Researcher: Shumethia S. — Thanks so much for always going the extra mile for me, even when it's inconvenient. I love you, woman!

Beta Reader: — Yorubia, thanks for all the work you put in...all the listening to the plots and developments with patience and anticipation. I know I won't hear from you for a few weeks until you call and ask about my next set of characters, but... WHATEVER!

LBTR — Afi, Angela J.J., Artemysia, Ash, Asha-kai, Ashleigh, Ashley, Ayanna, Ayo, Azaria, Bonita, Brittany, Courtney, Danielle, Dee, Deidre, Denise, DeVona, Diana, Diane, Diva Dee, Doresha, Doris, Ericka M., Gail, Grace, Heather, Heidi, Hezie-Ann, Hyacinth,

Jasmine, Jessica, Kamashia, Karmen, Katrina, Kendra, Kerry, Keyma, Kim, Kimmiko, Kita, Korei, LaLa, LaSonde, Linda R., Linda W., Lee, Malaika, Marshall, Michelle M., Michelle R.O., Michelle T., Mocha, Monique H., Monique N., Natoya, Nena, Nikki, Pamela, Rakia, Quan, Regina, Richell, Rose, Roslyn, Samona, Sharon L., Sharon F.W., Shaun, Sola, Sophia, Stacey K., Stacy M., Tamara, Tanisha, Tanya, Tara, Té, Teresa, Terri G., Tesha, Tia, Tiffany, Tineka, Tonya, Tralaina, Vivian, Wendi, Yolanda P., Yolanda U., and Yorubia, it's crazy how I'm finally convinced of how connected we are. I love you guys for teaching me the magic of Black women supporting our arts. I brag about you to friends and family, and feel the love you give me behind my back (I hear about it). Thanks for being that core of support. *Jemeka* & *Rita*: You two are like the proverbial smarter and more resourceful wives. You make me look so put together and organized. I can't say thanks enough for being by my side. Love you for real!

Christina C. Jones aka CCJ — Your friendship grows more valuable by the day. Thanks so much for all you contribute to my life and brand. May God continue to increase everything you touch! *And Lord, heal her road rage!*

Interior Artist: Cedeara Ardell McCollum — Thanks, baby girl, for the imagery you've designed for my books! Love you always!

Proof Reader: Tina V. Young — You've been a rock to me, a special gift. I hope to return the favor in some form or fashion. Love you so much, T!!!

Editors:

Zakiya Walden of *I've Got Something to Say!* — I appreciate your hard work and dedication. This process reminds me of our L.I.P. days. LOL! May we have many more!

Santisha Taylor of *AccuProse Editing Services* — I was an even bigger pain. I know! You were a trooper. I appreciate you greatly!

MDT: That break you're pushing... Ummm... Yeah. It's time.

Master, my *Jireh*, my *Rohi*, Proverbs 16:3 (AMP) "Commit to the Lord whatever you do, and he will establish your plans." *This, oh Lord, is my worship.*

~OTHER BOOKS BY LOVE BELVIN

Love's Improbable Possibility series:

Love Lost, Love UnExpected, Love UnCharted & *Love Redeemed*

Waiting to Breathe series:

Love Delayed & *Love Delivered*

Love's Inconvenient Truth (Standalone)

Love Unaccounted **series**:

In Covenant with Ezra, In Love with Ezra & Bonded with Ezra

The Connecticut Kings series:

*Love in the Red Zone, *Love on the Highlight Reel, *Determining Possession, End Zone Love, Love's Ineligible Receiver, *Pass Interference, Love's Encroachment, & *Offensive Formations (*by Christina C. Jones)*

Wayward Love series:

The Left of Love, The Low of Love & The Right of Love

Love in Rhythm & Blues series

The Rhythm of Blues & The Rhyme of Love

LOVE IN RHYTHM & BLUES series

The Sadik series

He Who Is a Friend, He Who Is a Lover & He Who Is a Protector

The Muted Hopelessness series:

My Muted Love, Our Muted Recklessness, & Our Reckless Hope

The Prism series:

Mercy, Grace, & The Promise

Low Love, Low Fidelity (Standalone)

~EXTRA

You can find Love Belvin at www.LoveBelvin.com
Facebook @ Author - Love Belvin
Twitter @LoveBelvin
Goodreads: Love Belvin
and on Instagram @LoveBelvin

Join the #TeamLove mailing list on my website to keep up with the happenings!

Click here (with WiFi) to join!